ATOMICA
BETWEEN SEA AND SKY

BOOKS BY HEATHER MCKENZIE

The Nightmusic Trilogy Series

Serenade

Nocturne

Rhapsody

The Atomica Series

Atomica – Between Sea and Sky

HEATHER MCKENZIE

ATOMICA

Between Sea and Sky

Title: Atomica – Between Sea and Sky / Heather McKenzie

Copyright ©2024 Heather McKenzie
All rights reserved.

ISBN: 978-1-7381530-6-0 (Print)
ISBN: 978-1-7381530-9-1 (Ebook)

House of Hebyzie Publishing, Canada
www.houseofhebyzie.com

HOUSE OF HEBYZIE

Young Adult Fiction / Fantasy
Young Adult Fiction / Science Fiction
Young Adult Fiction / Dystopian/Survival

Summary: Guardian Eva vows to protect Zoleya, a girl of extraordinary importance. But when a catastrophic shipwreck strands Eva on a mysterious tropical island and Zoleya vanishes, Eva joins forces with other castaways to survive.

Cover Illustration by: Emily Bueckert
Layout: House of Hebyzie
Editing: Haley Bueckert and Emily Bueckert
Interior: Damian Jackson

For Byran, Josh, Emily, and Haley

3055 CE, ALDIRA

One thousand years after The Burn...

PROLOGUE

First came the rats.

I was five. They mowed through the garden. Tunneled under the cabin. Made nests out of our bedding and burrowed into our walls. Mother told me it wasn't the first time it had happened. In fact, it had been a regular occurrence for decades after The Burn. But this time the rats brought with them the disease that claimed Father.

Next came the Black-Blooded.

I was six when they crossed the river and took what little possessions we had. Before then, their existence had been merely stories whispered in the dark hoping no child would overhear. While I hid in the cupboard with Mom and Delia as our tiny cabin was ransacked, I caught glimpses of their crippled bodies sick with radiation. Some were missing ears and eyes, some hunched as if spineless. Their long skinny arms deposited large items into their shredded clothes, and they swallowed the trinkets they could not hold. They left behind toxic puddles on the dirt floor.

I'll never forget the fear in my mother's eyes as she motioned for us to be quiet, smiling for little Delia's sake and trying to make a game of hiding. Months later, Mother's eyes conveyed that same terror once again, wide and red-rimmed, as a sickness left behind by the Black-Blooded brought down Delia's body, and then her own. It took me weeks to dig their graves.

Then came the wasps.

The river was bone dry, so I heard them far off in the trees, fleeing from the smoke or the radiation pockets that shifted around the continent. I was young, yet I knew I had to run. So I left behind the family that I'd buried next to the only home I'd ever known and willed my legs to carry me to the city of Nora. There, I starved. I was caught and beaten by Aldiran enforcers who didn't want a child sleeping on the streets. Treated no better than a dog, doorways and back alleys became my home, and soon, stealing was second nature. Even though the loneliness nearly stopped my heart many times, something kept me fighting to survive.

Then I came upon Zoleya.

A horse-drawn carriage rolled past me one blistering day as it traveled down a blackened street shadowed by slowly crumbling buildings. Garbage in the ditch stank in the heat, so thick my throat stung. I hadn't eaten in many days. I felt the start of a fever. Yet that carriage sent out a ray of hope like a lifeline, and I felt so compelled to follow it that I moved out of the shade and started weaving through the throngs of people to get to it. Whoever was inside needed me, and I needed them. I knew this as surely as I knew my own name.

I followed for days. When the carriage moved faster, I ran, even though my lungs hurt. When it stopped, I curled up against its wheels. And when my body could no longer endure another movement, I lay in the dust of its wake without even the strength left to cry. I was dying. I collapsed in the middle of the road, hoping death would come quickly.

"You're a tenacious little thing, aren't you?" said a soft and sweet female voice.

I stared up at the most beautiful face I'd ever seen. Long blonde hair draped around the rounded cheeks of someone in their early teens with vibrant blue eyes that sparkled in the light and skin so pale it was almost blinding. The person in the carriage had ventured out into the sunshine, and I wondered if she was an angel.

"My name is Zoleya. What's your name?" she asked.

Carts rolled by. A turnip fell from one and was promptly run over just feet from my head.

"Evangeline," I replied.

"And how old are you?" she asked.

I could barely speak. My mouth was dry and crusted with so many sores that my tongue throbbed. "Six," I squeaked out.

Zoleya knelt closer, put her arms beneath me, and picked me up like I weighed nothing.

"Would you like a job, Evangeline?" she asked.

I muttered yes in her arms, then fell asleep next to her in the carriage, her skin ice cold and soothing to my feverish mind.

Little did I know that the job was to become one of her Guardians. I would train every moment of every day to protect her from the threats we all faced, as well as from an ancient cult known as the Nihila, whose sole mission was to eradicate her and all beings like her from planet Earth. And, with the help of other Guardians devoted to Zoleya's preservation, I did exactly that—quite joyously—for thirteen years.

Until the Raiders came.

I thought I'd been prepared for the likes of them—I'd trained hard and learned from my mistakes—but the cutthroat rogues had caught us unaware in a meadow just before sunrise, and they had numbers and weapons we couldn't compete with. When Zoleya and I were captured, I came to learn that these Raiders who traveled across the sea to rape and pillage Aldiran lands were more determined than the Nihila, more invasive than the rats, more pissed off than the wasps, and more toxic than the Black-Blooded. At least their single-mindedness left them clueless to the fact that they'd taken the most valuable treasure known to humankind; the last remaining catalyst that could save the planet from dying in the form of a small, angelic-looking girl named Zoleya, whose abilities were far beyond their understanding.

Now we were both held captive in the hold of the Raiders' ship. I was completely helpless with my hands chained over my head and ankles bound together, unable to free myself and Zoleya from the cage we'd been locked in. Along with eighteen other people taken against our will, we were reduced to nothing but cargo heading for Cal de Mac. If we made it to the Raiders' homeland, Zoleya, along with the other women, would be sold to slavers, and I'd be forced to fight alongside the men in the arenas until my last breath.

I need not worry though. It was becoming apparent that we'd be dead long before that ever happened.

Because next, came the storm…

1

KADE

— JOURNAL ENTRY, KADE, AGE 19

I was born with the marks of the Nihila on my skin. The intricate web of ink-like patterns covering the right side of my neck and torso had charted my destiny before I even took my first breath. Today was their awakening—whether I was ready or not.

Firelight danced in the eyes of the five hooded figures staring down at me. My mother's eyes were among them, shining with a mixture of pride for her only son, and horror for what was to come. As my wrists and ankles were secured to the Anyan stone with chains, I dug deep to remain calm. Once awakened, the marks would use me for a purpose my ancestors had programmed a thousand years ago. My life would no longer be my own.

The raging fire sent thick columns of smoke up to the stars. The sea crashed onto the rocks hundreds of feet below. I tasted sand on my tongue from the recent dust storm that had stripped every living thing from the cliff on which we stood, leaving the rock smooth and gleaming much like the ceremonial blades in the hands of the Elders.

"Your blood will be spilled," said Mother, not one tear on her golden-olive cheeks.

I knew my purpose. "For the greater good," I replied.

One of the Elders removed a lid from a small urn, then dusted my body with its contents; the ashes of my father. My bare skin tingled, and a tremble started up deep in my bones.

"Protector of the Earth and all it holds sacred." The Elder drew the sign of the Nihila on my forehead with his fingertip. "This title now belongs to you, Kade Thorn."

"Protector of the Earth and all it holds sacred," I repeated.

And so it began.

The ground rumbled around the Anyan stone as if the labyrinth of tunnels and sandstone caves beneath it were eager for my blood. If I had any notion, no matter how fleeting, that the stories of how I came to be were just *stories*, I now felt the truth of my calling as clearly as I felt the first Elder's blade.

A sharp bite of steel. The stinging release of blood. The Elders began speaking in an old tongue as they started cutting into my skin, into my marks, thus releasing visions stored in my deepest memories. Suddenly, I could see the planet as it was before The Burn. Our beautiful blue world, pristine and thriving. I fully understood how we came to be, how the plants took root, how the land rose up from the sea and the moon found its place in the sky. I saw the magnificence of our Earth, with lush rainforests and crystal clear lakes, oceans teeming with life, and nature and animals living in harmony. I fell even deeper in love with it than I already was. So much so that I thought I might never breathe again.

But then I saw how humans ruined it, ignoring Earth's pleas for help and instead polluting, draining, and abusing, then creating machines that forced all life as it once was to succumb to a hundred years of hellfire.

And I was angry.

So angry I barely felt the knives now at my ribs, awakening the code stored in my DNA that was powering up my soul with fury and vengeance. With each drop of blood spilled, I became consumed with one thought; *eliminate Earth's last remaining threat.*

As the ground continued to rumble, one of the Elders working on my ribs dug in too deep. I wondered if he'd hit bone. By all logic I should have been screaming and pleading for him to stop, but the visions kept coming, showing me exactly why my pain did not matter.

"The final mission of the Nihila falls to you," said my mother, her hands slick with my blood as she raised the knife to the sky. "You must protect the world and destroy Atomica—the last of the machines."

It was like a switch inside of me flipped on. All at once, I could feel a tug against my skin as the marks seemed to come alive. They were active now, awakened, and they were forcing a powerful replacement for the spilled blood into my veins.

"Your marks are visible to all but Atomica, and they will conceal your identity." Mother bent to kiss my forehead. "You will be able to hunt for it undetected. They will not allow you to stray from your purpose. They will guide you to that which you seek. They will keep your mind focused and your heart loyal. If you stray, they will burn. If you lose sight of your mission, they will burn. However, if you need help, you can call upon them."

I hadn't yet received training on how to call upon them. There had been no time. The ceremony had been rushed with great urgency when the Elders had felt Atomica's presence for the first time in a century.

It began to rain, turning the ashes of my father into black rivers on my skin. As the Elders released me from my chains, I became acutely aware of how every part of my body was both hot and cold, new and yet intensely familiar. The pull of Atomica had increased so intensely that I longed to walk off the edge of the cliff to get to the sea; it was out there somewhere... I could feel it...

"I will not fail," I said, determined to fulfill my destiny.

The rain stopped as quickly as it began. The bloody and blackened ground beneath my feet stilled. I could see the silvery moonlight casting shadows under the eyes of the Elders as they positioned the points of their blades over their hearts.

"Wait, no. It doesn't have to end this way," I begged, body trembling.

My mother's eyes met mine. "It does. This is the only way, my son."

Before I could even mutter a strangled protest, they all fell dead at my feet.

At once, my marks glowed as they absorbed the light of my mother and the others who were now rising from their lifeless bodies. It brought me to my knees. The pain was unlike anything I'd ever encountered. The only family I'd ever known had sacrificed themselves to make me stronger, and now, not only could I *feel* Atomica, it was as if I could *taste* it, too.

I threw the ceremonial knives into the sea, then put the Elders on the stone—careful to smooth my mother's black curls away from her cheeks—and screamed up at the heavens for a very long time. When the sun came up, I built a fire around them big enough to rival The Burn.

Then I started walking, letting the marks lead the way. I stole bread from a thief who was trying to rob me. Hitched a ride with a leper on his horse-drawn wagon. Hid in an abandoned grain mill from corrupt Aldiran Enforcers. Spent two days and nights avoiding the mobs razing the city of Nora and the wolves scouring its ditches. While skirting the radioactive wastelands, I got caught in a dust storm, and then found myself navigating rat-infested alleyways in the town of Hel. When I finally got to Port Hayes and made my way through the seemingly endless trash to the docks, I knew exactly where I would find Atomica.

There, perched atop the oil-slick sea was a Raider ship, its sunbleached sails fluttering ominously in the sea winds.

I had to get on that ship.

For the greater good.

2  EVANGELINE

I had no idea how many days had passed when the ship began losing battle with a raging storm. All of us being held captive by the Raiders had gone through hell and back already, so this was an additional layer of torture. We were all hurting and scared to bits, yet the sea couldn't care less—it was going to drown us one way or another.

And maybe that was a blessing.

As I watched Zoleya from across the cage, water began dripping down from the oily planks overhead and between the unbreakable iron bars. We were in the belly of the ship, the women cowering in the corner either praying or crying, and the men moaning in agony and fear. I was helpless to do anything, only able to watch dried blood turn to tiny red rivers on Zoleya's skin as she became soaked to the bone. Our journey across Aldira had been hellacious, to say the least, but being responsible for the state she was in felt worse than a million knives slicing up my heart. I was supposed to protect her, and I had failed.

"We'll be okay," said a doe-eyed woman with arms and legs thin as toothpicks. All her front teeth were broken, making her hard to understand. "The storm will pass soon."

Normally I'd respect someone who was just trying to be comforting, but that was a bald-faced lie.

One of the men chained up across from me snorted in disgust. "Delusional," he said and spat, adding to the slimy water lapping at our toes.

We could all hear the Raiders up on deck losing battle with the violent weather and churning seas, panic thick in their voices as they yelled "Secure the lashings" and "Man overboard."

As water inched past our ankles and up our calves, Zoleya's gaze met mine. The light from the quivering lanterns danced in her irises. She was so pale. The sky-blue sundress she favored torn and splattered with filth. Her long white hair hung loose down to her hips, clinging to her petite frame—I hadn't had a chance to braid it for the day before we'd been captured.

"Calla is correct," she said, agreeing simply to provide an extra ray of hope. But Zo was bad at lying. Her lip always quivered. "Things will be just fine. Our journey will come to an end soon," she added.

Well, that was at least true. Soon we'd all be dead.

"If you mean that we're going to drown, then so be it," a giant of a man with sores all over his face practically growled at her. "I'd rather die at sea than on Cal de Mac. Drowning would be better than what the Raiders will put us through if we make it to their homeland."

He was right. The women would be sold as slaves, and the men and I, with our wrists chained over our heads and ankles shackled together, would be forced to fight in the arenas until our last breath. Being captured by these thieves of the land and pirates of the sea was a certain death sentence, and I saw no way out.

The wind howled like a million wounded Black-Blooded, shrill and curling up tight to my eardrums. As the ship seemed to break apart, I thought of Mom, of Delia, and of Father, their graves dug deep in the toxic Aldiran dirt. Then I prayed to a god who never had a moment to spare for me, begging her to magically transport me back to the cabin with the little woodstove and bury my body next to theirs.

Those who were not chained up in the cage toppled into each other as the ship crested a wave before dipping sharply downward and then leveling out. Lightning crackled through the sky. Someone let out a heart-wrenching wail... I couldn't just hang here like a carcass waiting to be gutted, I had to try to do something. Anything.

Tugging on my restraints caused the shackles to dig deep into my wrists. A sickly warmth trickled down my arms. I nearly passed out from the pain, but I kept tugging; at least I would die with honor trying to save Zoleya.

"They can't be barbaric enough to leave us down here to drown," said a woman with a small child clinging to her legs.

A man across from me with black greasy curls let out a pained laugh. "Oh, but they are." His voice was raw with hatred and his face was bruised, one eye nearly swollen shut. "Raiders are no better than the maggots swimming in your dinner."

Crates full of stolen food, weapons, silks, and spices slammed into each other, releasing a plume of crushed cloves into the dank air. Someone up on deck shrieked and the wind shrieked back. I wondered if we had minutes. Seconds even. If I had to rip my hands off I would.

"Eva. Stop that, please," Zoleya pleaded.

If I could only break some bones then maybe—

"Aye, stop for heaven's sake!" said a massive man directly across from me with hair as red as the blood leaking from his broken nose. His skin was black with filth. His clothes were rags. "It's bad enough we be trapped in here together. Watching ye torture yourself is making it worse. Besides, even if ye git free, there ain't nothing a wee missy such as yourself can do. You be just a girl."

My pulse throbbed at my temples; how many times had I heard that before? "Don't you think there's a reason I'm chained up like the rest of you?"

The redhead had some sort of answer perched on the tip of his tongue, but the sea spoke first. With another shriek, it dragged its salty claws along the sides of the ship, grabbed hold, and wrenched it to the left. A barrel tipped over, mixing brine and writhing squid into the rising water. More clearly than ever, we could hear the frantic voices of the crew dancing with death above while we waited for it below.

Despite being warned not to leave the corner, Zoleya made her way across the cage to grip my waist and press her head against my chest. The chill of her skin, the pulse of her energy, and that familiar scent of her hair—a mixture of sunlight and black tea—was all-consuming. Nothing else mattered. God, I loved her. So much so that I thought my heart might break clean in half.

"Stop hurting yourself," she said softly. "That is a command."

I grew still immediately, conditioned for years to follow her orders when her voice took on that tone.

She looked up and smiled in a way that I knew was just for me. "That's better. Be still now, Evangeline."

I allowed myself a moment to feel nothing but her body against mine, my mind racing. "Are you sure the Raiders don't know what you are?" I whispered against her hair, starting to shiver.

Her reply floated through my head. "Yes. They believe me to be nothing more than an unlucky Aldiran like all their other captives. We just got caught up in their looting, Eva. Nothing more."

That was a relief. If by some miracle we didn't drown, Zo wouldn't be tortured, mutilated, or sold to the Nihila so that they could do much worse.

"I'm so sorry I failed you." I could barely hold back the tears.

"You did not fail me. Of all the Guardians I have had, you are my favorite. Certainly the most loyal, fierce, and stubborn."

"And you... are everything to me," I whispered. I wanted her to know that I cared for her deeply and was not just bound to her by the oath I'd made all those years ago. I thought of the countless hours of training and all of the times I nearly died saving her, threats ranging from a solar storm to thieves robbing our carriage. My sacrifice of a normal life for a nomadic one devoted solely to Zo's protection was a choice I'd repeat in a heartbeat. "It's been an honor to serve you."

Her delicate hands cupped my face. "And you, sweet Evangeline, are the sister I never had. Thank you for that." Her voice was soft and eerily calm.

"We're saying goodbye, aren't we?" I asked, barely able to get the words out.

Her eyes were dimming and I could tell it was all she could do to remain standing. She'd been without sunlight for too long.

"Yes. This is goodbye. But maybe being lost to the sea is the perfect ending."

It was as if ice was rushing through my veins, shredding them to pieces and stabbing at my heart. I'd failed her. Failed everyone.

"I'll love you even in death," I said.

As I stared at her beautiful face—unlined and exactly the same as it had been when she picked me up off the street all those years ago—the overhead hatch was thrown open and four Raiders descended into the hold. They stormed toward the cage, unlocked it, and began ushering the women out of the corner. I struggled against my restraints again, unable to quell the panic stabbing like arrows shot through my chest.

"I love you, too," Zoleya said.

And then her body was ripped away from mine.

I watched helplessly as she was forced to go up the ladder and into the storm.

Then the hatch was closed, and we were separated for the first time in thirteen years.

I learned the meaning of madness in that moment, my body and mind saturated with the kind that drowned out any rational thought. My limbs thrashed as my heart exploded behind my ribs. I yelled out a solemn promise that if even one hair on her head was harmed, I would kill every single Raider over and over until the world ran red with their thieving, corrupt, barbaric blood. I swore that I would go to their homeland of Cal de Mac and slaughter their families so violently that every dead relative in their piratical depraved bloodline would feel my wrath. My anguish was as ugly as the water churning with filth sloshing around my knees, and I became determined to break the chains or my bones in one last attempt to at least die at Zoleya's side.

"If you don't stop struggling, I will have you beheaded," said an authoritative voice.

Through the bars of the cage and a crimson curtain of fury clouding my vision, I met the stone-cold gray eyes of Commander Rowan, the leader of the Raiders. This was the man I'd confronted in the meadow just weeks ago and lost everything including my pride to. This was the man who had ordered his followers to capture me, Zoleya, and anyone else he fancied, forcing us onboard this hellacious ship. I'd never hated anyone or anything more in my life.

I thrashed harder.

"I said stop it." His voice was as loud as the storm. "Or I'll bring those women back down here and torture each one, starting with the young blonde one you seem to have quite a fondness for. And you best believe that I'll make her suffer for as long as possible."

Commander Rowan didn't make idle threats. He was lithe and lean, and despite being slightly smaller than the men in the cage with me, he was more intimidating than all of them put together. There was an edge to him. An aura of indifference and chilling brutality clung to him like his wet clothes. Even the deckhand at his side—a massive man with hands like tree stumps—seemed wary.

I forced my body to be still.

Squid floated past my thighs. The lanterns quivered.

"I ordered all the women to be freed. Why is this one still in the cage?" Commander Rowan asked the deckhand, pointing in my direction.

The deckhand stuttered. "She's as dangerous as the men. Cap'n don't want no threats to be surviving."

The ship lurched horrifically to the side and the deckhand reached out to steady himself.

"Fine. Get back on deck where you're needed," Commander Rowan ordered, barely swaying. "I'll make sure the cage is secure."

The deckhand obeyed, fleeing up the ladder quickly and closing the hatch behind him.

For a strange second it became eerily quiet. The world stilled, as if the storm was gathering its breath.

"The ship is sinking," stated the commander.

That was obvious. I couldn't understand why he was down in the hold instead of trying to save himself.

After glancing around quickly, he headed for the cage. But instead of locking it and leaving, he marched straight in and headed for me.

"We have to hurry," he muttered.

What? Was he going to have a little sadistic fun before we all died? Gut me like a fish? Practice his jab to the throat and knife to the heart? He was capable of much worse.

The black-haired man let out what sounded like a growl and the beastly redhead began praying when the commander got close enough for me to smell—lemon, wet leather, and something spicy had blended with the salt of the sea. Bracing myself, I tried to maintain my dignity as I waited for the pain his hands were sure to deliver, but his body became hot as a fever against mine, pressing just as tightly as Zoleya's had.

"Pig!" I spat, not giving him the satisfaction of struggling.

"Leave the girl alone!" roared the black-haired man, and the voices of the other men rolled together into a swirl of threats.

Commander Rowan pressed tighter, his hands up over his head, knuckles white from gripping a set of keys… What was he doing?

"I'm not going to let you drown down here," he said to me. And me only.

Was this some sort of cruel joke? The thought of this man wanting to save *anyone* was absurd. Yet, I could see the worry in his eyes. I sensed the urgency of truth about him. And when he was thrown off balance, dropping the keys and then rushing to try and unlock me again, I had the overwhelming feeling that if I was released, he would leave the others to die.

"Unchain them first." My voice was stronger than I felt.

He blinked at me in confusion.

"The others… unchain them before me," I clarified. "Or the second I get free I'll tear you to pieces."

He laughed. Then his eyes lowered into a glare. "Like hell I will."

The ship tilted and threw him off balance again, so I used it to my advantage. With just enough slack in the chains at my ankles, I pulled my knees up to my chest and blocked him from getting closer, but I nearly blacked out from the pain in my wrists.

"No. Them first."

Eyes like hurricanes, gray as the stormy sky, met mine. "Stubborn," he muttered.

Then, miraculously, Commander Rowan went about unshackling his hostages, making quick work of unlocking the hands of the redheaded beast first. "Stand ready by the hatch," he ordered. "Hold it shut until everyone is free, then all of you get up on deck and jump overboard. We're near land and—"

The ship shuddered viciously, stealing his words.

The redhead burst from the cage, doing as he was told. I watched as the rest were freed, alarm bells going off in my head while the man with the black hair waited his turn. Water was coming in, fast. I began floating. The oil lamps were flickering out one by one. The black-haired man watched with urgency as the commander worked on his locks. Chest deep. Shoulder deep. Water lapped over my face as I gasped for air…

"Unlock her!" the black-haired man yelled.

And then I was underwater.

The swirling world became very quiet. As quiet as I supposed death would be. It wasn't calm and inviting or pillowy enough to rest upon, but a frenzied sort of silence that coiled and tightened around every pounding heartbeat. This was not like being on the streets of Nora all those years ago when I thought sickness or a turnip cart would end my life. Back then, as I lay dying, my child's mind still had a notion of hope—and Zoleya had saved me. Nursed me back to health. Given me a home and a purpose.

There was no chance of that happening again.

Resisting the overwhelming urge to suck water into my lungs in place of air, I closed my eyes and waited for the nightmare to be over. But a hand grabbing and shaking my arm prompted me to blink Commander Rowan's face into view. There was no malice in his expression. And when his mouth pressed down over mine, prying apart my lips and sharing some much-needed air, I inhaled greedily. Then I waited as he fumbled with the chains at my ankles before returning with another breath. It seemed that the very same man who took lives without any thought was risking his own for mine.

When he finally managed to get my hands free, he latched onto my fingers with a death grip and led the way out of the cage, pulling me with him, kicking fiercely through the water until our faces were upturned in a small pocket of air.

I greedily gulped oxygen into my lungs, and for a moment, with mere inches between our noses, I didn't see the commander as my captor or as the ruthless cutthroat that legends had been born of.

Someone else was staring back at me as the last oil lamp began to die —and it was no monster.

"Breathe…" the commander said. "Just breathe, Eva."

I gulped madly until there was no air left. Then Commander Rowan's grip became an unbreakable vise around my hand, pulling, tugging, guiding… a flash of blue… a burst of red…

pressure, so much pressure…

and then,

nothing.

3

KADE

I overheard Elder Grig saying to Elder Matthias that women are only good for breeding, and that they should keep their mouths shut unless they're pleasing their man. When I asked Mother what he meant by that, she threw him from Thalasa cliff.

Mother has unique ways of answering my questions.

— JOURNAL ENTRY, KADE, AGE 12

I pushed through waves and up onto a beach with her unconscious body in my arms. Atomica was pulling me in one direction and self-preservation in another, so I ignored them both and marched back into the sea to save a drowning woman—and why I'd done something so idiotic was beyond me.

Now the marks of the Nihila burned my skin as if it had been lit on fire. Mother had warned me that straying from my purpose would cause this to happen. I had a mission. An important task. I was to hunt Atomica and do nothing else…

But apparently my Nihila upbringing hadn't rid me of my humanity because now I was breathing life back into the lungs of the young woman whom Commander Rowan had called Evangeline.

Which, in hindsight, was most certainly a mistake.

4   EVANGELINE

During the delicate fragments separating life from death, I was caught between the loneliest shadows and the brightest lights. I felt a cold that could snap bones in half, then burned with a heat that surpassed the sun. It all came in bursts, along with a pressure on my chest like a swinging sledgehammer, until all at once a rush of liquid came up into my throat and out of my nose and mouth.

I fought to exchange water for oxygen, my entire body doing everything it could to purge the sea from my lungs and stomach. When I could finally take in a breath, I dug my fingers into the wet sand to verify that I was truly on solid ground. It seemed that the voracious deep that failed to claim me had been replaced with the moonlit face of my rescuer, and it was *not* Commander Rowan.

"That's good, cough it all up," said the black-haired man who had been in the cage with me. His eyes were wide as plates. "And don't try to kill me. I'm on your side."

I was confused; the last thing I could remember was Commander Rowan giving me life-saving breaths of air, and then gripping my hand as the ship seemed to break around us…

"Where are we?" I asked, coughing up more seawater, throat on fire. Waves licked my toes and I squirmed away from them like they were a demon's tongue.

"No idea," the black-haired man replied, breathing heavily. "I can't believe we… we—"

"Didn't drown?" I sputtered.

"Yeah."

My bones ached. Head pounded. Wounds stung. But as I rubbed at my eyes with unshackled hands I was hit with a sense of elation; I was *free*.

"Are you okay?" The man's dark eyes met mine as his words were marked with a crack of lightning far in the distance. The storm was receding and by starlight I could see the streaks of blood running across his tattoo-covered chest.

"I think so," I answered.

"I'm Kade."

I reached out with numb fingers to shake his outstretched hand, pressing my palm to his and unable to do much else. "I'm Eva. How—?"

"Commander Rowan," Kade said, rubbing water from his eyes. "He got you out of the ship and almost to shore. When he started going under, I took over and pulled you up onto the beach. Your heart had stopped."

I sat up slowly, now noticing the unmistakable shape of a human lying prone on the beach not far from us—and not moving. My heart jumped into my throat.

"I hope he suffered," Kade added, flopping onto his back in exhaustion. "It would be what he deserved."

Hoping it might be Zoleya, I stumbled toward the body. It was only twenty strides but it felt more like a thousand before I got a handful of fabric and tugged the unconscious person onto their back.

The deathly pale face of Commander Rowan came into view. His eyes were closed. Moonlight grazed the tips of his lashes and the ends of his blonde hair. He looked peaceful. Normal. Not as ugly as his sins.

"Hey," I slapped his cheek.

No response. No pulse, either.

I could still feel the heat of his mouth on mine and hear the panic in his voice; *"breathe, Eva... Just breathe..."*

It momentarily blinded my hatred.

And he was turning blue.

Without further thought, I straddled him and began pumping his chest just like I'd been taught. Then, pinching his nose, I blew air past his lips and into his lungs, watching for his chest to rise. I repeated this over and over, arms shaking and heart pounding madly, but I didn't stop. I reasoned that not helping someone was just about as bad as killing them in cold blood.

But I wasn't sure if what I felt was relief when his body jerked back to life.

His eyes opened. He blinked my face into focus. We were nearly nose to nose, water dripping from my hair onto his forehead. Our gazes held, and when his eyes widened with the realization that I saved his life, I wearily sat back to try and gather some more air into my own lungs.

He coughed. "Y-you...?" he exclaimed, clutching his chest. "Why?"

I could have slept for a thousand years right where I was. Never in my life had I been so tired. "I couldn't let the sea take credit for your death." A wave reached up onto the sand and tried to pull us both back in. "I wanted the chance... to kill you myself."

He smiled. *Smiled.* Then, wordlessly, he reached for me. The hands that had dealt death, caused pain, and taken the person I loved most, touched my cheek as if I was something precious. Something he cared for.

Oh. Hell. No.

I slapped his hand away and instinctively reached for the weapon I didn't have. He countered my intentions by getting to his knees and drawing his knife. It was then that I realized I'd made a terrible mistake by not leaving him to die.

"Come on, Eva." Kade had come up behind me and hauled me to my feet. He was trembling. I could feel the quake of his body rippling into his fingertips. "We have to get out of here. If he made it to land, then other Raiders did, too."

"He's right. You better run," said Commander Rowan, standing and then bending over, putting his hands on his knees as he coughed up more of the sea. "But, I will find you again."

"I should kill you now!" Emotion exploded from the very pit of my being. "What you did to me and the other Aldirans... you—you deserve to die!"

"Probably. So, this is your chance, Eva," he said. "You better take it."

Then he tossed his knife toward me.

It landed inches from my toes.

Suddenly nothing made any sense. The stars were blurring. The sand beneath my feet felt too thick to move in. The silver of the moon and the shadows of the earth played games with my vision. I bent down, scooped up the knife, then shakily pointed it at his face.

"If you come anywhere near me, I'll remove your limbs."

Commander Rowan seemed amused. "I would expect no less."

I had a thousand threats and curses, but not a single one made it past my lips. I was supposed to kill this man. I had the means and the reasons to. But, as his gray eyes met mine—unblinking and full of some sort of emotion I couldn't decipher—I wondered if I was drowning again.

"Eva, we have to go." Kade pointed to the water where shapes could be seen rising from the waves. "Those Raiders are undrownable cockroaches."

"Yes, hurry," said their commander.

Somehow, in a daze, I found the strength to run. With the waves on one side and an unknown mass of solid black on the other, Kade and I hurried hand in hand along the moonlit beach. We were both stumbling; him catching me, me catching him. At a mound of rock stretching out into the sea and up to the stars, we had no choice but to turn inland.

All kinds of plant life instantly surrounded us. After what felt like hours of pushing through vines and shrubs and walking into skinny trees, suddenly it was impossible to go any farther. The moonlight was gone. We were the blind leading the blind with pounding hearts and burning lungs.

Kade tripped and brought us both crashing to the ground. In what felt like years and seconds all at once, the plants beneath me became the most luxurious featherbed, and the background sounds of the strange island a soothing lullaby. I didn't care that my cheek made a pillow of Kade's bicep and my body, abused and exhausted, relaxed against his warmth.

I tried to remain alert, but just as fast as exhaustion took Kade, it took me too.

5 EVANGELINE

The hum of rapidly fluttering wings brought me out of a dream.

I awoke to see a dragonfly hovering on a thin ray of early morning sunlight, its wings gray and lacy black. It stared as if studying me while I got my sleepy eyes to focus. Above the creature was a lush green canopy of leaves, sparkling as if coated in diamond dust, framing a sky of the most vibrant blue. Feeling stunned by my surroundings, it took me a minute to remember where I was and why I was on the ground with a man's arm beneath my head. But the sudden sting of my wrists and the many new cuts and scrapes I'd earned from barrelling through a strange jungle in the middle of the night were a good reminder.

Damn, I hurt everywhere.

Birdsongs mingled with the dragonfly's wings, the air warm and fragrant with the scent of clean earth and something floral. I tipped my head to the side, noting a dizzying tangle of thick vines and green mosses stretching out around me like patches of worn carpet. Bunches of yellow and blue blossoms peppered the bases of robust trees, and delicate stalks of grasses stood tall and proud. Everything seemed lush and healthy, and nothing like the world I'd grown up in. Had I wandered into the pages of a fairy tale? I had never seen anything so beautiful in all my life.

"Is this real?" I asked the dragonfly, lifting my hand toward it and becoming even more vividly aware of how badly every part of my body hurt—which was enough to never want to move again.

As the dragonfly watched me closely, I wondered if Zoleya was using it to see me through its thirty thousand ommatidia. She'd told me all about dragonfly eyes once. One of her many gifts was being able to take control of tiny creatures and use their vision—and this would be the first time I wasn't freaked out by it. If it was her, that meant she hadn't been lost to the sea.

I spoke in the barest whisper. "If it's you, know that I'm okay. Stay where you are. I'll come and find you, I promise."

With that, the dragonfly took to the air and disappeared.

I eased up onto my elbows. Leaves rustled, crawly things skittered against wood, and odd chittering accompanied by what sounded like a hiss made the hair on the back of my neck stand up; I wondered if the beauty of the jungle might be deceiving.

"Holy hell," Kade moaned, awake now, too.

I glanced down at where he lay stretched out on the ground, shirtless, feet bare, and pants shredded at the ankles. Blood had crusted in patches on his face and stomach, but nothing seemed to be bleeding at the moment and all his limbs were intact. He was just hurting like I was.

Struggling to sit up, his jaw hung open as he blinked our surroundings into view.

"Whoa," he said, stunned, running his hand through his mop of black curls.

"Yeah. I'm not sure if I'm awake or in a really weird dream."

He sucked in a few ragged breaths and winced, then pressed his hands to his ribs—even beneath all the strange marks on his skin I could see that he was covered in bruises. I hoped the Raiders hadn't injured him too badly.

"I've heard stories about places like this," he paused, pulled a huge thorn from his palm, and shrugged off the sting, "but never imagined they truly existed."

"It doesn't seem real."

"It will when something bites you."

With that, we both jumped to our feet.

I swiped at a crawly thing on my arm, then tried to rub the dirt off my filthy hands and onto my pants but just ended up making my hands even dirtier. Kade shook his head, causing a few leaves and a twig to drop to his scraped toes.

"Where are we?" I asked.

After straightening the pants hanging around his hips and ducking away from a flowering vine that seemed to be wiggling, he spun in a slow circle. "I dunno. Somewhere between sea and sky, I guess. Certainly not in Aldira, that's for sure. And judging by how incredibly beat up I feel, apparently not dead."

"Between sea and sky," I repeated, clinging to that vague location to not feel *lost*. This wasn't the meadow. This wasn't a Raiders' ship. But we were still on Earth in a place that seemed to be thriving and not dying—and indeed nothing like Aldira.

"Have you ever seen so much green?" Kade muttered.

I pried my gaze away from a colorful bird to study him closer. Kade was much taller than me—and I was over five feet and nine inches when Zo measured me last—and he probably had a hundred pounds more weight on him than I did. Solid and imposing, broad-shouldered and toned, I could see why the Raiders took him. If he could fight he would bring quite an audience to the arena, and from the amount of healed wounds crisscrossing his arms and chest I suspected he must have won a few, or else he would be six feet under. He had interesting eyes, both a different color and unique enough to stare at for a while. The intricate swirl of what seemed like tattoos and scars that started behind his ear and ran down across his chest were intriguing and—

"They're birthmarks," he said, turning that side of his body away from me.

They most certainly were not, but I had more important things to worry about. Like finding Zoleya. She was alive. I knew this deep in my soul—whether she visited in the form of a dragonfly or not—and I wouldn't fail her a second time.

With no idea where I was going, I started walking.

Kade lunged for me. "Hey, we should address our wounds before we do anything."

I glared at his hand gripping my forearm just inches above my wrist, where the flesh was red and swollen.

"The last man who grabbed me like that lost a limb," I warned, tugging free and trying not to wince.

Respectfully, he put his hands up and stepped back. "Point taken. Carry on."

I took the lead, skirting strange sticky plants and pushing through thick walls of vines. The jungle was beautiful, but a total pain in the ass. It was almost too lush, too vibrant, and it was incredibly disorienting—not to mention *hot*. In certain places it felt as if the plants were little stoves throwing invisible flames. Pockets of air that seemed to turn to mud in my lungs came out of nowhere and were like hitting a wall. Within fifteen minutes I was sweating buckets, and gone were the yellow flowers and patches of blue sky. Everywhere was just green upon green. Even the birds, the odd bugs with the leaf-like bodies, and a colony of ants were green. I had to keep glancing at the filth on my hands to stay grounded.

Kade had been following closely. "Eva, let's slow down. We need to think things through and be smart. We can't just barrel on ahead without a plan."

"Plan shman," I said.

He sighed heavily. "Plans come in handy. Sometimes, they even make life easier."

"If you're not doing things the hard way, then you're not living," I said, punching through some waxy plants, lungs burning.

Kade remained somber. "Well, then I guess I've lived a helluva lot. Really, though, walking in circles doesn't get anyone anywhere."

"It does if you want to end up where you started."

"Well, who the hell wants that?"

I stopped, only because I felt like I was stuck and couldn't lift my arms. The jungle was thick and I was pretty sure I saw a snake ahead. "Somebody comfortable, I guess."

"Comfortable? Okay, Eva. You're not just walking in circles, you're talking in them, and I'm pretty sure you don't want to roam around this snake-infested jungle for no reason. So, let's take a second and just make—dare I say it—a *plan*."

He sounded like Crow, who liked to make schedules and notes for every training regimen, food-gathering mission and meal prep, right down to the second. Crow—who was dead because I'd failed. In fact, all Zoleya's Guardians had died that morning in the meadow because of me. I should have heard the Raiders coming. I shouldn't have been so complacent thinking we were in a safe place and that I could let my guard down. I'd been on watch duty. I should have sounded the alarm…

The lifeless bodies of my comrades would forever haunt me, but grieving them would have to come later.

"I do have a plan," I wheezed, breathing heavily enough to make my head spin, and I was starting to stumble. "My friend is alive and I'm going to find her."

"If our bodies fail us, we'll be useless and unable to find anybody," Kade replied.

I turned to face him. "What do you suggest?"

He ran his fingers through his curls, making them stick up in odd places. I liked the way they framed his angular face, enhancing his sharp jawline and full mouth. He was certainly attractive, and I ridiculously caught myself wondering what he'd look like not covered in sand and dirt, but clean and shiny and—

"When was the last time you ate something?" he asked, eyeing my flat stomach exposed by the soaked tank top that didn't reach my belly button.

The last few weeks on the Raiders' ship had wasted quite a bit of the muscle I'd worked so hard for. My clothes hung on me.

"I don't know." As always, I was far too aware of how ravenous I was.

Kade sucked in a breath—he was dizzy, too. "Listen, we do need to see if there are any other survivors, but first, let's get our bearings and try to find food and water, okay? This island, or whatever it is, seems to have a ton of plant life. Maybe we'll get lucky."

I nodded, feeling the threat of tears.

"Hey, we'll be ckay," he said.

"I know, I'm just—"

"Tired. Scared. Hurting. Hungry. Thirsty. I get it."

Yes, but the guilt of failing my comrades by losing Zoleya was much worse than any of that. This I kept to myself, though. I didn't know Kade from a hole in the ground and just because he seemed level-headed with a healthy dose of intelligence shining in his oddly colored eyes, I couldn't assume he was trustworthy.

He thrust out a calloused and scraped hand for me to shake, not noticing the massive spider inches to his left crossing from branch to branch. "Let's stick together. Okay? Work as a team?"

I'd be faster on my own but was unable in good conscience to leave him alone in this strange place. I was relieved when the spider crawled away.

"Yes. I've got your back," I said.

Hand still tight around mine, he calmly pulled me away from a low-hanging branch where a snake was moments away from dropping down onto my head.

"And I've got yours," he replied.

I watched the snake slither away—maybe we did need each other.

6 EVANGELINE

I discovered that Kade wasn't one for small talk as we pushed through the jungle in search of food. I asked a million questions but mostly got one-word answers. He was so tense, his every muscle coiled as if ready to strike at a moment's notice. When we skirted through some poisonous-looking plants with quivering waxy leaves and came upon a millipede as long as my leg, he tossed the knife at it faster than I could blink.

"Are you going to kill every creature in this jungle?" I asked.

"Only the ones that could possibly bite us," Kade replied.

"Well, then this whole place might become a bloodbath."

As the severed millipede stopped quivering, I glanced at Kade out of the corner of my eye to see something on his face that hinted at regret; he was just trying to protect us and was quick to react. I had to be patient.

"Well, I'm starved," I said, being truthful but also trying to lighten Kade up a bit. He was a gloomy dark cloud. "Almost seconds away from chomping down on that thing."

"Yeah. Well, have at 'er." He retrieved the knife, wiping the blade on his pant leg. "I've eaten enough bugs in my lifetime."

Geez. I'd been poor, and always hungry, but I'd never eaten bugs. "I would need some sauce. Do you think there are some magic trees with jars of bittersweet around here?"

"What the heck is that?" He tipped his head, curiously studying me.

"Bittersweet?"

"Yeah."

Where the hell had Kade grown up? In a cave? "Well, it's a sauce you can make with honey and vinegar, and it's sweet but also kind of bitter. Hence the name. I'm not sure how else to explain it."

"Huh," he said, then began walking again, leaving me with another batch of questions that I would file away and ask another time.

Kade stumbled. I reached to steady him, then thought better of it. He didn't seem like the kind of guy who would appreciate any sort of assistance. Instead, I put my head down and watched my feet, keeping an eye out for more millipedes—or, worse yet, *snakes*—and continued to follow closely. When he abruptly came to a dead stop, it was like slamming into a brick wall.

"The storm must have knocked them loose," he said, seeming dazed as he pointed ahead.

Averting my attention away from his intriguingly muscular back, I realized what Kade was pointing at.

Coconuts.

Loads of them. Scattered on the ground atop beds of rotting fronds.

"Whoa!" I rubbed my eyes to make sure I wasn't dreaming again.

"They're a type of nut," Kade said as he bent to pick one up. "I found a few washed up on the shore after a storm once."

I had learned about them in one of Zo's books—ancient tomes with pages stiff from the formula preservationists used to keep them from crumbling. They were called encyclopedias and contained information on anything you could think of including coconuts. I had some candy made of it once. It was the best thing I'd ever eaten. Years later, I still dream of how it tasted on my tongue...

"I read that they're a fruit." I shook one next to my ear and liquid sloshed around inside.

Kade seemed more shocked by my response than the free lunch at our feet. "You *read*?"

"Uh, you don't?"

His cheeks went a bit pink. "Yes. I do. It's just rare to meet someone else who does. Books aren't very common since they're illegal and all. Where did you get one? What was it about? Can you write, too?"

He was looking at me as if seeing me for the first time.

"My mother had a book of fairy tales, and she taught me how to write a few words. She's dead now," I said, choking slightly on the words. "Sickness from the Black-Blooded."

"Oh. I'm sorry, Eva," he said. "I lost my mother, too."

We shared the same pain. It was a tragic thing to bond over.

"Did you love her?" he asked.

He genuinely wanted to know, and I thought that strange. "Of course. Did you love your mother?"

"No." He looked to the sky and put a closed fist to his heart. "It's good that she's dead. I respected her though."

I wasn't sure how to respond. My mother had been my everything, and her adoration and love still clung to me. I would have done anything to save her life. Anything to stop the Black-Blooded from coming into our cabin and spreading their sickness…

Which was exactly why I had to protect Zoleya. Someday when the timing was right, she would fix this planet. She would cure all diseases and rid the air and oceans of the filth, then guide us lowly humans onto the right path toward making the world a better place.

Except, I was the last of the sect. Her only guardian. Possibly the only person on Earth who knew exactly what she was.

With a shaking hand, I pointed to the coconuts. I had to keep it together. Not let my emotions get the best of me. "Well, whether nut or fruit, we should eat them."

Kade nodded, clearly grateful for the change of topic. "Agreed."

The coconuts weren't easy to open. There was a technique—which we learned by watching an orange-haired monkey that threw its poop at us—and smashing the shell the right way against a rock eventually cracked one open, but it took a frustrating curse-filled hour. At least the hydrating liquid and white meat were delicious, and there was enough of it to numb the incredible hunger that had been making it hard to see straight. My body reveled in the rush of flavor and energy, and the millipede was left for the birds.

With happy bellies and as many coconuts as we could carry, we headed toward the distant sound of waves. Kade and I argued about which way to go. He wanted the straight path through the quivering trees, but I worried about snakes so we marched on ahead until the leaves began to thin. Eventually, we broke out of the green to set foot on white powdery sand—and fell to our knees.

A shimmering beach stretched ahead of us, rolling into a stunning turquoise sea where massive columns of black rock stood straight up out of the water like giants bathing in the waves. White gulls soared through a cloudless sky, drifting on a gentle breeze that swayed the fronds of massive palm trees. It was pristine. Not a soul or speck of garbage. The air was clean. With impassible walls of rock at either end of the beach, it felt like a fortress. A paradise. I thought the jungle was beautiful, but this… this cove? There were no words.

Kade cleared his throat. "Did we die and go to heaven?"

There were beaches in Aldira. Endless miles of coastline. But they were under layers of garbage and scum, the sand black with oil and decay, putrid with human waste. People from *Before* had used the oceans as garbage cans, quite selfishly and arrogantly not caring about who would inherit their mess. Most of the fish were filled with mercury and lead, and the people who died from eating them were tossed back into the water to add to the slime or feed the sharks. This place—this beach—was the exact opposite.

I was too stunned to move for a good long while.

"I'm going in," I said once I found my voice, letting the coconuts fall to the sand. "You should too, Kade. You smell like a pigsty. Actually, you smell more like hot garbage. Or the pits next to the Durban wastelands where the dogs don't even—"

He put his hand up to cut me off. "Yeah, I get it. I stink."

There was still dried blood on my greasy and matted hair, and itchy places of skin where scabs had formed over wounds that were surrounded by layers of dirt the sea had yet to wash away. I was a giant smudge of ick marring the otherwise perfect landscape, and weeks of sweat and dirt needed to be scrubbed off. So, I wrestled off my filthy shirt, peeled off the pants I'd had on for weeks, and then waded in, not caring one bit about how much of me Kade saw.

The water was warm and clear and felt incredible. Better than laying atop a bed of feathers or falling asleep snuggled up next to Zo in the winter sun. But I was still so hungry all I could think about was my stomach. Truly, though, I'd been a ravenous bottomless pit since I could remember, never full no matter how much I ate.

The black rock towering up into the blue sky looked like a giant stick of candy. I took a few long strides toward it, noting that the water began to cloud slightly and pull at my legs. I wondered if it would tug me under if I got any closer, because where the sand darkened there seemed to be the beginning of a trough. I quickly backed away, knowing how dangerous rip currents could be.

The salt stung my wounds, but I didn't mind. My shoulders ached when I rubbed at my hair and my spine screamed with every move-ment, but the bliss of the sea made it all bearable. I separated my long strands to release the muck at my scalp and used my fingers like a comb, ignoring the pain in my wrists and hands. Scooping up handfuls of sand, I scrubbed. Knees. Thighs. Armpits and face. Layers of dirt and grime came away and the green and purple splotches on my body stood out even more on my pasty-white skin. Patches of oil at my neck from where the chain had circled my throat took forever to come off, but afterward, I felt lighter. I kept pressing handfuls of sand every-where until my palms became raw and a feeling of exhilaration claimed all my senses. The words Zo often said in the wee hours of morning echoed through my mind; *You have a choice, Eva. You can be free...* Was this what freedom felt like?

Kade waded in, but he didn't seem happy about it as he nervously scanned the water for more things that might bite us.

"Careful. Don't get too close to that rock." I pointed to the dark patch in the sand. "There seems to be a strong current there that could suck you in."

Following my lead, he started scrubbing, using the sand like it was soap and creating a black cloud of filth around him. I couldn't help but notice that what he'd called a birthmark covered the entire left side of his torso and traveled up his neck, the swirls and symbols coming to life without the dirt... was it some sort of ancient text? Would it be inappropriate to ask? I'd never seen anything like it.

Since he seemed to turn that side of his body away from me whenever he caught me staring, I decided it best to keep my questions to myself.

"You should wash your clothes." He vigorously scrubbed at his neck. "They'll dry fast in this heat."

"Uh-huh," I muttered, tipping my head back too and floating, savoring my weightlessness as I watched the gulls soar into the sky from atop the rock. There was so much to take in, but I could feel Kade's gaze on me.

"What?" I said sharply, making him jolt.

"Your eyes… they're weird. A mix of gold and brown. And I didn't realize you were blonde. Without all that grease and dirt in your hair, it looks like a waterfall of honey."

"*A waterfall of honey*?" I rolled my 'weird' eyes. "Geezus Kade, I'm starving, too. I'm tempted to go lick that rock over there." I pointed to the column of black stone. "I think it looks like that licorice stuff you see at the market in Nora."

"What the heck is licorice? Is it some sort of—" He stopped short; something over my shoulder had caught his eye. "Whoa, there's something in the water."

"If it won't eat me and I can't eat it, I don't care," I said.

"Seriously, Eva. I think it's a body."

He was off, swimming frantically toward the unmoving mass, so I followed, then tried not to squirm at the gruesome sight of a bloated corpse. Even though I'd witnessed many dead bodies, it was still a shock.

"Damn. He was one of us," Kade said, panting as we dragged the body of a young man out of the water and up onto the beach.

The wounds around the man's wrists were the same as ours.

"Was he a friend?" I asked, dizzy with exhaustion.

Kade was on all fours, fighting to catch his breath, visibly stricken. "When I was taken aboard the Raiders' ship I hadn't eaten for days. This man gave me half of his slop."

In a world where every scrap was fought for, that was extremely generous.

Forcing myself to take a closer look at the bloodless, swollen face, I recognized the man's tattooed cheeks and long, hooked nose. "He was kind to me, too. He tried to stick up for me when one of the Raiders put a hand up my shirt. They broke his nose for it."

Kade took a deep breath and then sprung upright. "We have to bury him."

It was a massive effort to drag the man across the beach and into the jungle, and an even bigger one to dig a hole in a patch of dirt using coconut shells as shovels. It was hotter inland than by the sea and without a hint of a breeze. We sweated buckets as everything seemed to move above and below us, adding confusion to the heat with vines that looked like snakes, snakes that looked like vines, and leaves that turned out to be four-legged creatures.

"Should we say something?" Kade asked, sweat dripping from his forehead onto the mound of dirt he was patting flat. His cheeks were streaked with muck, and the start of a sunburn grazed his shoulders. He'd tied his hair back, but strands at his temples had pulled free and were stuck to his cheeks. I wondered how old he was. In his early twenties? It was hard to tell. His face was unlined, skin clear and tanned, and there was some softness of youth left in his features, but he was deadly serious in a way that meant he'd witnessed a good many years of bad things.

"Eva?"

Our gazes connected over the grave. "Should we say something? Oh, right. I suppose so."

He continued to stare.

I felt sweat drip down my spine. "What, me?"

He nodded. "Yes. Please."

It was nice that he was trying to do the right thing. Most people would have just walked away. So, I cleared my throat, closed my eyes, and put my palms together like Zo used to. She was always asking a higher power for things or muttering to herself with her eyes shut tight. She'd bow her head over the creatures she'd found dead in the meadow or thank whoever created the fish or the bird I'd set about cleaning and cooking. I didn't know what words were appropriate for burying people on strange land, so I just said what came to mind.

"We didn't know your name, but for a short while you made a difference in our lives, so we will call you 'Friend.' Thank you, Friend. We pray that wherever you are now, those you loved and lost are cradling you in their arms. Your journey is over. Now you can rest."

I felt Kade's heavy gaze. "Thank you," he said.

There was an intensity in the way we studied each other, our hearts full of sadness and fear yet coupled with the selfish zing that we were still alive and free amongst such beauty. We were still walking on the forehead of the Earth and not about to be rotting in its belly. We were *free*.

7

KADE

— *JOURNAL ENTRY, KADE, AGE 9*

I took the shirt off the dead man before we buried him. I wanted it. Not because I was cold but because Eva kept staring at my chest and she wasn't buying my explanation that the marks of the Nihila were just random birthmarks. She was very intelligent. She could see through my lie as easily as I could see through the damn tank top clinging to her wet skin.

I also hoped that if I covered the marks they wouldn't burn as much when I caught myself ogling her. I told myself that curiosity was the reason I stared, not because exertion had made her cheeks pink and the sun brought out the freckles on her nose, or that she was fascinating, intriguing, and maddeningly beautiful…

Gods above, I didn't need this kind of distraction. I needed to get up, walk away from this grave, and quit staring at Eva like a love-sick puppy. But I was stuck. Held in place to this very spot, under the spell of this strange girl.

"Kade? Are you okay?" she asked.

Her concern for me only made my marks burn hotter. They viciously gnawed at my ribs because I was straying from my purpose —finding Atomica.

I could barely swallow. "I'm fine."

But I wasn't. I hadn't been fine from the moment I resuscitated Eva on the beach the night of the storm. And as much as I wanted to walk away from her, I couldn't.

A silvery black dragonfly drifted between us.

"Ooh, pretty. Don't kill it," Eva said as it landed on her hand.

All at once an overwhelming feeling gripped me right to my bones, forcing me to zero in on it explicitly. It was as if something shoved my mind in the direction of the dragonfly, and the world around it simply fell away. I felt the pull of Atomica almost as fiercely as I had when I was taken aboard the Raiders' ship. An electric charge surged through my marks and my hands, while a feeling of rage coupled with acute clarity of purpose cleared my mind of all other thoughts; kill.

But Atomica could not be a damn dragonfly!

The thing fluttered its wings and took to the sky, and as quickly as that intense feeling had taken hold of me, it let go, leaving me nearly gasping for breath.

"Kade? Seriously. Have you got a problem with all of Mother Nature's creatures?"

Atomica is not a dragonfly... not a dragonfly... not a dragonfly... "No. I just don't—feel well. Or whatever." I closed my eyes for a moment, trying to see if I could sense the pull of Atomica again, but there was nothing.

"Maybe you've got heatstroke," Eva said.

Or maybe it was her. *Eva.* This golden-haired goddess who occupied too much of my thoughts. Maybe she was the cause of the pull. On the Raiders' ship, she was in the cage when I felt Atomica the strongest, so much so that I thought I might burst apart at the seams. But when we set out to sea, the pull had dissipated completely, not to return again—until now.

But Eva bled like any other human. She was not a machine. Not a monster. Just an infuriatingly beautiful girl.

"Maybe you should go lay down and—"

"Stop," I said, bolting to my feet.

My marks were misfiring somehow. They had to be. There was nothing but plants and sand and sea around me. I was just tired and not feeling things correctly.

"Are you hurt? You're kinda green," Eva persisted.

Gods above she was exasperating. "No, I'm not green," I said irritably. "That would be impossible with my skin tone." I started walking away.

She laughed. It was such a strange mix with the turmoil in my head.

"Right," she said, following closely. "Pale, then? Would that be an accurate description of your face when you appear close to puking? Just asking for a friend."

I spun around with every intent to tell her to mind her own damn business, but that sparkle in her eyes and the slight upturn at the corners of her mouth made me forget my annoyance.

"It's heterochromia, by the way," I blurted out, breathing a bit heavily and telling myself it was because of the hunger.

She tipped her head to the side. "Uh, pardon?"

"It's what I have. Why my eyes are two different colors. I noticed you staring."

"Oh."

I marched ahead into the green opposite the beach purely to get out some weird frustration that I couldn't explain for the life of me. Eva continued to follow.

"You sound disappointed," I said. "Were you hoping for a pick-up line?"

I regretted the words the second they left my mouth and didn't dare turn to see her reaction.

"Ha! Nope. I was hoping you were speaking code for 'there's beef stew in the trees'."

I stopped short. "Uh, not stew but…well…"

"More coconuts?" Eva asked eagerly.

How was this possible? "No. Bananas. Loads of them."

Tree upon tree laden with thick green bunches of fruit spread out as far as I could see, somewhat uniformly spaced as if planted intentionally long ago. Surely the universe was just playing some twisted joke and they were all rotting. Or this was a mirage. Or maybe my marks were filling my head with strange visions…

"Whoa!" Eva let out a delighted whoop. "Not beef stew, but I'll take it!" She strode into a pocket of sunshine in the middle of the trees and spun about in a circle. "Honestly, Kade, this whole place is one giant buffet. Breakfast, lunch, and dinner, all waiting to drop on our heads!"

She seemed so fragile and small among the massive expanse of green. A surge of protectiveness washed over me that I had yet to feel for anyone. "Be careful. We don't know anything about this island. There could be people here who wouldn't like us intruding. Or it could be a trap. Or there might be some sort of insect that—"

"Stop it, Kade." She put her hands on her hips. "Where I come from, you just say thank you and don't question the little luck that comes your way. Besides, the grass isn't broken or bent, so there hasn't been anyone here in a very long time. Now, help me get us some lunch."

I begrudgingly hoisted her up to cut down some fruit, ignoring the feel of her warm thighs against my palms. Along with a leaf that she proclaimed was the size of her dream house, we dragged more bananas than we needed down to the beach. Many trips in and out of the jungle yielded more coconuts, a vine filled with water, and some sort of root Eva claimed we could eat. With full stomachs, we made a small camp on the beach as the sun left the sky, then stretched out side by side, saying nothing to each other as the stars began to appear.

The jungle sounded different at night. I was nearly asleep when a yelp followed by what might have been a growl tore through the dark and jolted me awake.

"Don't worry, I'll protect you," Eva mumbled, moving closer.
When had anyone ever said such a thing to me?
For a very long time, I stared at the sky.

8  Evangeline

When I woke up the beach was still in shadows, the sea an inky black, and Kade was gone.

The sand beneath my aching body was heavenly, like a made-to-fit mattress, and the sound of the waves rhythmically lapping onto the shore where squawking gulls awaited the sunrise was comforting—and very different than the chaotic sounds of the jungle at night. I didn't want to move a muscle because for the moment nothing hurt. Not my many cuts and scrapes, the horrible bruising on my arms, or the possibly infected wounds around my wrists.

Where was Kade? I wished he was next to me, sleeping in like we had nothing to do with our day except breathe. Maybe he'd had enough of me. Or was plucked from the beach by some mutated island vulture while I was lost in a dream… Although he was hard to read and so serious it was nearly suffocating, at least he was company. He took the edge off of the loneliness I felt without Zoleya.

Zoleya… who had been absent from my side for too long. I missed tending to her needs, doing simple things like braiding her hair and monitoring her sunlight, or even standing guard while she rested. I wouldn't even mind the strange way she came into my mind and spoke directly to my thoughts, or the fascination she overtly displayed over every bug she came across. I'd even welcome the horrifying way her hands sometimes shifted from what appeared to be skin to liquid metal, or the way her eyes would become solid black while she fought some demon within her that only she could see. I loved everything about her, the good and the bad, regardless of how important she was to this world.

"I will find you," I said to the sky.

All at once, everything became eerily quiet. So quiet that I could hear my heartbeat. Back in Aldira, when the air became still and not one living thing made a sound, it meant that a storm was coming. Did that mean the same thing here?

I became keenly aware of a rustle in the trees and the crunch of heavy footsteps; a dark shape was coming out of the shadows, and I felt a wash of relief—until I realized it was *not* Kade.

I reached for the knife but it was gone, and my attacker was gaining ground faster than I could anticipate. Before I knew it I was swinging at a massive mound of flesh, then was pinned to the ground by an enormous weight.

A calloused hand pressed down over my mouth.

"Shush now…" said my attacker.

I recognized the strange accent and thick red beard of the man I'd likened to a beast. We were in the cage together on the ship.

"Be still, Missy." His breath was close to my ear. "Them Raiders will hear ya and we'll both be caught."

I nodded and he took his hand away. "Heavy…" I sputtered.

As he eased up to allow my lungs to expand, I heard the Raiders being issued commands by their illustrious leader—it was not an approaching storm causing the jungle to become quiet, it was Commander Rowan.

The sun was rising. Any minute now, we would be visible.

"I counted fifteen of 'em," the beastly man whispered. "We're gonna have to make a run fer the trees."

I grabbed hold of his shirt. "They're *in* the trees. Listen."

He tensed. "Aye. They're circling us. We be trapped."

Never again would I be trapped.

"Come on. This way." I motioned for him to follow me.

He shook his head violently when I started heading toward the sea

I grabbed his hand. "It's okay. Trust me."

The lights of many torches crested the rock and poured out of the green as Raiders stormed the cove from every direction. Had the beastly man not warned me, I would have been ambushed.

We waded into the water and then sank down so only our heads were above the surface. All around us were patches of black and I couldn't help but think of the creatures that could be swimming about —fish with teeth as sharp as razors, jellyfish with stings that could paralyze a man from pain or even kill him in seconds—and then I reminded myself that Commander Rowan's wrath would be much worse than anything the ocean could unleash. Judging by the way the beastly man stayed in the water, I think he felt the same.

Torches lit up the banana leaves I'd slept on. "Someone was here, Commander," said a voice that carried effortlessly to us across the water. "The sand is still warm. They couldn't have gotten far."

Rowan stood on the beach, his regal posture and imposing presence making it impossible to mistake him for anyone else. "Find her," he ordered in a tone more chilling than the murky sea.

Some men charged back into the trees while others scurried over the wall of rock. Rowan remained to inspect the makeshift bed. He kneeled, put his hands in the sand, and picked up a fist full of the grains, then let them sift through his fingers and fall back to the ground. As if the sand spoke to him, he straightened, turned, and stared right at us.

The beastly man and I went under. A light passed directly over our heads and then quickly vanished. When I could hold my breath no longer, I came up for air to see Commander Rowan standing at the edge of the water, gaze piercing, eyes meeting mine in the golden morning light.

"Can you swim?" I asked the beastly man.

"Aye," he said, backing away from the shore alongside me.

Rowan was yelling for his men to come out of the trees while pointing in our direction, and I hoped that wherever Kade was, he was safely hidden.

"Listen carefully," I said, wrapping my fingers through a hand more than twice the size of my own. "When the current takes us, *don't* swim. Understand? Don't swim, don't panic, and don't fight it. Just hold on to me and don't let go. Okay? Just float."

"Float. Got it," the beastly man replied.

I led him toward the towering licorice rock as Commander Rowan called my name and demanded that we come out of the water. I felt the trough in the sand with my toes and treaded an inch toward it, feeling the current warn of its powerful pull.

"Take a deep breath," I said, then moved forward another inch.

Suddenly the water grabbed my legs, and I heard the beastly man yelp just before it pulled us both under. The swirling water was too strong to fight even if we wanted to. All we could do was hold our breath and desperately cling to each other. Swirling, tumbling, lungs starting to scream… just before I thought I might pass out from lack of oxygen, the current shoved us to the surface. But now, at an alarming rate, we were being pushed out to open water.

"Don't fight it!" I yelled to the beastly man, who, in a momentary panic, released his grip.

"We're heading out to sea…"

"The current will bring us back. I promise."

Well, either that or we would drown, which was better than whatever Rowan had in store for us. Still, the approaching vastness of the ocean was alarming, and suddenly we were so far from the shore that the Raiders looked like ants. I watched one in particular fall to his knees and slam his fists to the ground.

"We have to conserve energy. Do you know the dead man's float?"

The beastly man took in a deep breath, nodded, then rolled onto his stomach and put his face in the water. I did the same, lifting my chin only when my lungs demanded air. The sea became colder. The surface rougher. I could sense the man next to me starting to panic.

"Breathe, we'll be okay," I assured him when he came up for air.

His eyes were wild, and I could tell he was about to start swimming for shore, but the current still had a hold of us. I could barely keep my hand wound through his as my own panic started to increase until, suddenly, we weren't heading out to sea anymore. The current changed direction and began pushing us toward land. We were a long way down from the cove and the towering rock, but at least there were no Raiders in sight on the approaching beach.

The push of the water suddenly ceased, and Beast and I began swimming to shore. At one point I heard him laugh and wanted to join in, but I was too tired. My body was feeling increasingly heavy, and my movements were sloth-like as I swam. I was too breathless to appreciate our bizarre escape, and when something sharp scraped against my leg I inhaled a mouthful of water and went under.

An intense, searing pain stole my ability to move for a moment; had I been bit? From knee to ankle, it felt as if my flesh was fluttering around the bone and lit on fire. When I finally came up for air again, all I could do was gather as much breath as possible and concentrate every thought and movement toward getting to shallow water.

"Well, I'll be darned," the beastly man said once we could stand in the waves. "How did ye know that would happen?"

Weak with exhaustion and shivering too hard to reply, I couldn't tell him that I'd risked our lives with a guess. Along with coconuts, the "C" section of Zo's encyclopedia had information on currents. There were theories about them, and although I'd read every word, I was pretty sure it was just plain luck that saved us.

A wave toppled me over. The beastly man grabbed hold of my arm and pulled me the rest of the way to shore.

"Something got me," I said, sputtering, noting a mass of red pooling beneath my legs.

"Oh, slam," he said, eyes widening in alarm.

Blood. Everywhere. Pouring out of my leg. Before I could even register what was happening, he had shredded what was left of his shirt and made a tourniquet with it just below my knee.

"Something got ye, all right, Missy. It darned well sliced ye open almost to the ankle. Looks a wee bit bad, not gonna lie."

It *was* bad. He was right. I could tell by the chill that flooded my limbs. "I'm fine," I said, but my vision was spotty, and when I stood, I collapsed into his arms.

"Relax, Missy, I gotcha," he said, then picked me up like I weighed nothing and marched into the green.

I wanted to yell at him for being so bold, but I had no fight in me.

When he set me down in a small clearing infused with sunlight, I looked away from the long gaping wound and instead studied the huge man who looked like he'd slept in a dumpster his whole life. Large stick in hand, he swept an area at the base of a tree, shooing away insects and what appeared to be a blue worm, then propped me against the tree as the jungle squirmed around us. He applied pressure to try and slow the bleeding but it wasn't going so well.

I wondered what sort of creatures might be attracted to blood.

"What be yer name, Missy?" the beastly man asked.

"Eva," I sputtered. "Yours?"

Clear blue eyes met mine. "Willard Plinket."

"Willard?" I repeated. "Is that your given name or fighter name?"

"Given," he said. "Why?"

"Doesn't really suit you," I said honestly.

A scowl came over his face. "And what *would* suit me?"

I laughed, because holy stars was I dizzy, and holy stars did my leg hurt, and if I didn't laugh, I might cry or scream… "Beast," I choked out.

He wasn't expecting that. Smiling, his shoulders relaxed, and I got a good look at his front teeth—white but slightly crooked—and a portion of his upper lip that hid beneath a thick mustache. Curious, he studied me for a moment, too, then remembered my leg and got back to his task.

He pressed his palm tight over the wound and turned the laughter I was digging for into an agonized moan.

"Sorry, Missy," he said. "Ye been cut right to the bone. Must have been coral that got ye. I've heard it be razor sharp."

He tightened the tourniquet, then grabbed some leaves and pressed them over the gash. I couldn't contain a yelp and had to put my head back against the tree to keep from passing out.

Breathe, I reminded myself, and I tried to focus on anything other than what was happening to my leg. Beast was muttering something but I tuned him out, concentrating solely on a patch of green that had begun swaying. Leaves were shaking and branches were parting, and now I could see the unmistakable glint of a knife; Kade. His mismatched eyes were wide and glaring, and the strange marks all over his chest and neck seemed to glow. Did he think I was being attacked? He angrily marched toward us with a look of pure hatred and murder in his expression, ready to drive a blade into Beast—or, quite possibly, me.

9 KADE

My ancestors believed that Atomica was created in the shape of a human, but during the thousand years of it being hunted, it transformed into something more easily hidden. I've been told that I must suspect everything, trust my instincts, and kill without question.

But, what if I'm wrong?

— *JOURNAL ENTRY, KADE, AGE 17*

When I was asleep next to Eva on the beach, the presence of Atomica jolted me awake and I nearly stabbed her in the heart.

But, no sooner had I positioned the tip of the blade over her chest when the pull shifted as violently as my thoughts. Then I was running after some unseeable thing, my marks taking over and telling me where to go, filling my emotions with a dark rage that consumed me to the core. I was barrelling into the dark jungle without any thought other than *kill*.

Then I felt insane when the pull suddenly stopped altogether, sending me to my knees in a damn near fit of hysterics. There was nothing around but plants and bugs. Nothing that was a weapon of mass destruction. Nothing that posed any threat. Was Atomica taunting me? Could it do that?

"Where the hell are you?" I roared into the shadows of vine-covered trees and coiled plants that seemed to squirm.

I still felt nothing. My marks were dead asleep on my skin. This made no sense.

"What form did you take? I will find you, Atomica. I will not disappoint my family. *I will not fail.*"

I felt the pull again as if the abomination heard me, and it lit up my marks, making them dig deep into my muscles and bones to propel me forward. I don't think I could have fought it even if I wanted to. It led me out of the jungle and onto a beach where I ran a mile, only to head back inland when it changed direction before vanishing once again.

"Damn you!" I yelled, making an animal with a white stripe scurry away from me. "Show yourself!"

Nothing.

I stood for a long while and waited.

Still nothing.

I was just about to head back to Eva when I heard voices, specifically the shrill pitch of someone in pain, so I made my way through the jungle toward them as the morning sun broke through the canopy of leaves. The voices grew louder. Suddenly, the pull hit me over the head like a sledgehammer, once again so strong I could barely see straight. It led me to a small, blood-covered clearing where I was positive I would find Atomica—in whatever form it took—waiting for me.

But it was Eva. Being attacked by a massive man. And I was very aware as the rage exploded within me that I was not charging toward her with the knife to save her.

Except when she put her hand up and told me to stop, I did. I could clearly see the blood pouring from a gaping wound on her leg, from the flesh and blood of someone completely, certainly, and undoubtedly human. My conscience took over for one moment and warred with my DNA, my marks, and my years of grooming to hunt without question, and suddenly I didn't know who to kill.

I didn't know who to kill.

I gripped the knife as the ancient technology buried into my skin sent messages to my muscles to react—

Again the pull disappeared, leaving me gasping for air.

Eva probably thought I meant to protect her, that I was about to kill her attacker, but I wasn't sure *what* I'd been about to do.

"*Trust your marks*," Mother had always said. "*They are never wrong.*"

But Eva was not Atomica, and I refused to be a monster like the cursed thing I'd been bred to hunt—if I even had that choice.

10 EVANGELINE

Clarity came to me just in time. Kade was charging toward me and Beast with a murderous look on his face and the knife in his hand. Did he think I was being attacked?

"Kade, stop! He's one of us," I said.

The look in his eyes was unearthly making his irises seem ruby red as he paused as if trying to make sense of what he was seeing. He stared at my leg, and the blood, and then honed in on my face. His expression gave me chills. Were his marks glowing? They seemed to shift around on his skin…

I blamed it on the pain that was making it hard to see straight, but for a moment I thought he meant to kill *me*.

"This man is helping me," I said, fighting to stay conscious. "He was in the cage too."

Kade's eyes returned to their usual mismatched color of blue and brown, and his marks now looked like his regular—albeit intricate and hella weird—tattoos. He dropped the knife as if it had turned to lava in his hands and wavered off balance, then rushed forward and got down on his knees next to me.

"That doesn't look good," he said, breathing heavily, sweat beading on his forehead and dampening his hair.

Beast looked up from my leg to give Kade a quick once over then shrugged his shoulders with a huff as if he was nothing more than a pesky fly.

"Whadya go by?" Beast asked, pressing more leaves to my leg.

"Kade Thorn."

Beast maintained pressure. "Well, don't be causin' me any problems, Kade Thorn. Missy here is gonna bleed to death if we don't be workin' together to sort her out."

Kade paled slightly—yes *paled*. Olive-skinned or not, the pallor of him lightened considerably.

"What happened?" Kade asked.

"Something got her in the water." Beast shooed away some ants. "Coral maybe? It's deep. To the bone, I think."

"I knew the water was dangerous." Kade took in a deep breath—his hands were shaking as he wiped his forehead. "And you… what do you go by?"

"Will—" Blue eyes met mine briefly. "Beast. You can call me Beast," he said with a small smirk.

"Beast," Kade repeated. "Not your real name, but fitting."

The two men locked eyes for a moment, silently having a conversation I wasn't part of. I felt like they were communicating "she's gonna die", because their body language was panicked and hurried but their voices were maddeningly calm.

"Have you come across any others?" Kade asked as he quickly plucked more leaves and handed them to Beast.

"Just the Commander and fifteen or more of his men. We're lucky that Missy here outsmarted them in the sea, or we'd be goners."

I was losing focus, the movements of the men becoming a blur. Pressure to my wound was released, more leaves were applied, and then more pressure. I winced with a jolt of pain, and the world suddenly got quite fuzzy.

Kade pressed his fingers to the inside of my wrist, probably because he wasn't sure what else to do. "Eva, I'm so sorry I left you alone."

I wanted to ask him how he found us so easily amid the endless green, but I was too tired. "I'm not yours to protect," I muttered, my head not wanting to stay on my shoulders.

There was regret in Kade's voice. "I got up because I couldn't sleep. I thought I'd scout the area and—well, dammit. I shouldn't have left you."

I was the protector. I was the one trained to care for others. Although I liked Kade's company, I didn't need him babysitting me or feeling responsible. Besides, I wasn't alone, I had Zoleya, and I could feel her now, alerted by my pain. She'd taken over a butterfly this time, and it nervously danced on the breaths between Kade and Beast, hovering, assessing me head to toe.

"I'm okay. Don't worry," I said to it, *to her*, but the world was starting to spin and slip away. The canopy of green was becoming black.

"Darn straight," said Beast. "We'll make sure of it."

"I promise I'll do everything I can to help you," said Kade, but he was gritting his teeth and staring at the butterfly as if it had grown teeth and claws. When it flew up and into the trees, he took in a deep breath and returned his gaze to mine. "I—I mean *we*. We will get you fixed up. Right, Beast?"

"Aye," said Beast.

We. Although I didn't need help, I liked the word.

"I'm okay," I said. But what I should have said was thank you.

11  KADE

Day one of my first journal. I'm gonna write all the things. Keep all my ideas in one place so that when I'm done killing Atomica and my marks erase all my thoughts, I'll know exactly who I used to be.

— JOURNAL ENTRY, KADE, AGE 6

We moved deeper into the jungle and made camp as the sun moved directly overhead. Beast went about building a fire while scrutinizing me out of the corner of his eye; I was still trembling from what I'd nearly done. Guilt was crushing me into a thousand pieces. Had I listened to my marks without any reservation, Eva would be dead.

"She's a brave one, ain't she?" said Beast.

Eva—sound asleep on the ground and so deathly cold I kept checking her pulse to see if she was alive—was brave, yes, but so much more. Why had the Raiders chained her up inside the cage like the men? Did they intend to put her in their arenas to fight? And why was she so important to their commander that he risked his life to save her? It wasn't simply because she was *brave*...

"I guess." I sucked on a vine filled with water to satiate a strange thirst and tried to not look too hard at Eva... would the wound kill her? *Would I?*

"Ye can have a lay down beside the Missy if ye like," Beast said, stepping back from the flames. "Rest for a bit. I'll keep watch."

The island buzzed and hummed, every sound keeping me on high alert. From a homemade holster at my thigh, I retrieved the knife Rowan had tossed to Eva's feet and inspected its sharp edge. It was finely made. The blade sturdy. The weight and length similar to the knife my mother had used to pierce her own heart—my mother, whose body I turned to ash on the Anyan stone. My mother, who died so that I could take her strength and fulfill my destiny. And I would do exactly that.

But I had also promised Eva I would look after her, and I meant it.

As if reading my mind, my marks burned, stabbing and digging into my ribs with vicious force, warning me that I could not stray even one moment from my purpose, that there was no time to worry about the welfare of some insignificant human. My family—quite possibly the last of the Nihila—had died *for the greater good*. Nothing I was feeling mattered.

I rubbed the lower part of my back where raised scars from whip marks peppered my skin... I didn't know how to *not* feel. It was one thing Mother had failed to teach me.

12   EVANGELINE

I was vaguely aware of Beast and Kade circling me like sharks as I drifted in and out of consciousness. They kept asking me weird questions. Poking my shoulder. Feeling my wrist for a pulse. Certainly not hiding their concern or panic when they thought I'd expired in my sleep.

But I hadn't been beaten. Not yet. Some random coral slicing me open wasn't going to be the end of me—that much I knew.

Someone had built a fire. The sound of it brought me back to my childhood and I let my mind drift to a memory of the old cabin with the crackling woodstove, sitting on Mom's lap while she read to me and my sister from one of her favorite preserved books. Delia was too little to understand words, but she'd react to Mom's animated voice by giggling and momentarily forgetting about the itchy spots all over her tiny body. Mom would lovingly touch the pictures and then guide me through the letters, teaching me how to sound them out. I loved how cozy and warm we were, and how the stories blocked out anything remotely bad, sad, or painful.

The day Delia died, Mom built a fire in the old stove so big that flames licked out around its hinges, and then she put in every book we had, singing to me as the flames burned them to ashes.

Crackle, sputter, heat and color
The fire's a singin', the fat birds a spittin'
Baby will eat soon, Mama will feed her
and the only cryin' will be the bowl gettin' a lickin'

After Mom died too, I mumbled those lyrics whenever I felt scared on the streets of Nora and needed to tune out the sounds of the terrifying city. I used them to sing myself to sleep. To find comfort or distraction from horrid things like the rats and the stench…

Whoa. Why could I smell the city again?

"Come on, wake up, please," said a gruff voice.

I looked up at the worried face of Beast. He was holding a coconut shell inches from my mouth. Was he the source of the smell? My eyes watered.

"Ah. That's good. Now drink," he ordered.

His hand was under my neck, lifting my head to the brown husk. I had no choice but to let the sweet coconut water make its way down my throat.

"Thank you," I muttered.

Looking past his alarming size and breathing through my mouth, it took a moment to get my bearings. A twilight haze washed over the green, which was humming, wiggling, buzzing, and yelping. I was extremely relieved to discover that I wasn't on the ground. Beneath me were long, split pieces of bamboo, their curves rather comfortable under my aching body. Beast had built a platform that seemed to be a good few feet up off the dirt, and it felt like a palace.

"How did you build this so fast?" I asked.

He grinned. "Ah. Ye has mostly been asleep fer a night and a day. If'n I had the proper tools, they'd be a roof." He sat next to me and put his fingertips to my forehead, feeling for a fever. "More importantly, how ye be feeling, Missy?"

"I'm fine. I think." I did a quick head-to-toe assessment; many parts hurt or throbbed painfully. My toes were tingly, my palms a little too sweaty, and my shin… oh, it was bad. I tried to ignore its wretched complaining.

My pants had been cut away mid-thigh and the removed fabric was fashioned into bandages around the wound, replacing the shredded pieces of Beast's shirt that were now washed and hanging by the fire to dry.

"Thank you for looking after me," I said, choking slightly on my gratitude.

Although his eyes didn't meet mine, his concern was obvious. He fiddled with his beard, pulling at the curly red strands, and shrugged like saving my life was no big deal. "I did have some help. And ye ain't out of the woods yet."

I realized with a start that Kade was stretched out next to me, his eyes shut, the fire casting golden hues over his cheeks. I tried to put together more fragments of the day but could only remember wanting to help set up camp and passing out when I tried to stand, then jolting awake to see Kade impale a noisy bird with a knife. At first, I thought he was securing us dinner, but the bird's body was tossed into the trees. It hadn't been attacking, nor was it big enough to worry a man of Kade's size, so it was a strange reaction. I knew Beast felt the same thing when I saw him shaking his head at Kade, and I was glad Zo hadn't witnessed a winged creature needlessly killed. She would have taken a stab at Kade herself.

Zo…

Zo! I had to find her! I had to set aside my aches and pains and start moving, start walking. She was alive, and she needed me.

Beast's hand shot out, gripping my shoulder. "Whoa there. Whadya think yer doin'?"

My mind was racing. "I can't just lay here. I've got to go find my, uh, *friend*." I tried to push his hand away, head spinning and leg screaming with the movement.

Beast wasn't having it. He pressed me back down, not letting up until I was flat again. "Just stay where ye be, Missy. I'm sure yer friend be fine."

Kade rolled onto his side and the platform wobbled beneath his weight. His hand fell to my arm and he gave it a gentle squeeze. "Beast is right." He sounded sleepy. "You'd just be easy prey for the wildlife with that leg of yours, and getting eaten isn't going to do your friend any favors."

My leg was bad. I knew they were right. But what if something lurking in the jungle was after Zo? Or… *had* her? She was completely defenseless without me. What if she was injured? Alone and vulnerable? What if she wasn't getting enough sunlight, or worse yet, too much…

Oh, stars above. I had to keep it together and remember my training. What would Crow tell me in this situation?

I closed my eyes and tried to channel the vein of common sense he always thought I possessed. Since I had already failed Zoleya most epically, I knew I couldn't find her or protect her on my own. It was painfully obvious that I needed help. I needed *numbers.*

Kade and Beast were strong, healthy, and lethal, which was why the Raiders took them in the first place. They could be excellent recruits. I knew Crow would be telling me to keep them close and gather my strength, bide my time and gain their trust, then build an army of Guardians—just like he had in Aldira.

But time wasn't necessarily on my side.

I took in a deep breath. The fire crackled. I clung to the sound as I got a lungful of smoke along with Beast's horrid smell.

"How did you build the fire?" I asked.

He rose from the platform and picked up a bundle of branches. "Them Raiders have been scouring the shoreline and scavenging stuff that's been washing up after the storm." He broke branches and tossed them in the flames, then stabbed at something crawling past him with a pointy stick. "I done stole a fire starter while half of 'em were tugging crates out of the water."

Beast had an illegal object. I had to remind myself that we weren't in Aldira and he wouldn't be hung for it if caught. "Oh."

"Ye know, their ship hit a reef. Ye can see it from the beach. Waves be crashing up all around its busted bits, and how any of us survived is beyond me. Anyway, them Raiders, they ain't afraid of useful items like these fire starters." He held up the strange device.

"You call it a *fire starter*?" Kade sat up, rubbing his eyes.

"Yup." Beast held out the contraption, a small column-shaped thing the length of his thumb. He moved something on the top and it produced a tiny flame. "What would ye call it?"

"Trouble," said Kade, tensing.

Beast shrugged and slipped the gadget into his pocket. "Meh."

"How many Raiders did you see?" I asked, picturing the ship, once an imposing and terrifying sight on the coastline, now landlocked and destroyed—it made me smile a little.

"I done lost count at thirty," said Beast.

Kade ran his fingers through his hair, but the unruly curls sprung back up. "Damn."

"Yeah."

"How are they?" I asked.

The few lines on Beast's forehead crinkled. "What ye mean?"

"Well, how did they look? Are many of them injured, or were most of them up and moving about? Did they appear organized, or scattered and scared?"

"Oh." Beast scratched his beard, then began twisting its ends in concentration. "Well, there certainly be more able-bodied men than injured as far as I could tell. And nasty as always, stinking up the place with their cussin' and such. They seem to be organized the way them Raiders are, ya know, efficient to the extreme. Many fires lit, lots of people giving orders, and they have food too. I smelled meat cookin'."

"Did you see any people that *weren't* Raiders?"

Beast nodded. "Aye. Fer sure. I saw a few men in chains."

I looked Beast in the eye, wishing I could see inside his mind. "How many?"

"I don't know, Missy. Eight? One looked kinda dead, though."

Numbers... "So, you think you saw at least thirty able-bodied Raiders and eight Aldirans."

"Hmm, yeah, but it was at night, so they probably be more."

Kade cleared his throat. "Eva, you know there were more cages on that ship besides ours, right?"

My stomach flipped. "Uh, no. I didn't."

"We were in the hold with the cargo. There were six cages up top, too. All full."

I didn't want to ask, but I had to know. "How many people, Kade?"

"Twenty to a cage, if I were to guess. All ages, it seemed. Probably being sold as slaves by the looks of them."

I felt my blood boil. "How many crew members do you think were on that ship?" I asked, hands shaking with anger.

Kade rolled off the platform and slowly lumbered over to the fire, kneeling before it as if every movement caused him great pain. "It's rumored that the ship, The Whydall, employed one hundred and forty-seven men."

More than I thought. "Plus our twenty-four in the cage, and possibly another hundred and twenty on the main deck, makes—"

"Two hundred and ninety-one people," Beast said, spitting at the dirt. "Plus their captain and Commander Rowan. That be making two hundred and ninety-three possible survivors."

"Minus the man we buried," I said. "So, two hundred and ninety-two possible survivors."

We all contemplated that for a moment. There was no way even half that amount lived through the storm and the ship breaking up, or the swim to land.

"We need to check out the Raiders' camp." My heart was racing. "Find out how many of them we're dealing with and see if we can free any of our people."

"Our people?" Kade repeated, eyes meeting mine across the flames, confusion clouding them.

"Yes," I said. "You, me, Beast, and anyone taken against their will and dragged through hell on that ship are our people." And possible Guardians for Zo.

Kade, unreadable, lowered his gaze.

"I will never be held against my will ever again," I said, voice stronger than I felt. "And I will do my best to make sure no one else is either. Are you guys with me on this?"

"Aye," Beast stated.

Kade just stared at the fire.

"Kade, are you with us?"

His eyes met mine. For a moment I thought he might tell me to shove it and head off on his own. His hands were shaking. His teeth grinding together as if my question was causing him great turmoil. But, eventually, he stood, crossed his arms over his chest, and took a deep breath.

"Yes," he said firmly. "I'm with you, Eva."

13  Evangeline

By firelight and a full moon, Beast joked as he dragged the knife through my other pant leg.

"If we keep cutting up our clothes, we're gonna end up naked, and although I look amazing in my birthday suit, I don't wanna be shooing off ladies swarming me day and night."

I laughed. Kade's somber expression didn't change.

"Well, Beast, maybe you've invented a new island trend," I said. "Cut-off pants could become high fashion."

His eyes crinkled with a grin. "Ugh. I'd rather be blind than see any more of Kade Thorn than I gotta, Missy."

We'd been trying to get Kade to lighten up just a little, but it seemed he didn't have a lighthearted side to him. I wondered if the weight of the world that he seemed to be carrying on his shoulders ever lifted, or if he remained trapped in reality, bound to it so tightly he couldn't let go and have a laugh for one second.

At least Beast was uplifting. I appreciated him finding the brighter side to our otherwise dim situation.

"Don't worry, guys." I braced myself as Beast began re-wrapping my wound, tying the fabric around the still-seeping gash. I saw stars for a moment. "There are things in the jungle perfect for weaving into clothes…" I breathed through the pain, mouth dry. "I'll make us all some grass skirts."

My leg looked dreadful. Beast tried to hide his concern. "I wipe my arse with grass. No way am I *wearing* it." His eyes met Kade's and the mood of the entire jungle seemed to darken significantly.

"It's bad, isn't it?" Kade asked.

Beast cleared his throat. "Her leg? Well, it sure ain't pretty."

I patted Beast's arm, which, if I didn't know any better, could have been a boulder warmed by the fire instead of flesh. "It'll be okay," I said. "I'm a fast healer, and I'm tougher than I look."

"Aye." Beast's voice was pained, but there was a glint in his eyes. "Yer pretty durable, *for a girl*," he said with a chuckle, noting the glint of annoyance in my clenched smile.

"And you're a big ol' marshmallow *for a Beast*," I teased.

Kade's eyebrows drew together. "What the hell is a marshmallow?"

My jaw dropped to the bamboo platform. Had Kade never had a treat in his life? Gone to the market and drooled at the candy stands? What kind of life had he been living?

"Never mind. Don't care." Kade put his hands up abruptly. "I've got other things to think about."

Right. He was going to spy on the Raiders' camp and come back with a full report. We'd planned—to his restrained elation—and discussed everything at great length. He knew to mark his trail so he could find his way back, as well as what signs to follow if Beast had to move our camp farther inland.

But he was worried about the task. I could see trepidation tugging at his angular features. Maybe he was intimidated by the jungle.

"You'll be okay, Kade," I offered. "You've survived worse than this. Plus, you'll have a torch to light your way."

He looked at me like I'd spoken a different language. "What?"

"You're strong and—"

"I'm not scared of the damn jungle, Eva. I'm worried about you," he blurted out, and as if the words caused him great pain, he lurched forward and clutched his ribs.

"Whoa, Kade…are you hurt—?"

He put his hand up to silence me. "No." Gathering a ragged breath, he tugged at the black shirt tight across his chest. "Listen, I'm going to find us some medical supplies. In the meantime, just, uh, don't die."

I forced a smile and swallowed a lump in my throat. "Uh, no prob."

His somber expression lightened ever so slightly.

"I'll wait until you get back," I added with a grin.

His eyes darkened. "Not funny."

He stood. The makeshift bag made from my other pantleg was full of food we'd gathered and strapped to his back. Skin gleaming with a thin sheen of sweat, he faced Beast. "If anything happens to her—"

Beast put his hand to his heart. "It won't on my watch."

Then Kade disappeared into the dark, and I felt a strange tinge of longing for him brush across my heart.

"What kind of person don't know what a marshmallow is?" Beast grumbled.

"A very stern, no-frills kind of guy, apparently. Maybe he was raised by goats."

Beast snapped a branch in two against his knee. "The boy gots no sense of humor. He be serious as a heart attack. Makes it hard to breathe."

Huh... that it did. I pulled air in now, deeply, filling every inch of my lungs.

"Can ye sleep now, Missy?" Beast asked, stoking the fire and swatting at something crawling too close to the platform.

I was so tired I could have cried. "Maybe."

He sat down and hugged his legs with arms as thick as trees. "I don't think I can. I just have so many questions. I mean, how could this be?" He made a sweeping gesture to the surrounding jungle. "I just don't get it. Our whole lives we been told that the only places capable of sustaining human life are Aldira and the Raiders' island of Cal de Mac. I mean, some get talkin' of Carlina, as they do, ya know, drunks mostly, but I done think it might be a hoax just to give us blockheads something to dream about. So, I'm quite flummoxed, Missy. It's been drilled into our heads that everywhere else be nothin' but ruin and death. All laid waste by The Burn. Yet here we be with clean air, green plants, and scads of living things. This ain't a barren wasteland trapped beneath radioactive clouds. It's not dead or dying. It's... plentiful."

"I know, I feel like I'm in a really good and bad dream."

"Aye," he said with a snort. "All of my years traveling between Nora and Port Hayes, suffering in them stinking cities and risking my life to earn a coin just to buy some bread, and notta once did I even think about going anywhere else. But… all this time, there be *this*." Yet another hand gesture to the trees. "Maybe back home, the Council be lying to us. They be hiding the fact that beyond our mountains are fields of green, places fer food to be growing and such. Maybe they gots it wrong about the radiation, and them warnings to stay away from the West Coast be false and—"

"I've been to the West Coast," I said, unable to suppress a shudder, "and I've trekked through the mountains. There's nothing but dirt and rock, and any humans you encounter are either long dead or a mutated version that should be. You've seen the Black-Blooded, yes?"

"No. I been lucky so far."

"The creatures by the coast are worse than they are. And besides the dust making it too thick to breathe, the waves that come up to the shore are tinged red with sickness. Not even rats can live there. The Council isn't lying about that. Our continent is truly divided, and the west coast of Aldira is nothing but a wasteland." I remembered having a good look at a red, frothing sea as a child, coughing up a lung in Crow's arms. Our tribe had been seeking a new home for Zoleya and had to turn back when we were attacked by slimy-looking creatures that seemed to be nothing but teeth and bones. I had nightmares of us nearly dying there for months after.

"Well." Beast scratched his neck. "I can safely be saying that we ain't in the likes of Aldira, that's fer sure. So, where the raspberries are we?"

I pictured one of those old maps that Crow liked to stare at with little red X's all over the brown parchment, edges ragged from use. "How about since we're not sure, let's call this place Island X until we have a better name."

"Island X, eh? Well, that be good enough for me. Paradise sounds fitting but kinda lame." Beast's icy blue eyes met mine, the unfathomable kindness he possessed making them sparkle. He was nothing like his intimidating exterior; there was a thoughtful, deep thinker on the inside.

"Ye need stitches," he said, changing the subject.

"I know." The new bandage he'd wrapped around my leg was already soaked through, but it didn't matter; we had a knife, the fire starter, the clothes on our backs, and not much else. All we could do was wait and see if Kade returned with a healer's kit.

Beast stretched out by the fire, not in the least bit worried about whatever was crawling around him—but only after giving my surroundings a thorough check.

"Do you think there are snakes nearby?" I asked.

I heard him laugh. "I be a heck of a lot scarier than a snake, Missy. Ye can be sure of that. Now sleep."

In seconds my mind was fading with the knowledge that I was, at the very least, safe from the island's beasts under the protection of my own.

14 EVANGELINE

While Beast snored by the fire, I found myself replaying the morning that the Raiders ambushed me and Zoleya in the meadow. Funny, but I'd felt the same sense of calm then that I did now. Like I had no reason to worry—but I'd been so wrong.

The day had started like any other, with me asking Zo the question that always haunted me through the night; "Do you think there are snakes around here?"

Zo had sighed and straightened the skirt of her dress. We'd spent the night under the stars beneath the chestnut tree, and she sat upright with her back against its trunk. "Like I told you yesterday and the day before, there is only an eleven percent chance you will run into one in this meadow."

I suspected the smarmy critters lay in wait in the tall grasses surrounding the dilapidated cabin and in shadowy crevices along the river, their beady little eyes watching, bodies coiled and ready to strike. They could venture out of hiding and slither into a sleeping blanket at night, or crawl up the tree and drop onto our heads.

I couldn't suppress a shiver. "Eleven percent. I don't like those odds."

Zo laughed. It sounded so human. "You should be more worried about what new regimen Crow is going to put you through when he returns from scouting the perimeter. You're still injured from yester-day's training."

Our illustrious leader showed no mercy to any of the Guardians, forcing us all to continually train when not on duty. But I liked that he was purely devoted to Zo's protection and that nothing else mattered. It suited me just fine.

"My ankle will be quick to heal," I said. "Truly. I'm more worried about what's lurking in the outlying mountains than anything else."

Zo pulled her knees up to her chest and rested her chin on them. The first rays of morning light played with her pale blonde hair— which I would soon braid into the intricate plaits she loved.

"You don't have to worry about a thing," she said, voice echoing through my head. She plucked a daisy and put it beneath her nose, inhaling deeply. "We are safe here, Eva. The Raiders don't travel this far inland, and I have not felt the presence of the Nihila for a very long time. It's also too cold for the Black-Blooded and the snakes. Besides, Crow and the others are securing the perimeter. You can rest. Close your eyes and relax."

That was funny. "I'll relax when I'm dead."

Zo turned to face me, her unblinking eyes staring intently into mine, unimpressed. "You know, Eva, you can leave whenever you want." Her small hand brushed aside a lock of my hair with genuine affection. "In fact, I think you should do that right now. Leave here and go live a normal life."

I had a good chuckle over that. Zoleya was unfathomably important, and her preservation far exceeded the wants and desires of a nine-teen-year-old nobody.

"You're my family." I pressed a kiss to her forehead and, even after all these years, still found her abnormally cool skin a bit of a shock. "And besides, I love you."

Her gaze fell to her hands, which were white as paper. "You cannot love an abomination."

She was in a mood. I had to tread carefully so she wouldn't shut down completely.

"You are a phenomenon of biological and technological marvel that I'll never pretend to understand," I said. "But an abomination you are not."

She turned her hands over and, with a scowl, retracted the skin covering her palms. Somehow equally horrifying and intently beautiful, there, glistening and moving as if alive, were hands of what I could only describe as liquid metal. A small ocean of shifting colors, mostly silver, pulsed and flowed over unbreakable bones.

"Then what the hell am I?" she asked.

I reached out to touch her fingertip. "You are a beautiful soul with razor-sharp wit and a unique view of the world. Someone excited about bugs and flowers, a generous teacher, a fair and wise leader… and most certainly the most incredible person I know."

"You think of me as a person?"

"Yes. A very unique one."

"Why?"

"Well. You've mentioned that not all of you is man-made, for starters."

"Only my brain."

"You have a heart too, Zo, I can feel it."

She shrugged. "That's just my nuclear fusion processor converting solar energy. Simple physics based on the theory of—" She stopped short and tipped her head to the side as if listening for something, then returned her gaze to mine. "Listen, Eva, I need you to promise me something." Her hands had become 'normal' again as she changed the topic.

I would never get used to her drastic mood changes. "Okay?"

"If you can free yourself from this life—from me—you must do so. It is what I want."

The tree over our heads rained pink petals as I stifled a laugh. "Yeah, right. You'd be miserable without me. And as much as I hate to admit it, I'd be miserable without you."

"Not necessarily," she said. "Let me show you why…"

I felt my body grow weak and my eyes involuntarily shut, then suddenly I was swirling through a cacophony of colors toward an endless sea of black. Zoleya was dragging my mind out of my body and taking me to a realm that no human should be forced to go. A vast never-ending continuum of time and space that was unreachable in the physical world. I sensed that I was at her side as we soared through muted puffs of what appeared to be smoke in dizzying shades of reds and blues before coming to a halt in an area of infinite darkness. Zoleya pulsed next to me, her essence—or her mind, I wasn't sure what to call it—vivid gold like the sun. The thread tethering me to her quivered.

"Why do you keep doing this to me? I asked. "I hate it here!"

To an onlooker, my body in the physical realm would appear lifeless, crumpled in a heap at the base of the chestnut tree while Zo sat next to me wide-eyed and catatonic. In reality, though, I was very much alive, albeit terrified and totally pissed off.

Ah. But I do like it here, Zo said, her golden light trying to envelop me completely and blur out the alarming expanse of black. *I know it bothers you, but it's pleasing for me to be free of physical constraints.*

"Well, I think it sucks," I said, or thought, or whatever it was that one did to communicate to another being in a strange realm without a voice.

I just wanted to show you that if you left, we could still be together once in a while.

"I prefer talking to you with actual sound waves. Please get out of my head."

Zo sighed. *We've discussed this, Eva. I'm not* in *your head; rather, I've taken you out of your head. Only a very rare kind of Sage can communicate directly to someone's mind, and I'm not that kind of Sage. I merely brought you to this place to show you that we can be together. In this realm.*

"Realm shmelm. How would you feel if I yanked you out of your body? This is so not cool."

She laughed and her light shimmered and pulsed around me. I could feel her emotion just as clearly as I could understand what she was saying.

Oh, Eva. That would be impossible. You do not possess the ability to come to this realm on your own. You must be brought here by a Sage. You are merely a Receiver and nothing more.

"No, what I really am is annoyed. And this place… is horrifying."

She sighed. *I'm just trying to tell you that you can go and live the life you deserve and still be with me. You have a choice, Eva. You can be free.*

"I don't want to be free if that means living without you!" I yelled. Or angrily projected. "Now, take me back."

As you wish.

As quickly as she'd yanked me from my body, she shoved me back into it—a bit forcefully—and I sprung upright with drool running out of the corners of my mouth and a fly crawling up my nose.

"Save your party tricks for Crow," I said, wiping my chin.

Zo smiled. "Oh, Eva. So stubborn. So—"

"Choose your words carefully or I'll braid your hair into the shape of a turd."

"And funny," she said, eyes flashing that brilliant blue. "You can always make me laugh."

"Well, life is pretty hysterical, isn't it?"

I stood, stretched, then kissed her cool forehead—and that was when I heard the Raiders. But I heard them too late to do anything about it.

"Eva…" I blinked my eyes open to see Beast towering over me. "Ye all right there, Missy?"

I wasn't in the meadow anymore. I was on a strange island, and I'd failed to protect Zo, and there was no going back and changing that.

I shrugged off the memory. "Yes, Beast. I'm fine."

"Okay. Good." He brushed a spider off his arm. "Because we need to git ourselves some fresh water. And food. The kind ye cook, not them bananas and mangoes and such. Any more of that crap and I'm gonna turn into a fruit salad."

He had come to stand beside the platform, his massive body blocking out the heat from the rising sun. I awoke earlier to him cracking coconuts, and now a dozen were lined up next to me on the bamboo bed. I could see that it was killing him to sit idly by when our survival depended on so much.

"I gots to head deeper into the jungle where I can build a better shelter," he added. "If a storm done came a fussin' up this way, we'd be too exposed. We're too close to the water, and there are not enough trees between us. And—"

"You go on, Beast. I'll be fine on my own." I inched up onto my elbows and flinched; my leg was hot and red.

Beast anxiously scratched his beard. "Kade should be back soon. In the meantime, if ye needs me, ye scream, aye? My ears are good and my feet be swift."

"Yes. You got it."

A bird, or monkey, or island zombie screeched in reply, and Beast froze mid-step. "Maybe ye'd be safer on the beach closer to me. I'll comb the shore first and see if anything useful washed up."

I knew what he was thinking; there weren't as many creatures next to the water that might sniff me out for a meal, and hopefully not as many insects trying to invade my wound.

"I'll be fine. Go do what you have to do," I said.

But Beast grunted some unintelligible reply, then plucked me up off the platform like I was a feather pillow. The smell of him! The entire city of Nora was right under my nose. I couldn't get enough breath to complain about him picking me up without asking.

"Ye can keep a lookout for me on the beach, aye, Missy? Alert me if ye see any Raiders."

I had no choice because in a blur he was marching out of the trees toward the sea, and soon we came out of the green onto a pristine, white beach with towering mounds of rock like the ones in the cove. They rose out of the water like kneeling giants. Birds. Blue sky. Shimmering water. Soft breeze.

"Whoa. It just keeps getting better," I muttered.

Beast set me down under a towering palm tree and took a moment to admire the stunning beach.

"Island X, eh? I like it here," he said.

Then he stomped off.

Leaning against the tree, the sand soft and warm beneath me, I studied the rocks that framed the tiny alcove... or was it a lagoon? From what I'd seen of the island so far, the beaches were guarded by these fortresses of stone. Had they protected this little piece of paradise from The Burn all those years ago?

The water was glassy with barely a ripple and looked good enough to drink. I imagined wading in and guzzling the sea dry. My throat had become parched, lips puffy as if blistering, and all at once out of nowhere, I felt like I was coming apart. Was it because I'd lost so much blood? Or was this the beginning of a fever?

"Here," said Beast.

I almost jumped out of my skin. He'd returned, so drenched with sweat it looked like he'd been showering in it. Now he reeked like the dumpsters of Nora on a blistering summer day.

I took the cracked coconut he was holding out to me and downed the juice, eyes watering, breathing through my mouth as much as possible. "Thank you."

He grunted something and kneeled next to my leg. "Agh, she don't seem to be wanting to clot. Looks a wee too red as well. Is it hurting ye?"

It was, but I didn't want to admit it. Instead, I feigned interest in a vividly blue bird and realized that the sun was much higher in the sky than it seemed a moment ago. How long had I been sitting here? "So many interesting birds here, don't you think?"

Beast looked at me as if I'd grown horns. "Sure. I guess. But, Missy... yer leg?"

"It's fine."

"Ye either be putting on a brave face or ye gots no feelings," he said, peeling bananas and shoving them in his face, breathing heavily around the chewing.

"Let's go with happily delusional."

He grinned. "I'm okay with that."

"How's the scavenging coming along?" I asked.

"Good. I got a nice pile of odds and sods for the new shelter, and the base be finished. The platform is wide enough to stretch under all the arses of the stinkin' lot of us, and more if we be finding any strays. Gotta git a good three feet off the ground, aye? It's no palace, but it'll do."

"Is there a bathtub?"

Beast smiled, his teeth barely visible beneath the scraggly mustache. "Aye, and cotton towels."

"Marble floors and feather beds?"

"And a kitchen brimming with honey cakes."

"Cake…" I had some once and had dreamed of it since. Vanilla, fluffy, and sweet… my mouth was watering.

Beast insisted I eat a banana. It was delicious but nothing like cake.

He moved me to the base of a different tree when the sun shifted, and the shade beneath the towering palm leaves made the silky heat of the morning rather blissful—or was it afternoon? I was nodding off.

"I'm gonna head to the next beach and see what's been washed up," Beast said, startling me awake. I watched him move about like a cat, fluid and graceful. "I don't much like the water, but maybe I'll give myself a good washing up while I'm there. No peeking," he teased, dumping an armful of cracked coconuts next to me.

I smiled, relieved that he might return smelling better and also happy for the coconut water—I was so incredibly thirsty.

"Scrubbing with sand worked well on me and Kade, by the way. It got the remains of the voyage off our skin," I yelled after him. "Works on clothes, too."

"I'll give it a go," he yelled back.

He disappeared for a moment and returned with some bananas and massive leaves. "Shield yourself from the sun with these if ye have to. You're getting a wee pink. And eat some more."

Then he was off.

I was jealous of his seemingly boundless energy and strength. I felt like a putz just sitting, staring off at the horizon, picturing all sorts of things that weren't there; ships, whales, a giant dog? Doing nothing was playing tricks with my mind and the bloody bandages on my leg were attracting flies. I had to do *something*.

Dragging myself to the water's edge felt like an endurance test. I knew the salt water was going to sting, but I had to get the wound and the bandages clean. Untying the strips of cloth holding my flesh together brought forth a gurgle in my throat; my leg looked worse than I thought.

The water around me turned pink and the salt stung enough to make my vision darken alarmingly. Forcing back a scream as I soaked the wound, I could only hope that the ocean salt would pull out any infection.

The bandages I removed were not only filthy from my blood, but from being my clothes for the last few weeks. Scrubbing them with sand, I rinsed and wrung out the colors that shouldn't have been there and then rubbed them again. Tucking them under my chin, I dragged myself out of the water, barely able to catch my breath.

I spread out the bandages to dry on top of the huge banana leaves. When I looked toward the water, a trail of dark red marked my path in the sand—there was no hiding where I'd been.

And the flies were back.

I couldn't leave the wound uncovered, so, in desperation, I peeled a few bananas and laid the inside of the skins over top. The cool flood of relief was overwhelming. Flopping back on the sand, I peeled more fruit and covered my sunburned chest and arms with the skins, even draping a few over my face.

"Stars above, what happened here?" Beast said, returning and dropping something he'd been dragging behind him. "There's blood everywhere… and, well, I wanted ye to eat them bananas, not wear 'em."

"I thought I might look good in yellow," I muttered, sitting up and realizing the sun was much lower in the sky and the peels were now brown and sticky; had I passed out?

"What's going on, Missy?"

I peeled a peel off my peeling forehead. "I just had to get the wound clean," I muttered.

Propping myself up on my elbows, I noticed that Beast had gotten himself clean, too. His clothes were soaked, he smelled like the sea, and he'd scrubbed himself pink. There were no questionables crawling in his beard, and the stink of his horrific body odor was gone—thank heavens. But there was a scowl on his face that was new.

"Maybe just git to waiting' and don't do stuff like that by yerself," he said gruffly, snatching up the bandages and tossing the banana peels behind him into the green.

He was worried, and rightfully so; I was a huge liability to his survival.

"Sorry," I said, hating the feel of that word on my tongue.

His brow relaxed and he began re-wrapping my leg. "Ah, it be fine."

I watched him tend to me, hair drying quickly and beginning to spring up from his head. When he looked up to catch me staring, I saw eyes like Zoleya's, as blue as the sea.

"You know, back there on the ship. Well..." he sighed. "I didn't mean to insult ye, Missy. Ye know, with the 'yer only a girl' comment and all that."

I smiled. "Really, it's okay. You're just a boy. You didn't know any better."

He stood and a smile crept over his face. "Ouch," he said, playfully clutching his heart.

In that moment, I knew I'd found a friend for life. I think he did, too.

"So, what did you find?" I asked, noting that the knife in his hand was new as I pointed to a pile of what appeared to be a bundle of fabric on the sand.

"What? Oh, that! I done cut as much as I could 'cause I couldn't drag the whole thing outta the water. Can ye believe my luck?"

I blinked a few times, trying to make sense of what I was seeing.

Excited, Beast lifted a corner of sun-bleached canvas. "The ship's sail," he said triumphantly.

"How the... " I sat up too fast and made everything throb. "It's like this island is trying to help us *not* die."

"Aye. Here we be shipwrecked and not had it this good in weeks."

"And you said there's more?"

"Sure as the nose on my face. I'll go back for it and—"

A hair-raising *clap* broke through the sky. Dark clouds were moving quickly across the horizon and the wind picked up—hadn't there been sunshine a moment ago?

Beast sent a wordless scowl to the approaching storm. "Maybe we spoke too soon."

He made quick work of bundling the heavy canvas as best he could. The temperature dropped and the energy in the air became electric; this storm was going to hit us hard.

I refused to be carried and instead limped along next to Beast into the green until his patience ran out. I was too slow, he was in a rush. My protests fell on deaf ears as the canvas was thrust aside and I was gathered up in his arms.

"I'm not okay with you completely ignoring me when I say no to you, Beast," I said angrily, but truly I was angry at myself for being weak—all this bleeding had really sapped the energy out of me.

"Ye be tough, Missy Eva, but yer—"

"If you say 'just a girl,' I'll feed you to the fishes," I threatened.

His heavy breath surrounded me as he barrelled ahead, stomping down waxy plants and skirting moss-covered trees. "I was gonna say 'injured,' and it ain't nothin' to be ashamed of. Happens to the mightiest of us. Besides, I'm not just letting ye lounge about in a self-made grave of banana peels to die under the might of nature. Now shush and git to watching' where we be going' so ye can find yer way back to the beach if ye gotta."

It all looked the same to me—and I think I might have dozed in his arms—until we came to a small clearing where Beast had built an impressive shelter.

He'd split four stumps into Y joints and used them as the base to anchor felled trees. The structure was about three feet high and crisscrossed with split bamboo. He'd even filled in the gaps between the bamboo with pieces he'd smashed flat. He'd also "swept" the ground, built a stone barrier for a fire, and amassed a small collection of coconuts, bananas, mangoes, and passionfruit.

"Holy smokes," I muttered in awe. "You truly did build my dream house."

It was nearly dark. Beast shrugged his shoulders and went back for the canvas.

"How did you do all this?" I asked when he returned as a loud *boom* ripped through the sky. For once I was happy to be in the green. The trees started rustling and the temperature of the air dropped another ten degrees, but we seemed protected here.

Beast hacked at the edge of the canvas, tearing off a long piece and handing it to me. "Fold it in half and twist. It'll do for rope."

I suspected he was too tired to talk so I just did as I was told, making rope with the torn canvas pieces he kept handing me. Soon there was a makeshift roof over the platform, the remaining section of the ship's sail secured and sturdy enough to keep the rain off our heads. With a fire roaring, Beast collapsed next to me, and I was pleased that the platform didn't crack or sag under his weight.

"You are amazing, Beast," I said.

Another *boom* ripped through the sky.

"Ah, thanks, Missy. This bed be good and strong beneath us, don't worry." He wearily patted the platform that would keep us dry and off the ground. "It won't break. Tomorrow I'll head back for more of that sail, make some walls for ye to hang art upon and angle another piece over the fire so we not be in danger of losin' her to the rain—I hate cold food and I hate the dark."

He put a hand to his forehead and I noticed the masses of blisters, nicks, and scrapes from fingertip to wrist. I felt a massive wave of gratitude.

"Thank you for this," I said. "I'm so truly grateful for you. For… everything."

He grunted some sort of reply.

A moment stretched to a minute, just me and him, simply breathing, lulled into a state of relaxation beneath the patter of lightly falling rain. I thought about Kade. Was he caught in the rain or, worse yet, by the Raiders? And Zoleya…

"How'd ye know that rip current would bring us back?" Beast asked out of the blue.

I adjusted my spine on the bamboo bed. "My friend had a book she used to let me read. It had information on rip currents. And… once, I tied a ribbon to a bottle and tossed it into a dark swirly patch of water. It went out to sea then came back."

"A book ye say? I'd like to see one someday." He scratched his beard. "But what yer telling me is that ye made an educated guess. We actually could've drowned."

"Yes. But I thought that was a better alternative than being caught and chained."

Beast nodded his approval. "Aye. For sure."

I could tell he had more questions, so I waited.

"And, Zoleya… the white-haired girl," he said after a while. "What is she to ye?"

My jaw clenched at the mention of her name. "She's my sister."

He stole a glance, no doubt comparing our appearances. "Not by blood."

"No."

"But ye feel responsible for her," he intuited. "Like ye would a sister."

"I don't *feel* responsible for her, I *am* responsible for her. She is my only family."

"Somethin' be different about her," Beast said, rubbing his temples. "I'm not sure what it is, but—"

"She's just pretty," I said quickly. "All men are enchanted with her."

He didn't skip a beat. "Ha, nope. That's not it." He waved away a plume of smoke. "I can't be explainin' it right, but I feel like—well this might sound weird—like I could feel her energy or something like that. And I know she ain't dead because every once in a while I think I feel it again. Which don't make no sense."

If I were standing, my jaw would have hit the ground. Was Beast a Nihila?

"Does that feeling make you angry?" I asked, holding my breath.

"Angry? Geez, Missy. What a strange question. But no, if anything, it made me feel like I needed to be protective of her or somethin'. Like she be special. I dunno."

A Nihila would feel rage and a lust to kill. That much I knew. Besides, Zo purposely kept her power too low for a Nihila to detect her in the first place. So, had Beast experienced the same thing I had the first time her caravan passed me on the streets of Nora? Rendering me unable to do anything but *follow?*

"Sounds dumb, but fer some reason I want to help ye find her," he added nonchalantly.

"Do you think we're going to get a bad storm?" I asked, desperate to change the subject. He had me rattled. "It's cooled off drastically."

"Huh? Oh. The storm. Nah, we're just gonna be getting the edges of it. A wee dusting of rain is all."

"How do you know that?"

"I can feel it in my bones."

Maybe Willard really was a beast and just more in tune with nature than most people. Nothing more.

Although, Zoleya wasn't technically *natural.*

"I'll help ye find Zoleya," he said with a yawn. "I'll make that promise if ye will take it."

Maybe Beast had a higher purpose and was destined to be one of her Guardians—just like me.

I smiled inwardly. "I'll take it."

15 

"It seems a bit hypocritical," said Elder Mathias to Mother. "Implanting circuit threads into the boy to make him more adept at hunting a machine from Before, when the threads themselves are born of machines. It also seems cruel, does it not? He didn't choose this life."

Mother sliced my torso open like I was a side of beef. "Choice is what nearly broke this planet. It has no right to exist anymore."

— JOURNAL ENTRY, KADE, AGE 12

I came to a standstill in the dead of night, my torch casting weak light into the thick jungle surrounding me. I hadn't felt the presence of Atomica in a long while, and after a thorough inspection of every fluttering creature I came across and killed, I was at a loss. Where the hell was it? And what was I even looking for?

From somewhere in the distance, I heard the sound of voices. Many voices. I knew by the strange cacophony that it was Raiders. Their camp seemed to be due north of where I stood, and since I was nowhere near finding Atomica, I decided it was time to make my way there and steal a healer's kit for Eva and get her the information she wanted.

Suddenly my marks lit up brighter than my torch and the pain they forced upon my body brought me to my knees. I could barely breathe.

The world was dimming as panic surged through my heart and blood throbbed at my temples. The marks were hurting me for deciding to stray from my purpose. Gasping, tears rolling down my cheeks, the pain was so bad I was nearly ready to take my own life.

"Stop," I begged, clutching my ribs and rolling onto my side. "That's enough!"

I was sure they were going to kill me. Never in my life had I experienced this kind of pain. Not when the elders began enhancing my marks as a child, and not when they dug into them during their awakening. I could barely breathe as I curled up like an infant, feeling helpless.

"I'll cut you out of me," I warned, hoping that a threat might sedate them.

It did not.

My life seemed to flash before my eyes; the caves in which the Nihila hid, the smell of smoke in the air as they conducted whichever ceremony that they thought might enhance my senses, and the cruel 'life lessons' taught by my mother. Mostly, though, my mind was flooded with stories told by the light of a flame about how man created a machine and married artificial intelligence with a human mind, then weaponized it for the war that caused The Burn. The complete disregard for the destruction this weapon caused was a legend in its own right. I was reminded why I didn't have a childhood. Why I wasn't loved and nurtured but groomed to kill; so that the planet would never experience another near-cataclysmic event brought on by humans ever again. And fuck the humans. The less of them the better. I had to do whatever it took to ensure the survival of the planet and the creatures on it that *deserved* to thrive.

At least, that is what had been drilled into my mind since birth. I hadn't been prepared to hear life-changing words that had me questioning everything I thought I knew. Because Eva shook my foundation the first night on the beach when she'd said, "Don't worry, I'll protect you."

As if *I* was worth saving, too. *Me*.

I'd felt something other than sadness and rage just then. Like I mattered to someone in a different way than what the Nihila had groomed me for.

And I'd craved it since.

But the marks weren't having it, and the agony was driving me mad.

I tried to get my knife out of my holster, trembling, thinking that I would at least try to cut the marks off of my skin or attempt to dig them out. I would bleed to death, but it would be a welcome release from the torture. But, as if knowing this, the marks simply increased the burn and tightened around my neck, making it nearly impossible to breathe. Could they read my mind? Or could they just sense what I was about to do by my emotions?

"I will… n-not let anything get between m-me and my mission!" I yelled, frantic for a solution, hoping to say what they wanted to hear as they continued to drive spikes into my bones. "But I need allies. I need others around me to… to survive, or I will never be able to fulfill my destiny."

The burning lessened; the marks were listening.

Fighting to stay conscious, I continued. "This land is foreign to me. The odds of succeeding are slim to none if I am alone."

The marks released their hooks from my bones, allowing me to take in a full breath. I sensed that they wanted me to explain my actions, so I did.

"My body has been battered and beaten." I stared at the waxy plants beneath my hands as drool, snot, and tears dripped from my face. "It needs time to heal. To regain strength."

The burning lessened even more.

"Eva is imperative to regaining that strength, she can gather resources and people around her. She thinks logically, is trustworthy, and can lead a tribe. Also…" I sucked in another breath and wiped my nose with the back of my hand. "I believe that Atomica is attracted to her." I did not add that I was as well. "So, I am using her to lure it toward me. She is bait."

The burning stopped. Completely. I panted for a minute, hands on the earth, feeling the pulse of the jungle around me.

"Eva is injured and might die. I must keep her alive... for now," I said, barely a whisper, no need for yelling anymore. "And that means going to the Raiders' camp and doing things that might seem like I am going off course, but I can assure you that I am not. You must trust me, just as I have trusted you."

Suddenly I felt light as a feather. Like the weight of a thousand Anyan stones had lifted from my shoulders. I could stand. Straighten my spine. The marks dimmed and then resembled nothing more than a maze of what could have been ordinary tattoos. Unhindered by pain, I stood and stared up at the heavens. *For the greater good* had suddenly taken on more than one meaning.

"Thank you," I whispered upward, pretty sure that wherever Mother and the Elders were, they were listening.

Determined and with unhindered objectives, I headed for the Raiders' camp. I would steal supplies, free any prisoners I could find, get the lay of the land, and take a healer's kit back to Eva. For the moment, I was in control of my body and in charge of my destiny. But I knew that wouldn't last long.

16 EVANGELINE

The fire was merely embers when I heard footsteps growing louder in the trees. Someone was approaching our camp in the dim light of morning.

"Beast," I whispered, shaking him. "Incoming."

He awoke and bounced upright, then followed me as I limped into the trees. Crouching, we waited until the faces of three men came into view; one of them Kade's. His black hair was soaked in sweat, nearly flat to his head, and his cheeks were pink from exertion. He looked tired but all in one piece, and I was shocked by how relieved I was about that.

I stood, unable to hide my smile despite the horrid feeling in my leg.

"Ah, good. You didn't die," he said.

Was that a grin tugging at the corners of his mouth? He seemed a bit different somehow. Eyes brighter, jaw and shoulders more relaxed. Maybe he'd discovered marshmallows.

"Glad you're back." My voice trembled. I cleared my throat. "Who have you brought with you?"

Dropping an armful of supplies to the dirt, Kade motioned to the two newcomers, both reeking and filthy.

"They were in the cage with us," he said.

Funny, but I didn't recognize their faces. Maybe my mind had blocked out that hellish experience.

Kade wiped the sweat off his brow with a corner of his shirt, revealing his marks for a moment. They looked different too.

"Many Raiders survived," he said. "More than I thought. They're salvaging things from the wreck and combing the beach and jungle for food. Unfortunately, they're better off than they should be. But at least we managed to pilfer a few items."

The men behind Kade had their arms full but seemed hesitant to set anything down.

Kade continued. "The Raiders have guards posted everywhere, fires up and down the beach, stations set up for food prep and an area to tend to their injured. I was able to free these two because they were at the edge of the camp. Four others are being held more in the center. I couldn't chance it."

Numbers. More able-bodied men to help me find Zoleya. I was elated.

"Did you see any of the women?" I asked.

Kade shook his head no.

I was relieved and upset by that at the same time. "How about the people in the upper cages? Did you see any children?"

"Commander Rowan ordered them to be freed. They could have been lost to the storm."

I felt sick. Beast let out a huff, feeling the heavy loss too.

"And what about the captain, did you see her?"

"Yes. Captain Vera Vallerik is alive and well," Kade said. "Preening in a chair on the beach and barking out orders. She rules her crew with the edge of a sword on the sea and is no different on land."

"And Commander Rowan?" I asked, pressing eagerly. "What about him?"

Kade's lip curled in a slight snarl. "Unfortunately, Commander Rowan is alive and appears uninjured as well."

My chest felt tight. My leg throbbed. "I'll need a full report, Kade. Of everything you've seen. A map of what you can remember." My scalp tingled. "I need to know every single detail completely."

Kade nodded. Beast smiled. One of the two strangers made a mocking snorting type of sound, but I couldn't tell which one.

"I'm Eva, by the way," I said, eyeing them both.

The taller of the two stepped forward. He was thin and wiry with eyes like black holes, somehow reminding me of a starving fox. His brown hair had been cut close enough to the scalp to be almost nonexistent. A tattoo of words in a language I didn't recognize covered his forearm and was the only part of him not coated in filth. I suspected he was in his early twenties, but lines around his eyes and creases on his forehead suggested hard living had aged him faster than his birthdays. He set down a healer's kit and a machete then reached to shake my hand. For some reason, I hesitated to oblige… but then noticed the wounds around his wrists that mirrored my own.

"Thank you for saving us," he said.

I was confused. He noticed.

"On the ship… you had the commander unchain us first, and, well, that was very stupid," he clarified. "But, very brave and kind."

His hand remained wrapped around mine, which garnered a step forward from Kade.

"Respect," he said, letting go and placing a fist over his chest. "I'm Dominic Falkosky."

"Nice to meet you, Dominic Falkosky." I put my fist over my chest too; I knew what this man had gone through, and the respect was mutual. "And this is Beast."

Handshakes were exchanged.

The other male stepped forward and peered at us with heavily lidded eyes. His clothes were practically rags, feet scraped and bleeding, and right arm in a sling. He looked about my age but there was no ignoring the mounds of lean muscle achieved by years of hard labor. Springy auburn curls crowned his head and streaks of dried blood showered his neck and chest, but for some reason, I didn't think it was *his* blood. There was a sharp glint of intelligence, and—despite obvious weariness—intense vibrancy in his eyes.

"Max," he said, wincing when he offered his hand.

More wrist wounds like mine… I took his hand gently. "Nice to meet you, Max."

There was an awkward silence as we all assessed each other. Standing amid these four men taken by the Raiders for their sheer size, brute strength, and ability to kill, I suddenly felt quite small. I had to remember that I was taken because I, too, was a fighter.

"By the way, Dominic Falkosky *is* my real name," said Dominic. "Just to clarify."

Silence.

"My father was a Falkosky. His dad, too. Bastards, all of 'em."

More silence.

"Dominic means 'belonging to the Lord.' It's Roman Catholic or one of those obscure religions, but let me assure you, I don't belong to nobody. I'm not sure what the name Falkosky means, maybe 'like a falcon' or something? I am rather intelligent and quite fast."

I wondered if it meant 'talks a lot when nervous.' But Dominic did have a rather sharp, bird-like nose.

"Never had a middle name, though," he prattled on. "I think my dad ran out of ideas since I was the third kid. That man didn't have a creative bone in his body. He grunted most words instead of—"

"So... what's the plan?" Max interjected.

Dominic's mouth snapped shut.

Beast tipped his head to the side, eyeing me expectantly.

"Eva loves to make plans," Kade said with the barest hint of a grin.

Why was this on me? I took in a deep breath, mind racing. There were so many tasks: the need to find fresh water and a source of protein, address injuries and fortify the shelter, and—

These were all things they knew.

These men wanted the *bigger* plan.

I looked each of them in the eye. "We're going to get all our people together and take control of this island. We won't bow to any Raider— they'll bow to us. Our plan is to go beyond just surviving; we are going to thrive."

And all of you will help me find Zoleya, I thought but did not say.

Dominic snickered. Max rolled his eyes. Kade said nothing, but I could see that he doubted my words too.

I glared at all of them. "One of you equals, what... four or five Raiders? You were all taken because you can stand your own in an arena against the mightiest men of Cal de Mac. The Raiders want to bet their hard-earned money on you because you're scarier and stronger than the average male. Am I right?"

"Darn straight," Beast grumbled.

The others nodded.

"Well, that means something," I said.

"What about you?" Max had a scowl on his face. "You were in the cage chained up like the rest of us. Were they going to put you in the arena too?" He laughed, showing his ignorance. "Or were you gonna bake bread for the crowd?"

While Max spouted the same sexist crap I'd been hearing all my life, I tuned him out and watched the spider that had been staring us down for the last five minutes drop from its silk just inches from his shoulder. Zo's books had many sections on dangerous spiders, and I always made sure to read up on any potential threats—no matter how small. This furry arachnid with yellow-striped legs and red fangs could kill a man in seconds.

Knife in hand and not giving it any further thought, I lifted my arm and whipped the blade forward through the air.

My aim was true.

Max stumbled back, shocked. "What the hell! Were you trying to kill me? Are you insane?"

I motioned to the spider now impaled on the tree next to him and his face turned white.

"Whoa, a phoneutria," said Beast. "I seen one before. One bite from that bad boy and it's game over."

I put my shaking hands behind my back—my body was close to giving out as the pain in my leg was becoming unbearable, but I couldn't show weakness.

"Word of advice, Max," I said, forcing my voice to be calm. "Never judge based on appearances. Sometimes the most unassuming can be the deadliest."

17 EVANGELINE

Dominic liked to hum while he worked. Face expressionless, he dove a needle into my flesh, slowly pulling the gaping wound on my leg back together with thread as his tune carried through the camp. It was eerie, silencing even the loudest birds as he methodically went about his task, patching me up like I was a torn quilt he'd fixed a thousand times. The fire smoked with the husks of coconuts, sunlight streamed through the trees, and I bit into the stick between my teeth, sweating bullets and fighting to stay conscious.

Then it was Max's turn, his auburn curls sweat-soaked and clinging to his cheeks, hands balled into fists as Dominic sewed up a large gash across his ribs then maneuvered his shoulder back into place, still humming that tune.

After the stitching, Max and I lay recovering, stretched out on the structure Beast had built beneath the shade of the ship's sail.

I snuck a look at the young man next to me, wondering how he'd managed to not scream or even shed a tear from the torture he'd just endured because, despite a few moans, he'd remained silent. His fists were still clenched though, and he stared up at the canvas roof as if wanting to rip it to shreds.

"Where are you from?" I asked.

Max took his time answering. "Carlina."

I noticed Beast's head jerk up and a smile spread across his face.

"Oh? Most people don't believe it exists," I said, grinning back at him.

"Well, I'm living proof that it does."

"Do you have family there?"

Max squeezed his eyes shut. "Not anymore."

My heart sank. "Oh. I'm an ass for asking."

"No, it's okay." He shifted his weight, the ropy lean muscles of his arms flexing. "I want to remember every moment of why I am alone. I want to remember my family's faces and the way they screamed in terror when the Raiders attacked."

Clouds rolled in, darkening the sky.

"I'm so sorry—"

"The guard was tripled after that," he said, lost in thought. "The wall was built, and no invasions have happened since. But it was too little too late."

I hated to ask, but I had to. "Your family... were they—"

"Father killed. Mom, sister, and older brother taken. They were loaded onto the ship *The Annamarie,* along with another one hundred and eighty villagers, gold, weapons, and livestock. Homes were burned to the ground. Entire families were wiped out."

I lowered my eyes in respectful silence.

"But it's okay," Max said with a snarl. "Because I'm going to get my family back."

He was delusional. Nobody taken to Cal de Mac had ever been rescued. It was unheard of. Impossible. Like sending a moth into a bee's nest to kidnap the queen, or coming face to face with a Nihila and thinking you might win against them in a fight.

"And now that I'm free from that cage, I'm going to kill every Raider I come in contact with," Max added.

Commander Rowan's face flashed across my mind. His storm-gray eyes darn near rattled me upright, and I couldn't stop what burst from my mouth. "They can't *all* be bad."

Silence. A cutting copper glare from the young man next to me.

I cleared my throat. "I mean, some are forced into that life, and others... well, there probably aren't many career options for men born in Cal de Mac. Maybe they have no choice but to do what they're told."

"*No choice?*" Max said, choking as if the words were poison. "I call bullshit. Every man has a choice. Are you sticking up for the Raiders?"

He'd propped himself up on his good arm and his tanned face was now red as cherries, the freckles splattering his nose and cheeks darkening. The anger and pain in his expression made my chest tighten— mostly because I knew I was being a hypocrite. I'd wanted to kill every Raider when I was in the cage and Zoleya was taken from me. I'd felt that same unfathomable rage.

"They took everything from me, Max," I said gently. "And I, too, carry the weight of revenge. But does one bad apple truly spoil the whole lot? Are they *all* evil?" I recalled the feel of Commander Rowan's mouth on mine when he gave me life-saving breaths of air as the ship was sinking... and the look in his eyes when he threw me his knife on the beach and told me to run...

I could feel Max's glare increase but couldn't stop myself from continuing.

"I mean, if revenge and hatred harm those that are innocent, is it worth it? I think that for us to get what we want, we must conquer the Raiders while entertaining the possibility that they might not *all* be evil."

Did I truly believe that? Or was I trying to quell the ire of the man next to me? One good deed didn't fix a past riddled with a thousand sins. Commander Rowan embodied evil from head to toe. He kidnapped people. Killed people. Sold people. And... the bastard took Zoleya from me. Maybe he was the bad apple of the bunch. Maybe his people would be saved if that one bad apple was disposed of—but deep in my heart, I didn't think so.

After a second of silence passed between us, Max's glare centered on me and he simply said, "Your 'possibilities' can fuck right off. I'm killing them all."

18  EVANGELINE

We all fell into our respective tasks of gathering food and expanding the shelter, but it was hot, humid, and the sky was just broken pieces above the smothering ceiling of leaves. Brown spiders as wide as the palm of my hand often got too close, while lizards in dizzying shades of blues liked to launch themselves from tree to tree and startle me senseless. I didn't like it in the green, so when Beast suggested we hit the beach to cool off, I could have hugged him.

The sun was low in the sky when we stepped onto the sand. As the wind blissfully brushed our sweat-soaked bodies, we all spent a moment in awe of the island's beauty before wading into the water.

My shin stung but was bearable, and I was rather pleased with Dominic's handiwork; the stitches were going to leave a ghastly scar, but at least I kept my leg—and my life.

"This will never get old," said Kade, and there was the tiniest hint of a smile on his face. It looked good on him. He also didn't seem so worried about the too-small shirt barely covering the birthmarks or tattoos on his chest.

"This is actual paradise," I replied.

"It is," he said, stretching his arms up over his head.

"Hey…did something happen on your trek to the Raiders' camp?" I asked, studying him a moment. "You don't seem so—grumpy."

He splashed water on his face. "Grumpy?"

"Yeah. You know what that word is, right?"

"Yes. But I'm still not sure what a marshmallow is. Care to share?"

Avoiding the question? Huh. Well, whatever happened, it must have been significant.

With a heavy sigh, I tipped my face to the sun. "Well, Kade, a marshmallow is a really soft—"

I felt Zoleya at the edge of my mind. She was prodding, warning me to get my body safe so she could steal my mind away.

"Problems?" Kade asked, concern clouding his eyes, grin disappearing.

I had seconds to get out of the water or I'd drown.

"Cold," I said quickly and waded out as fast as I could. I heard Kade saying something but didn't even pretend to listen. The edges of my vision were narrowing and any second now my body would become slack as a noodle.

I barely made it underneath the shade of a palm tree when the world darkened. I could only hope that it looked like I was just napping and not having my consciousness detached from my physical body.

"Zoleya..."

Sweet Eva. Please don't be upset that I brought you here.

I would never get used to the way Zo's golden light circled me in the vast expanse of darkness, and how the thread of my consciousness trailed out behind me into the realm. It was overwhelming and far surpassed what my puny brain could comprehend.

"No, it's okay. I'm just completely freaked out and confused about the logistics of this place. You know, the usual."

Rightly so.

"Where are you? Are you okay?

I'm in a safe place, yes.

Her light seemed to pulse with tinges of pink and purple, which I had never experienced around her before. I realized that her energy felt... different.

Are you sure your body is safe? she asked.

"Yes. I'm with people who will protect me if need be, and—oh, Zo. I'm glad you finally came to me. I have been worried sick. Are you monitoring your sunlight? Do you know where you are? I'll start making my way to you and—"

Stop, Eva.

The purple hue seemed to expand, almost pushing me away. "Zo?"

You don't have to worry about me anymore.

I laughed, but it didn't project accurately. It was a foreign, forced feeling that muddled the light. I had to change the topic; she was in 'that' mood, which was always best avoided.

"Have you been coming to me in the form of insects?" I asked.

Yes. Butterflies are the easiest to commandeer. Their minds are small, so I can project into them directly... I had to see if you were still alive.

I felt like I needed to keep her talking. "Maybe with enough practice, you'll be able to commandeer a human someday. Communicate directly instead of using this freaky meeting place. Wouldn't that be something?"

Eva, we don't have time for chit-chat.

No, we didn't. "Okay."

Listen, I am very well and I am not alone. Many of the women made it to land with me, and they have become my caregivers.

I couldn't help but feel a tinge of jealousy. "Oh. That's excellent."

They are extremely competent. I am well taken care of.

"Good. Yeah, that's good. But I will still come to you."

We are separated by a vast amount of water—

"So, I need to build a boat or learn to fly?"

Now her light pulsed with bursts of gold. *Oh, Eva. You always make me laugh.*

"Well, at least I'm good for something, because keeping you safe from Raiders sure wasn't my strong suit."

What's done is done. Now, tell me, is there a healer among you?

I sighed. "Yes, Dominic. He sewed up my leg. It's healing."

Yes. Without stitches, you would have bled out. I am glad you were tended to.

"I'll be back to running in no time."

Now her light pulsed with a pink hue. *I saw a man with black hair and strange marks on his neck. There is something familiar about him that I can't place. It seems odd, but he hates butterflies. Birds too. His behavior is very erratic.*

"That's Kade. He pulled me out of the water when the ship sank. He has a temper it seems, but I think I can trust him. There are two others with me as well. Max, who is hell-bent on avenging the death of his family, and Beast, who I think might be Guardian material. He says he felt a connection to you on the ship."

Beast has a strong aura, just like you. From what I've seen, he would make a good Guardian.

"You've picked up a lot of info through the eyes of a few bugs."

Yes. But I have to access energy reserves to do so, so I must abstain for a while.

Right. It was most important that Zoleya maintain a certain level of stored energy. Not too much, not too little; whatever necessary to keep the artificially intelligent side of her dormant.

"Noted."

I am glad you are at least safe and with good people, Eva.

"I'm fine. Don't worry about me, Zo."

Noted.

Her light shifted again, a magenta hue now tinging the edges of her gold light. A feeling of dread came over me because I suddenly could sense that she was about to tell me something I didn't want to hear.

Eva, remember in the meadow when I told you that you could be free…

Oh, stars above. This again. "Yes. I remember." I hoped I sounded as agitated by this topic as I truly was.

That time has come.

I tried to convey the feeling of a heavy sigh. "Zo, stop it, please. I am your Guardian until the day I die because I want to be, not because of an oath. Now, give me a rough idea of your whereabouts so I can start making a plan to get to you."

That won't be necessary.

Panic was creeping in. "Why is that?"

Will you allow me to show you?

I trusted her explicitly, but nervous tension shook my light. "Yes."

Suddenly visions—or memories that were not my own—poured through me. Zoleya was showing me a clear blue sky while she sat cross-legged on a patch of soft, long grass. She was surrounded by the other women who had been in the cage with us, all protectively guarding her, one shading her face, another letting a bit of sunlight brush her toes. A dress of dusty rose fabric was tucked in around her, and I could see the ends of her hair—clean and brushed—waving in a breeze. I sensed that she was content. Calm.

"Do those women know what you are?" I asked.

Yes.

"Can they keep you safe?"

Her light shimmered. *There are no threats here, Eva. We are on one of many islands adjacent to yours and it is plentiful. There are no Raiders. No Black-Blooded. My sensors haven't picked up any radiation either, so it is optimum for human life.*

She showed me more; a field of white flowers not far from a rickety fence and thick green stalks holding star-shaped fruit above tilled earth. Worms on a shovel, birds on a tree, and… a house? Peeling paint, a crooked porch, broken windows, and a tree growing out of the roof, but a house nonetheless.

A human dwelling abandoned not long ago, she clarified. *And it appears that The Burn never touched this area. So… do you see now?*

I did. "You're saying goodbye."

Only in the physical realm. You finally have the opportunity to go and live your life, so you can forget about me and—

"No!" I yelled or bellowed without sound—either way, it was forceful enough to make Zoleya's light shimmer madly and expand. I felt this massive wave of terror and screamed the word 'no' again to make sure I got my point across. I felt the agony of my despair ripple through the realm, felt it spread and lash out with claws. If someone could unravel in this freaky place, I was going to be the one to do it.

Eva, please calm down…

"You're everything to me, Zoleya. You're all I've ever known. I can't say goodbye. I need you in my life…"

Shush now. Words can carry in this place…

"But we're not even talking! Out loud I mean. I don't under-stand…" the darkness seemed to twinkle, like a night sky full of stars.

You are panicking.

"Damn straight I am! I'm your Guardian. And I'm going to find you and keep my oath whether you like it or not!"

Fine.

Did she just agree? The light around her shifted. "No more talk of not needing me. No more trying to say goodbye. I can't bear it."

Oh, Eva. I do love you, too.

"Yeah. That's right, you do. And you'd be lonely as hell without me."

A laugh. *You might be right.*

Somehow, I didn't feel like I'd won this conversation, but I left it behind. "Tell me what direction you are in. Give me co-ordinates."

She was silent for a long while, contemplating telling me, and if I had knees in the realm they would have buckled with relief when she finally spoke.

I am due south. Longitude—

She was about to say more, but a light was barreling toward us with colors in more dizzying shades of blues than I thought existed. I felt Zo's mood shift into high alert and her defenses tightened around me. I hadn't given much thought to what might be in the realm besides us—assuming it was just a tea-for-two sort of situation—but my agony had alerted someone.

Another Sage is heading our way…

"Zo, I'm sorry," I said as she pulled my thread tight to her light.

I must take you back. This Sage is a presence unlike any I've ever felt. It can travel between realms just like I can but possesses a great deal more power. It too, is Earthbound.

"Nihila?"

I don't know.

The light was growing brighter, getting closer. "It can't be allowed to follow you to your body," I said. "It can't find out what you are!"

We will talk again when it is safe, Eva… Zo said.

She began dragging me through the realm, then, with a mental shove hard enough to imagine I was physically feeling it, my consciousness was slammed back into my body at breakneck speed.

But the Sage had not followed Zoleya, it had followed me. I could feel it at the edges of my mind, probing, clinging to my thoughts as I opened my eyes to try and force it out of my mind.

"Hey!" Beast was shaking me. Hard. I blinked his worried face into focus. His hands were on my shoulders, cheeks splotchy from exertion.

"What the raspberries be wrong with ye, Missy?" he asked franticly. "Ye looked catatonic. Did ye get a bite from somethin'?" Half the ocean poured off his thick beard. "What's going' on?"

Kade was behind him, face a waxy sheen of sweat and pulse racing at the base of his throat. "Are you sick?" he asked.

I could feel the presence of the Sage trying to get into my head, his mental fingers prying, digging, and hesitant to let go. It was male, and infinitely more powerful than Zoleya. I didn't know how I could sense that, but I did. So, I silently and politely asked him to leave me alone for now, and quite astonishingly, he obliged.

Beast gave me another shake.

"I'm fine," I snapped, stomach queasy.

"Heat stroke, maybe?" Kade asked, rubbing his forehead in dismay.

Zoleya had come to me to say goodbye, and in my panic, I had alerted another Sage. Of course there would still be some human Sages left in the world. They wouldn't all have been exterminated… Dammit, I was screwing up again. Maybe Zo was better off without me.

"Ye seem a little rattled," said Beast.

I had to laugh; that was an understatement. "I'm just hungry." I got to my feet and shook my limbs awake. "And I need a moment to myself."

I headed into the green where no one would see me cry.

19 EVANGELINE

Night fell over our camp.

We all sat around a roaring fire while Beast and Dominic cooked fish and boiled water in a long tube of bamboo. Both men butted heads over the cooking, then argued about the difference between crows and ravens even though we hadn't seen a single black bird on the island. They only stopped talking when they were eating, and then their only sounds were groans of satisfaction.

I felt like I was in a dream with so much to eat. A whole skewer of fish and coconut just for me. And warm water, too, made into a tea with what I thought I heard Beast say was a type of bark. It was like swallowing heaven. I think we all thought the same.

"We need to find a source of fresh water tomorrow," I said, wanting to gulp down the entire contents of the bamboo but instead passing it along. "The little pool we found could dry up, and we're going to deplete our supply of coconut and—"

"And too much coconut water makes ye piss like a racehorse," said Beast. "It's a… I don't know whatchama call it."

"Diuretic," said Dominic, patting his flat belly. "The young, green coconuts are anyway. We certainly can't rely on them or nasty shit is going to happen."

"Aye, 'cause it's a laxative, too," said Beast.

Dominic's eyebrow arched upward. "Ha. Good one."

Beast looked confused but let it pass. "Hey, how did ye come to have so much medical knowledge?" he asked, leveling his eyes on Dominic.

Dominic shrugged, rubbing the top of his shorn head. "I thought I might get into medicine when I was younger. That was the dream anyway."

Beast brightened. "What? Ye be wanting to be a *healer*?"

"Yes. Do you have a problem with that, Beast?"

Beast put his hands up in defense—they were covered in cuts. "Goodness no. My mama was a healer. Best in town. She delivered half the kids I grew up with."

"I've only ever delivered one," said Dominic.

A hush fell over camp. Kade and Max looked up from their fish, also eager to hear what Dominic would say next.

Beast cleared his throat. "Sounds like ye might have a bit of a story that needs tellin'."

"I guess." Dominic ran his hand wearily across his face, leaving behind streaks of fish grease. "I was fourteen. Sitting outside a clinic one morning waiting for it to open. I was going to beg the healer who worked there to take me under his wing when a young girl showed up. She was a mess, probably living in the streets, and had a baby in her that was itching to come out. I tried to calm her down, thinking that would stop the contractions, but that baby wasn't waiting for doors to be unlocked or business hours to commence. Before I knew it, I was helping the girl give birth right there on the steps. Imagine, I got to witness nature's greatest miracle and hold a brand-new human in my bare hands. I've never experienced anything so beautiful in my entire life. And I haven't since."

"What happened to the girl?" I asked, intrigued.

"I don't know." He looked down at his forearm, to the tattoo of words in thick black ink mottled with dirt. "She spent the day in the clinic and the next morning was gone. I searched the streets for a while but turned up nothing. No one had seen her."

"Does your tattoo have something to do with her?" I asked, sensing some connection by the way he kept glancing at it.

"That's kind of personal."

"Oh. Sorry—"

"Ha. Kidding!" Dominic's birdlike nose crinkled with a wide grin, taking an edge off his otherwise harsh exterior. "I'm an open book, Eva. Got nothing to hide." He ran a finger over the ink. "It's one of the old languages—which was what the girl spoke. I didn't understand a damn thing she was saying while she pushed the baby out, but I did recognize her trying to thank me afterward when I wrapped the baby in my jacket and handed him over. She gave me a piece of cloth with pretty gold embroidery—probably something she'd been saving for her baby—and insisted I take it. After a month of carrying it around, I found someone to interpret it for me."

"What did it say?" Beast asked.

Dominic cleared his throat and spoke:

You are love, light, and honesty at your beginning,
A pure being facing a path of many directions.
Remember how you started your journey
So you can always find your way back.

"That's beautiful," I whispered.

Max continued to gnaw on the stick his food had been skewered on, staring at the fire like he might argue with it or kill it.

"Or something like that. I don't remember exactly," Dominic said after a moment.

Trying not to stare too hard at his arm, I repeated the beautiful phrase in my head. I was about to ask Kade about his marks, too, but the way he pulled his shirt across his chest to cover them up was a fairly big hint that he still wasn't interested in sharing. At least he didn't seem to be in so much pain anymore.

"Anyway," Beast cleared his throat, eager to get back to some good-natured arguing with Dominic, "thanks fer letting us know what be the meaning of the writing on yer arm, otherwise I'd continue thinking it said, 'I'm a yappy asshat who overcooks the fish'."

Dominic laughed. "It says that too, Beast."

"How about yours?" Dominic pointed at Kade with a fishbone. "You have some pretty intricate markings on you. What do they mean? I've heard of some people who have a 'birthbrand', or whatever you call it. Something they're born with that is then enhanced by some sort of ritual. I'd say that's what yours looks like. How long have you had it? Does it say something? Why—"

"It says 'none of your damn business'." Kade grew tense and glared challengingly.

Dominic wasn't even remotely fazed. A wry smile crossed his angular face, and he just shook his head, crinkling his hawk-like nose. "Right. Got it, bro."

"So… who wants to venture deeper inland to find water with me tomorrow?" I asked, feeling the need to change the subject, because the longer the silence, the moodier Kade became. "My leg is better and I'm up for a hike."

"I'll go," said Kade.

Beast threw a log on the fire, sending glowing embers up into the air. "I'll stay behind and see what can be found fer food, and maybe Dominic can set some of them traps he's been blabbering about all day."

Dominic nodded eagerly. Max continued to gnaw on the stick.

"We need a latrine too. Somewhere civilized to be doing our business. We ain't better than the monkeys if we're just pooping all over the place," Beast added.

I laughed; Beast had been furious earlier when he got too close to a lively orange creature hanging from a tree and it threw a wad of excrement at his face; I'd been sworn to secrecy.

"We need to rescue our people, too, and get started on a proper shelter. One with walls maybe." I thought that it would be nice to have some privacy, being the only girl.

"Walls?" Max threw the stick in the fire and cracked his knuckles. "You talk like we're going to be here for a while."

None of us knew how to reply to that.

"What?" he said, sitting up a bit taller, eyeing us curiously, a thin sheen of sweat breaking out on his bare arms.

"No one's coming for us," Kade said. "We need to approach our situation like it might be permanent."

"Yeah," huffed Beast. "Besides, I'd rather be dying here than in the stinking pits of Port Hayes or Nora, or, stars forbid, in them arenas on Cal de Mac."

Max leaped to his feet, forgetting his ribs and doubling over just as quickly. When he got his breath back, his tone was scathing. "Haven't any of you got someone to go back for?"

I didn't—Zoleya was here, somewhere.

Kade shook his head.

Dominic bit his lip and stayed quiet.

Beast toyed with his beard and spoke up. "My mama be six feet under, and the land she left me was taken when I couldn't pay the taxes. I headed north to start a new life in Nora, and the girl I set about marrying sold me out to them Raiders. So, nah. I be good here."

Max's eyes widened in utter disbelief. "You can't be serious! We're not going to just sit around reminiscing about our old lives while sun-tanning and fishing forever. We need to go back. If there's no rescue, then we'll build a raft or something. I guarantee you that Captain Vallerik isn't growing roots here. Hell, she's probably got her people building a new boat already. We can steal it... find a way—"

"Dammit, Max, your family is gone." Kade stabbed his knife into a log. "If your brother was put in the arena, he's dead. And your mom and sisters... there's no finding them or saving them, *if* they're alive, which is highly unlikely. So, unless you've got land and goats and a brood of children running about in the magical land of Carlina, you've got nothing to go back for either."

Max exhaled like someone had punched the air out of him. He dropped the bamboo and the last of our water gushed out.

"You're all assholes," he said, then stomped off into the dark.

I stood, wanting to go to him and offer some sort of comfort.

"No," Kade said, catching me by the wrist and then promptly letting go. "Leave him. He has to come to terms with this."

"Then you go," I said, turning on him. "You just took away his hope. You can't do that, Kade. You can't take away someone's hope when that's all they have left. Did you not think of that?"

"Yeah, it was a dickhead thing to do," said Dominic.

"Whoa. Are you all that sensitive?" Kade put his hands up defensively.

We all stared at him in silence.

Kade shook his head in disgust. "Fine. Okay. I'll go after him. Whatever."

And with that, he angrily stomped off after Max.

The camp instantly seemed a few degrees cooler.

"He's kind of a jerk sometimes," Beast said, poking at the fire.

I nodded but said nothing. I could hear Kade calling for Max, but the sound suddenly became muffled in an odd way. As if my ears had become filled with mud. I got that feeling at the edge of my mind like someone was slamming their fists against my skull, wanting to come in. I knew it was the male Sage who had followed me from the realm.

With what seemed like a massive effort, I pushed back in my mind while picturing slamming a door shut, and said out loud "Wait" as forcefully as I could.

Remarkably, the Sage backed off.

"Wait for what, Eva? What's wrong?" Dominic's voice was loud and clear. He was kneeling next to me and gently pushing on my skin next to the stitches, feeling for swelling in my leg.

My head was swimming. "What? Oh, sorry. Nothing. I'm fine," I said robotically.

He cleared his throat. "Right. Well, we'll clean your leg in the morning. Use fresh bandages and make sure it's sealed up tight as a fly's ass."

"Do flies even have arses?" asked Beast.

Dominic snickered. "Well, they have to do their business somehow, don't they?"

Flies, crows, ravens... their words came in and out of my ears because the Sage had returned and was pressing more forcefully. I knew he was being polite and alerting me to get my body safe—because he could just barge on in if he wanted to—but I didn't have enough time to wander off into the green before I was pulled from my body and dragged through the dark and into the realm.

Circled by colors more vivid than I could ever imagine, blues of every shade wrapped around me, prodding and poking, testing, then morphing into a distinctive shade of the deepest indigo that was near as black as the infinite space surrounding us. This male Sage was nothing like the feel and familiarity of Zoleya. His presence was heavy, sizzling, and electric. His power radiated off him in waves.

I would like to speak with you, he said.

"Yeah, I figured so since you dragged me out of my body."

I gave you time to prepare. His colors pulsed terrifyingly. *You are safe?*

Beast and Dominic would be wondering why I had collapsed in a heap. Hopefully, they would take care of me for a few minutes.

"Yes," I replied. "Who are you?"

More importantly, who are you? he asked in answer. *I didn't think there were any Receivers left in the world, but I felt your agony so strongly it pulled me out of the physical realm to find you in this place. You were with another Sage and she—*

"I think I'll be asking the questions," I said, trying to portray strength even though I was completely at this Sage's mercy.

Annoyed, he headed for the place in my consciousness that held my memories, and I pushed back at him with more force than I knew I had. "Don't you dare steal your way into my thoughts…" I warned, stunned that he could even do that. Zoleya was powerful but not *this* powerful.

I won't hurt you. I promise, he said.

"I'm not scared of being hurt. I just don't like my privacy invaded. It's rude and uncalled for." I tried to remain calm, not wanting to alert Zoleya—if that was even possible—or worse yet, another Sage.

His light shimmered and danced between shades of blue. *You realize I don't need your permission.*

I had to tread carefully. I could do nothing in this realm but speak. Moving was like running underwater in total darkness, and I would never find my way back to my body on my own. If I pissed off this Sage, he could leave me here, lost forever.

"Yes. But I suspect that you are not an immoral monster."

Some would beg to differ.

"What do you want?" I asked, trying to sound bored and subdue my fear. "Because I was kinda in the middle of something back in the physical world."

I want your name. I want to know why your agony brought me out of a dead sleep to see what the fuss was about. You were upset with another Sage...why?

"That's a lot of questions."

Start with the first one.

As if to show me why I'd better start talking, he pried at the wall of my memories.

"Quillene," I said, using my last name because it was impossible to lie in this bizarre realm. "And if you want the answers to anything else, you will take me back to my body so I can make sure it's safe. First things first; prove that I can trust you."

My name is Alexander, and I'll come to you again tomorrow night at sundown, Quillene. Until then...

Without giving me a chance to reply, I was hurtling through the vast darkness of the realm, then eased gently back into my body.

I blinked the roof of the canvas shelter into view.

"What the hell! You scared the shit out of me, Eva," said Dominic.

He was at my feet, eyes wide as saucers in the firelight. He was checking for infection, worrying that I had become unconscious due to fever, and rightly so. My head was swimming and I was dizzy, but infection wasn't the reason; the feel of the strange Sage lingered right down to my bones, the intimate connection of Sage and Receiver leaving my mind reeling.

"Eva?" Dominic's hand was on my forehead.

"I'm okay," I mumbled, shaking head to toe.

He wiped his damp forehead with the back of his hands, then sat on the platform with a sigh. By the sag of his shoulders, it seemed the day had caught up to him. How long had he been sitting here worrying about me?

"You should rest, Dominic," I said, letting him know it was okay to lie down.

After briefly contemplating my words and getting a nod from Beast, he stretched out next to me and was snoring in seconds.

But Beast was awake.

"I know what's happening to ye," he said after a long while.

He'd been watching me from across the fire, blue eyes sparkling, hair so red it could have been flames.

I just stared back.

"Yer being contacted by a Sage," he said quietly.

I tried to conceal my shocked expression.

"I didn't think there be any left alive. Who is it?" he asked, voice barely a whisper.

I bit my lip—there was no sense lying. "I don't know."

He said nothing, processing the information with heavy concentration. Time ticked slowly. "Ye passed out cold, ye know. Just about fell face first into the fire."

I couldn't hide my shock. "I-I can't block, uh, *him*."

"Huh." He sucked on his teeth a moment. "That's not good. Sages can be very dangerous. If Dominic wouldn't have been sitting next to ye—" he trailed off.

"I would have woken up with a fried face."

"Aye. Care to share what the Sage wants? 'Cause they always be wanting something."

"He just wanted my name."

"I hope ye kept it to yerself."

I nodded.

"Them Raiders will put yer head in a jar if they find out what ye be," Beast said, looking over his shoulder to make sure we were alone and that Dominic was still snoring. "And other people... well, folks don't understand people like you. They be scared—ye know, fear of the unknown and all that. Yer minutes on earth would be few to none if word gets out."

I knew that, but still, I gulped. "And, what about you?" I asked. "Now that you know I'm a Receiver, should I be running?"

Beast's eyes darkened. "Yer friend with the white hair, she be a Sage, too. That's why I had them feelings on the ship."

Being a Sage was the reason Zoleya was able to share a body with an artificially intelligent being. Science needed a special kind of human mind to make a successful hybrid, and this was one of the reasons Sages were hunted to near extinction after The Burn.

I moved my hand to the knife at my waist.

"But she not be the one communicating with ye just now. She wouldn't have put yer body at risk like that."

I did not move, just stared.

"My momma was like ye, Missy," Beast continued, gritting his teeth. "And when those she healed found out, they done turned on her. She was as normal as anyone else, ye see, but she could receive messages from Sages, too. One came to her at the market one day and pulled her from her body, just like what happened to ye, Missy, but my momma had no body to return to afterward. The villagers… they burned her bones to ash."

I let go of the knife—it was clear that Beast wouldn't hurt me.

"I have a million questions, but fer now, just know that yer secret be safe with me. Till death," he said, placing a fist over his chest.

I let go of the breath I'd been holding.

I woke up many times in the night with the essence of the male Sage lingering in my mind. I couldn't get comfortable, first too warm, then too cold. Things were skittering, leaves shaking, and a hissing sound followed by a low growl repeated somewhere in the jungle.

Then Kade returned. He stretched out on the platform and squeezed in between me and Dominic. His chest pressed up against my back was oddly comforting and seemed to quiet the disturbing sounds and regulate the heat.

"Did you find Max?" I asked, already knowing the answer.

"Nuh-uh," he replied as sleep beckoned him. "We'll keep an eye out for him when we search for water tomorrow."

His arm flopped over me, and I contemplated snapping it in a few places, but when it grew limp and his breathing became even, I found myself relaxing beneath it. My mind floated on the rhythmic waves of his lungs contracting, and the stories the fire was whispering became a lullaby. When I thought I felt the Sage pressing against my mind, I drifted off into sleep before he could push his way in; Sages couldn't invade the unconscious, only the fully awake. There was a process, and for that I was grateful.

20 KITKUN

I smelled the strangers before I saw them. Anxiety, fear, arrogance, and illness mingled with their unwashed bodies and tainted the air. Their black clothes, intricately woven hair or shaved heads, and necks and limbs circled by leather-bound amulets and chains of gold made them like nothing I'd ever seen before. They walked without grace, stomping over everything in their path. They yelled instead of speaking. They carried weapons and often threatened each other with them; barbaric, the whole lot of them. In my village, people like that would have their severed heads bouncing down the altar in no time. The gods would not approve.

But the strangers were fascinating. I was glued to the tree I'd climbed up into as I spied on them from above, my tunic blending in with the leaves and making me nearly invisible. I only hoped my rumbling stomach wouldn't give me away; my eldest sister had withheld breakfast this morning because I'd spilled beet juice on her ugly embroidery. As far as I was concerned, it looked better after.

Straining my ears to hear over the constant rush of the sea breeze, I was happy to discover that the strangers spoke my language. They called themselves Raiders, and I learned that their leader was a tall woman with skin darkened by the sun nearly to the color of her leather clothes. She barked orders from a chair, mindlessly shredding red flowers with fingernails shaped like daggers, sending precious hibiscus petals fluttering off into the breeze. I disliked her instantly. Didn't she know those flowers were full of nutrients? That they could help some of her people who looked to be in the throws of scurvy?

A little boy was brushing the wasteful woman's hair, which was black like mine but curly like coiling snakes instead of straight. No one questioned her. In fact, most seemed thoroughly terrified of her. They said 'yes, Captain' as they obediently retrieved scraps of their broken ship from the shore, and when she slapped the boy for tugging too hard on her hair, no one paid any mind.

If that woman was in my village, she'd have a few stinging thistles in her bed. And maybe an itch frog or two.

A blonde-haired man seemed to feel the same way that I did. His dislike was obvious, his bows to her lackluster, his smile forced and disingenuous. He, too, was in a position of power and was given a wide berth by his people, but their heads nodding in passing seemed more out of respect than fear. There were black markings across his bare hands that did not come off when he washed, and strips of corded leather adorned his wrists. His body was lean, muscles defined, and he moved with the grace and finesse of some of the finest warriors in my village. His eyes, though, were like nothing I'd ever seen. Even from this high up in the trees, I marveled at how they matched the gray of the sky just before a storm. Sharp, watchful eyes, so full of intense sadness I wouldn't want to stare too long.

The Raiders had a strange device that released a flame, and they used this to make fire with no effort. I choked on the smoke of fish flesh burning and marveled at their lack of skills—had none of them ever cooked before? The food they'd scavenged from the Sea was sending off unpleasant smells, and none of them gave thanks before eating. Portions were brought to the woman in the chair, which she wolfed down without second thought, and I was sure that any moment she'd be stricken with illness or spontaneously combust right there in her chair—the God of the Sea did not tolerate disrespect.

But I watched. I listened. And nothing happened to any of them.

I used my hook and rope to maneuver through the tops of the trees, shifting as the sun moved through the sky to remain hidden. I watched the blonde man with storm-gray eyes give orders around the camp. He demanded odd structures to be built and land to be cleared, while his people sang songs with no discernible melody. Wounded were tended to. Torches made. When they dug holes for a select few of their dead instead of burning them, I waited for the Goddess of the Sky to shower them with the skin-peeling punishment of Mordorain, but the sky remained clear. And when a group of them were ordered into the water to scavenge their broken ship, I sat on pins and needles, waiting for the God of the Sea to drown them... but nothing happened. They all walked out of the water in one piece.

And this made no sense.

My whole life I'd been told that if I went in the water I'd never come out, yet these people were thrashing about in it like fish, dragging things to shore and carrying on as if it were a perfectly normal thing to do. Were they a special human?

My legs were nearly numb, my stomach screaming in agony, but I couldn't look away. I wanted to know more about these sea people. Who were the men they kept in a cage and treated no better than dogs? Were they being punished? And the women tied to a tree, so frail and frightened I felt embarrassed for them...who were they? I settled in to observe closer, but I heard a sound ever so faintly in the distance; the call of the drum.

Drifting my way from the edge of Black Mountain, rhythmic thumps were sending a message for me to come home. *Kitkun*... beat the drum, my name mixed with the breath of the clouds... *Kitkun*... the beat tripled as I imagined Hanuk's meaty hands wielding his stick against stretched hide. The Raiders did not notice the sound, but I could hear our Chief's impatience, his pompous arrogance oozed its way into my ears. *Kitkun, Huntress, come home...*

Either the village was under attack, or Hanuk had a craving for fresh fish, and I was not to keep him waiting. Waiting made him angry, and anger made him slam that stick onto other things besides the drum

—people, pets, trees—and I would be the one to blame for any bruises. "That girl of yours is more hassle than she's worth," he'd say to Muma.

To which Muma would reply, "If she feeds even one mouth it's better than none, and that mouth might be yours one day."

It always amazed me that Muma still had her head.

21 EVANGELINE

It was slow going through the jungle. The farther we moved inland, the denser the vegetation. Kade took the lead, hacking vines out of our way, and I stayed a safe distance behind, marking tree trunks with my knife so we could find our way back. As the Sage still lingered at the edges of my mind, I had to fight to keep my wits about me because I didn't need any distractions—the intense green was so disorientating that twice I had to climb a tree just to see what section of the sky the sun was in.

At least I had the strength to climb now. Two days of rest and more food than I'd eaten in the last month had done wonders.

We trudged ahead and often Kade and I would pause and listen, hoping to hear a trickle of water. We were in sync with each other. Moving in unison. There was an undeniable camaraderie between us that increased with each step. I thought of how it felt when we slept side by side, his arm resting over me, the heat and bulk of it and the way it offered protection…

"Does it seem like the air is thicker somehow, or is it just me?" he asked.

Out of the blue, my chest felt heavy. "Yeah, suddenly it's like breathing mud."

"And everything just seems even more *green.*"

"Ugh. I hate it." Odd flowers of red and blue were the only other colors, and they were sparse. Even the tree trunks were covered in mossy green. I should have been admiring the beauty of the place but a chill raced up my spine instead.

"I wouldn't want to be lost in here," I said.

"What if we are?" Kade teased.

"Well, at least the company is nice."

He grinned ever so slightly, then shivered, too, despite the rivers of sweat pouring down his back. He motioned to a fallen log and we both sat down in exhaustion. "This place certainly has a strange vibe."

I nodded in agreement, pleased that he felt like chatting.

"I wish I had a nice cold beer right now," he added, sighing.

I fished the last banana out of my makeshift bag. "It's not beer, but—"

He put his hand up, a signal for me to be quiet. "Listen."

At first, all I could hear were the annoying chittering bugs up high in the trees, but then there was something else. Something rhythmic. Something *human*.

"People!" Kade jumped to his feet.

Then the sound was gone. I spun around madly, trying to locate it again, but it was as if a switch was hit and it had just turned off.

"It was coming from that direction, I think." Kade swung the machete at some thick brush and then stomped forward—only to leap backward with a startled yelp. "Holy shit... what the—?"

A thin, black snake scurried away from his feet.

All the hair rose on the back of my neck as I reached for his shoulder and spun him to face me. "Kade, are you okay?"

He was instantly pale. "It got me."

The world spun a moment, then stopped in alarmingly clear focus; I knew right away the bite was deadly. The snake slithering away had its photo in the 'B' section of Zo's encyclopedia and was venomous. I'd read up on the black mamba and knew I only had seconds to save Kade's life.

"Sit down," I ordered.

He was in shock, trying to process what had happened, staring down at his ankle.

"Kade!"

In a daze, he lowered himself to the ground. I lifted his pant leg to see the skin around two neat little holes just above his ankle already starting to swell and turn red.

"Give me your belt," I ordered.

He was so slow and clumsy I shoved his hands away and ripped it from the loops at his waist. I circled it above his knee and pulled as tight as I could to stop the blood flow to his heart.

"Keep it tight," I ordered.

What I had to do next was going to hurt, but I didn't have time to warn him. I ran the sharp edge of my knife across the snake bite, then put my mouth over the cut and sucked as hard as I could.

It should have been thoroughly disgusting and turned my stomach, but when you're desperate to save someone's life, gross things don't matter. I spat mouthful after mouthful of Kade's blood into the grass, fighting to stop the poison from entering his bloodstream. I knew I had mere moments—seconds—before his heart pumped the deadly toxin into his every cell.

Kade was saying something but I tuned him out, concentrating, mouth filling, spitting, repeating… repeating…

"Eva—" his hand was on my head. "Eva stop. I can't feel my toes."

What if I missed some of the venom? What if I hadn't done enough and he—

Died.

What if I failed someone I cared about yet again?

And…did I feel something more for him than friendship? He was incredibly good-looking. Strong, capable, and intelligent…

I kept my mouth firm over the bite, drawing more blood from him.

"Eva… stop."

He pulled my head away and I spat out another mouthful of blood onto the grass.

Tentative to look at him and find that shadow of death creeping across his face, I took a moment and dug my nails into the soft earth. Dizzy. So dizzy. The memory of Commander Rowan's voice fluttered through my mind; *just breathe, Eva… just breathe…*

In. Out. Lungs expanding. Pulse slowing… I sat back on my heels and chanced a look at Kade's mismatched eyes; they were wide, alert, and blinking back at me in astonishment.

Wiping my mouth, I undid the belt, allowing the blood to flow back into his leg, rubbing the thick muscle of his thigh to get the circulation back. His heart was pounding evenly—I could see it flutter at the base of his throat. Minute after minute passed, and when I was positive he wasn't dying, I crawled away from him and threw up.

Then we sat for a long while, saying nothing, just breathing in the thick, muddy air.

"You saved my life," he said, stunned.

Kade is okay. I repeated it in my mind like a mantra until my hands stopped shaking. There was something besides gratitude in his eyes when I chanced another look, and it did something strange to my chest.

"Thank you," he said.

I bounced upright, dusting dirt off my palms. "No problem."

"Without you, I—"

"We better get moving," I said, cutting him off. I had the strangest desire to run my fingers through his hair. Pull him to my chest and hold him protectively—and that seemed inappropriate somehow. "Can you walk?"

After clearing his throat, twice, his voice still cracked when he spoke. "Yes, of course. I'll wrap it up good and tight and Dominic can give me a stitch or two when we get back."

After tearing a piece off the bottom of his shirt to wrap the gash, he got back to hacking away at the green, delivering fatal blows to unsuspecting vines. I was relieved that he'd recovered quickly from the incident, barely even limping.

"Thank you again, Eva," he said, his back to me. "I didn't even see that snake. The only thing not green in this entire place and I missed it."

"No problem." I stopped to carve an X into a tree to mark our trail, and when I looked up, Kade had turned to face me.

I gave my full attention back to the tree.

"You amaze me," he said.

I etched a bit deeper. "Yikes, I need to sharpen this knife…"

"Eva?"

"Yes?" I didn't look up.

In three long strides, he was before me, putting his hands on my cheeks and demanding my attention. "There are so many things I want to say right now." The gentle light pouring through the trees lit up his eyes and the tips of his midnight hair. "But I'm not so good with words. So… please allow me to show you."

I pressed the palm of my hand flat to his chest, keeping distance between us. I was human too, and the desire to touch and be touched was flooding my veins. But I wasn't sure if that was because I wanted him or because I just wanted *someone*.

"We're friends," I said, staying calm beneath his burning gaze. "If you need to tell me something, you're going to have to *say* it."

He was staring at my mouth, breathing heavily. "Friends," he muttered, then his hands dropped to his sides and he took a generous step back. "I… I want—"

He bent over as if something had stabbed him in the ribs. Did I miss some of the venom? Was it just now making its way through his heart?

I couldn't conceal the panic in my voice. "Kade?"

He straightened. "I'm fine. Really. It's just… a cramp is all."

"You're sure? It's not the snake—"

"Honestly. I'm fine." He pulled in a long breath, then cast his gaze downward. "And… friends it is, Eva. It will be the word of the day."

"And water," I said, relieved he was still standing, still alive.

"Huh?"

"That's the other word," I said. "It's why we're out here wandering around in this weird place in the first place."

He nodded and turned away. "Right, of course. Water."

22  Evangeline

"How do we even know we're on an island?" I asked, needing to lighten the mood and get my mind off my thirst and the lingering metallic taste of Kade's blood. Zo had said that her sensors indicated as much, but sometimes when her power was low they were wrong. "I mean, we've just made that assumption. We don't know for sure."

He was slowing down, tiring. The oppressive heat had become a new opponent to fight through. Once in a while we heard that rhythmic sound again—drums?—but it was gone as soon as it started. And it seemed like the air only kept getting thicker.

"What are you talking about," he asked breathlessly.

"Well, maybe this isn't an island. Maybe we're on a continent."

He shook his head in annoyance.

"Why can't that be a possibility?" I pressed. "We've been taught that anywhere besides Aldira and Cal de Mac is uninhabitable. Yet… here we are walking on ground that technically should be a complete wasteland. I don't know what to believe anymore."

"Wishful thinking. I mean, come on. Somehow this place was spared and not burned to a crisp or made unliveable by radiation, but it's an anomaly. The Burn wiped out nearly everything on this planet a thousand years ago, and the hole in the ozone layer ensured that most things never healed. There's a reason nobody goes outside the safe zone… there's nothing there."

"Yeah, I know, but what does that have to do with this being something more than an—"

"I mean, don't you think greedy bastards like the Raiders have searched for liveable land? Don't you think that they, of all people, would know about this place? No, this isn't a continent. It's an island and nothing more."

It seemed like he was trying to convince himself of that.

"But what if we walked inland," I said, skirting a bearded iguana hanging from a branch. "and kept walking and walking, and weeks turned to months, streams turned into rivers—"

"False hope, Eva. The same thing that Max has about his family being alive, and I'll have no part in it. None. So drop it. Please."

There was finality in his tone. He was done with the subject. I wondered what he had lost that made him so guarded. Why was he scared to dream or imagine that things could be good? I worried that his desire to be so firmly rooted in reality could bury him.

"We should head back to camp," I said, not wanting to anger him further. "I don't want to be stuck sleeping on the ground when night falls." I also needed to make sure I could sneak away and be by myself when the male Sage returned. I didn't want to be falling face-first onto the fire, or having everyone think I was narcoleptic.

Kade agreed. So we turned around and began following the X's on the trees—until there weren't any.

"Eva, I thought you were marking our path?" Kade said, whirling on me.

Behind him, the trail he had just tamed with his machete seemed to have grown over in seconds. There weren't even any broken vines or footprints to be seen.

Baffled, I threw my hands up in the air, circling the area over and over for my Xs. "I was. I swear. This makes no sense." Suddenly, I was so turned around I almost didn't know which way was up. "I'll climb. Have a look."

Forcing my exhausted body up a tree made Kade nervous. I was getting clumsy. The heat was almost strangling. The view from as high up as I could go revealed that the sun was much lower in the west, lighting up what looked like a mountain of black to the east, where thick columns of gray spiraled upward... I tried to get in a breath, feeling that the air must be cooler and cleaner up here, but it wasn't.

"Smoke..." I said, wheezing. My leg was really aching now, and I wondered if I'd torn a stitch. "Looks like it's coming from the base of a mountain or something. According to the sun, our camp is that way." I pointed north.

"Smoke?" Kade echoed.

We were thinking the same thing: Raiders. Or, maybe another tribe just as nefarious was making the drum-like sound we kept hearing. Either way, we didn't want to cross paths without backup.

We blundered ahead, neither of us saying anything, the silence between us uncomfortable for the first time. Kade stumbled and coughed, and I put my hand on his back to steady him—but he stopped dead in his tracks as if he'd hit a wall and couldn't go any farther.

I tried to walk around him to take the lead, but then I hit it too; the air, thick and caustic, seemed to become practically impenetrable.

"This is insane," he said, throwing out a fist into it, punching ahead with one arm and now dragging me behind him.

A cough started in my throat as a tickle, and soon we were both coughing like we'd inhaled a hundred campfires.

"Should we go back?" I sputtered, bent over, not being careful about where I was putting my feet and stepping on something sharp.

"No..." Kade's lips were slightly blue. "We have to get to the beach—air..."

He pushed aside a barrage of green to reveal a maze of leaves tightly woven into other leaves amongst a net of vines and branches. As he slashed out with his machete, I realized there were no other sounds. None.

"Listen," I sputtered.

His arm dropped to his side. "Nothing, not even chittering."

Struggling in a breath, he was about to swing again but stopped. His entire body tensed, and he pointed ahead; bones. Most certainly of the human variety.

They were scattered across a patch of neon green earth, picked clean and sparkling like they'd been polished. There had to be ten bodies, maybe more, and it prompted an urge in me to scream, but my breath was lodged in my throat like an immovable mass; whatever this thick air was, a few more minutes of breathing would kill us.

Kade and I gave our everything, slicing and coughing and lashing out with our blades to get through the endless walls of green that seemed to be closing in.

When we thought we couldn't move another step, we fell forward as if released from unseen hands into cool, breathable air.

We lay quiet for a while, savoring the oxygen in our lungs.

"Are you okay?" Kade asked, lips no longer blue.

"I think so."

"What the hell was that?"

"I don't know," I said, finally able to draw in a full breath. "But judging by those bones, I think we're lucky we didn't find out."

We sat up, taking stock of ourselves and each other, then got a good look at the vegetation that had become somewhat normal again. It was still green but not a creepy, glowing, silent wall of it. The sounds of the jungle were back in full swing too, and the foreboding energy was gone.

Kade and I got to our feet.

Stumbling slightly, we both carved double X's on four trees as a warning to not go back that way—ever—then diligently marked our way as we moved ahead, hopefully in a favorable direction.

"We're close to the beach, Eva. Can you hear the waves?"

I could hear water… but weren't we far from the sea? I also heard monkeys howling and so many birds singing it was almost other-worldly.

"Yes. Still thirsty, though."

I was painfully aware of how dry my mouth was now that the sound of water increased. I could have licked the dew off a frog's back when we emerged into a clearing bathed in intense sunlight. I was barely able to focus on marking more trees. When Kade went on ahead, I veered off slightly to the left and… what I saw in the distance through a break in the trees left me speechless.

Couldn't be. Not possible. Was I hallucinating? "Uh, Kade? Can you come here?"

With hurried steps, he rushed toward me, voice edged with concern. "What's up? Everything okay?"

All I could do was point, because whether continent or island, what I was seeing left me completely speechless.

23  KADE

I had tea with sugar for the first time today. Mother even kissed me on the cheek before handing it over and said that she was proud of me because someday I would become the Nihila's greatest hunter. I don't know if her kindness was because I followed orders and killed a puma for no good reason, or if she drank too much mead.

Either way, I realized I don't like sweet things.

— JOURNAL ENTRY, KADE – AGE 13

I couldn't believe what I was looking at.

A waterfall. Picture perfect. Surreal. Just like you might see deep in the pages of an illegal book hidden in the Nihila's archives.

Cascading down a tower of rock flanked by vines and thick green moss, birds of many colors fringed the surging rush of water, ruffling their wings in its mist. Some dove into the wide pool that churned and bubbled at its base, returning to the surface with tiny fish… How was this possible? In Aldira, places as pristine and breathtaking as this didn't exist anymore.

But they did here.

I was awestruck. It was nearly as beautiful as the golden-haired goddess who was beaming and vibrating head to toe.

"Kade, can you believe this? An actual waterfall with fresh water! Is it real?"

"Uh, I don't know."

Maybe it was just a cruel joke. A dream I'd wake from to discover that Mother had poured one of her tonics down my throat to sedate me before a ritual. Or just a mirage in the desert to distract me from my bones turning to dust…

"Beat ya to it!" Eva said with a smack to my shoulder, beelining ahead of me without thought.

"Slow down," I warned, but she was off, weaving down across the slick stone bordering the edge of the pool at the point farthest from the falls.

I followed, mainly because she was careless and it made me crazy, and as I watched her crouch at the waterline—probably gauging the pool's depth—I had barely enough time to tell her she was being reckless before she stood, stretched her arms up over her head, and dove in.

The stupid girl! She was putting us both in danger, because if I had to dive in and rescue her I would. After the whole snake bite fiasco, I realized I would follow her to the depths of hell if need be.

My marks nipped at my ribs in warning.

"Must keep her alive," I reminded them. "It's all part of my plan."

It seemed like forever before Eva's head broke the surface. I watched as she drew in a deep breath, shaking water from her hair in a ray of sunshine that lit up the droplets like scattered diamonds.

"Kade, it's glorious," she said, golden eyes flashing.

I wanted to give her a piece of my mind, but suddenly all I could think of was how her tanned cheeks were more freckled than this morning and her skin luminous while wet, and that I hated how badly I wanted to crush her body to my chest and find out how her mouth would feel against mine…

The marks gave me a subtle zing.

"Come in," she said, grinning.

"Are you crazy?" I had to rely on anger, an emotion I knew how to deal with. "You don't know what's in there. Besides, waterfalls create currents that can pull you under and trap you. If this pool of water was shallower, it would be even more dangerous. You'd most certainly be caught in the current and dragged under. Not only that, you could have broken a bone, or—"

"Chicken," she said, laughing.

I was stunned. The liveliness in her voice rattled me out of my head. "Did you just call me a chicken?"

Her giggle echoed across the rocks. "Yup."

I dragged my fingers through my sweat-soaked hair, ignoring the gash on my leg that had started to sting. "You sound like you're twelve years old, Eva. I'm not a damn chicken."

"Then prove it," she said and went under.

My body lurched forward, but I caught myself, hovering on the edge of the rock. I was forgetting my place. Completely sidetracked by a female. Had Mother ever taught me what to do in this circumstance? I didn't think so. She wasn't the kind of parent to engage in small talk about affairs of the heart. When she'd found the first journal Elder Matthias had gifted me, she scolded me for trying to understand my thoughts and the world around me, then burned my fingertips. I was to think only of the destruction of Atomica. Nothing else mattered. Especially not my *feelings*.

I was very careful about where I hid the next journal, and the one after that. Not that anything I ever wrote would help me now.

I watched Eva tread water, tipping her head back and letting the mist from the falls fill her mouth, then, without further thought, I dove off the rock and swam over to her.

Then I shoved her under.

She came up sputtering. "What the—"

"Chicken?" I asked.

"Well, I had to get you in here somehow." Her smile was infectious and wide.

I foolishly reached for her waist, bringing our hips together, and her expression darkened.

"The current is strong beneath our feet. We better not get any closer to the falls," I said.

She tensed. "Listen, Kade. Your arm over me at night is okay. But this is not. So take your hands off me or you'll risk losing them."

Was it horrible that the fire in her eyes turned me on so aggressively it became hard to breathe? It took every bit of strength I had to let go. "Sorry. I just—"

"No need to explain." She put some distance between us. "Snake bites, piles of human bones, almost suffocating for no reason, and then finding this place… it's been a weird day."

"Weird. Yeah. That's it." My whole body ached for her so badly it was agony, and the marks, recognizing this, retaliated.

"We need to get back to camp before the sun goes down," she said. "I don't want to be out here in the dark."

I swam to the edge of the pool and hopped out. "Agreed." I had to calm down. Get myself under control and not allow my emotions to take over, lest my marks burn me right to my bones again. *It's all part of the plan…* I whispered again, hoping to pacify them.

"We're still friends, right?" Eva asked, worried she'd offended me.

I forced a smile. "Yes. Of course."

Wordlessly, we followed a stream that snaked away from the waterfall directly to the sun lowering in the sky. The swim had made my clothes stick to my body, and the blood loss had really sapped my energy. Twice I bent to scoop up water from the stream and drank like it was a lifeline.

After what might have been a half hour, the stream led us out of the jungle and onto the beach, where it flowed over black rock and collected in clear pools before merging with the sea.

"Thank goodness," Eva muttered. "I hate it in the green."

To the north was a recognizable tower of rock that stretched out of the jungle and into the water.

"Are you kidding me?" Eva said, mirroring my shock.

She started marching toward the rock, and I practically had to run to keep up with her. Crossing into the green to get around it, we came out onto a familiar spot, stopping when we could see a fire on the beach—our beach.

"So, we could have saved ourselves an entire day if instead of walking straight into the trees we walked up the beach another ten minutes?" she said, slapping her forehead.

I started laughing from exhaustion and the stupidity of it all, then reached for her hands as if it was the most natural thing to do. I tightened my fingers around hers and got lost in that fire in her eyes, knowing I was crossing the line but doing so anyway.

"Come on, let's go tell the others about our discovery," Eva said, smile gone as she pulled back.

I tightened my grip, wanting her to myself for a few more minutes, needing to say something but not entirely sure what that might be.

"You know that's Beast up there risking his neck with a bonfire to let us know where he is," she added.

My body reacted before my mind did, and I leaned in and attempted to kiss her, desperate to feel those ruby-red lips against mine. But, in a rather impressive move, my arm was swiftly twisted behind my back and the knife Rowan had gifted her was held against my jugular. I was awestruck. Stunned that this exquisite woman had me in such a vulnerable position.

"You saved me from a snake bite, and now you're going to slit my throat?" I didn't counter her move because I was fairly certain she'd slice me ear to ear if I did.

"Maybe I'm overreacting, but I have clearly stated my personal boundaries and you keep choosing to ignore them."

I felt the bite of the knife and winced. "Okay. Okay, I'll remember to *ask* before I attempt to kiss you… alright?"

She twisted my arm a little harder. "Damn right, you will."

"You're going to break my arm, Eva, or cut me open."

She let me go and stepped back, glaring. "It would serve you right."

It would.

I put my fingers to my neck and checked for blood, surprised there was none. "Stars above," I sputtered.

"Oh, you're fine." She sheathed the knife, her hand slightly shaking. "If I wanted to kill you, I would have."

"But you didn't. Because you feel something for me too, right?"

She straightened her shirt and looked me dead in the eye. "All I *feel*, Kade Thorn, is hungry for supper. Got it?"

I stared at her backside as she marched off to where Beast sat waiting for us by the fire, marks stabbing at my ribs.

 24 Kitkun

When angered, only human blood can quench the God of the Sea's thirst.

— THE BOOK OF IMATLA

The sound of the beating drum grew louder, its rhythm more aggressive. It was calling me; *Kitkun... Return... Now...*

Chief Hanuk was an impatient bastard. Surely he knew that I couldn't snap my fingers and transport myself back to the village. There was a bit of a process to making my way through the jungle and back to Black Mountain, and I almost made a fatal mistake by missing my marker and heading into the Wejukah. The shiny face of my carefully placed jade rock sloped in the direction of the stream, a warning to turn away from the band of poison air that sliced through the island like an impenetrable fence. Long ago, I had placed many smaller stones with my hands, lining the perimeter just in case the jade rock got moved somehow, and was glad I had. They alerted me to turn south, where I walked until I came to the safety of the stream, where the Wejukah could not cross.

I thought of those strange sea people who called themselves Raiders. Their odd way of cooking and their lack of respect for the gods. With birds chattering above me, I said a silent prayer to all the gods I could think of just to stay on their good side, and then I checked the first trap I'd buried and disguised with ferns and muck; empty. My underwater traps were empty too, the hollow bamboo with the putrid remains of a bird hadn't enticed any fish, eel, or monitors. All I could do was hope the net I'd strategically placed at the base of the waterfall had fared better. It had taken months to make. The fine threads woven together by my sisters and my mother were strong enough to trap fifty fish. I'd promised them that I'd only use it in the stream and never go near the sea—and certainly never come *here*—but the deep pool was full of the tastiest fish, and when one was sputtering and cooking over a flame with sliced mango, no one would question my hunting grounds. Heck, it might even shut Hanuk's mouth and earn us all a reprieve from hearing him constantly quote from The Book of Imatla.

My hopes were high when I wandered up the stream and came to the clearing that held the first and deepest pool. Nobody from the village came here; they feared that there were creatures that lived in the deep that could climb out onto the rocks and swallow a person whole. I knew it was just a story, so I always had the place to myself.

Except for today.

Voices carried to me through the mist... sea people?

Dropping to my knees, I crouched behind a boulder, watching as a man and woman came out of the trees from the other side of the pool with awe and wonder on their faces. The woman, tall and lean, clutched her chest, blinking her eyes as if she didn't believe what she was seeing. Scrambling down closer to the water, she moved far more freely than the man, who stood firm and cautious. I had the sense that they were not of the same tribe as the sea people on the north beach. Their clothes were very different, and they weren't as sun-weathered.

I put my nose to the air, trying to get a sense of them, but all I could smell was the man's anger and tension mingled with a hefty lust for the woman. He watched her closely as she made her way down the rocks to a flat stone at the water's edge, warning her to stay back. Large and muscular, with thick black hair soaked from sweat, he seemed bossy, like the men in my village. I liked that the woman paid him no mind. She didn't even blink at his words.

Dressed in strange pants with many pockets that were cut off mid-thigh, and a tight white shirt that was sleeveless and sweat-soaked heavily enough to see through, the odd clothes barely covered her, and she didn't seem to care. Golden hair flowed down her back, untamed and free, and a wide smile revealed white, straight teeth. I thought she was quite pretty.

The man followed the woman to the water's edge, his movements purposeful, calculated, expression unchanging as every tendon visible on his body remained tense. He was unsure of what might be beneath the surface of the water, but the woman seemed positively fearless and moved as if at any moment she might dive in. But… nobody was crazy enough to do that. It was deep. There was no bottom. If you weren't a fish, you would drown.

Drown! That's what the male thought was happening when the girl jumped in, headfirst.

The pool swallowed her whole, the surface instantly flat as glass and sealing her into its depths. The male was unsure what to do, and I had half a mind to pull in my net and use it to retrieve her. But somehow, she broke free of the surface, and… was floating? And, then the man was jumping in, too? What sorcery was this? How were they keeping their heads up in the air and not sinking to the bottom like the rocks I'd thrown in? Were they part fish like the sea people?

I was so stunned I almost leaped to my feet for a better look.

They were laughing, splashing each other, their cheeks no longer pink but instead golden in the sunlight. There was something different about them, very unlike the barbarians on the north beach. The man looked at the woman the same way Avda looked at my sister; like he would like to eat her and kiss her and kill her all at the same time. Something about it made knots in my stomach. The hair lifted on the back of my neck when he spoke her name. *Eva*, he said, the sound rolling off his tongue in a way that made his eyes light up. *Eva*.

She called him Kade, and even though there was affection for him in her tone, at one point I thought she might slice him open when he got a bit too close. At her warning, he backed off respectfully, and I wished that's what my people had for me; respect. I wished that when I walked by, instead of feeling sorry for the village girl who lost her father, they looked at me with admiration.

Maybe I would bring home these strange sea people. Capture them in my net and march them through the main street of my village. Hanuk would be impressed with the fair-haired girl. He'd drag her around like a prized pig and there would be a big celebration in my name and much cheering as her head rolled down the temple steps in a sacrifice that would please all the gods.

But that would be wasteful. She was interesting. And, maybe if I observed her closer, I could learn how to attract respect and not sink in the water.

I would keep this discovery a secret for a while.

Leaving my net behind, I followed the strangers back down the stream to where the sands met the sea. I wanted to follow them to their camp, but those drums started up again, the rhythm furious now, conveying that Hanuk was angry.

Kitkun, come home!

25 EVANGELINE

The male Sage never came for me. The sun slipped behind the horizon, and I hadn't been dragged off into the freaky realm by he who called himself Alexander. In some way, I was grateful for that, happy to not have to experience that unsettling feeling in the other-worldly place that made no logical sense. But, in the dead of night when everyone was asleep around me, I wondered why. It created a gnawing feeling in the pit of my belly that wouldn't settle, made worse by the fact that Zoleya had kept her distance, too.

When morning came, I was on pins and needles. We were all going to spy on the Raiders, and I could only hope that the male Sage wouldn't yank me from my body at some inopportune moment.

With Kade in the lead, Beast, Dominic, and I headed deep into the jungle. After hours of sweating and stepping on thorns and fire ants, we could finally hear the Raiders, and now we waited in the trees for the sun to go down so the dark would conceal our presence.

"If we get separated, we meet here at this exact spot," Kade said. "And remember, we don't want to fight any of them, okay? As far as they're concerned, we don't exist, and we want to keep it that way."

He was looking at me in particular when he said this, as I was absentmindedly patting the knife Commander Rowan had given me— freshly polished and sharpened—in its holster at my thigh.

"I'll behave," I said and rolled my eyes mockingly. "I'll follow 'the plan'."

Beast cracked his neck and ran his fingers through his beard, giving away clues that he was nervous. "If we can't git our people out, then let's take as many supplies as we can, aye?" The apple-red sunset made his red hair redder. "We be needing somethin' for boiling water in, and —" he looked at my chest, the shirt I was wearing nearly threadbare. "A change of clothes."

"I just hope Max is okay," I said quietly, taking a step closer to the Raiders' beach, trying to see around a huge palm tree that stretched lazily out over the sand. "It worries me that he never came back. Maybe they caught him again."

"Ah, he be fine, Missy," Beast said, patting my shoulder. He was about to say more but the smell of roasting meat wafted toward us on the sea breeze and his thoughts clearly turned to his stomach. "Them Raiders be cookin' up a boar."

My mouth started watering so badly I couldn't swallow fast enough to keep from drooling.

Beast eagerly rubbed his palms together. "We might have to steal some dinner and—"

"Hey," said Kade sharply, getting all our attention. "Don't get distracted. We have to remain alert and focused. Rowan will hunt us down relentlessly if he knows we're alive, and there are too many of them and not enough of us. I don't want to be a prisoner on this island any more than I wanted to be one on that ship."

"We understand, Kade," I said, holding his gaze for a brief moment. "Food can wait."

Beast muttered an affirmative response. Dominic knuckle-rapped his heart with his fist. Then none of us moved or said a word until the fires on the Raiders' beach mingled with the light of the moon and the stars.

Slipping out of the trees, I hadn't realized how cold my feet were until they hit the still-warm sand. A texture different than on our beach, this sand wasn't as powdery and smooth, and the shells and stones littering the surface stabbed with every step.

Beast stumbled and stifled a yelp. "Let's steal ourselves some darn shoes, too," he whispered.

Dominic placed his fingers to his lips as a signal to be quiet, then pointed; coming toward us was a man holding a torch. In moments we'd be lit up plain as day. I bolted behind some sort of tent-like structure and everyone followed closely, then we held our breath until the man with the torch passed by.

"They're patrolling," Kade whispered from behind me.

"Why?"

"I don't know. Maybe there are threats here that we aren't aware of."

There was another tent a few feet away, so I made a beeline for it and the others followed. Someone inside was snoring.

"It smells like death here," I whispered, covering my mouth and nose with my hand.

Getting low and peeking around the corner, I counted eleven men around a fire, all flat on their backs, some moaning, some wide-eyed and vacantly staring at the stars. Broken limbs, missing limbs, head wounds, and one most certainly dead. Was this where the Raiders put their injured? On the edge of their camp with no one to tend to them? What monsters.

We carefully moved toward the next fire, crouching along behind a massive piece of driftwood. Slowly, we stalked toward a livelier bunch of Raiders who sat around a heavily smoking fire pit. Ten or so other fires peppered the beach, flames broken by the moving shadows of Raiders and the structures they'd erected, sticking up out of the sand. A few boisterous groups farther down the beach were singing the kind of songs one would hear in Port Hayes creeping out between pub doors in the dead of night, and it was unsettling to me that the Raiders seemed content enough to sing.

"You'd think they could find a better song," I heard a man say, his hair so slick with oil it shone in the moonlight.

"Darn straight. It seems that the whiskey has muddled their judgment," replied an extremely short man next to him with arms that barely reached his waist. "But hell, I'd do anything for a mug of it right now. How come *we* ain't the Cap'n's favorites?"

"Cause we ugly as that boar's ass," said the greasy man. He waved away a plume of smoke, then stood to turn the spit of one of three boars crackling and smoking over the fire. There must have been enough meat to feed sixty hungry men, and we all quickly realized that when the dinner bell rang this would not be a good place to hide.

A fourth boar—still living—snorted and tugged at a rope around its neck that was tethered to a post dug deep in the sand.

"Old Hairy over there is pissed that we're cooking up his whores," joked the short man, who then stood and threw a rock at the irate boar. "You're next," he said with a laugh.

Greasy coughed. "Commander Rowan ordered that one to remain alive. He says the scent of the male will attract the ladies, and more chicks means more food."

"How the hell does he know that?"

"I dunno, but he's been right about everything else, so who cares? We'd all be sun-baked bags of bones without him."

I pointed to a large, empty pot behind the short man, and Beast gave me a nod of understanding. Then I motioned to the tent that smelled of death, reminding him to steal more medical supplies as well. He curled his lip in a snarl and then disappeared into the dark.

We crept back into the trees because there was too much light on the beach to go unseen. Sidestepping branches or anything that might crackle or swish was almost impossible, but every Raider who perked up and looked in our direction barely gave the sounds a second thought before going back to drinking, singing, or cooking. I held Kade and Dominic's hands, and we moved as one, skirting a near inferno of a fire where men and women sang at the top of their lungs, thankfully drowning our muffled shrieks when sharp things seemed to catch our bare feet at every turn.

I couldn't believe my eyes when we came upon a clearing where the Raiders had managed to fell a mass of trees that were now nothing but stumps being burned away by small fires. Moving like ants, efficiently and swiftly, they were hacking at the earth and building structures out of the trees along with the wood they'd scavenged from their ship. By the light of lantern and fire, someone had even woven mats out of massive palm fronds and hung clean laundry on a long rope. It seemed that every Raider had a job—and there was a whole lot more of them than I'd anticipated.

My spirits fell. I'd been hoping to see chaos and suffering. These men and women were fit, well-fed, focused, and eager to thrive. How was this possible? I lost count at fifty able-bodied Raiders in this clearing alone.

Fifty.

Kade pointed to a young man standing in the midst of it all and a chill rolled up my spine; Commander Rowan. He stood straight as an arrow with his broad shoulders squared, looking every inch the leader that he was. I felt the knife quiver in my hand, recalling the speech I'd given to Max about revenge. I realized now that those were words spoken from a muddled mind and a temporarily numbed heart. Rowan was the reason Zoleya had come to me to say goodbye. The reason we were separated and all her other Guardians were dead.

He would pay.

I could hear him giving orders, voice rising above the clamor of bodies but never yelling. He pointed and directed while consulting some sort of book in his hands. He was the eye of the storm, calm and centered while massive amounts of energy swirled outward from around him. Raiders didn't blink at what they were told to do and went about their tasks without delay. Were they that scared of him? So fearful for their lives that they would still follow their commander's orders even though they were off the ship and far from the laws of Cal de Mac?

"The sun rises and sets around that man," Kade spat.

His hate seemed as deep as my own.

"Why don't they resist? Or rebel? What reason is there for them to do what they're told?" I was stunned.

Kade was silent a moment, watching intently too. "They don't follow Rowan for lack of choice, they do it because they respect him."

Respect? That word rattled around in my head for a bit.

"Well, there is a bit of fear there too, for sure," added Dominic. "Believe me. If a man decides he might not agree with the commander, then good ol' Captain Vallerik will have said man's head on a platter and hunt down his entire family 'just cause'. She's one nasty bitch, and Rowan is her right arm. I wouldn't mess with either of them."

I looked closer. Watched and listened. Through bits of words caught here and there, it became clear that Rowan was building a shelter for the wounded. "Ten beds," he kept repeating, consulting his book and then using a stick to draw diagrams in the dirt. "Two feet off the ground and sealed off from predators and those damn sand flies," he said to someone, shoving away a plate of cooked boar. He was approached by an old man with a deeply lined face and thick gray hair. "Move the wounded here immediately," Rowan demanded of the old man. "I want them tended to around the clock. They shouldn't be on the beach."

He *was* caring for his wounded. Huh.

The old man shook his head. "It's getting late, Commander, and everyone is tired."

"This is more important than sleep." There was urgency in Rowan's voice, and it made my hand nearly lose grip of the knife.

"Cap'n also don't want them stinking up the camp, Commander."

"I don't care what Captain Vallerik wants. Do it anyway, Cyrus," Rowan ordered.

Cyrus looked like he'd been marinated and seasoned by the sea. He had ancient, barnacle-like skin, his body stooped and slow but eyes still sharp as a blade. He sighed heavily and placed a cup in Rowan's hand. "As you wish, Commander."

Rowan was about to take a sip but instead stopped and looked in our direction. I nearly jumped out of my skin; did he see us? My fingers weren't even visible in front of my face, but those gray eyes were staring this way as if he knew exactly where we were.

I felt Kade tense next to me. Dominic had long ago disappeared.

Rowan tilted his head slightly to the side as if studying the exact spot where we were hiding in the trees, then took a long, slow slip of the contents in the cup. Abruptly, he turned away, marched over to a pot hanging over the fire, dipped in the cup, and then handed it to the man next to him.

Kade tugged on my arm. "Earth to Eva."

I'd forgotten where I was for a moment. "What? Were you saying something?"

"Yes... our people. *Right there.*"

Being dragged toward Rowan, struggling in the grasp of two men with a glaring female close behind, was someone I recognized from the cage. A massive man—bigger than Beast—was thrashing, cussing, and spitting-mad as the boar. Bruised and bloodied, skin rough and red, his entire body seemed beaten.

Rowan wrote something in a notebook before addressing the glaring female. "Is this him?"

"Yes." Her voice carried through the camp toward us loud and clear. "He claims that 'Prominus' is his only given name, Commander."

Prominus had his hands chained and ankles shackled. I feared for his tongue when he spat at Commander Rowan's boots. "Low-life fucking Raiders," he said, voice booming.

Completely unaffected, Rowan pondered the man for a moment. "Unfortunately for you, Prominus, we don't give third chances."

Then he drew his weapon. And not just any weapon; a kopis. A massive, curved blade with most of its weight at the tip, capable of cutting a limb clean off or decapitating a human with one swipe. I jolted upright only to have Kade pull me back down.

"Be still," Kade warned with a whisper. "Or it will be your head."

A group of Raiders circled Prominus to watch with wide-eyed enjoyment as their respected commander readied his blade, measuring the distance between it and Prominus' throat. The world spun madly out of my control—how could I stop this without putting all of us in danger? I couldn't let one of our people die...

I unsheathed my knife; I had an aim that was good and true.

"I'll kill him," I whispered.

But at this distance, there was no way my knife would enter Rowan's back. I had to get closer.

Kade grabbed hold of the back of my shirt. "Wait. Don't be an idiot."

Rowan sliced open the front of Prominus' shirt and had it removed, then ordered Prominus to be strung up between two trees. Once Prominus was secure, Rowan motioned to the glaring woman with the sword to come forward. As tall and sturdy as any male, she bowed her head and took from Rowan's hand a long, thin, green branch—which was meant to be used as a whip.

Rowan gave her a nod and stepped back; it was an affirmation that she may go ahead and cause Prominus as much pain as she wished. The woman seemed to be enraged with fury. Delivering lash upon lash, she breathlessly tore Prominus' skin to shreds, and even when he passed out, she kept swinging.

I would kill Rowan for this a hundred times over. And that woman, too.

26 · EVANGELINE

Hours passed.

By the time most of the camp had fallen under the spell of sleep, I couldn't feel my legs when I stood.

Kade and I took our time sneaking around the outskirts of the clearing, getting closer to the smell of blood and vomit that clung to Prominus' battered body. I kept feeling like I was being watched and almost welcomed the idea of a Raider pouncing from the trees so I could let off a little steam.

The woman who had whipped Prominus had fallen asleep with her sword and was cradling her arm, snoring softly against a tree. I wanted to slit her throat—but Kade's steady hand on my shoulder kept me focused on the task at hand; rescue.

A few guards were roaming about, but their bellies were full of wild boar, their eyes heavy-lidded and hands nowhere near their weapons. One sitting next to the fire kept nodding off, head bobbing up and down comically.

"Those chains are going to make some noise," whispered Kade when we managed to get about three feet from Prominus.

The guard at the fire had the keys. I could see them dangling like golden carrots from his pocket. Before Kade could protest, I was on my belly, slithering across the clearing toward them. The fire was down to embers, and since I was filthy from head to toe, I was merely a slug on the ground. It was easy to swipe the keys and crawl back, so easy that I almost felt like laughing.

Kade slapped Prominus' cheeks to wake him while I slipped the key into the locks at his ankles. His chest and back were a mess, bleeding, red, and swollen, but his eyes were wide and clear when he awoke and realized what was going on.

"I know you," he said to Kade.

"We're here to rescue you."

Prominus nodded, almost falling to his knees when I released his wrists. We quietly dragged him into the trees, barely able to see a thing as we moved into the safety of darkness. Kade gave Prominus some water from a bamboo tube and allowed him a moment to collect his breath, then, stepping as lightly as possible, we winced our way back toward the beach. My hands were grossly sticky with Prominus' blood.

"Thank you," he said, leaning on me and Kade, the weight of him staggering.

"We have a camp." Kade spoke quietly. "It's a long hike through the jungle, but we have shelter, food, and water. Can you walk?"

"Hell yeah," Prominus replied, and his arm slipped off my shoulder. "It will take a lot more than a beating from some angry bitch to keep me down."

Something about the tone of his voice made my stomach turn. Or maybe it was just the smell of him.

I heard a cracking sound from up over my head but ignored it. Weaving our way alongside the beach, keeping tight to the trees, Prominus gained strength with each step. The sky was growing brighter, the tips of the trees lighting up with the first rays of the morning sun. Through the gray-blue light I could almost see my feet, as well as the horrible wounds on Prominus' bare skin.

Another crack.

I pulled my knife from the holster. Someone was following us and not being discreet about it. I stopped, looked around, put my nose to the air and waited to feel the vibration of footsteps. Then came another crack, this one loud enough for Kade and Prominus to drop down into a defense position. I could see Kade's mismatched eyes flash a warning to be quiet as the trees rustled overhead. A whistle—softly made but loud enough to get my attention—made me look up to see long black hair framing a round face and wide eyes; a girl was urgently pointing at something behind me.

I spun around and threw my knife before the Raider ten feet away could throw his, and the blade he was about to kill me with fell to the ground before his body did. It was a clean hit. Right through the heart.

The girl in the trees had saved my life.

I glanced back up in awe, realizing by her clothes that she certainly was not a Raider. I caught a glimpse of bare feet as she moved up higher, now out of sight in the shadows.

"Holy shit," said Prominus, staring between me and the dead man. "Good aim."

"Remember that," I warned instinctively, regarding him with unease despite his circumstances.

Kade gave me a respectful nod and then motioned to the very dead Raider on the ground.

"Get his weapons, Eva."

Kade and Prominus moved on ahead, but I stood there a moment, stunned, wondering where the girl had gone. Without her, I'd be dead. *We'd* be dead.

I scanned the leaves that were silver in the morning light, the breeze from the sea shaking them slightly, throwing off any visual trail I might have had.

"Thank you," I whispered upward.

Then I turned to retrieve the dead man's weapons, along with my own knife, and came face to face with Commander Rowan.

All the air left my lungs in a rush. There he was. Mere feet away. Gaze slicing through me.

"Eva…" he breathed.

The way he said my name made every hair on my body stand on end.

I was fairly certain I could take him in hand-to-hand combat, but there was that kopis at his side, and I knew full well that it wasn't his only weapon. I waited for him to make a move, but his arms remained straight at his sides, hands not reaching for anything to kill me with.

We stared each other down, and after a moment, he took a step back and motioned to the dead man. "There's a blade at his ankle, take that too."

What? Had I heard him right? Was this a trick? The second I bent down would he swing that kopis and remove my head?

Someone started yelling from behind him.

"Hurry," he demanded.

I could fight him. Try to kill him. But instead, I lunged forward, pried my knife from the dead man's chest, and snatched the blade that was indeed at his ankle.

When I looked up, Commander Rowan was gone.

27 EVANGELINE

It was slow going getting back to camp, and I sensed that the girl was following us the whole way, but I said nothing. When the men were busy boiling water and tending to Prominus' wounds, I snuck off on my own.

In a small clearing, I found a fallen tree to sit on and tipped my chin upward. The morning sun was burning my cheeks and shoulders to a crisp, but I stayed put and waited, knowing that the girl who had saved me at the Raiders camp would approach. Sure enough, I soon sensed her standing before me and lowered my head to look into a beautiful face.

Her hair was down past her waist like a long sheet of black satin, she was of medium height, very fit, and had an intriguing glint in her dark eyes... were her irises black? I sat still, not wanting to scare her off.

She eyed me curiously, gaze drifting to my sunburned shoulders. "Aloe," she said, pointing to a spiny-looking plant growing out of the ground next to my feet.

I broke off a piece of what seemed like a cactus and held it up, giving her a questioning look.

"For burns on the skin," she said. "Open it."

I was relieved that we spoke the same language. "Oh, thank you." I eagerly split open the plant and pressed its gel-like substance to my shoulders. The relief was so great I wanted to cover my whole body with it.

"Wounds as well," she said, noting the horrible stitches on my leg and my wrists that were finally healing.

I nodded, holding the impressive plant with reverence. "My name is Eva."

"Kitkun," she replied, pressing her hands to her chest—which I noticed were covered in scars, but purposeful ones. Intricate branded circles reached up her arms and across her shoulders. They were beautiful.

I repeated her name, enunciating slowly. "Kit-coon… am I saying it correctly?"

She nodded, eyes darting around, making sure we were alone. "Yes, Eva."

"Are there others like you?" I asked.

She bit her lip and stared at my hands and the scars I'd earned fighting for my and Zoleya's life.

"I won't hurt you, or your people," I added.

"Mine would hurt you," she said. "The Ouray would not like your kind near our village."

Village, meaning many more like her.

"But I won't tell them about you," she added quickly.

I hoped she was being honest. "Thank you." I choked a bit on my words, wondering what kind of people—besides the Raiders—we were up against. "How many are in your village? Where do you live?"

She pointed north. "On the other side of Black Mountain, where there are as many Ouray as there are stars in the night sky."

I felt my stomach flip. "That's a lot."

"Forty-two tens. Or seventy hundreds. One of those numbers I suppose."

Her knee-length dress was finely made of silky fabric the color of the trees, the stitching intricate at the seams, with patterns of flowers and stars embroidered at the waist. Leather straps across her chest held a knife and pouch, and leather bands circled her bare ankles. "How old are you?" I asked.

She crinkled her forehead. "Oh. I've had sixteen summers."

Something slithered past my feet and I jumped up off the log.

Kitkun's eyes widened. "It's just a jade snake, nothing to fear. The only snakes you need to be wary of are the black or brown ones because they're aggressive. If you don't get their poison out of you, you'll die. Everything green—except the toad with the bloodshot eyes—is pretty much harmless."

I smiled inwardly, knowing that I'd saved Kade's life and hadn't been overreacting.

"Thank you for helping me at the Raiders' camp. That man would have killed me without your warning."

She bowed her head a moment, then lifted her eyes to meet mine. "Was he a bad man?"

"Yes."

"Are they all? Those men dressed in black that go in and out of the sea… are they of your village? You and the men you are with seem different from them."

"We are Aldirans. Those other people are Raiders. We're two separate groups, some of us good, some of us bad."

"Are you? Good?"

Sometimes I wasn't sure. "I'm trying to be."

She was about to ask me something but instead crouched and froze, putting her finger to her lips as a warning for me to remain silent; someone was approaching.

In a flash, she was at the edge of the clearing and up a tree, blending in so seamlessly she all but disappeared. I wanted to ask her if she had seen Zoleya and had many questions about the Ouray people and her village, but Kade was marching toward me with utter rage.

"What are you doing, Eva?" His nostrils flared slightly when he was angry, which was often. "We don't know this island well enough for you to be out wandering alone. Stars above, you can't just sneak off like that."

It was all I could do not to look up and scan the trees for Kitkun. Instead, I concentrated on Kade's oddly colored eyes and the way his teeth were bared as if he might choke the life out of me.

"Don't tell me what I can and cannot do," I said, squaring my shoulders, gripping the aloe in my hand and feeling it gush.

"Just let me know where you're going next time." He turned to walk away. "We are all we have on this island."

"No," I said.

He stopped and spun back around. "What do you mean, 'no'?"

I got up and stood before him, lowering my eyes into a glare that I hoped rivaled his. "Just because you have a dick doesn't mean you have to act like one, nor does it give you the right to tell me what to do. The sooner you understand that, the better."

"I'm just trying to look out for you, that's all."

"I can look after myself."

"Oh really? You think you can protect yourself against... against someone like *me*?"

He had muscle upon muscle and a ferocity that would have most people shaking in their boots. But I could take him, of that I had no doubt. "Yes."

He pulled the knife strapped to his waistband from its holster and dropped it to the ground. "I'm defenseless," he said.

I was confused. "So?"

In a blur, his hands grabbed my wrists, and the only reason he got hold was because I'd thought he was joking. But when his body pinned mine against a tree and his mouth sought my neck, I knew this was no joke.

"You're no match for my weight," he breathed, body burning against mine. "I can do whatever I want and you can't stop me. You realize that, right?"

Fury, pure and undiluted, flooded my senses; this wasn't the first time I'd been attacked by a man, and I knew exactly what to do.

I let my body relax, pretending for a moment that I had begun to enjoy the feel of his mouth on my neck, and this disarmed him entirely. He pulled his head back to look into my eyes, searching them now with something more than just desire—and I slammed my forehead into his nose.

Blood. Instantly everywhere.

Kade's shock gave me the opportunity I needed to execute a move I'd worked into perfection, and in no time he was flat on his stomach, broken nose to the ground, with his arm pinned behind his back.

"Dammit, Eva!" he yelled.

Pulling hard on his arm elicited a deep groan. "You see... I can look after myself," I hissed. "I don't need *anyone*... I—"

Before I could finish my rant, Kade flipped upward in a move I had yet to encounter, and suddenly the roles were reversed. Now I was on my back, arms pinned up over my head as his nose dripped thick gobs of blood onto my chin. He was breathing hard, the look in his eyes terrifying. His legs clamped mine together in a way that rendered me helpless, giving me no way to leverage him off.

"Get off me," I said, barely able to breathe, feeling my heart race.

He just stared, something unreadable flashing through his eyes. "There are others my size on this island, and tough or not, you are goddamn beautiful and desirable. Your confidence could cost you your life, Eva."

"I've fought more than just one man. You're nothing to me," I said, gritting my teeth, squirming, and trying to find a way to break free.

"You mean when the Raiders came for you and Zoleya in that meadow? Yeah, I heard about your valiant efforts. You made a mess of quite a few of them. Killed twelve? But they were just playing with you, Eva. *Rowan* was just playing with you."

I felt tears behind my eyes as I continued to struggle; I was helpless. I couldn't get to my knife, I couldn't use my legs. I truly was at Kade's mercy. He could deliver one solid blow to my temple and knock me unconscious.

Breath hot on my cheek, I could feel his hands loosening their grip on my wrists ever so slightly. He put some of his weight on his elbows so I could breathe.

"If I had to get my nose broken to drive it home to you that we need each other, then so be it," he said. "Notice how I said 'we,' Eva? That's because I'm not indestructible either." His nose poured. "Obviously."

I pretended that what he said didn't affect me. "I'm going to kill you."

I had half a mind to head butt him again, and he must have seen that in my eyes because he put his head down as a precaution. I could feel his heart hammering, his breath grazing my collarbone, and every single inch of my body where it pressed against his squirmed with heightened sensitivity to his touch. But I quit struggling when I realized Kitkun was sneaking over to us, lifting her arm, ready to drive a knife into Kade's back.

I shook my head, *no!*

She paused, confused.

"You won't hurt me," I said to Kade, but for Kitkun's benefit.

He lifted his head to look into my eyes, deadly serious. "I'd give my life for you," he admitted, then winced as if the words caused him physical pain.

I wasn't expecting that. Neither was Kitkun. She put the knife down, gave me a subtle nod, then disappeared back up into the trees.

Kade let go of my wrists, but I left my arms where they were, stunned by his comment and too tired to move. His face was a mess of emotion as he looked down between us to where his blood covered my chest. As his eyes bore into mine, he rubbed his thumb ever so gently alongside his bleeding nose. "I'm sorry," he said, then he sat back on his heels.

My knife was easily within reach now, and he knew it. Yet still, I didn't move. I understood what he'd been trying to do. 'Tough love' Zoleya liked to call it. In his weird angry way, Kade was trying to protect me.

"Do I have to kill this guy?" said a thunderous voice.

Beast had stormed toward us and stopped a foot away, a murderous expression on his face. I knew if I gave the subtlest nod there would be a fight, and only one man would remain standing.

Kade sighed and stood, eyes never leaving mine as he backed away into the green. "There might be a time when you have to kill me, Beast, but not yet."

I didn't want to sleep in the shelter.

Kade's eyes kept meeting mine from across the fire, his nose red, eyes darkening with bruises, and I didn't know whether to comfort him or yell at him. I hated to admit that he'd rattled me, and now I felt more than an appropriate amount of fear because I realized I *did* need to be more careful. He was right. I wasn't as tough as I thought.

I pondered what he'd said about how Rowan had just been playing with me that morning in the meadow. All the other Guardians had been ambushed on their perimeter check before the Raiders came for me and Zoleya. I'd fought my hardest, thinking I had a breath of a chance, and only the fact that I had actually killed twelve and held my ground kept me from believing that although I was a failure, I was not entirely useless.

But now?

"I need to talk to you, Zoleya," I said under my breath as my self-esteem took a thundering crash. "Please. Come for me. Take me into that freaky realm."

Nothing. I couldn't feel her at all. Nor could I feel the male Sage who said he'd return to me at sundown yesterday and never did. With a shiver, I realized that despite the company of Kade, Beast, Dominic, Prominus, and possibly Kitkun hiding in the trees, I felt truly and utterly alone.

Dominic and Prominus were having a good laugh over Kade's face, teasing him about being bested by a girl, and neither he nor Beast corrected them. I had the feeling they wanted the newest members of our group to think that I could defend myself against someone like Kade and that trying to take advantage of me would result in getting something of theirs broken, too. And if that was the reason Prominus wasn't staring at me quite so much anymore, I was grateful for the lie.

Still, I curled up by the fire with my hand on the knife strapped to my leg.

I was close to nodding off when a screeching noise not too far behind me pierced the night. I was quietly relieved when Beast came to the fire and stretched out next to it, his head resting a few feet from mine. His presence was comforting, and the selfless act of leaving the shelter to sleep on the ground next to me was a gracious display of loyalty and friendship.

In the morning when I awoke to embers in the fire pit, Dominic was on the ground as well, sound asleep, his head inches from my feet. I blinked the shelter into focus but only saw Prominus stretched out and snoring, and that's when I realized that Kade was on the ground too, behind me, an arm's length away.

28 — EVANGELINE

We raided the Raiders for a third time and had a really good laugh about it. The bag of salt, cooking pots, clothes, and blankets all made a difference in our little camp. But no item was more life-changing than soap; never in the world would I have imagined I'd be so grateful for the stink of us to be replaced with the scent of cedarwood and lemon.

The only disappointment of the raids was that we never did find Max, and we only managed to rescue one other person besides Prominus; a young man who said his name was Lucky—who seemed to be anything but.

Lucky broke my heart. Soft, sad eyes, meek, and painfully thin, he'd been held captive on the upper deck of the ship. I wondered if that experience had horrified him into silence. He would barely speak, and I had the strongest motherly instinct to cradle him against my chest and rub his back.

Lucky wasn't wounded, but the long brown hair that hung to his shoulders was pulled out in patches—either by his hands or someone else's, he refused to say—and he had a horrible rash on his back. After Dominic gave him a thorough check-up, Beast sharpened his knife and shaved Lucky's head to the scalp. We left him staring into the fire when we headed off on another raid.

I was grateful to be doing something to distract my mind from Zoleya. She'd made no effort to come to me and neither had the male Sage. It made me wonder if maybe I'd lost my Receiver capabilities. Was that possible? Or had the distance between us been spread too thin? I knew there were limits to how far a Sage could reach someone, but I wasn't sure what they were.

Or, maybe Zoleya *had* said goodbye for the last time. She could have been sparing my feelings by agreeing that we shouldn't be apart. Perhaps she was well and truly happy with those other women tending to her and no longer had a use for me.

That made my chest hurt in the worst way.

No. She was just trying to stay safe and hidden, and the male Sage most likely had better things to do than talk to someone who believed herself to be a complete failure. Nothing more.

We made it to the Raiders' camp with the moon and stars hidden behind a blanket of clouds, allowing us to keep to the shadows. But even with the dark on our side, we only managed to steal a bag of grain and some rope before the sun started coming up, forcing us to return to camp tired and defeated.

"They're onto us," Kade growled when we returned to our camp and a pot of stew Lucky had made that was salty, sweet, and entirely delicious. "The Raiders have more guards posted and more fires lit. They moved their wounded to an enclosed structure as well as the people we're trying to free. We need to lay low for a couple of days or we risk getting caught or accidentally leading one of them back here."

"Bastards," Dominic said, spitting at the ground.

I leaned back against a tree, exhausted. "The women that are being held are in danger, and so is the little boy that Captain Vallerik keeps at her side. He's certainly not a Raider by blood and shouldn't be a servant to anyone, especially that monster."

"Brother." Lucky's voice was barely a whisper.

Kade jerked his head toward Lucky. "The kid is your brother?"

Lucky nodded. Lowered his red-rimmed eyes. "*Little* brother," he clarified, suddenly shaking so violently I thought he might stab himself in the face with the spoon.

I wanted to keep him talking. "We understand. How old are you?" I asked softly as the others at the fire remained quiet.

"Fourteen." He dropped his spoon to the dirt.

"You were held captive in a cage with some women... do you know them too?" I asked, hoping one wasn't a sister.

Lucky shook his head and pursed his lips together, not wanting to say anything else. He ignored the rapid-fire questions from Kade and Dominic, body becoming still as stone and shutting down completely. Lucky was going to need some time to heal from his ordeal, and I would have to remind everyone to give it to him.

"We need to go back to the Raiders' camp as soon as possible," I said, addressing everyone and getting the focus off of Lucky. "I don't think we can wait a few days."

Prominus had a snort over that, which we all thought strange. He glanced up from his bowl of food, and when he realized all eyes were on him, he shrugged and got back to eating. I wondered if anyone else got the same ugly feeling from him as I did.

His skin was healing thanks to the aloe plant, so at least he didn't appear quite so monstrous. I wanted to thank Kitkun for the tip about the medicinal plant but hadn't seen her since. I'd kept my word and not said a thing about her, but I wasn't sure how long I could keep the secret—we might need to defend ourselves from the Raiders *and* her people, the Ouray.

"Let's head out tonight and make one more attempt at rescue, and if we aren't successful, we'll wait a few days and come up with a better plan," I said, hoping all would agree.

"Fine," said Dominic.

"Sounds good to me," said Beast.

Kade shook his head. "I don't agree, Eva, but I'll go with you."

Prominus snorted again.

"Got a problem with that, Prominus?" Kade challenged.

"Yeah," said Prominus. "Why are you all taking orders from a chick?"

Lucky's eyes grew wide, and if he could have disappeared into his own skin, he would have.

"Why *wouldn't* we?" Kade asked, glaring.

Prominus sneered. "Cause chicks are only good for two things. Cooking and—"

"Don't say it, Prominus," I warned. "Not if you want to keep your head."

Prominus stood, his massive body a mountain unfolding. "Keep my head?" he said with a laugh. "Why? Do you think you could take it?"

He was challenging me, so I stood too, something fiery in my veins propelling me upright even though I knew it was stupid. Prominus had been looking for a fight with all that snorting of his, so maybe I'd give him one. "Yes."

"Oh boy," said Beast.

"Eva..." Kade started.

I put my hand up to silence them because I had something to prove to myself. I was trained to defend and kill and if I truly could do neither of those things, then what good was I? Why would I bother finding my way to Zoleya?

"Fight me," I said to Prominus.

Kade jumped to his feet. "Whoa! No goddamn way, Eva."

Prominus cracked his neck and smiled wickedly, his red, weather-beaten cheeks crinkling. "You know, if I hit you you'll be dead," he said matter-of-factly.

"Walk away, Prominus," Kade warned.

He said something to me, too, but all I could hear was that little voice in my head telling me to go for Prominus' knee, the one that bowed a bit when he walked, and I could see the moves play out in my head; I'd fake him out with a fist but take a lunge at his kneecap, feeling fairly confident that I could snap it good and hard. Then, as he was bending over, I'd land an elbow to his eye and slam an open palm against his throat. He was slow—solid muscle—but slow. Yes... I'd go for the throat...

Prominus let out a low, primal growl, and his red cheeks became redder. The excitement in his eyes at the thought of hitting me was so disgusting it made my blood thrum in my veins with anticipation.

"I can take him." I said, pulse racing eagerly, ignoring the lingering memory of how easy it was for Kade to pin me to the ground a few days ago. I'd gone over *that* scenario multiple times in my head and knew what I did wrong; I'd trusted him.

Well, I sure as hell didn't trust Prominus.

"Maybe…but you're going to walk away." Kade positioned himself between me and Prominus. "*Please.*"

It was that tone in his voice that brought me out of my arrogant, stupid head; Kade would step in. He'd take a knife to Prominus' throat to defend me, and Beast would certainly get involved too. They would be injured for no good reason except to satisfy my need to prove my worth. I was being an ass.

My pride was a hard lump in my throat to swallow. "Fine," I said after a while.

There was a collective sigh of relief from all but Prominus.

Angry, guilt-ridden, and struggling to hold back tears, I turned and walked away.

Heading for the beach—because I didn't know what else to do—I stomped down the west path, taking a wide berth around a thin brown snake and dodging a beetle the size of my hand. When I hit white sand, a breeze cooled my overheated cheeks as the sea beckoned with open arms. The sun was low in the sky and about to set any minute now, but I was pretty sure the male Sage wasn't going to take me from my body, nor was Zoleya. So I marched determinedly into the sea as if it would cure me of all emotional distress.

I swam. Lapped back and forth to expend my copious amounts of anxious energy, and was soon tired in a way I couldn't explain. I dragged myself out of the water to see Kade standing on the beach with a blanket. He held it open, eyes watching mine as I headed straight into his arms.

I put my head against his chest and didn't resist when he wrapped the blanket around me.

Then I told him I was sorry.

EVANGELINE

As exhausted as I was, sleep wouldn't come. There was an unsettling feeling in the air, and I couldn't shake the notion that something was wrong. It was making me crazy not hearing from Zo—who hadn't contacted me in days—or the male Sage. Was that a good thing, or bad? And where was Max? Was he all right? And how would we rescue the other Aldirans held at the Raiders' camp—we learned that there were at least four men, eight kids, and three women—and what would happen to them if we didn't? And—

"Relax, Eva," Beast said softly, so close to me on the platform that his beard tickled my cheek as my forehead pressed against his bicep. I was glad Prominus slept on the ground by the fire. "Everything will be okay."

Eventually, I succumbed to the cocoon of warmth and must have drifted off, because when I next opened my eyes, the sun was low in the sky and a voice I hadn't heard for a while boomed through the camp.

"Hello, Aldirans," Max said happily.

I sat up to see a massive grin on his angelic face, auburn curls soaked with sweat, his amber eyes flashing with excitement even though there was blood all over his neck and bare chest. Was he wounded? He had something in his hands, but in the low light I couldn't quite make it out… had he caught a couple of animals?

"I did some raiding, too," he said proudly, marching up to the fire and into better light.

Then he lifted the severed heads of two humans.

Beast leaped over me out of the shelter faster than I could blink, and Kade jumped upright in horror. Dominic made some strange gestures with his hands and swore. Prominus laughed.

"Max, what did you do?" I asked, wondering if I was in some sort of nightmare.

With blood dripping from the heads to the ground—the sight intensely gruesome—I tried to focus only on his horrifically delighted expression.

"Well, I've been watching you all trying to rescue 'our people' with no success, so I decided to help even out the numbers. Now, come on… don't look at me like that. They never saw it coming. These two were drunk and giggling to themselves, singing songs while others worked around them. Brothers, too, and quite possibly Captain Vallerik's favorites. She's going to be pissed."

There was a collective gasp from all of us except Prominus—who laughed even louder. Lucky bolted for the trees.

"Max! You can't just go around killing people!"

His forehead furrowed in confusion. "What? They're just Raiders. I thought you'd be proud."

I shook my head. It hurt. "No. No, I am not proud!"

His eyes darkened and he tossed the heads into the fire. "You know as well as I do that if we don't kill them first, then we're just sitting around waiting for them to kill us. They would have no problem taking *our* heads." He swallowed loudly, dropping his brave disposition for a brief moment as he recalled some vision that haunted him. "I know that for a fact."

"Killing in self-defense is different than killing in cold blood." Emotions swirled through me like a storm, making it hard to see straight. I felt Beast move next to me, his hand gentle on my elbow as if reminding me that I wasn't alone and should remain calm.

Max pointed to the fire. "When those two bastards were beating me senseless on the ship, would it have been okay to kill them then? Or how about when they were feeling you up and you were unable to do a thing to protect yourself? I know you recognize them, Eva, because I for one will never forget the faces of the men who put their hands on you and the other women in that cage."

I needed him to stop talking. I'd blocked the assault out of my mind and tried to make it disappear because it had hurt me on a level I had no time to acknowledge.

"I saw the pain on your face," Max continued. "If you would have had a knife in your hand—"

"All right, that's enough," said Beast, stepping forward. "What was done on that ship be done."

Dominic kicked at the fire, uttering more curse words.

"I didn't know…" Kade said softly, jaw dropping slightly as he regarded me carefully. "Eva, I… I didn't—"

"Well, I *did* know," Max said, voice booming. "So, when I had the upper hand, I used it."

The fire popped and sizzled in the worst way. The eyes of the brothers were now forefront and center in my mind as I compared the way they looked while they hurt me, to the way they did now melting over the flames… and it was sickeningly, abhorrently, satisfying. Better than the scenarios I'd briefly imagined where I was dicing them into pieces.

"It's still not right," I said, swaying away from the fire a bit and feeling Beast reach for my arm.

"Why?"

"You just… can't kill someone in cold blood," I sputtered, being a hypocrite yet again.

Prominus snorted.

"What now, Prominus?" I asked the red-faced mountain staring me down.

"The Raiders tied me up and whipped me until I was shredded," he said. "And you know what? They were going to do it for seven nights. Now, do you think if I came upon that bitch who wielded the whip on me I'd just walk away and not kill her in 'cold blood'? Hell no. I'd do worse. I'd hurt her in a way that would make her remember me for every painful second of her worthless existence."

I shivered, head spinning slightly. "About that, Prominus, why, out of all of the prisoners, did the Raiders decide to torture you? You're strong. They could have put you to work like the other Aldirans we've yet to rescue. Why were you singled out?"

"Because they're all maggots!" Prominus spat.

Max scoffed. "Maggots. Yep, they are. And I'll eliminate as many maggots as I can before they can hurt us again."

That meant killing Commander Rowan.

"Murder should be punishable," I stated.

Max laughed but it wasn't genuine. "Punishable how, Eva? Are you going to put me over your knee and spank me?"

With a deep breath, I centered myself, suddenly far too tired for male posturing. "I'd like to suggest that as long as we're here, punishment will be in the form of complete exile from the camp. Said murderer will be left on their own to fend for themselves and have no contact with any Aldiran."

I'd read something like that in a book once. It seemed fitting here.

Prominus glared.

Max tried to smile but it didn't reach his eyes. "We don't even know where 'here' is."

"'Here' is *Island X* until named otherwise," I said. "And here on Island X, we have our first law."

"And who will uphold it?" Max looked around the group, expecting opposition.

Beast cracked his neck and his knuckles. "I'll uphold it."

"As will I," said Dominic.

Kade nodded.

"And who determines if someone is guilty or innocent?" Max asked.

"It'll be a majority vote," I offered.

Max backed away, his smile gone and replaced by a nervous glare. "I'm here to slaughter Raiders, and that's what I'll do. I'm here for a reason, and nothing and nobody is going to get in my way. You wanna hang out here and have a vacation while our people back home are suffering? Then you go ahead. I'm going to get rid of as many Raiders as I can, take the ship they're most certainly building, go to Cal de

Mac, find my family, and then head home where I can make a difference."

I could start an all-out war with Max, or try and placate him. In the end, we all wanted the same things. Freedom, peace, and safety. But it was how we went about achieving those things that would define us.

Are you good or bad? Kitkun's voice was in my head, the question echoing…

I wanted to be good, desperately so. My morals were something I valued. But maybe rescuing people wasn't about just getting bodies freed and comfortable, but minds as well—starting with Max's.

Kade had started to pace. "You know, Max, even when the path ahead is clear, sometimes we have to change direction." The words seemed to cause him pain. "You need to adapt. It's the only way to survive."

Max shook his head and started to walk away.

"Max, stop," I said, head a bit dizzy and trying not to look at the fire.

He let out a heavy sigh. "What?"

"I *am* being a hypocrite. I've felt those same things you're feeling, yet somehow I'm able to brush over them with rainbows and unicorns. I can't expect you to do the same."

"Oh?"

"And I am ignoring the bigger picture. So, maybe you're right."

He turned to face me, amber eyes drilling into mine. "How so?"

"Our people back home *are* suffering, just like the ones here on this island being held captive by the Raiders. I've been wearing blinders, thinking only of those I could see and not of those left behind. Thank you for reminding me of that." I felt the world spin around me for a moment; Zoleya was a part of that bigger picture. She was the catalyst for change, and fighting for her meant fighting for everyone. "But we need the Raiders in order to get out of here and take you to Cal de Mac to find your family. We need them to help us get home so we *all* can make a difference. Now, whether that means waging war and taking over their camp or magically converting them to our ways, I don't know. But I do know that we must try something. So, I agree with you

Max, we will not treat this as a vacation. But killing just to kill isn't going to solve anything. If and when we wage war, we have to know that we can win, and right now we're outnumbered. We need to work together. We need to work smart. And since this is new to all of us, it's going to take some navigating to get everything working smoothly. So, let's figure out how to get back home together, and in the interim, let us be your family. Deal?"

I offered my hand for him to shake.

Max looked thoroughly stunned, eyelids fluttering rapidly as if he might cry. The tender years of youth shone briefly on his face, and his façade of stern bravery slipped away. I'd given him what he needed most; hope.

He marched toward me and put his hand in mine, eyes glistening with tears. "Thank you, Eva."

Prominus swung his head back and forth, his weather-beaten face screwing up in disgust. He'd been huffing and puffing like a volcano about to blow.

"You're all idiots," he said, spitting at the fire and then marching off into the green.

I wasn't sad to see him go.

30  EVANGELINE

Nobody said it, but the camp felt lighter without Prominus. His energy had been oppressive and kept everyone on edge. Even Max's dark mood had lifted slightly, and he was doing his best to pull his weight by fetching water and fortifying the shelter. Now when I caught Max eyeing me, his gaze felt more innocent than dangerous— even though he'd decapitated two defenseless men.

When the sun went down and the temperature dropped—still with no contact from Zoleya or the other Sage—I was grateful that the shelter was solid, enclosed on three sides, and the bamboo slats we slept on were covered with an extra piece of the ship's sail. No bugs or snakes could sneak in between any corners or come up beneath us, and the smoke of the fire kept them away from the open part of the structure. With Prominus gone, there was more space in it for us while one kept watch on the ground—a decision we'd made collectively when a panther came a little too close for comfort.

Tonight, Beast had the first shift. He came back from the beach freshly washed, his red hair gleaming in the firelight, wearing a black shirt and trousers he stole from the Raiders.

"Wake me in two hours for my shift," I told him.

He nodded, raking his beard with his fingers. "Yes, Missy."

I didn't think I'd be able to fall asleep, but it came on hard and fast. Before I knew it, Beast was giving me a gentle shove. "You're up."

I took my place by the fire, barely able to keep my eyes open. Knife at my side, the green rustled and rang with strange sounds that should have put me on edge but the flames were mesmerizing with patterns of wavering light. I was drifting off—until a sound, soft and close, pulled me awake.

A small rock was tossed to my feet, and my first thought was that Prominus had come back. Then I saw a female shape briefly step into the light of the fire. It was Kitkun, her fit body adorned with a leather butter-yellow tunic covered in beautiful embroidery, and her long black hair shining like silk. She waved at me to follow her, so, knife in hand, I took a few steps away from camp into solid darkness.

Without the assistance of a torch, it took a moment for my vision to adjust. Eventually I could see her before me as I inhaled the scent of mint coming off her skin. The clouds overhead scattered and made way for moonlight, and I blinked into focus a string of small shells she was holding out to me.

"A bracelet. For you," she said and pressed one of the shells to her lips. It made a high-pitched whistle. "If you hear that sound, it means you are too close to poisonous air or water."

Had I heard her correctly? "Poisonous air?" My head was fuzzy, barely awake, and all I could think about was getting back in the shelter.

"You and Kade survived it the other day near the bones of the dead. By the waterfall. You are lucky you escaped." Kitkun's voice was firm. "You must be more careful."

When we'd come across the bones, Kade and I felt like we were breathing mud. "What is it?"

"Think of it as a fence, or a barrier protecting the interior of the island. We call it the Wejukah."

"Oh."

"We worship it for keeping us safe from… well—"

"People like me," I offered.

"Yes. I have found a few 'doorways' though, which is why I can come and go safely. And there are places where it can be weak. The Wejukah doesn't cross water, so you can always follow a stream safely inland if you need to—but don't. You will be caught." She glanced around, on high alert, speaking too fast. "My people won't go anywhere near the Wejukah. It brings death, just like the rain does when the sky turns green." The jungle shifted around us, and for a brief moment, the clouds blocked the moonlight and I was staring at utter darkness.

"Poison fence," I said. "Follow a stream if I have to. Got it."

The clouds shifted again and Kitkun's beautiful face came back into view. "Don't go into the Wejukah ever again, Eva."

"All right," I said, touched by her concern.

"And you must always listen..." She reached for my hand, hers warm and sturdy as she tied the shell bracelet around my wrist. "If it whistles, turn back or seek shelter and do not stand in the rain."

What the hell? A poison fence, and now... "The rain?"

"Sometimes Nvula cries tears of Mordorain. It comes from above and strips your skin from your bones. The only warning is the green sky and this bracelet, Eva."

Her words were making me dizzy. "Nvula? Who is—?

"The Goddess of the Sky," Kitkun replied patiently.

For some reason my knees had begun to shake—I didn't feel so good. "Oh."

"Do you understand? She casts death from above. This island has many dangers. You must be careful. This is most important."

She was speaking quietly and my exhausted mind was having a hard time comprehending. "Okay. Green. Yes. Whistling. The Wejukah and Nvula. Got it. Thank you."

She sighed heavily. "You are tired, but there is much I have to teach you if you are going to survive here. I will come back when you're rested. And when I do, can you tell me how to not sink in the water?"

"You mean, swim?"

I could see her eyes light up. "Yes! Swim."

"Of course."

Drums started up, distant and haunting. I could see the expression on her face change and her body tense.

"What do the drums mean?" I asked.

"They are from my village, calling all the hunters home."

"You're a hunter? Huntress?"

"Yes. I provide for my family and—"

My name was spoken and Kitkun froze; Dominic was awake, calling out to me.

"Get some rest, Eva. But remember…" Kitkun pointed to the shells at my wrist. "*Listen*."

Then she disappeared into the dark so fast I wondered if I'd dreamt her.

"Eva," Dominic repeated. "You talking to yourself? Where you at?"

I practically fell forward out of the green toward him. "Here, sorry. I had to pee."

He'd fashioned a scrap of a shirt over his brush cut and tugged it down over his ears. "I can't sleep, so I might as well keep watch. You go ahead and get some shut-eye," he said.

Grateful to be off duty, I climbed over Beast and wedged myself between him and Kade, neither of them moving a muscle. They were sound asleep—but Max wasn't.

"You weren't talking to yourself. Who was it?" he asked.

I was too tired to give him a plausible lie. "Just the moon."

I woke up shivering even though someone had put a blanket over me. Lucky was stirring something in the soup pot, Max was whittling sticks to a lethal point, Dominic and Beast were sharpening knives, and Kade was pacing, arms crossed over his bare chest, his clean shirt hanging to dry. He looked worried, but not as shy about the birthmarks covering his muscular torso—which was rather something to behold. He was a work of art. *Beautiful,* I thought.

"Good morning," he said, catching me staring.

I felt my cheeks blush. "Morning." My saliva seemed sticky and my bones ached in a way they usually only did after a full day of training. The sky was gray, the air cool and damp. I pulled the blanket up to my chin.

"We be gettin' a good storm today, Missy," said Beast. "The jungle be quiet as a drunk skunk and the wind has a good bite to it."

Indeed it did. And that 'good bite' turned to a mighty chomp the moment breakfast was done and the dishes cleaned. We all scrambled to secure clothes drying on lines and angle the remaining sail high over the fire—Beast was adamant it not go out—and fortify every nook and cranny of the shelter. The wind was ripping through the camp, picking up everything not tied down, and then, all at once, it just stopped.

The air became still as stone.

Not one living thing made a peep.

And then came the rain. Not pouring like it had a few times since we'd been here, but raining nonetheless. We piled into the shelter, sitting knee to knee, shoulder to shoulder. The patter on the roof was like a song attempting to soothe frayed nerves. I liked the sound. Always had. When I was a kid it would put me to sleep.

But it was one thing to be so close to the men when we were all sleeping and another when we were all awake. Kade's thigh was touching mine, hot as blazes, and Dominic's arm brushed my shoulder every time he rubbed his shorn head. It was close. Too close. I contemplated sitting out in the rain.

"I have a comb," Lucky said out of the blue.

He hadn't spoken in days. "Would you like to use it?" I asked.

He nodded eagerly, his face so young and pained that my chest hurt for him. I braced myself to have my hair mangled to bits, but he moved to Kade.

Kade flinched comically. "Whoa… No way in hell, kid."

I pinched Kade. Hard. Beast snickered as I gave Lucky a nod. "Go ahead, Lucky. Comb Kade's hair."

Lucky tentatively inched closer to Kade's back. "Lice," he said.

Kade lurched again. "*What*? I have bugs in my hair?"

"No. Combing prevents lice. No comb and you get bugs. They itch. Hurt."

Ah. That's why patches of Lucky's hair had been missing.

The realization crossed over Kade's face. "I can do it myself." He reached for the comb.

Lucky snatched it back quickly; it was precious to him.

I pinched Kade again, and Lucky's hair salon was soon in business. With nothing to do but huddle in the tent, Lucky wielded his magic. Even Beast's beard got a makeover. I had to say, I was incredibly impressed that the men all succumbed to Lucky's desires. Even Max, who now looked more angelic than ever with his auburn hair tangle-free and flowing in waves.

Then Lucky drew up close to my back as the wind picked up again and began unwinding the long braid I'd tried to maintain. Sorting through my strands, his hands on my head were almost euphoric, the kind touch sending delicious chills up my spine. With Kade's roaring body heat on one side and Dominic's on the other, I found myself nodding off.

"Eva is hot," Lucky said after a long while.

I lifted my head off my knees—had I been asleep?

Kade laughed. "Uh, yeah. You're just noticing that?"

Lucky took Kade's hand and placed it on my forehead. "Hot," he repeated.

"What? Oh, whoa. Eva, you're burning up."

"Not hot," I said, realizing I'd been gritting my teeth because the pleasant chills had become uncomfortable. "I'm just really... just... cold."

Things were happening in the shelter and I found myself flat on my back while Dominic inspected my leg. I felt like a lab specimen with the men hanging over me.

"Does it look infected?" Kade asked.

"I can't tell." Dominic was probing around the wound on my calf. "It's warm, but with all the dirt I can't see anything."

Lucky bounced up out of the shelter. "Water," he said.

Something about the rain churned in the recess of my mind, but Lucky was fine as he stomped toward the pot we'd left out in the open to fill with rainwater.

"Stick out your tongue, Eva," Dominic ordered.

I did. I said 'ah,' Beast complained that he didn't think Dominic knew what he was doing. Dominic told Beast to shut up.

"No red throat," Dominic said.

Then he was picking up my hand, examining the wounds around my wrists where the chains had made permanent scars. If he noticed the bracelet, he didn't say a thing. Max, however, raised an eyebrow in curiosity; he knew someone had given it to me last night but thankfully remained quiet.

All the fuss was embarrassing. "I think I'm just tired," I said.

But Lucky had washed away the dirt on my leg and the mood in the shelter darkened dramatically.

"What?" I asked.

"It's infected." Dominic ran his hand over the crude stitches. "Given our situation, I'm not surprised."

No one said a thing for a very long time. I almost fell asleep. Then I heard the word 'amputate' and I was up, feeling *way* better.

"I'm fine," I said, but I knew that the sickening sting in my wound was the reason for my exhaustion. I'd been ignoring it, pretending it would go away, but now that it was exposed it was all too real.

"We're not amputating her leg," Kade put his hand on my shoulder. "What else can we do?"

"Cut it open," said Dominic. "Let the infection out."

Beast laughed. "That's barbaric! Did ye learn medicine in a back alley?"

"Well, I never really *learned* medicine," Dominic confessed. "I got in a fight with the healer's son and was thrown out on my ass five days in."

"What? Have ye even stitched anyone besides Eva before?"

Dominic bit his lip. "No. Not really."

"Holy shit," said Kade.

This was maddening. They were fighting and being ridiculous. "Listen, I'm fine." I crawled to the edge of the shelter, got out, and stood. I was shaky but determined to be okay. The rain continued softly pattering on the canvas overhead, keeping me and the fire dry. I was okay. I moved out from underneath the canvas and felt the rain dust my shoulders, making my chills dig a little deeper.

I was not okay.

I pulled in a deep breath of air, feeling my lungs expand exactly how they should. I was okay.

But I was not okay.

Suddenly the rain stopped. The wind stopped. *Everything* stopped. It was as if the weatherman hit the pause button. I was dizzy. Cold. Confused. Because the sky was turning green.

Green.

Everything on this blasted island was green.

I was okay?

Something was whistling. Kade was saying something. Beast and Dominic were arguing. I wanted to tell them all to shut up, but the sky was *really* strange. It wasn't the same shade of green as the plants bursting with life, or the algae on the pond, or those feisty lizards that jumped from tree to tree. It was sickly. Deathly. It looked how I felt.

Kade was insisting I lay down as he put a blanket around my shoulders, but all I could do was get back under the canvas and sit on the edge of the platform where I could peer out at the sky. Kitkun had said something about the rain... what was it?

"Well, I can't sit on my ass a moment longer." Max grabbed the pot that was now filthy from my leg being washed. "I'm going for fresh water."

"No..." I said, but I wasn't sure why.

"You really should lie down." Max was a blur of auburn hair and fiery irises as it began to pour. "You look really pale."

Then he crawled out of the shelter and marched off.

And I realized it was my wrist making that whistling noise. Whistling. Warning...

Green sky—

Max started to scream.

The rain!

I used every ounce of energy I had to race toward him, my skin instantly stinging as if being sliced by knives. I made it five feet from Max and thought I might not be able to go any farther... but he was stunned, trying to figure out why his skin was on fire, so I kept going, somehow getting close enough to throw the blanket over him. Grabbing him by the arm, nearly blind with pain, I started dragging him back to the shelter. The bracelet was whistling, Max was screeching, and I was up and in Kade's arms just feet from the shelter seconds after my legs gave out.

"What the hell?" Kade yelled as he got us both back under the safety of the canvas roof just before the sky opened up and all hell broke loose. "The rain is like acid!"

With a confirming crack of lightning, death fell from above.

31 EVANGELINE

The pain was so unbearable I couldn't control my shaking body. I knew I was crying and hated myself for it. The fever was making the world come in and out of focus, concerned faces were hovering, words were being spoken, and all I wanted to do was scream and try to run away from the acid burning into my skin. So, when I felt the pressure of the male Sage at the edge of my mind, probing, prodding, asking to be let in, I welcomed the break from the physical realm wholeheartedly.

Is your body safe? asked the Sage.

I was in Kade's arms… "Yes."

My consciousness drifted alongside a brilliant blue light into the freaky realm.

I fully realized that to everyone in the shelter, I would appear dead. Beast might know what was happening but he would keep it to himself. He'd understand that I was taking a respite from the pain for just a moment and would protect me, of that I had no doubt.

For the first time ever, I embraced the weird and welcomed the light of the male Sage. Alexander was a powerful presence yet oddly comforting, and I was so relieved to be free of the pain that if I had arms I would have hugged him.

"You're late," I said, or thought.

And you're hurt, stated the Sage. *Why is it that I am alerted to your pain?*

"I don't know. Why is it that you broke your promise to visit me at sundown? That was days ago."

This question irritated him. *Because I've been busy with matters of life and death. They took precedence.*

I reminded myself to be careful. I didn't know this Sage, or his capabilities. "Fair enough."

Where are you hurt? he asked. *The last time it was your emotional agony that brought me here. This time I was alerted by harm to your body. Your physical pain led me to you like a wailing beacon.*

"It's nothing, I will be fine." Would I, though? I'd known many people who died from infection, and the acid that seemed to be burning straight through my skin to my bones wasn't helping matters much.

Where are you, Quillene?

Quillene? Oh. Right. I'd given the Sage my last name. "I'm not exactly sure," I replied honestly.

A Sage can only link to a Receiver that is within a few hundred miles, so we are relatively close. What is around you? Are there any landmarks?

"Where I am is not something you need to know." The Sage could be from Kitkun's village, and divulging that kind of information could put my people in danger.

I could dig around in your thoughts and find out for myself, he warned.

"But you won't, because that would be a terrible start to our relationship."

Relationship?

"Correct, which will be nonexistent if you don't care about continuing to establish trust."

I sensed that everything around me was slowing down, becoming soft and warm even though I couldn't actually *feel* anything.

Tell me about the Sage you were with. Who is she?

I had to hold my ground and be careful. "Until I know a lot more about you, that topic is off-limits."

Even though you know it might anger me and I could leave you here in the Between forever?

I thought of Beast's mother. "Yes."

Hmmm, are you brave or stupid?

"Uh, neither. I'm loyal. I'm someone who keeps her promises."

I respect that. He paused, his light pulsing around us. *Would you like to know more about me, Quillene?*

Anything to keep him from digging around in my memories. "Yes."

Go ahead.

My thoughts were a bit scrambled, so I simply asked; "Where are you?"

How about instead of explaining, I show you what I am seeing at this very moment?

"Uh, okay?"

All at once there were too many colors. An exploding rainbow of dizzying pinks and oranges. It was as if I was being pulled apart and put back together over and over. Then, suddenly, as if I was awake during the strangest dream, I was seeing through Alexander's eyes and had to block out all rational thought of how this was happening or end up a blubbering mess of crazy.

"You're on a beach."

Yes, he said.

Mostly, all I could see was water and the horizon far in the distance. He wasn't showing me much else besides that and waves crashing up onto the sand, but I could feel how the sight and sound affected his emotions. He treasured the water, grew up with it, and knew it intimately, yet was also awed by the beauty of the island like I was. I decided at that moment that I liked him.

But something was off.

I actually never imagined this to be possible. You're able to see... through my eyes...

"Yeah, and your sky is green," I pointed out.

Falling apart, coming together, falling apart... my thoughts were snagged on that green sky... my words stuck, not quite computing what it was I needed to say. I could feel Alexander in a way I could never explain, as if his very essence was flowing through me, and all that was good about him was making itself known far too fast—but he was in danger.

In all my years, I've never thought this possible. I'm in both realms and I can feel you in my head and it's like nothing I've ever—

"Your sky is green," I said, cutting him off.

He laughed. *Yes, it is a bit odd.*

It hit me; acid rain. "This is bad!"

I sensed his confusion.

Words began tumbling through my head, or my mind, or… "You can't get wet. You must seek shelter when it's green…" It came back to me fully; throwing a blanket over Max, feeling as if my skin was being stripped from my bones. "Alexander, you must get out of the rain. Run!"

Pain exploded through me like lightning as I was slammed back into my body with such force my breath rushed in with a gasp.

Kade's face was hovering over mine, eyes wide and full of horror.

"You're not dead," he said breathlessly.

The shell bracelet at my wrist kept whistling.

32 KADE

Two days ago, Elder Mathias caught me trying to free a banned book from the Forbidden Cave. Oddly, he wasn't angry. In fact, he helped me unchain it and open it up on the altar. "It's a history book," he said. "Of the world long before our time. Considered dangerous information lest it be repeated. You see, back then, technology was both a gift and a curse."

I snuck back to read that book, but it had gone missing. A day later, so did Elder Mathias.

— JOURNAL ENTRY, KADE, AGE 17

A midst the chaos of the sky unleashing holy terror, I ceased to exist the moment I thought Eva was dead.

Red streaks peppered her arms, shoulders, and bare feet. Her body was limp. Eyes rolled back in her head. The only thing that kept me from ripping apart the shelter in utter despair and rage was that, upon putting my ear to her chest, I heard air moving in and out of her lungs and her heart beating—she was alive, but barely.

Max was splashing water out of the cooking pot onto his arms. "The water isn't helping," he said frantically.

Where the rain had hit him, his skin was turning white and making a sizzling sound. Only when Dominic squeezed the goo out of some sort of spiny plant and slapped it on did he stop hyperventilating.

"It works," Max said, holding back tears. "That plant is neutralizing it somehow. How did you know to do that? And... oh my God. What the hell is up with this place?"

The sky let loose, and now the rain came down in buckets. If Max had been out there—if *any* of us had been out there—our skin would have been stripped from our bones.

"Kade." Dominic nudged me. "Put this stuff on Eva's face."

He placed a tiny piece of the plant in my hand. I had her head on my lap, and the marks on her cheeks were turning white, too. I squeezed out the slimy stuff and rubbed it all over, touching the bridge of her nose, her neck, her lips... I felt the marks at my ribs give me a little bite and under my breath told them to fuck the hell off.

Dominic was rubbing the plant on Eva's feet, and Max had taken the remainder of his and was working on her hands. A long streak beneath her eye was like the trail of a teardrop. I pressed some gel to the burn, and I could have sworn I heard it sizzle like oil on a hot pan.

We worked together, pressing the gel to her skin, collectively trying not to panic as we eyed the corners of our structure for leaks. The sky had become lost to the rain, and we could smell the acid in it. It was metallic, like blood.

"Why isn't she waking up?" Max asked, seeming frantic. "The burns on her are turning from white to pink, and that's a good thing."

I applied more aloe because I didn't know what else to do, and said her name, gently shaking her. "Eva, open your eyes..." I was feeling frantic, on the verge of ripping everything and everyone around me to shreds. This girl was more important to me than I thought, and I couldn't picture a life without her in it.

"She's okay, you guys," Beast said. "Relax."

His hand was on my shoulder. I shrugged it off and looked up to meet his eyes as the sky tried to break through the canvas. I had to yell over the noise. "How do you know that?"

He just stared back, unblinking. "She'll wake soon. I promise."

There was something he wasn't telling me, and under different circumstances, I'd beat it out of him. For now, though, all I could do was hope he was right.

I gathered Eva's body closer to mine. Never in my life had I felt so protective. So distraught. So… *useless.*

"What be that whistling sound?" Beast asked when there was a second of silence between us.

I hadn't noticed the string of shells on Eva's wrist until now. They weren't there yesterday…

As I picked up her hand, fingers so petite in mine, I realized the larger shell was making the whistling sound. Had it been doing that this entire time and we were all too frenzied to notice?

"Does anybody know where she got this bracelet from?" I needed to keep my mind off the marks giving me little jabs again; they sensed that my heightened emotions had nothing to do with my destiny or my 'plan.' I practically growled out my question. "Did one of you make it for her?"

I stared hard at Lucky. He'd been following Eva around like a lost puppy, always watching her and at her side. Had he taken it from the Raiders to give her a gift? The pink and pearly shells were not like the ones on our beach.

Lucky looked me right in the eye. "No," he said softly.

Dominic and Beast shook their heads.

But Max had gathered Eva's other hand to his. The gel from the plant was all used up, but he was rubbing the green innards of it on her fading burns regardless, and if he didn't stop touching her I might kill him.

"You know something about this bracelet, don't you, Max?"

He returned my glare with one just as steady. "I know that this girl just risked her life for mine, so I wouldn't tell you shit if my mouth was full of it."

I could threaten to hack off his limbs, but I had a feeling that wouldn't make him talk. As I looked down at the girl in my arms, I realized that her decision to run to Max and cover him with the blanket while somehow knowing the rain would burn her in the process had cemented unfaltering loyalty and devotion from everyone. Since I felt the same way, it was the only reason anyone still touching her had their hands.

"Uh oh," said Dominic, getting all our attention. "I didn't notice this burn on the bottom of her foot. It's… oh, yikes. It's bad."

All thoughts of the strange bracelet disintegrated. I looked down Eva's body, past her bare thighs to the leg with the stitches draped over Dominic's lap. He was pressing the innards of the green plant to the ball of her foot as beads of sweat poured from his brow.

"Not enough plant goo left," Dominic added.

Lucky whimpered when the rain came down even harder, and there was no mistaking his words. "Cut it out."

He meant the burn. The acid was eating into her.

Beast was swearing. A mad string of words burst from his mouth. Max kept holding her hands, his eyes meeting mine, full of rage and horror. The roof above us was holding, but one corner kept lifting and Lucky was in that corner. I had to look twice to realize he'd cut out a small notch of skin on his arm to remove a burn, obviously saving whatever we had of the plant for Eva. Up until now, I'd thought the kid was a total useless putz. But the blood dripping down his arm proved otherwise.

"He's right," said Max, gritting his teeth. "Lucky is right."

My head swam, barely able to connect my brain to my mouth. But Dominic, calm and collected, removed his knife from its sheath and began working.

"Do it fast, while she's out," huffed Beast.

Dominic began humming, laser-focused on his task and nothing else as he dug the knife into Eva's skin. I felt her jerk.

"She's feeling this on some level," I said.

Dominic broke his tune. "Hold her leg, Beast. If she wakes, you keep it steady."

I memorized every line of Eva's beautiful face and ignored Dominic's haunting melody. Lucky whimpered and I suspected he was removing another burn. I didn't look up.

"This is all part of my plan," I whispered to my marks, my voice impossible for anyone to hear over the pouring rain. "I must keep her alive and I must be emotionally invested to do so."

The marks quit biting at me. So, I took a deep breath and held Eva tighter, elated when her eyes finally opened.

Beast grabbed Dominic's arm. "Stop!" he roared.

Dominic quit digging at her foot. Lucky froze. Max said a prayer to some god while patting her hand. Beast clenched his hands into fists.

But although Eva's eyes were open, she wasn't seeing anything. She didn't blink. Her gaze was unfocused. Face frozen as if turned to stone. Had she died?

"Eva?" I slapped her cheeks, then put my hand over her heart—it was still beating.

She barely seemed to breathe, the rise and fall of her chest hardly perceptible. I closed her eyelids because I couldn't bear the vacant look and tried to control the excruciating rage and sorrow at the thought of losing this beautiful girl.

"She'll wake up," Beast offered. "Just give her a moment."

I wanted to believe him. We all did. So, we waited on pins and needles, and when Eva drew in a deep breath and her eyelids fluttered open again, I nearly collapsed around her in relief.

"Is this real?" she muttered, trying to focus.

"Yes. The rain is being a real bitch," I said.

"Oh."

She shivered and winced, squeezing her eyes shut and digging her nails into my arms as if to stay grounded. The canvas above us was shaking, and now lightning cracked like a whip through the sky. When the wind changed direction and blew in the rain, we all scrambled away from the opening and huddled together in the corner.

"Where is Max? Is he okay?" Eva asked, voice barely audible above the bedlam as she tucked her face into my arm.

Max was on his knees in front of her, guarding her from whatever rain might make its way in. "I'm right here and I'm fine. Thanks to you."

"And Kitkun?" Eva asked. "She told me about the green sky and the whistling shell, but I forgot—"

"Who is Kitkun?" I asked.

"Is that who you were talking to last night?" Max interrupted, avoiding my glare. "Did she give you the bracelet?"

Eva looked up, but as if she hadn't heard either of us, her gaze centered on Beast. "He told me his name," she said.

Him? There was a Kitkun and a *him*?

The world around me seemed to explode in my ears.

Beast tugged at his beard nervously. "Now, Missy, we be talking about this later, aye? Get some rest now. Ye might be a bit delirious."

"Okay," she said, turning her face back into the crook of my arm.

"Who are you talking about? *Who* told you his name, Eva?" I asked softly, close to her ear.

"I don't—oh… it's so cold," was her reply.

Her body had broken out in a sheen of sweat, and since the blanket was on the ground being pounded by the rain, there was nothing to warm her with. So, I just held her tighter and kept my head about me when Beast and Max pressed closer to share their body heat as well.

"I wonder why the heck the blanket isn't dissolving. Or our hair," Max said, nervously rubbing his forehead, hands shaking. "Or the plants."

After a long minute of contemplation, Dominic spoke. "Maybe the acid only interacts with living human tissue. I suspect that this island probably has a lot of anomalies that we're going to discover the hard way."

Anomalies… If anything, I was comforted by the fact that this place wasn't perfect. It had its flaws and shortcomings and wasn't simply a magical wonderland of food and beaches. It hit me that the anxiety which always loomed over me like a dark cloud was justified. I could remain on edge. Look over my shoulder. Keep an eye on the sky…

A flash of light whipped through the shelter, illuminating the panic and terror on every wide-eyed face.

"We're going to die," said Lucky.

I patted him on the head and forced a smile. "Nah. If there's one thing that Beast can do, it's build a shelter. We're safe in here, kid. I promise."

"Darn straight," Beast said.

The rain poured. I briefly thought of Prominus, hoping his skin was shredded right down to his disgusting bones. I thought of the Raiders, most likely suffering great casualties. And I thought of Rowan... the mighty commander who, on his sinking ship, risked his life to save the girl in my arms because I was pretty sure he felt the same way about her that I did.

Then I could think of nothing else but surviving the night.

The shell on Eva's wrist continued to whistle until the sky cleared.

When the sun finally came out, we all remained in the shelter, tentative to test the wet ground, silently acknowledging the fact that we made it through the night but Eva might not make it through the day. She was so pale. Blue veins visible under her skin. Fevered, sweating, barely conscious, and the infection spreading up her leg was far too visible. I kept ignoring Dominic's suggestion to cut it off.

"It might be the only way to save her," he said, bringing it up again.

Beast agreed. "If those red streaks reach her knee, then we'll have no choice. We can't be letting them reach her heart."

"We can't do that."

"Then what do you suggest?" Dominic asked, his voice so calm I wanted to shake him.

"We have to find help. Surely there is someone who can—"

"Hey..." Eva said through chattering teeth, the pain in her voice gut-wrenching. "You guys k-keep talking about me like I'm not here, and it's... pissing me off."

Every once in a while she'd have a lucid moment, like now. Eyes flashing, focused and boring a hole straight through my chest.

"I don't w-wanna lose my leg," she added. "Then I'll never f-find *her*."

She was talking about Zoleya, and had been deliriously muttering her name over and over. But she had said nothing again of Kitkun or *him*—whoever they were.

"We're going to get you fixed up. I promise you won't lose your leg," I sighed, brushing my fingers across her cheeks and looking up to see four grim faces.

"Don't lie to her," Dominic mouthed.

"Fuck off," I mouthed back.

"And Kade…" Eva pulled my attention back to her. "I've n-never had an orange."

She was delirious again. "An orange?"

"Yeah. I'm going to die and never had an orange. What does it taste like?"

All eyes and ears were on me—it was a little too close in this shelter.

"Tell me?" Eva pressed.

I didn't know what a darn marshmallow was, but she thought—correctly—that I could describe an orange? Ironically enough, it was the only gift my mother ever gave me. A full, round one with a small heart she'd carved into the peel. I thought I'd never had anything so perfect in my whole life.

I had to smile. "Well, the smell alone will make your mouth water, so fresh and clean and tangy it puts all your senses on high alert. The segments are soft and burst in your mouth, the juice a bit sour but sweet too—not as sweet as a ripe banana—but balanced perfectly and just acidic enough to make your taste buds dance. Pretend lemons and limes have a magnificent great aunt who is just as enthralling but proper and reserved in all the right ways. That's an orange."

"Mmmm, I can taste it now," she said, then passed out cold in my arms.

I felt the heavy stares of Max, Dominic, Lucky, and Beast. "What?"

Lucky spoke for everyone when he simply said, "I want an orange."

Well, I wanted Eva to be well and for us all to get the hell out of this shelter…

An echo of Mother's words came rushing through me. "It's not your purpose to *want*, Kade Thorn, it's your purpose to *do*. Remember that."

Do. Yes. You're right, Mother.

"I'm taking Eva to the Raiders camp," I stated.

This was met with confused silence.

"I need to get her some help. Who's with me?"

"Those heartless assholes will just laugh at us," Max said in disgust. "They'll put us in chains or feed us to the sharks."

"Maybe. But Rowan won't hurt *her*. You all know this."

They'd been in the cage with me when the ship went down—well, all except Lucky, who had gone through his own private hell in a cage on the upper deck—and they all knew who Rowan came to rescue first. They knew I was right.

Beast released a breath that sounded like a lion's huff. "Well, it's not like we have any other choice. The infection be reaching her heart if we don't remove her leg, and even then…" he looked down at the girl between us, "that alone probably be killing her. We done have no sedatives, nothing for pain. Missy be strong, but…"

He didn't have to finish that sentence.

"Do you think you could do it?" Max asked, facing Dominic, his hand moving to Eva's arm a bit too protectively for my liking. "Answer honestly. Could you *actually* do that sort of surgery… successfully? You keep talking about it, but do you have the knowledge? The skills? The right tools?"

Dominic had kept a calm and assured air about him—until now.

"I, uh, don't know," he admitted.

"Well, that's answer enough for me." Max crawled across Beast and Dominic, slipped out of the shelter, and dug his toes into the still-wet earth. We waited for screaming of some sort, or tears, but instead he said, "It's safe. Let's go."

Activity broke out at an intense rate. It seemed that in minutes we'd collected some of the aloe plants just in case there was more rain, sucked back water and as much food as we could for fuel, then made a stretcher with the blanket. As Eva drifted in and out of consciousness, we headed toward the beach.

"What we be doing when we get there? Just go marchin' up to one of them Raiders and be askin' fer help?" Beast said, leading the way once we got back into the green, the machete in his hands lashing out furiously at the plants that were constantly trying to overtake our path.

"We'll need to find Commander Rowan and get him alone somehow. Two of us will go into the camp, two will guard the perimeter, and one will stay with Eva."

"We're walking toward our deaths," said Dominic.

"Then go back if that bothers you," Max replied with such ferocity I felt the hair on my arms lift. "At least it will be an honorable way to die."

He had one end of the stretcher and I had the other, and if I'd been worried that he'd stumble or let go, I wasn't now.

We stopped to catch our breath and wipe the sweat off our foreheads. The sun was high in the sky and heating up the jungle, taking away any trace of the rain. The birds were back, along with the snakes, lizards, and howling monkeys—all seeming unscathed. How did the rain not affect them? They didn't have shelters and aloe plants, so was it really only human skin that burned? I noted the bloody bandages Dominic had tied around Lucky's wounds as the question lingered a moment, and then I decided that I didn't have enough brain power to care. All I could do was concentrate on moving ahead.

"I don't like all this green," Eva said when we stopped for water. "It makes me uncomfortable."

We all laughed at that because we felt the same way. But then she said; "I'm going to die, aren't I?" and we picked up the pace.

Marching ahead, ignoring the thorns and rocks stabbing at my feet, I felt her shift on the stretcher and bent over to check on her. Her body jerked and then became completely limp, but her eyes remained wide and unseeing, just like they had been when she'd collapsed against me when the rain first hit.

"Stop," I said to Max. "Put her down."

I knelt next to her and the makeshift stretcher, then put my fingertips to her wrist to check for a heartbeat; there was barely a pulse.

"Don't die on me…" I said, patting her cheeks.

No response, just that dead-eyed stare.

"Eva!" I shook her, feeling close to a complete meltdown.

"Stop, Kade," demanded Beast, hovering over us, sweat pouring off him. "She be fine."

"What?" I stood. "First you agree with cutting off her damn leg, and now her eyes are rolling back in her head you say she's fine? What the hell do you know that I don't, Beast?"

His top lip curled up in a snarl and he crossed his arms over his massive chest defiantly.

"Say it," I ordered.

"I'm just trying to keep ye calm, Kade Thorn. Yer acting like ye might explode."

"Maybe I might! You're holding something back from me, and Max knows something about that damn bracelet, and there's—"

Eva took in a shuddering gasp and her body jolted back to life. Her unsteady gaze took in every face staring down at her before settling on Beast.

"His name is *Alexander*," she said to him. "He said he can help. Take me to him, okay?"

Then she was out cold again.

Beast wordlessly marched back to the front of the line and got back to swinging his machete viciously.

"Who's Alexander?" I asked, unable to disguise a thick wave of jealousy that shocked me to the core.

All I got was a growl in reply.

33  KADE

— JOURNAL ENTRY, KADE, AGE 6

Raging bonfires throughout the Raiders' camp lit the night, the smoke issuing a stern warning for intruders to stay away. Torches were lit all along the beach, and next to those were armed guards; our enemies were on high alert but seemed a bit beaten and weary.

"Don't go killing them," I said to Max.

His eyes had lowered into a glare, every tendon straining with rage. He was younger than me and certainly less experienced at fighting, but there was a deep-rooted fury in him that I wouldn't want to test. He was a wolf in sheep's clothing guided by an extreme sense of loyalty, and that made him tremendously dangerous. As my marks seemed to bite into me a bit more every hour—despite my attempts to silently remind them of my plan—I was glad to have him on my side.

"I know what I'm supposed to do, Kade," he snapped.

"Good. Because if Beast and I aren't back by sunrise, that means we're either dead or captured, and the rest is up to you."

"Yes, and if that happens I will take Eva back to camp and let Dominic remove her leg. But it won't come to that."

Was Max that trusting in my capabilities?

"Because she'll be *dead* by then," he clarified. "So don't screw this up."

I had every mind to put the punk in his place, but I swallowed my anger and snuck forward, tentatively leaving Eva behind with Max, Lucky, and Dominic.

As Beast and I inched our way into the Raiders' camp— avoiding the beach even though there were new structures to hide behind—I asked him about Alexander. He replied that Eva was just delirious and spouting off names.

Beast was a terrible liar.

The Raiders had surrounded the perimeter of their camp with long piles of spiky plants and brush they'd cleared away. We had to survey the outskirts many times before we found a spot we could get through without being ripped to shreds. Beast, as huge as he was, moved like a cat through the jungle, not even making a peep when a thorn nearly went straight through his foot.

When we were finally under the cover of night we slipped up tight behind a tent. The occupant inside was making a horrifically unsettling moaning sound that made the hair on my arms lift. It heightened the reality that Eva's last precious minutes were ticking by. When I tripped over an axe that was leaning up against a tree and swore under my breath, Beast scolded me with his eyes.

"Sorry," I mouthed.

The moaning stopped; the person in the tent had heard us.

We bolted off toward another tent, and then another, and almost stepped on a man sound asleep in the shrubs. From behind what certainly smelled like the camp kitchen, Beast and I listened to the hive of activity surrounding us; one group cooking over a smoldering fire, another sharpening tools on flat stones.

"Where the stars would Rowan be?" I said, frustrated.

A new structure had been erected in the center of the camp and guards sat around it staring off into the night, watching and waiting. It was fashioned from wood that had been plucked from the shipwreck, and the remnants of the Raiders' insignia was visible in the firelight.

"He probably be in that shack," said Beast, pointing to what we both assumed were the captain's quarters. "No way to sneak up though. We could be polite and mannerly and just go knock on the door I suppose."

I would have laughed, but really, was there any other way? If we couldn't find Rowan alone and out in the open, then we were going to have no choice but to sacrifice ourselves to get his attention.

We waited. Watched. Hoped for the guards to fall asleep. No one came or went out of the building for a long while.

Beast met my gaze; Eva's life was in our hands. We had to do something. But what? Both of us were frozen in limbo, legs numb from crouching.

When our worry was nearly unbearable, Commander Rowan emerged from the shack at last. He headed straight toward the beach. Even in the dim light, there was no mistaking him for someone else. He moved so regally and with such authority that it sent people scattering out of his way. His presence made the guards straighten while others paused what they were doing to watch him pass by. I felt Beast tense next to me. He'd never admit it, but Rowan made him anxious, too.

It seemed to take forever for us to skirt the edge of the camp unseen and get to the beach, and I worried every second that Rowan might be gone by then. Maybe he just went to give the guards their orders, or wanted to take a piss in the sea before bed...

My haste made me careless, and before I knew it I'd stepped right out onto the sand and into the path of a man with a sword strapped to his back. Beast swung before I had a chance to lift my hands in defense, knocking the guy out cold with one punch.

"Damn, Beast, that's quite the right hook you got there," I said, impressed.

He grumbled something as we dragged the unconscious man into the bush.

Beast then made quick work of removing the man's sword, strapping its leather holder across his own chest. Twisting the end of his bright red beard into a point, he glared. "Ye best be more careful, Kade. Get yer head together."

Ribs burning. Bones throbbing. The marks were fighting me, making me weak. But how could I explain that I was being hindered by some ancient technology carved into my skin that could sense my emotions?

"If you continue to cause me pain, I will be caught by Raiders and will never be able to complete my mission," I said to the marks. "Now back the hell off."

Remarkably, they obliged, so I took in a deep breath and stood taller.

"That's better," I said.

Beast eyed me curiously but didn't ask why I was talking to myself. I appreciated that he was single-minded and didn't give two shits about what was going on with me. He took the lead as we snaked through the Raiders' camp, back to the south end of the beach to where we hoped to find Rowan. Stars twinkled. There was no breeze. A small group of tents we came upon were minimally guarded, and the smell of death hung thick in the air. I realized rather quickly that this was where the dead awaited their send-off, and the only man standing watch here seemed a little worse for wear. We stopped and waited behind a boulder a few feet from him and a row of dead bodies laid out on the sand. When I thought my legs might fall asleep again, we finally saw *him*.

Commander Rowan exited the last and largest tent and strode to the water's edge. He looked up and down the coast, his shoulders slightly hunched. After what seemed like forever, he turned and walked back to the tent, pausing a moment to look at the dead before going inside.

Beast motioned me to follow. We got up close and strained our ears for voices or any indication that there were others in the tent with Rowan. We heard nothing. I readied the axe while Beast held the machete. Taking a deep breath, we pushed back the tent flaps and barged inside.

Rowan was kneeling before someone on a makeshift bed with his head in his hands. He barely flinched when he turned to see Beast and I standing behind him. Slowly straightening his spine, he merely appeared irritated by the intrusion, and that alone was rather unnerving. I glanced around quickly to assess the level of threat to find only us, some lanterns flickering weak light into the shadows, and drying plants hanging from the timber holding up the tent roof. I noted that the person on the bed was a female wearing full Raiders fighting gear and assumed she was injured by her labored breathing.

"Kade Thorn," Rowan said, giving me and then Beast the once over. "And Willard Plinket." The tone of his voice was smugly self-assured. "To what do I owe this pleasure?"

Was Beast's real name *Willard?* I shook it off. "We need your help."

"Oh, do you?"

Rowan stood and Beast readied the machete. I reached over to lower his arm.

"One of our people is hurt and we need medicine," I said, sounding a bit too desperate for my liking.

"I would imagine that many of 'your people' are hurt, Kade Thorn. Much like mine." Rowan motioned to the woman behind him. Along with many bruises, her arms were covered in white marks that were indented, the skin around them red and swelling.

"The rain?" I asked.

"Among other things, yes," Rowan replied, his hand moving ever so slightly to the kopis at his waist.

"Why isn't she in the infirmary with the others?"

Rowan slowly began drawing his blade from its sheath. "You know the layout of my camp, I see. Does that mean that you are familiar with The Keep? The place where you are going to be chained up two minutes from now? My captain wants to spill the blood of every Aldiran in exchange for the brothers you decapitated."

Max... the heads he'd thrown into the fire...

I put my hands up in defense, letting the axe fall to the ground. "It wasn't us."

Rowan and I regarded each other while my heart hammered in my chest; if I messed this up, Eva would die. Of that, I had no illusions.

A flicker of concern flashed across Rowan's face when the woman on the bed moaned.

"I know how to help her burns…" I offered, "The wounds from the rain."

Rowan cocked an eyebrow. "I'm listening."

"As I'm sure you've realized, water doesn't neutralize the acid, it only continues burning into the skin. You need the gel of a certain plant."

Rowan took a large step in our direction. I stood my ground, as did Beast, but it was the first time I felt truly threatened by another human. Rowan wasn't as large as either of us, but there was something intimidating about him on a level I could not comprehend. Maybe the reputation that preceded him had gotten in my head, or my hatred was muddling up my senses. Either way, I'd never met anyone so sure of himself—Mother would have liked him.

"Tell me which plant," he demanded.

"Will you help our friend?" I countered.

"No. I will not. But I will let you walk out of here alive."

"It's Eva," I said, saying her name slowly so he felt every vowel. "Evangeline."

Silence. Stone-cold gray eyes stared hard into mine, conveying only the slightest flicker of emotion.

"She's sick. Dying," I continued. "Maybe has hours left to live. Minutes, even."

Rowan barely blinked. "And she is the only one you want me to help? There are no others?"

"Only her."

He drew in a steady breath. "Where is she?"

"Close by." I tried to unclench my hands that balled up into fists as Rowan's stare became so intense it weighted the air. "Please, help us and we will help *her*…" I motioned with my chin to the woman on the bed. "We have the plant. We brought some just in case there was more—"

"Rain," Rowan said, sheathing his kopis.

I was winning him over. "Yes."

The woman on the bed spoke softly, her voice muffled by what I now realized was a very swollen lip. "Rowan, you know what will happen if you help an Aldiran—"

"That's enough, Amari," he scolded, then, without another word marched right between me and Beast, lifted the flap of the tent, and left.

At once we could hear his voice. He was giving orders. Sending away the guard to clear the way for us to bring Eva to him unseen. When the tent flap was pulled back open, he directed us out onto the beach with a look that said "Get her."

I didn't trust Max to refrain from decapitating someone, and Lucky was scared straight out of his shorts being so close to the Raiders, so I left Beast behind to keep watch over them. With Dominic assisting, we moved Eva as fast as we could toward the tent where Rowan was waiting. Once inside, Dominic went straight to the woman on the bed and applied the gel of the aloe plant to her burns.

I placed Eva at Rowan's feet like an offering—or a sacrifice. He didn't even glance down at her, only focusing on me even as I put my hand on her forehead, unable to hide my alarm over the increase in her body temperature.

"She's burning up," I said, feeling my voice catch. "Help her. Please. She sliced her leg open on a reef and it's infected. She got hit by the rain, too, and we managed to treat most of her burns, but—"

Rowan put a hand up to cut me off, glare breaking away to briefly look at Eva's leg. It was swollen and hard, and now her knee was puffed up and red. He knelt and pressed gently. She winced, but her eyes remained shut. He pressed his fingertips to the inside of her wrist, on edge as if ready to draw his sword on me in case it was a prank, and only when he felt how truly weak her pulse was did he acknowledge the gravity of the situation.

"Is she the only female in your camp?" he asked.

"I'm not telling you that."

"How many of you are there, Kade Thorn?"

"I'm not telling you that, either. It would be suicide."

"I could kill you both in one breath."

The smug bastard. "You won't."

Rowan's fingers twitched. It was the first sign of nervousness I'd seen from him, but it wasn't because he felt threatened by me. "Is the plant helping you, Amari?"

"Yes," said Amari as Dominic broke open another long stem of aloe and pressed it against her shoulder. "The relief is almost instant."

Rowan shifted foot to foot, then stepped over Eva toward the exit. "Do not leave this tent, Kade Thorn. Understand?"

I hated that I had to listen to him, obey like a dog when I really wanted to slit his throat. "All right," I replied through gritted teeth.

Then Dominic and I were alone with the woman, Amari.

"I can't believe you survived the storm. And the... rain," she muttered.

I was surprised she could speak at all with the amount of damage and swelling to her face. Someone had beaten her bad enough to completely seal one of her eyes shut, but the one that remained open mirrored Rowan's cold stare. I decided to hate her just as much as I hated him.

"It takes a lot to take down an Aldiran," Dominic replied bitterly.

She tipped her head to the side and studied Dominic's angular face, shorn head, ratty clothes, and the tattoo on his arm. I pulled the shirt tight across my chest when she then eyed me.

"Oh, I remember you..." she said, tensing.

I reached for the axe; suddenly I remembered her as well. Back in Aldira when I'd become certain that Atomica was on the Raiders' ship, I started a fight outside of a bar in Nora to prove I was worth taking. After I won, I offered Amari my wrists to shackle and boarded her vessel of my own free will. Then I marched up to Captain Vallerik to try and bargain my way into her good books— which resulted in being beaten by her minions and forced into the cage.

"You…" Amari's fingers twitched and she coughed. "You came aboard—"

"That death trap you called a ship," I said, completing her sentence as a warning for her to shut up.

Amari knew too much about me. My marks surged with a powerful anticipation of bloodlust that made bile rise into my throat. I needed to remain calm. Breathe. I could not lose my cool here.

Dominic misread the tension. "You *should* remember us, Amari. You locked us up in the hold of your ship. Left us for dead. You took us from our homes against our will."

"Not *all* of you," she said.

Dominic shook his head, confused. "What's that supposed to mean?"

Amari was about to give me away, so I lifted the axe ever so slightly and leveled my eyes on hers, silently sending a message that I would kill her if she said anything about me. She was vulnerable. Her neck in just the right position for taking off her head…

Quite wisely, Amari quickly changed the subject. "So, why are you risking your lives for *her*?" she asked, eyeing Eva.

Kneeling next to Eva's lifeless body, I put down the axe and glared. Dominic moved into position next to me. We said nothing.

Amari struggled up onto her elbows and spat at the cold sand. "It took us ages to find that girl." She coughed and swore under her breath, wheezing slightly after. "We had to go inland and trek across your cesspool of a country—for a month."

"What?" I was intrigued. "Why?"

"I guess Rowan figured she'd be good entertainment. Just like you two."

Right. I suspected Rowan wanted to capture Eva for another reason but kept that to myself. "You put women in your arenas?"

"You don't?"

"We don't force people to fight to the death *for sport*."

Amari was struggling to keep her head up, body shaking. "Maybe you should… instead of letting everyone just off each other in the streets for no reason."

"You Raiders are barbaric," Dominic hissed.

Amari's arms gave out and she collapsed onto the bed. "And you Aldirans are delusional scum."

I put my hand on Dominic's shoulder as a silent demand for him to not enter into an argument, and for a long while only the sound of Amari's labored breathing filled the tent.

I was relieved when Rowan returned, carrying a strange case made of metal, which was most likely ancient and just the sort of illegal item you'd be hung for owning in Aldira. I hoped it had something to do with getting Eva healthy, and with a nod, he subtly let me know that's exactly what it was for. I breathed a sigh of relief so heavy it brought forth an excruciating wave of exhaustion.

Rowan quickly went about pushing a sequence of buttons on the top of the case, and I couldn't help but recoil slightly when it opened. It seemed to be lit from within, casting an eerie glow on all sorts of vials filled with swirling liquids of greens, blues and reds.

Dominic's jaw dropped and he appeared ready to bolt from the tent. I was sure the rules of our country echoed through his mind, but the part of him desperate to be a healer was frozen with intrigue.

"What the hell is that?" he asked.

"Medicine," Rowan replied.

"From… *Before*?"

"Enough questions." Rowan removed one of the vials very carefully, as if it might explode if jostled. "Amari, are you recovering?" he asked, not taking his eye off the vial of swirling blue liquid as he placed it on the lid of the case. When it was stable, he opened a cloth sack that he had slung over his shoulder.

"Yes, Commander," she replied weakly.

"Then get off the bed."

Amari struggled to sit up, displaying more injuries than just bruises and burns. What appeared to be claw marks ran from her neck down her arm, and I suspected that she had broken ribs and other internal injuries by the way she moved. I made the motion to help her, and she shrugged me off, curling up on the cold sand by the canvas wall.

We maneuvered Eva onto the bed, and Rowan made quick work of swabbing the back of her hand with alcohol or something I assumed was for killing germs. From the cloth sack, he took out a strange bag filled with glowing liquid and told me to stand and hold it while he eased a long needle into Eva's vein. Dominic watched with great interest while Rowan attached a long tube to the bag I was holding, joining it to the needle.

"For hydration," Rowan simply said.

"Don't you have a healer that does this?" Dominic asked.

"Yes," Rowan replied but didn't elaborate. He was working quickly, noticing—as the rest of us were—the alarming advancement of the red streaks moving up Eva's thigh.

"How will this help her?" Dominic pressed.

"I'm giving her something for the infection. It will go directly into her bloodstream."

"What is it? Where is it from?"

Dominic was ignored.

Eva was so lifeless I wondered if she was dead. Her eyes were shut, her body limp, and her chest barely moving. Rowan added the contents of the vial to the liquid in the bag I was holding, and we watched a blue substance head down the tube and into her veins. She stirred slightly, opening her eyes but not seeing anything.

"Are you sure you know what you're doing?" I asked.

Rowan shot me a look. "Shut up, Kade Thorn."

I bit back a reply, swallowing my pride for Eva's sake.

Rowan pressed gingerly at the hot skin around Eva's wound, then made quick work of unpeeling the bandage from around her foot. "Gods above, what sort of barbarity is this?"

"The rain," Dominic said flatly. "We were afraid the acid would keep burning into her, so—"

"So you *cut* it out?"

"Yes."

Rowan was about to unleash a torrent of reasons why that was a bad idea, but the words seemed to stall on the tip of his tongue when he noticed our bloodied bare feet. Shaking his head, he got back to the task at hand and removed another vial from the case. After filling a syringe with green liquid, he jabbed it into the most swollen part of Eva's wound without warning.

Eva gasped, her eyes flying open as Rowan pressed the plunger of the syringe, sending the green substance deep into her leg. To my horror, he yanked free the needle and dove it into yet another spot. Pain stole Eva's screams as she tried to catch her breath. Her eyes widened in terror at the sight of Rowan and what he was doing.

"Cover her mouth and hold her down, Dominic Falkosky," Rowan ordered. "If she screams, the whole camp will come running."

Eva was panting, looking from me to Rowan as the words I was trying to soothe her with were lost. Rowan stabbed at her leg again, pressing the plunger and forcing the liquid deep into another spot of her wound. Eva screamed behind Dominic's hand.

"Give her something for pain!" I felt close to losing control.

Rowan motioned to the bag of liquid in my hand, his voice devoid of any emotion. "I did. It takes a minute to work."

"Then stop and wait!"

He filled the syringe again and was now pressing with his fingertips around her knee, trying to find the right place to jab her. I felt my stomach twist as this cold-hearted human went through the motions. Eva was even more pale and now sweating, eyes brimming over with tears.

This was torture, and I knew firsthand what it felt like. I'd been jabbed, sliced, prodded, beaten, and everything in between. Could I put Eva through this? Maybe it would be better to let her die than force her to endure any more pain. Besides, what if Rowan was just playing us? Having some sick, twisted fun? How could I truly trust a... *Raider?*

I grabbed his arm. "Stop."

I saw it in his eyes just then. That this was killing him to hurt her. But he had no choice.

"Do you want her to die, Kade Thorn?" he motioned to the red streaks moving rapidly.

No. Of course I didn't want her to die. "Just... give her a minute."

"We don't have a *minute*. I have to hit bone. Now."

Right. Mother's words seemed to fill my ears; *Sometimes you have to hurt what you love to keep it alive…*

I gave Rowan a nod and let go of his arm, then I said Eva's name and told her it would be okay while she fought against Dominic, terror in her eyes as Rowan lifted his hand—and jabbed again. Another muffled scream, then her eyes rolled back in her head and she passed out.

"That bag has to remain above her heart," Rowan said when he was finished, completely emotionless. After packing up the case with the used vials, he handed Dominic a roll of gauze, some antiseptic, and a needle and thread, then pointed at Eva's foot. Dominic, needing no explanation, got to work.

Rowan stood to leave.

"Why her?" I asked, and the question hung between us like the fine line between life and death.

Rowan's eyes met mine, and I realized that not once had he even looked at Eva's face. Not once had he acknowledged who it was on the bed. "I'm not heartless," he said.

But he was. He'd sentenced many to die on his ship, put children in cages, and would have no problem stabbing one of us, unprovoked, just because he could. I'd learned firsthand how 'heartless' Rowan was.

Amari broke the silence. "Hurry and get the case back to the healer," she said, her tone respectful and full of admiration for her commander. "They'll hang you for helping an Aldiran, brother. Please don't get caught."

"*Brother*?" I repeated.

Rowan handed me his kopis. "Guard them with your life, Kade Thorn," he said, then he left the tent with the case of medicine and a bundle of the aloe plants.

I felt Amari's stare and looked down into her eye that wasn't swollen, gray like Rowan's and flecked with blue. Her sharp jawline gave her that same air of regality, but brother and sister had different coloring. Amari's hair was black as night and her skin white yet heavily freckled, while Rowan was golden-skinned and blonde. Despite this difference, I suspected they shared many other traits, like extremely quick reflexes and ingrained lethal capacities—otherwise Rowan would not have left her alone in this tent with me and Dominic.

"Why aren't you with your healer?" I asked, so tired I thought I too might collapse to the sand, but needing to feel her out—would she hurt Eva? Stab us in the back if we fell asleep?

There was a note of sadness and wounded pride in her voice. "I've been exiled."

I hadn't been expecting any sort of reply, but then again, the end of life usually made the dying loose-lipped. "Why?"

Amari dragged in a ragged breath. "I disobeyed my captain's orders."

"And did the bitch beat you for it?" Dominic asked, wrapping clean white gauze around Eva's foot.

Amari closed her eyes, gripping the handle of the knife at her thigh. "No. But I wish she had."

I was about to ask more questions but heard voices outside of the tent, rising in pitch as they neared. Dominic and I crouched before Eva, ready to defend her in any way we could, but I realized my disadvantage as I held the bag of liquid dripping into her veins over her heart...

The voices grew louder, then trailed off. I hadn't realized I was holding my breath until I damn near passed out.

"If I can sense your fear," Amari mumbled. "They will too."

Ignoring her, I turned my attention to Eva. She didn't look any better. Her breathing was still shallow. My ribs ached.

"Hey." I wanted to pat her cheek and urge her awake, but I had a kopis in one hand and the bag of liquid going into her veins in the other. "Can you hear me? We're getting you fixed up. You're going to be all right."

No response.

"She's going to be asleep for a while," said Rowan, appearing behind me from out of nowhere. His cheeks were lightly flushed from running, yet before I could even blink he had his kopis back and sheathed at his waist. Taking the bag of fluid from my other hand, he hung it from the tent beam with a rope. "Now, leave and let Eva rest."

It was a command, but he was not my commander. "I'm not going anywhere."

"She'll be here for a while," he replied.

I sat down defiantly, as did Dominic, and the wave of exhaustion that stole over me was enormous.

"Suit yourself," Rowan said, not arguing but drawing out a small knife that gleamed madly in the weak light of the lanterns.

I put my hand on my own blade as my heart pounded, getting ready to spring to my feet; I would do what I had to do in order to stay at Eva's side.

Rowan simply cracked his neck. "Relax. You may stay, Kade Thorn," he said. "And you as well Dominic Falkosky. You are both safe under my watch. Take rest." Rowan handed Amari the smaller knife and then straightened his jacket. "I will check on Eva every fifteen minutes and Amari will not harm you if you leave her be. It is my word that until sunrise, I will not leave this post."

Could I trust a Raider? All logic said no.

But while Rowan stood guard outside the tent, I slept harder than I had in years.

34 

To bathe in sun and starlight and forget the need to breathe is to be truly blessed by the gods.

— THE BOOK OF IMATLA

The smell of so many people in the confined space was unbearable. I didn't mind the rats and spiders in the tunnel, or the odd snake slithering up out of the black water running like an anemic river six feet below our ledge. But all the villagers with their sniffling and farting, some hyperventilating or worse yet singing songs as they cooked parts of the goat that smelled as vile as pig shit in the heat of summer, fried my nerves to a crisp.

"Someone has angered Nvula," said Hanuk from his red-painted platform, voice booming like thunder past the arched concrete walls. "Our Goddess of the Sky punishes us with Mordorain. We all must pray. Now, repeat after me…"

His incessant blathering was as inescapable as the stink. Hanuk aimed to strike fear in the hearts of everyone in the village, and, for the most part, he succeeded. But I always thought he sounded as stupid as he looked. His massive muscled body was adorned with gold at every joint, even circling his neck. Beads, shells, and stones were woven into the hundreds of greasy black braids pulling at the top of his scalp, and the shaved sides of his head were painted red. He wore tight leather clothes no matter how hot it was, and weapons I'd seen him use far too often were strapped around his chest and thighs, completing his 'I'll kill you and dance on your face' persona.

He was awful. Sometimes I thought I'd rather take my chances and go stand in the rain.

"We'll make sacrifices at sunset after The Goddess Nvula has grown tired," he roared, the slick arched walls of the tunnel channeling his voice deep into the never-ending dark. "All of you think about what you have done and beg to be forgiven."

I noticed Muma glance up at me from where she sat huddled with my sisters; of course she would assume that I was the reason the entire village had to hide down here. That I'd been up to no good and angered a goddess with nothing better to do than watch me. Little did she know that it was the sea people I'd spied on at the north shore who had caused the relentless downpour. Those who called themselves Raiders, who had dug holes for some of their dead instead of burning them.

But I kept that to myself.

The Mordorain fell in waves, as if the sea itself crawled up to the sky and jumped off the edge of a cloud. We could hear it pounding, see it sneak down the stone steps to collect in the trench the warriors had carved and spill into the black water below. Our homes were well suited for regular rain—roofs were repaired daily and gutters were kept clean to whisk the water away from the streets—but when the sky turned *that* shade of green—the one that made the insides of my eyelids ache and the shells on the wrists of every villager whistle in unison—we took no chances. We hid. Down here. In the ancient tunnel I'd affectionately named the Hell Hole.

The only thing I liked about the Hell Hole was the strange pink and green symbols that decorated the walls and stretched for miles into the dark. Hanuk claimed they were warnings to not venture too deep into the tunnel, but I didn't believe him. So, months ago, I told Muma I was going hunting for a few days and snuck down into the Hell Hole with enough supplies to last me a week. Then I started walking. But after four days of descending downward into total darkness, the crawly things became poisonous, the rats ravenous, and my torch wouldn't stay lit to keep me from tripping over them. Things moved in the black water. Animals that could see in the dark hung from the roof. Stairs that led to nowhere offered no way out. So, when my lungs would not stop screaming for oxygen, I had to turn back and accept that Hanuk might be right.

"Will this rain ever end?" said Elke, hanging on to Muma's skirt as always, eyes wide as she watched the murky water rising below us, the trench filling rapidly.

I thought of Eva and the sea people; had they found shelter in time?

"Of course," said Muma, patting her head lovingly. "Eventually, Nvula runs out of tears, just like people do. We just have to have patience."

Patience. That was funny. It was something the gods did *not* have but demanded from us. They were such hypocrites.

"Or the tunnel could flood and every single person down here will die," I said, being honest.

Muma cast me a disapproving glare. "Watch your mouth, Kitkun, lest you anger the gods even more than you have."

The rain fell harder. Hanuk preached louder.

It seemed an eternity until the Mordorain stopped. When we were back home and safe, Hanuk's voice was ringing in my ears while I scrubbed at a pot that never seemed to come clean. As I tuned out my sisters fighting over something at the kitchen table, I couldn't help but continue worrying about Eva and those sea people, wondering what I'd find when I went to their camps...

"Kitkun!" Muma yelled, startling me.

I put down the pot, turning to see her standing in a bit of light coming in through the murky window. "Yes?"

Muma's hair was trying to escape the bun on the top of her head, the ends as dry and frayed as the broom she was sweeping the floor with. Both were nearly the same wheat color as her skin, making her resemble a washed-out painting you'd disregard—until you were hit with the backside of her hand.

"Are you listening to me?" she asked.

I hadn't heard a word. "Of course." My throat tickled from the dust that always seemed to be present in the musty cottage.

"Hanuk wants one sacrificial offer from each family before the sunset. Pick the skinniest of the chickens and then help your sisters with dinner." She pointed to the yard.

Sacrifices were horrible but unavoidable. The only thing anyone with a heart could do was push their feelings as far down into the gut as possible. I did so today as I begrudgingly tugged on the gnarled wood gate of the tiny paddock that protected our family's livestock— but nothing was inside except an empty square of dirt.

My heart sank to my toes. I looked around, hoping a chicken would appear from out of nowhere, but had no such luck.

This was not good.

I took in a deep breath before heading back inside.

"There are no chickens out there," I told Muma, using my calmest voice.

A fresh log crackled in the hearth and sent smoke into the kitchen.

"They were there yesterday before the rain," I continued. "I know because I put them in the coop. The gate is still closed, too, and there are no signs of foul play—no blood or feathers—so I have no idea what happened to them."

Four pairs of eyes met mine from across the kitchen table. Muma had stopped sweeping, Elke and Nita quit arguing, and the knife Hesutu was about to jab into a mango hung mid-air.

"Chickens don't just disappear." A pained expression pulled at Muma's delicate features.

I had to agree with that. "Maybe a neighbor, uh, borrowed one?"

Preparing for sacrifice often pitted family against family. Each man for himself. There was no sharing. No helping hands. Stealing happened.

"You are sure we have *none*?" Muma pleaded with her eyes for me to be wrong. "Not one chicken?"

"Not one."

"But Hanuk demands a sacrifice," said Elke, starting to shake. "He said so. In the tunnel."

Muma knelt and put her arms around my youngest sister. Elke couldn't stand to watch animals being hurt, and she once almost starved over her refusal to eat them. But she wasn't worried about a chicken being beheaded today, she was worried about Hanuk demanding that Muma sacrifice one of *us* in its place.

"Don't worry," I told her, picking up my hunting knife and strapping it to my waist. "I'll go catch something. Besides, Hanuk wouldn't want you anyway, Elke. If anything, he'd like to see my head rolling down the temple steps. I am the troublemaker, remember?"

Elke started to cry.

"We can ask another family for help," Hesutu said, ignoring me—and Hanuk's rules—and rising from the table. She was the only sister with common sense enough to try and think of a solution instead of bursting into tears. "I'll ask Avda."

Her boyfriend was *not* going to help us. If anything, he was probably the louse who stole our chickens.

But Muma didn't stop Hesutu from leaving, and her usually stoic expression was close to unraveling in a fit of tears.

"What can I do?" she muttered.

We all knew that the hunters would be spared, as well as the warriors and the women of birthing age. But my youngest sister was a good offering. Just as acceptable as a goat or a chicken.

"I'll fix it," I said, but I was met with silence.

"I'm all you have to give," Elke sobbed. "I'm the youngest."

Mother hugged her tighter. "Now, that's enough. We'll figure something out," she said, but fear shone in her eyes.

Was I invisible? I grabbed my boots—just in case it rained again—and headed for the door. If a sacrifice was demanded, there was no bargaining our way out of it. If we didn't present our own offering to the Goddess of the Sky, Hanuk and his followers would come stomping into the house and take all of us.

I needed to hunt.

Elke sobbed harder. "They'll take me."

Muma tried to soothe her. "No, I won't let that happen."

I patted the knife at my waist. "No, *I* won't let that happen," I said, then ran out of the cottage and headed for the jungle.

35 · EVANGELINE

A heavy substance flowed in my veins, filling my bones with lead, numbing my pain and terror, making what was happening around me confusing. Commander Rowan had been trying to kill me, but Kade was there, and some strange girl with black hair was talking, and Dominic was humming…but I couldn't focus. Couldn't sit up. Move. Speak. Nothing made sense.

So when I felt Alexander come for me, I practically held out my hand, welcoming his blue light as it fit around me like a snug envelope; the freaky realm was more appealing than whatever was happening in the physical realm.

Is your body safe, Quillene? Alexander asked.

"I'm very ill," I replied, relieved to be momentarily free of my body and embracing the calm depths of the vast darkness. "So I'm really not sure."

I'll be quick then, said Alexander. *I just wanted to thank you for the warning.*

He sensed my confusion.

I was able to get my people out of the rain. We suffered a few injuries but no deaths. Some memories were fuzzy and difficult to recall. "Oh, right. The green sky."

Yes. Tell me, are you wondering why you're not thinking straight at the moment? I sense something is off about you…

"Yes. Sorry, I'm not sure what's happening to my body, or where it is and why… or… ugh. I'm not even sure if I'm awake or dreaming or—"

You are awake and this is real.

I wasn't sure if that was a good thing. "Okay. Because it feels like pieces of me are breaking off and about to drift away."

Your light is strong and intact. But it is my understanding that sometimes your flesh and blood can play havoc with your synapses in this realm too, and this is usually brought on by illness or extreme stress.

"Stress, most likely. Because someone is trying to kill me."

What? Who?

"A very horrible human."

Tell me where you are. Let me help you. Or, if you don't know, then let me see your memories. Maybe I can make sense of—

"No!" I had to keep Zoleya a secret. "Put me back in my body, right now!"

The response was instant.

I startled upright to see Commander Rowan staring back at me with tears in his eyes. Tears? What the hell were those for? His odd display of emotion caught me off guard—but only for a second.

I swung at him with everything I had, but besides my complete lack of strength, something was preventing my fist from connecting. There was some sort of strange wire at my wrist, taped to my skin. I swung again anyway, and Rowan stepped back but didn't try to defend himself. The silver device he'd been stabbing me with was next to my leg, so I lunged for it and aimed it at his eyes—only to come within inches of hitting my mark before being stopped.

"Calm down, Eva. He's trying to help you," said a male voice.

The fighter in me was raging. My limbs were flailing, desperately trying to escape the hands that were now holding me down; I needed to kill Rowan before he killed me.

"Eva, stop!" Kade demanded.

I took in a breath and a familiar face came into focus. "Kade?"

He was between me and Rowan, and he was the one holding me down with tears in his eyes, too. What was he doing? I yelled at him to move… swung at him…

Then I felt a rush of warmth flood my veins. That heavy liquid moved through them again, turning my limbs to lead and clouding my mind. I had no choice but to give in to what I knew was some sort of drug, so I closed my eyes and let the darkness take over.

I woke to find myself on a strange bed in what seemed like a tent. Warm fingers grazed mine, and I tipped my head to see Kade's thick mop of black hair. He was hunched over, his forehead resting on his arm next to mine, sound asleep. It was quiet. A lone lantern dangled from a post, casting about weak light.

I assessed my body, not moving except to breathe, and the first thing I felt was that my feet were warm and not bare. Odd. And my leg wasn't stinging and throbbing madly with every heartbeat, it was just a dull ache that I might be able to forget. I felt something nestled into a vein in my hand, and a bit of the confusion in my mind cleared; Kade had gotten medicine somehow and was trying to help me. Maybe he killed Rowan.

Easing my head up ever so slightly caused my heart to pound, but I held it up long enough to see that I was wearing boots. The same kind of soft black leather ones that Raiders wore.

Raiders…? Maybe Kade wasn't helping me and we'd been captured. I had to get up!

Kade felt me struggling and wearily patted my arm. "Eva, relax," he said, speaking softly, moving his other hand to my shoulder to gently hold me down.

"We're in the Raiders' camp!"

"I know. And we're okay."

I tried to get up but he pushed down harder. I had no strength. None. "We have to get out of here."

Kade appeared to be in pain, wincing as he moved closer and pinned my arms to my sides. "Listen, you were dying. I needed help.

The infection in your leg was spreading, and I had no choice. I brought you here, and —"

"Are you *crazy*?"

"Keep it down," said someone in the tent behind Kade. Black hair, short, face beaten and arms covered in bruises—a female in Raider clothes was curled up on the ground in the sand, armed, and *not* trying to kill us. "You'll wake the camp and we'll all be dead."

I looked to Kade for verification. He nodded.

"Who is she? And... what's going on... I don't understand," I asked.

Before Kade could answer, the entrance to the tent fluttered and in marched Rowan. My breath caught in my throat; he was decadently dressed in black leather trousers, and a black silk shirt, and had a holster of weapons strapped to his chest. I was sure the temperature in the tent cooled by a few degrees.

I reached for the knife at my thigh—but it had been removed. That meant I would have to kill him with my fists, and the odds of that were not in my favor. I struggled upright regardless, seeing stars for a moment, and for some stupid reason, Kade stood between us and put his hands out to block my attack.

"Stand down, Eva," Kade said.

My mind did a backflip and barely made the landing. "What?"

"Just lay down and relax, okay?"

I looked hard into Kade's mismatched eyes to see if he'd been drugged too, but he merely seemed to be exhausted.

"Are you protecting *him*?" I asked.

Kade nodded, shoulders sagging. "Yes. He saved your life, Eva. Without Rowan's medicine, you'd be dead."

I noticed that there were boots on Kade's feet, too—the same style as mine, the same style as Rowan's. Was he a traitor?

"Wait... are you *one of them*?" I asked.

Kade's forehead wrinkled in a moment of confusion. "What? A Raider? Hell no."

This was ridiculous. Kade was protecting Rowan—a man who

could eliminate every single one of us in a heartbeat—*from me*. Maybe he'd been brainwashed.

I had to tread delicately. Feel out the situation. If Kade thought our enemy wouldn't stab him in the back the second it was turned, he was also delusional.

"Where are the rest of my people?" I asked, focusing on Rowan. "The women you chained up… I want them freed."

His eyes wouldn't meet mine. His gaze was focused on a bag hanging from the ceiling that was dripping liquid into my veins—ah. That's where the drug was coming from. The one keeping me weak.

"You are in no position to make demands," he said, stepping out from behind Kade with a small blue vial in his hands and the silver device he'd stabbed me with.

I tried not to show my fear, but I was shaken to the core, fairly sure that Kade would allow Rowan to stab me again. I needed to keep Rowan talking so I could come up with some plan of escape…

"And you have no right to hold people against their will," I said. "What we went through on your ship was beyond hell. Let my people go, they've suffered enough."

Silence. I had the feeling Rowan was about to give me a nod as his gaze nearly connected with mine, but the female who was curled up on the floor spoke first.

"You can't do that, Rowan. Don't even think about it. If you get caught freeing Aldirans, you'll be tortured until nothing remains of you. Helping the girl—helping *me*—is treason. You can't risk—"

"That's enough, Amari," Rowan said, dragging his fingers through his hair, golden ends sticking up all over his head. I now noticed that he was slightly disheveled, which seemed unusual. His shirt was unbuttoned, revealing a toned chest, and his artfully stitched leather pants were slightly wrinkled. There was a hint of fatigue in his tone, which unsettled me somehow.

The woman he'd called Amari was sitting up, elbows digging into the sand. "Please, Rowan, you have to walk away. Kade can take the girl back to their camp, and I'll disappear into the jungle. You'll never have to see us again and—"

"Stop it, Amari. Do not tell me what I must do."

"Yes, brother," she sighed obediently.

Kade's eyes met mine; Rowan and Amari were siblings? Kade's nod let me know I'd heard correctly.

Rowan lowered himself to his knees before the bed, positioning himself over my legs, which allowed me perfect access to his throat— if I had a weapon. He poked at my leg where the skin was hard and red, and I grit my teeth and fought to not flinch. I didn't want to let on how much it hurt or show I was too weak to stop him.

"You are not going to stab me again," I said when he picked up the silver device and filled it with blue liquid.

"That's exactly what I'm going to do if need be," he said coldly, inspecting the device. "Your fever has reduced and so has the swelling, but if either return I'll have to, or you will die."

A wave of nausea hit me because in my heart I knew he spoke the truth. He'd saved my life, and I now realized that he'd been jabbing my leg with a needle to deliver infection-fighting medicine. He was the reason the fog had lifted and the pain was subsiding. He was the reason I was still breathing.

"You're much better, but you're not out of the woods yet, so to speak," he added. "I will deliver the medicine to your body through the vein in your hand and see what happens. If the streaks on your thigh don't keep receding, I *will* jab you again."

Did his voice have a tone of softness to it? I tried not to cringe as his hand met my forehead to feel for a fever, and then his fingertips pressed at my wrist, taking my pulse. My whole body tingled with the desire for a sharp blade, and I was reminded of my hypocrisy when Max had been adamant about slaughtering every Raider he could.

"You need to rest," Rowan stated.

Rest. Here. In the Raiders' camp. With him?

Hell no.

I sat fully upright and in one fluid motion yanked the tube out of my hand. "I'm getting my people and we're getting out of here," I said, swinging my legs over the side of the bed.

Without any intervention, I stood... then crumpled to my knees, barely able to see through the spots in my vision. My body defied me. Worse yet, my leg began to throb, and blood was gushing from my hand. All I could do was get back on the bed and catch my breath, shoving away the hands that came in to assist. Everything hurt; my leg mostly, but my foot too… what the heck happened to my foot? I felt like I could sleep for a thousand years. I would have cried like a baby if I had the strength.

"I have to re-attach the intravenous, Eva," Rowan said flatly, and when I searched his face for ill-intent I saw none—even though his eyes wouldn't meet mine.

"Just let him, Eva. Please," said Kade. "It's what's keeping you alive."

And taking away the pain.

My common sense warred with my heart.

Trust him, said a voice in my head.

I stayed still while Rowan lifted my hand, swabbed the back of it, and eased in a clean needle. The fierce Commander of the Raiders was gentle and precise, finding the vein he wanted as his calloused fingertips annoyingly brushed over my skin. As much as I didn't want to say how I felt, I couldn't stop my words when a warmth came over me and the pain subsided.

"Thanks," I muttered.

His gaze met mine ever so briefly. "You are welcome."

36 KITKUN

The gods grew bored watching leaves and flowers wither and die, so
they made man.

— *THE BOOK OF IMATLA*

I set traps as I headed toward Eva's camp. Although I was on the
hunt for some poor creature to bring home for the sacrifice, I had
to know if she had heeded my warning to watch for the green sky, or if
her skin was melted from her bones.

It was dreadful that I cared. Sometimes I wished I was cold-hearted
like Hanuk and his warriors because life would be so much easier.
There would be no worrying about the well-being of a girl who was no
more than a stranger, or the fate of a sister who thought little of me. I
would be able to see the jungle and the world around me in black and
white and mow it down without any thought. I could tune out Muma's
continuous blatant disappointment in me and, in turn, not care about
the dark circles around her eyes or the limp in her step.

But that was not to be.

Eva's camp was empty. Her shelter was covered with some sort of
sturdy fabric that appeared water-tight, but judging by the used aloe
plants on the ground, there had been some injuries. Thankfully, no
bones were being picked clean by birds, nor did I hear the moaning of
someone barely clinging to life. It seemed they'd either left in a hurry
or had been taken.

I turned to leave but something caught my eye; on a stump sat one of the devices the sea people used to make fire. Gingerly picking it up, I wondered how it worked. It wasn't stone or wood, nor was it bone. It was smooth like the metal of my knife and just as thin. I contemplated the strange mechanism on the top but dropped it into my pocket when a loud snapping sound rang out behind me. Had one of my traps been triggered?

I hurried back the way I came and found a tortoise caught in my snare.

"It's not your lucky day, my friend," I said.

Its patterned shell was as wide as my hand with my fingers outstretched, chunky arms and legs wiggling as I held it up. "I don't want to hurt you, but I must keep you for a while in case I catch nothing else. Hopefully you won't end up being sacrificed."

But the tortoise's fate seemed sealed when all my other traps turned up empty. The drums started sending out a message to the Nvula that a sacrificial ceremony was starting soon, and I had to run as fast as my legs could carry me back to the village.

I blew through the front door and into the kitchen as the sun started leaving the sky.

Muma had twisted Elke's long hair into tight coils on her head, painted her face and arms with the swirling designs meant to please the gods, and dressed her in her finest clothing. Beautifully woven silk the color of cream fell to her feet, making her look like an angel. Gold bangles adorned her ankles. Her eyes were puffy and red, vacant and hopeless.

"I got an offering," I said, breathless, emptying my sack on the table.

Muma's eyes lit up—until she realized all I had was the tortoise and a few mangoes. Then her expression folded and she quietly returned her attention to my emotionless little sister. Hesutu stifled a sob, appearing defeated—so, obviously there had been no help from Avda's family—and Nita just wore her usual stunned expression, uselessly babbling nonsense to herself.

"You'll be fine, Elke," I said, tossing the mangoes into the sink and pointing to the tortoise. "I've got an offering."

"Hanuk won't accept a tortoise." Hesutu's hands trembled as she picked up the hard-shelled creature and guided him away from the edge of the table. "He will say that it's the same as an iguana or a worm."

"It's a living sacrifice. Just as good as any."

"It's a *tortoise*."

"So?"

"It doesn't mean anything."

"What? It's a life, Hesutu. How can you say it doesn't mean anything? Because it doesn't have feathers? Or isn't warm-blooded? Or doesn't follow boys around with its tongue hanging out of its mouth all day like you do?"

"That's enough, Kitkun," Muma said flatly, standing back and assessing Elke's appearance. "Don't aggravate the situation. Go get cleaned up and change into your best dress. It will be time to go soon."

I bit my lip to keep my mouth closed—but I could only bite so hard. "Why don't we leave here?" I said.

It was as if the air in the room disappeared.

Muma's eyes finally met mine. "Kitkun, really. You say the strangest—"

"I'm serious. Let's leave. Now. We can make a home away from here where there are no sacrifices to worry about and no Hanuk ruling over us. We can take Elke far away and start a new life by the sea—"

Muma's hand lashed out and slapped me hard across the cheek. "How dare you speak of such things, Kitkun! We cannot leave the safety of our village. If the Mordorain doesn't get us, the animals or starvation will. And don't forget that the gods would strike us dead for abandoning our people. You know this! If sacrifice is the price to pay for keeping our people from completely dying out, then so be it."

"So be it?" I said incredulously, cupping my stinging cheek. "Hanuk will have no problem sending Elke's head down the steps if he doesn't like the tortoise, and you're okay with that?"

Elke buried her face in Muma's skirt.

"Elke knows what she must do for her community," Muma said,

eyes lowering into a glare. "She also understands that if your father were here, we would not have this problem."

Bringing up Father was an underhanded, double-fisted, solid punch to the gut that disabled the muscles needed to take a breath. They all blamed me for his absence—for his death—and it took a moment to recover from such a blow.

"I don't want you putting any ideas in your sisters' heads, Kitkun," Muma added, petting Elke's blood-drained cheeks. "This is the life we were born into. There is no hiding or running from it. Now, do not speak further of such blasphemies or Elke and others like her not will be honored in the afterlife."

I blinked back my tears and picked up the tortoise. "This is as good of an offering as any. Elke will not die today."

37  KITKUN

The gods sectioned off their limbs, cut locks of their hair, and scattered pieces of themselves all over the Earth. From them grew all living things. The gods created life, so we must honor their wishes without question—lest they take it away.

— THE BOOK OF IMATLA

Hanuk stood atop the altar flanked by six warriors decorated in the same fashion he was; leather and beaded weapon holders, hair greased and braided, chests shaved, muscled arms gleaming and faces set in an expression as fierce as they could muster—if the situation wasn't so dire and I wasn't worried about losing my own head by being disrespectful, I'd have laughed out loud.

As mist seeped in and the sun sank in the sky, Hanuk began calling the names of each family, the leader of which had to march up the steps to the towering altar where Hanuk was waiting to slit their offering's throat. The first blood drawn was released into a giant silver bowl, then the animal was handed off to a warrior who would finish the gruesome process and toss the head down the left side of the steps. The body would be placed on the altar's blazing pyre, and Hanuk would mutter words that would ooze out of him like pus from a festering wound.

Muma was shaking next to me as the crowd steadily moved us closer to the base of the altar. Animal heads were piling up, and the stink of death was in the air. I had high hopes for the tortoise when

225

Avda's family got away with offering a tenrec—apparently, Hesutu's boyfriend hadn't taken our chickens.

"See? You'll be all right, Elke," I muttered, feeling confident and mighty proud that I had saved my sister with my hunting skills. I would present the tortoise on behalf of my family. Everything would be fine.

But as the tiny pointed nose of the tenrec bounced down the temple steps, the sky sputtered and began to let loose a fine dusting of rain— not a good omen.

Clutching the tortoise, I began the ascent up the slick stone steps toward Hanuk as a collective hush washed over the crowd. We all felt our skin dampen, but at least no shells whistled.

"Are we not pleasing you, Nvula?" Hanuk roared upward.

I paused on the twelfth step—I could smell blood. The tortoise squirmed. With a heavy gulp, I gathered my courage and the skirts of my dress, then forced my feet to take me the rest of the way up.

Hanuk glared at the tortoise in my outstretched hands. "The Goddess of the Sky does not want tenrecs…" His black eyes studied the creature in my hands. "Or vermin from the sea."

A tortoise wasn't vermin, or from the sea! Hanuk was so stupid.

"I can assure you that this tortoise is a worthy life," I said as confidently as I could.

Hanuk scanned the crowd and found my mother staring back at him with pleading eyes, but no emotion registered on his face. I wasn't surprised. When Hanuk stood atop the altar, he was a man of the gods. One who would do their bidding. And no amount of crying, begging, pleading, or bribing would sway him.

When he then stared down at me, I knew that the tortoise would not suffice.

And my heart dropped into my stomach.

"Please…" I muttered, begging anyway, quietly so only he could hear.

Hanuk's eyes rolled back in his head, and he tipped his face to the sky as if it were communicating with him. His warriors grew uneasy, shifting foot to foot as he bellowed; "The gods require more than tenrecs and turtles. Family of Kitkun and Avda, you must send up your youngest."

"No!" I cried, and was grabbed by a warrior and shoved brutally to my knees. I felt the cold blade of a knife at the side of my neck and knew that one wrong move would end my life, and it would be a wasted death, not even considered a sacrifice or made in place of someone I loved.

My mind raced while the youngest of Avda's family—Sera—was sent up the steps. Sobbing and trembling, she tripped on the skirt of her dress and was dragged up to the altar by one of the warriors. Elke tried to run, but Mother and those around her pushed her forward until one of the warriors could get hold of her braids. She too was dragged up the steps as if she was nothing more than a sack of breadfruit.

The altar—the stones of our ancestors—transformed the minds of the men in our village into emotionless machines, even though machines were the very thing that angered the gods and nearly destroyed the earth all those years ago.

Elke hyperventilated as she was shoved to her knees before Hanuk. Avda called out for his little sister until, suddenly, he stopped.

I had closed my eyes and waited for the nightmare to be over when a jolt of pain stabbed my hand. I looked down to see that the tortoise had bit my thumb and was staring at me, big eyes blinking slowly as if to say "Do something."

I pulled in a deep breath and lifted my head despite the metal pushed to my neck. "Take me instead," I said to Hanuk.

The misting rain stopped. The sky pressed down, gray and ready to unleash a torrent of rain as the knife in Hanuk's hand hovered in front of Sera's neck.

"Hanuk, I am worthy," I said, speaking as loud as my quivering voice would allow. "Give our sky goddess a huntress instead of two plain little girls. Give her someone brave enough to offer her own life."

I found Muma's eyes in the crowd, thinking that she would scream or yell or react in some horrified way, but she just blinked in confirmation. A small part of me broke; she probably thought that my life in exchange for the husband she blamed me for losing was fair.

Hanuk took a moment to process my offer. "It is a noble request, Kitkun. But we don't sacrifice hunters."

He had a handful of Sera's hair and used it to tilt her head back; he was about to slit her throat.

"I am much more than a hunter," I said loudly, setting the tortoise down and slowly rising to my feet, mind scrambling. The air was still and thick, the light dim under the hovering clouds. I reached into the pocket of my dress for the firestick. "I can make fire... *with my hands*."

My voice traveled down the altar steps, over the heads of the people and into Black Mountain. There was a collective gasp. A stunned hush. Hanuk eyed me warily, but he didn't tell me to get back onto my knees. I knew that the sudden disappearance of the rain made him think Nvula was intrigued.

The problem was, I didn't know how to use the firestick.

A breeze wafted across the altar, fluttering the hem of my skirt. I bent over and picked up the edge of the finely sewn fabric, exposing my legs for all to see. Then, hoping the device was hidden from all eyes, I rolled my thumb over the top of the firestick like I had seen the sea people do.

But nothing happened.

I tried again. And again.

Then I rolled my thumb the opposite way and a little flame burst upright—

So, I set my skirt on fire.

Which, in hindsight, probably wasn't a good idea.

The delicate fabric caught quickly and flames began to dance around the edges. I released it back to my feet and my ankles were instantly hot, then searing. My skin was burning, and not only did I feel the heat of the fire but the reality that death was about to consume me in the most horrific way. A scream was on the edges of my tongue, but I held it back even though the women in the crowd began to howl. My dress was going up in flames. I was going to burn to death, right here on the altar.

But the Goddess of the Sky had other ideas—bless her almighty heart.

She opened her palms and let go of a solid sheet of rain—the nurturing and healing kind of rain there was no need to cower from. Thick and powerful, it put out my flaming clothes as well as the sacrificial pyre turning headless bodies to ash. I felt hot tears of relief as I fell to my knees, thanking Nvula over and over again for her mercy.

Then, as suddenly as the rain came, it stopped.

And if there was the slightest part of me that didn't believe in the powerful beings that lorded over us, it did now.

The whole of my village stared up in awe as the clouds disappeared, and the sky, now so clear that the stars and the moon were nearly blinding, brought tears of reverence to all who beheld it.

"Kitkun has pleased you, Nvula, Goddess of the Sky!" said Hanuk, his voice a thunderous roar. "You shower us with the gift of clean water to voice your pleasure, so we will spare her, as you have. We will honor her gifts as a huntress and a firestarter!"

The crowd cheered as Sera and Elke ran back into their mothers' arms. Relief and joy washed over everyone in the village, even the warriors. I caught Hanuk's eyes as I stood, legs shaking and covered in burns, feeling faint when his gaze traveled from my face to the firestarter still squeezed tight in the palm of my hand. He knew.

38 EVANGELINE

I heard muffled voices outside of the tent along with lapping waves and a crackling funeral pyre. Since the Raiders burned their dead at high noon when the sun was the fiercest, all Amari and I could do was be still and hope that we would remain hidden.

But it was like being in an oven. Hour by hour I felt my strength come back, but I quickly sweated out any liquid left in me. With Kade waiting in the trees and promising to keep Max from killing anyone, there was no one to talk to, because Amari certainly wasn't having any of my chit-chat.

I thought of Zoleya. How I had woken by her side for so many years and how her friendship had fueled me every day, making my life feel full and purposeful. I missed her telling me about butterflies and different kinds of plants or explaining how to read the constellations. I missed her strange hands that revealed liquid metal when exposed to the sun… and I missed knowing exactly what it was that I was supposed to do each day; protect her.

What if she was actually saying goodbye for good the last time we talked, and she didn't want me as her Guardian anymore?

My heart would never recover.

"Zo, please come to me," I said, staring up at nothing, thinking of her angelic face and long blond hair that probably needed a good wash and braiding. "You might not need me, but I need you. I don't know who I am without you—"

"Stop talking to yourself," said Amari. "I'm trying to sleep.

I found it difficult to think of anything else but Zo, so when my sadness became as suffocating as the heat, I rolled off the bed and onto the cool, damp sand.

"This sucks," I said, not expecting Amari to chime in.

Her clear gray eyes examined every inch of me. "Yup."

I didn't know how many hours passed until the air began to cool and the sun started leaving the sky, but I was shivering when Rowan returned to the tent, wordlessly plucking me up off the sand in one fluid motion and putting me back on the bed. He fed me and Amari salty fish and water from brass cups, then was gone as fast as he came.

Amari struggled upright and opened the tent flap for a bit of air. She managed to get to her feet and take in a raspy breath before crumpling back down onto her knees.

"What happened to you?" I asked.

Wincing with every movement, she started digging a hole in the sand, then squatted over it to pee, covering it up like a cat would afterward.

"You really want to know?" she asked, breathing heavily as she tried to remain sitting up.

I felt horrible for her and then reminded myself that she was a *Raider.* "Um, yes."

"One of your people did this to me," she said bitterly.

I inched up onto my elbows, then sat up fully too, fighting the spots in my vision, needing to see her face more clearly. It took a second for the world to stop spinning. "Are you saying that one of the Aldirans that *you* captured, beat you up?" I may have been secretly thrilled at the thought.

"Not quite." She worked herself into a cross-legged position. "He assaulted one of the women we'd put him in the hold with, and I had the pleasure of whipping him as punishment. Somehow, he got free and came back for revenge."

"Assaulted? As in—"

"Beat her bloody for no reason. She was no more than ninety pounds at the most. He broke her ribs and an arm...and she was tied up, too. Couldn't even defend herself. Not that it would have mattered."

I could barely contain the horror I felt on every level as a chill rolled up my spine. Was Amari talking about Prominus? I'd seen that look in his eyes, the bloodthirsty stare of a man eager to cause pain for no reason…

I suddenly recognized Amari; she was the woman who'd whipped him.

Her voice was barely a whisper. "He called himself Prominus."

I felt every hair rise on the back of my neck.

"I was caught off guard the night he snuck back," she continued. "I didn't even have a chance at a fair fight because he attacked while I was sleeping. While he hit me, he kept saying that by the time he was done I would never speak again, but I'd live to choke on every breath I took. He even raked his nails down my—" she stopped short, voice lowering as she touched long wounds on her neck. "Anyway, Rowan stopped him from breaking every bone in my face."

Horrified, I swung my legs over the bed and flopped down before her. I could see now that she not only had a wounded body but wounded pride as well. "I'm so sorry that happened to you, Amari." Trying to offer comfort, I put my hand on hers without thought.

She recoiled and glared. "Are all of you Aldirans so barbaric?"

It was an honest question, I suppose. If one came upon one of the port cities on the Aldiran coast and took a stroll, you'd think that every human was a breath away from being feral. The filth, the language, the blatant disregard for laws and lack of morals certainly made us seem barbaric. But really, we were all struggling to survive.

"No. I promise. There are some bad, of course, but there are some good." I thought of Kade and Beast, the family of Guardians I'd grown up with, and Zoleya… "Some are also a very intriguing mixture of both."

Amari wasn't listening, her gaze had drifted off. "Prominus killed two of my people before he took his revenge on me. Their deaths were my fault."

"Why do you say that?"

"Because when I caught him beating that young woman, I bargained with Captain Vallerik for him to be punished by whip instead of executed. Had I not gotten involved, that bastard would probably be dead."

I didn't say a word, just listened as she gathered her breath before continuing.

"So, when he was caught again after attacking me, I was given orders to execute him myself and prove my worth."

"But you couldn't do it?"

Amari bit her lip. "No."

"Because you were too weak?" I suspected she couldn't even have held her head up after what Prominus did to her.

Her eyes met mine and she growled. "Certainly not."

I put my hands up in defense. "Hey. It was an honest assumption."

"I am not weak. I've been loyal to my people, doing what I've been told and following orders my whole life. I've trained and starved just as much as anyone else. But I cannot kill in cold blood. I cannot behead a man who is restrained. So, according to my captain, I am worthless. She exiled me, knowing that if left on my own I would die."

"So, Rowan hid you and brought you medicine."

"Yes. He is a good brother."

I was stunned that Amari was offering up so much information. Eager to keep her talking, I asked, "How is he getting away with this? How have you—we—not been found?"

Amari rubbed at her swollen eye. "This is the corpse tent. My people believe the souls of the dead hover above their bodies until they are burned and that someone must guard those souls and keep them safe until they transcend. Rowan offered to guard the dead on this island, so my people fear and respect him even more than they usually do. No one dares enter without his permission."

"Telling secrets?" said a deep voice.

Rowan stepped into the tent. His presence filled every inch of space and all at once I had the feeling I was free-falling from clouds into a raging storm. I hated that I noticed the dark shadows under his eyes and the day's worth of stubble on his chin, and that he smelled of smoke and salt. Mostly, I hated that I couldn't look away as I wondered how someone so beautiful could be so… so…

So *what*? Monstrous? Evil? A good brother? A healer?

Amari grew nervous. "No harm in that, is there, brother?"

"Depends on whom those secrets are shared with." Rowan's eyes met mine.

A rush of cold flittered up my spine. "You can trust me."

"I know that. If I didn't believe you were a person of your word, Evangeline, you would have died long before my sister had a chance to spill her guts."

Amari hung her head with no reply. I, however, stared at Rowan, trying to pick which one of a thousand questions, insults and compliments to hurl at him first. After much debate, I thought I would start with 'why are you helping me?' and then morph into 'so… what's your favorite color?'

But before I could say a word, voices rang out on the beach not far from the tent, and Rowan was gone in a flash.

I felt as if the wind was knocked out of me as I crashed back to earth.

"There are no dead left to transcend," I heard someone say. A male. His voice was clipped and mixed with the caw of a gull. "So, I'm wondering why you're still here, Commander Rowan."

Amari crawled across the sand toward me and crouched into a fighting position. She motioned at me to be quiet while the conversation outside the tent continued.

"Better yet, why are you questioning your commander, Terens?" Rowan replied, voice authoritative and menacing.

Terens seemed to trip over his words. "Uh, Capn's orders. She wants to know why you're spending the evening, uh… guarding souls when they've all transcended."

"Maybe they haven't *all* transcended," said Rowan.

"Oh?"

"The Aldirans attacked and killed two of us this morning. How is it you do not know this, Terens?" Rowan countered, and I could hear the rustle of more Raiders marching down the beach. Four? Five? Too many to fight were heading our way. "They are to transcend tomorrow at noon, and their souls must be guarded. You can take over this position from me, though, if you would like. I wouldn't mind spending a night by the fire on a soft bed."

A dare. I imagined that nobody wanted to stand next to dead bodies in the dark for twelve hours.

Terens cleared his throat. "Forgive me, Commander, but Cap'n is still in bad spirits over the loss of the Grakke brothers. She's, um, not taking their decapitation too well. I'll need proof of these bodies you speak of."

The Grakke brothers. The men Max had killed. The ones who assaulted me while I was in chains… As I pictured their heads in the fire, my stomach lurched around the salted fish.

Amari crawled over to me. "*Play dead,*" she whispered.

As an argument ensued outside, Armari ripped the intravenous bag from the ceiling and the needle from my hand, then moved next to me onto the bed and furiously rubbed her face and mine with the blood spurting from my open vein. The bag and my bleeding hand were then shoved beneath her thigh.

"If you wish to anger the spirits, then go on in," Rowan said to Terens, and I imagined him motioning toward the tent.

Amari and I lay still, not breathing. A gust of air brushed over our skin as the tent flap opened.

"Two women?" Terens muttered.

"Yes. Feel free to go on inside," said Rowan, and I could hear him drawing his blade from its sheath. "Just know you are disrespecting the dead, and it is my job to act on their behalf."

Terens was suddenly desperate to be anywhere else. "So much blood… how did they die?"

Rowan's tone was cold enough to freeze hell. "You will join them if you ask any more questions, Terens. I am your commander, not your informer. Now go back to Captain Vallerik and report to her that I am busy doing my job and she will lose the heads of her other favorites if she bothers me again."

Terens left amongst the audible swooshing of many arms and legs marching off down the beach.

Amari and I lay still for a long while before Rowan marched back into the tent. His eyes widened briefly at the sight of us.

"That was close." Amari crawled over me to make her way back to the sand. "Do you think Terens recognized me?"

Rowan didn't reply. Instead, he strode to the bed and pressed his thumb over the gushing vein in my hand. "Bury that," he said, tossing Amari the IV bag and needle.

"We need to go, Rowan," she replied, struggling to do as she was told.

Rowan softly cursed under his breath. "Eva isn't strong enough to leave yet."

"It's either that or we all die."

"You're not strong enough either, Amari."

"Do I have a say in it?" I asked but was ignored.

Rowan concentrated on tending to my hand, and I held my breath against the intensity about him. I didn't even notice Kade had entered the tent until he was standing directly behind Rowan with an equally unsettling look on his face; a mixture of fury, jealousy, and worry.

"That was too close for comfort, Rowan," Kade said, his eyebrows drawn together, hand raking through his inky curls damp with sweat as he kept glancing at the tent entrance. "You can't keep Eva in here another minute. There were ten Raiders on the beach just now, and I doubt you could fight off all of them. What did you tell the one that came in here?"

"That he was disrespecting the dead." Rowan didn't even glance over his shoulder to see if Kade had a weapon and might stab him in the back.

"What if he wanted to make sure they really were dead?" Kade was pacing, displaying a huge crack in his composure.

"Shut up, Kade Thorn," Rowan ordered. "I'm fully aware of what could have happened."

My leg began to throb—whatever was flowing out of the bag and into my veins had been keeping the pain away and my head clear. I was keenly aware of its absence.

"Without the IV, I'll have to give her three more injections,"

Rowan said, his eyes firmly focused on where his thumb remained pressed over my hand. "Three hours apart."

"You mean *stab* her in the leg?" Kade asked.

I nearly leaped off the bed.

With a shake of his head, Rowan sighed. "Don't be so dramatic. It's a needle. Direct into a vein will do."

"Okay. Well, I can do that," said Kade. "Show me how."

Conflict shadowed Rowan's eyes, but he quickly dismissed it. "If you don't, she will die. The infection will come back twice as virulent."

Kneeling by the bed, Kade's dark eyes met mine, and what he felt for me was practically written on his face. He cared about me. I meant something more to him than just a tribe mate or even a friend. What he conveyed without words made my heart skip a beat and my stomach fill with butterflies.

"The medicine is special," Rowan was saying. "You must get rid of the evidence after. You must not share it or show it to anyone, or speak of where it came from, Kade Thorn."

"Which is where, exactly?" Kade asked, eyeing the weird liquid.

I was wondering the same thing, but Rowan just grumbled a non-response.

"Whatever." Kade put his hands up in defeat.

"Look, I'm fine," I said, moving to sit up, only to be stopped mid-motion by four large hands.

Neither man acknowledged my complaints as I lay there like a pincushion while Rowan showed Kade how to find my veins, poking and prodding, slapping my skin gently to expose the blue lines. Kade's hand was guided and a clean needle sent heavy liquid into my blood and made the pain in my leg and foot subside. Almost instantly, my body became leaden, complaints forgotten.

"That was just for pain. She needs the medicine administered the same way three hours from now. And she must be kept warm." Rowan was pressing down on the small needle wound to stop the bleeding. "Go now and get one of your men to help carry her. You'll be too slow on your own and…"

Someone was approaching the tent. Moving the flap aside. Stepping in—

A man with a neck as thick as his thigh, holding what must have been supper for Rowan, drew his weapon at the sight of us. "Commander?" was all he managed to say before Rowan lashed out and sent a blade through the man's neck.

The man dropped to the ground, clutching his throat and bleeding out, eyes widening in the throws of death. And just like that, I was reminded of what Rowan was capable of. He *was* a monster. A cold-blooded killer. And I had no reason to think otherwise.

"Couldn't you have just *talked* to the guy?" Kade said after a stunned second, dragging the body away from the entrance.

There was a trail of blood across the sand, and following closely was the stink of the dead man's bowels letting loose. The tent suddenly felt too hot to breathe in. The pain medicine was making things confusing.

"No." Rowan glanced at the sister he was trying to protect, who in turn nodded her approval.

Then his gaze met mine. Those storm-gray eyes of his had almost made me forgo common sense. But now? I didn't bother concealing the disgust I felt for him on every level. As beautiful as he was, as kind as he pretended to be, he'd just proven that he was as dangerous as the dark and quiet sea, and like it, all the things that could kill you lurked mere inches beneath the surface.

39 EVANGELINE

Kade had given up trying to keep the shirt closed across his chest. It flopped open as he paced from the tent entrance to my bed, and either those strange designs on his skin seemed to shift around or the drugs were really messing with my head.

"I have to get Eva out of here," he said, stopping and facing Rowan. "I doubt you're willing to murder your whole camp, and it looks like they're all heading this way."

Rowan made a fist around the vial of medicine he was about to hand over to Kade. "You'll never be able to run fast enough carrying her. You'll be caught."

"Got any suggestions then?"

"Yes. She stays here," Rowan replied. "I'll tell my people that I caught her trying to sneak into our camp. I'll get her out when the coast is clear and—"

"What about Amari?" I asked.

Amari looked up from the knife she'd been toying with, shocked at my concern. "I can hold my own," she said bitterly.

Rowan clenched his teeth, turned to his sister, and knelt before her. Gathering her bruised and scraped hands in his, he steadied his gaze on her swollen face. "Are you well enough to run, sister?"

Her black hair stuck to her bloodless cheeks "Yes," she replied, eyes glassy. "Of course."

Run? She could barely breathe!

The voices of those approaching on the beach grew louder. Rowan put his forehead to Amari's as if to say goodbye, then he stood and faced Kade.

"Look after Amari. Take her to your camp. If you can ensure her safety, I'll make sure Evangeline remains alive. You have my word."

Kade's face darkened. "No."

"You must do this," Rowan countered. "Or you'll kill all of us. You must trust me, Kade Thorn."

Every part of Kade's body was tense, the corded muscles of his arms straining against his shirt trying to stay together at the seams. For a moment, I thought the two men staring each other down might start throwing punches, but to my surprise, Kade nodded and took a step back from my bed.

"If any harm comes to her, you will pay, Rowan," he said, voice thunderous. "I'll come back and kill every single person you love, as well as those you don't. Then I'll tear you to pieces."

"Seems we have a mutual understanding, then," Rowan replied. "Now take Amari and go. Lead the guards away from here and don't get caught."

Before I could protest, Kade grabbed Amari by the arm and yanked her upright, then bolted out of the tent with her and into the waning light.

I could barely breathe. "Are you mad? There's no way they can escape."

Ignoring me, Rowan stepped out of the tent and yelled. "Capture them! The intruders have headed south!"

Judging by the sudden shouting, Amari and Kade were running and now being chased. The feet of many Raiders rushed past the tent as Rowan continued shouting orders.

Spitting mad, I sat up and swung my legs over the bed, needing to do *something.* I got to my feet, legs shaking violently—before completely giving out. On my hands and knees, I tried to calm my pounding heart.

"They had a head start," Rowan said, spinning around to face me. "Thorn will be fine. And, even wounded, Amari is fast. Do not worry, Evangeline."

He was appalling. I tried to get up but the pain—not only in my leg but in my foot as well—was staggering. "You threw your sister to the wolves. Fast or not, she's injured."

"Do not ever underestimate Amari," Rowan said, dragging the body of the man he'd killed across the sand and maneuvering him onto the bed. "Or me."

"Oh, I've never underestimated you. I just don't trust you."

He bowed his head a moment, sighed as if my words hurt him, and then fixed me with that cold stare. "Listen, we don't have much time. My captain will be sending her first mate to check on me and inspect the dead."

"Terens," I said, remembering the man's name who had peeked into the tent before to see if Rowan was telling the truth about having two corpses to guard.

"Yes. Terens. So, I need you to get back on the bed and play dead, just like you did with Amari."

If I could get to my feet, then surely I could make it out of the tent and create some sort of diversion... I needed to give the Raiders a reason to abandon Kade and Amari and come after me instead.

As if Rowan could see the plan forming in my mind, he blocked the exit. "Don't even think about it," he said. "Now, go lay down."

I shook my head and the tent spun in the worst way, but I got to my feet. "No."

"Evangeline, please do as I ask, and then when it's safe I'll move you somewhere else. Okay?"

The way my name sounded on his tongue made my head spin even more. Why was I having such an intense internal battle over my feelings for him? Was it because he was trying to save my life and I felt like I owed him? Was his odd desire to play the hero in my story winning me over? Damn, not only was my body weak but my mind as well.

"You killed one of your men..."

"I did what I had to. For you and her. Now please—"

"No!"

I bolted for the exit, but an arm like an unbreakable vise wrapped around my waist. "I don't want to hurt you," he said. "Please don't struggle."

Rowan's body was so warm against mine that I blamed the drug in my blood for nearly making me forget why I was struggling in the first place and was now practically melting against him.

"Let me go or I'll... I'll scream," I warned, although rather feebly. "I'll scream loud enough to alert your whole camp and even wake the dead."

Suddenly, I was limp in Rowan's arms. My vision began to cloud over, and my legs seemed to disappear from beneath me. Rowan's face hovered above mine as he deposited me back onto the bed next to the dead man, and the next thing I knew I was heading into that damn freaky realm with Alexander.

"Your timing sucks!" I yelled, pushing back against the male Sage with every bit of mental power I had, but the vast expanse of darkness in the Between was soon broken only by his indigo light. "I have friends that need my help. Put me back into my body."

If Alexander heard, he paid no mind.

"You can't just abduct my psyche without asking. It's really... well, it's rude!"

Did he laugh? I felt his mood shift from a panicked urgency to a maddening calm.

I'd hate to be considered rude. I do apologize.

"Oh. So, you are listening. Take me back then. I don't have time to chit-chat with you right now." That feeling of coming apart and unraveling started to creep in. I needed to be back in that tent, with Rowan, fighting for my friends...

Again, I apologize, Alexander said. *But I need you here for a moment.*

I had to remain calm. Be careful. "Why?"

I need to try something. But don't worry, you can trust me. I would never put you in harm's way.

Weirdly enough, that was true. There was some sort of means of understanding in the freaky realm that surpassed anything one might discover about someone in the physical one. It was as if I could shine a flashlight into Alexander's soul and see the bits and pieces that shone, honesty being one of the brightest. I wondered why Zoleya couldn't sense this about him. I wondered why she fled so quickly…

"My friends need me," I said. "They're in danger."

Please. This is important.

If he sent me back right now, could I really scream loud enough to get the attention of all the Raiders and lead them away from Kade and Amari? In my current physical state, admittedly, probably not. So, maybe it was best to remember my place, which was, forever and always, as Zoleya's guardian. I couldn't risk putting her in any danger by angering this powerful Sage and having him steal into my memories. Complying with whatever it was he desired was the wisest thing I could do.

"Okay. Do your thing, but make it fast, please, and stay out of my memories."

As you wish.

Alexander's light deepened and he drew me closer to him until the color of my golden light mixed with his at the edges. I could never explain the shade, but if I had lungs to breathe with I would have gasped in awe at the startling hue. I'd never experienced anything like this with Zoleya. We were always just two separate lights in the Between. But with Alexander? We were connected in a way that was baffling on a deeply spiritual level. Somehow, I knew that he was good to the core. Misunderstood, deeply loyal, a perfectionist with heavy self-loathing and a secret he would die to protect… and I could sense his awe as he too began to understand me. The connection was all-consuming. Like a drug I would never get enough of. I had the sudden desire to know how it would feel if his light completely engulfed mine. Would we become one? What shade would that be?

I suspected we could do this but never thought it was truly possible. You are… astounding.

"This is nuts, it's like I *know* you. Like, really know you."

We could only just be for a long moment, both marveling at the discovery.

Then I had the thought, "I wonder if this realm is where we go when we die."

He shimmered. Pulled me in a little closer. *I don't know.*

I realized then that if I had to spend an eternity with Alexander, I didn't think I would mind.

He sighed against my thoughts, *I just want to try one more thing if you'll let me.*

Let him? That was funny. At the moment, I'd sell him my soul if he offered half a penny.

"And what might that be?"

I want to see if our conscious minds can remain connected in the physical realm. It was easy for me to allow you to see through my eyes before, as if playing for you a memory in real-time. But our connection is unique, so I wonder if I can take us both into your body and—

"See through my eyes."

Yes.

Since Zoleya was able to commandeer small creatures, this somehow didn't seem like an undoable request—which meant I might be losing my grip on reality. "That's the most bizarre thing anyone has ever asked of me."

The disconnect from your physical body might be quite strange, especially since I would be in control—if it works. You'd be merely an observer, and, in essence, seeing and feeling... through me. I think.

"So, you've never done this before."

No. But I have the sense that it can be done.

If he saw Commander Rowan as well as the tent I was in, would he know I was in the Raiders' camp? Could I take a chance that maybe he was someone who could help me? "If I let you do this, will you try and help my friends?"

Yes.

I had nothing to lose. "Okay. Then, go for it."

Suddenly, I was tagging along with Alexander as he moved through the realm and into my body.

The sensation of being back in the familiar domain that had housed me since birth but having no control over it was rather horrifying. I wondered if this was how it felt to be paralyzed, being able to see what is going on around you but unable to move, as if there is no body at all, just vision. As I remained psychically snuggled up with Alexander, I soon witnessed the stormy eyes of Commander Rowan as they moved in front of my physical face and widened in horror.

A tremendous surge of awe rippled toward me from Alexander. *This is incredible. I see the world through you.*

It was like looking through a bubble. "And, you know that man staring back, don't you?"

A pause. *Yes.*

I could only watch as Rowan's hands moved to my cheeks, his face so close to mine that I could see a tiny scar above his eyebrow.

"He is not a good man," I said, although it suddenly didn't ring true.

You're right. He isn't.

"And...you're a Raider."

Yes. I am. But maybe we can discuss that later?

I felt a ridiculous rush of worry for Rowan. "Are you going to turn him in?"

No. That would jeopardize your safety.

Rowan began covering my face and hair with something red. Blood? Yes. The blood of the dead man. His face disappeared from view, and I could see he had something else in his hands when it came back; sand. He alternated covering me with blood and sand as he kept glancing over his shoulder at the tent entrance.

"Now that you know you can steal your way into my body, I think that's enough insanity for one day. I need to get out of the tent. Help my friends escape."

Rowan is disguising you, Alexander pointed out. *He is keeping you safe. It's better that you are with me right now and not in control so you truly appear deceased.*

Faces other than Rowan's came into view. I could see them poking, prodding, checking to see if I was indeed dead—which I'd started to wonder myself.

"I don't know if my mind can handle this."

We could see that Rowan was alone again, wiping sweat off his brow and rubbing his temples. I could tell by the look on his face as he glanced worriedly at my lifeless face, that he truly thought he was doing the right thing. That he was genuinely trying to help me.

I want to try one more thing, Eva. Then I will take you back.

My guard went up instantly. "Whoa, wait a sec... I told you my name was Quillene. Have you gone into my—"

You would know if I dug into your memories because you are seeing and feeling the same things that I am. I simply observed Rowan calling you Evangeline, nothing more.

He wasn't lying. "Okay. Do what you need to do and be quick about it."

Thank you. Let's try this...

As I watched, I noticed that my hand had moved. It was up and away from my body, and the backs of my fingers had brushed Rowan's arm. His eyes widened in alarm.

"Alexander, are you doing that? Moving my body?"

Yes... Eva. And I feel your pain. I understand how the medicine is affecting you.

Rowan, probably thinking I was awake, reached for my hand, the look on his face so open and soft, so curious and in awe...

"Good looks can be deceiving, can't they?" I said.

A laugh washed through Alexander. *If you think so.* He was turning my hand toward my face, dragging my fingertips across my lower lip. *Bliss... I can feel—*

"Alexander, stop."

He lowered my hand. *All right.*

"I don't want to do this anymore. Leave me now, please. I can't take another moment of this madness."

As you wish, Evangeline. Thank you for allowing me this incredible experience.

In a flash, Alexander was gone, and I was back in my body—by myself.

I pulled in a few rapid lungfuls of air just to feel my chest rise, and then the ache of my wounds came crashing in, reminding me that I was very much alive. I turned my head to see the dead guy next to me—the man who Rowan had killed without any hesitation—and my senses jerked in response.

"It's okay. You're okay, Eva," said Rowan.

"Am I dreaming or awake?"

"Awake."

"Are you good or bad? I need to know. Answer honestly."

"That depends on who is asking."

"Me. An Aldiran. Someone who can't decide if she wants to kill you or thank you for risking your life for hers."

"Then, I'm good."

I had to believe him while the lingering feeling and longing for the Sage whom I'd never even met stood like an elephant on my chest. This was real. Here, with this scary commander of a tribe of Raiders. Not some weird dreamlike plane of infinite darkness with a being who could take over my body at will…

I shivered, realizing my arms were covered in blood and my hair caked with it, and there was sand everywhere. It felt like my skin was crawling.

"I had to cover your hair and disguise you." Rowan ran a hand across his face in exhaustion. "There aren't many blondes among our people, and I needed the guards to believe you were one of us. You did a very scary-good job of playing dead."

I couldn't look away, feeling grounded somehow by the angles of his face and the shadows under his eyes that made my chest hurt in a way I couldn't explain. What was wrong with me? Was I so lonely without Zoleya that I was falling for any man who paid attention to me? Was I delusional and this strange feeling I had for Rowan and now the male Sage just a bandage for the gaping wound of loneliness she had left upon me? And then there was—

"Kade." His name burst from my mouth.

"My men have not found him or Amari, so they will be long gone by now. They have escaped, Evangeline. You can rest."

Rest. Close my eyes—and be in darkness again. "I can't," I said, sounding whiny.

"Why is that?"

"So many reasons, but mostly… there's a dead guy's blood in my hair," I said, fighting back tears. "All I can smell is… blood… death… I'm breaking into pieces. Itty bitty bits of fluff, or… dust… or…"

I was losing my mind.

"Let's go in the water." Rowan stood and brushed the sand from his trousers. "Now that two bodies have been verified in this tent, no one will come near here. The sun is down, and my people don't like the mixture of the dark and the dead. They will break off into two groups. One will fumble through the jungle, and the other will center around the middle of camp and the captain's quarters. We will be unseen."

All that mattered at the moment was getting clean. I couldn't have cared less if rabid dogs were nipping at my heels. I needed the blood *off*.

"Yes," I muttered.

Rowan watched me struggle to stand, and then without asking scooped me up into his arms. I didn't want his hands under me, but I didn't want them to let go of me either, and the contradiction of feelings was maddening alongside the lingering connection with the Sage that clung to my every synapse.

"I got you," he said, heading out of the tent.

40 EVANGELINE

We could hear the faint singing of Raiders and warnings from the jungle's creatures, but Rowan was a man on a mission, ignoring it all as he carried me toward the sea under the cover of night. The water rippled sleepily, silver waves parting as he headed in. I noted that he could easily drown me here. Force me beneath the surface for mere seconds and end all his problems. But I sensed that, for the moment, I was safer than I'd ever been. And it was so oddly confusing.

I tensed.

"Too cold?" Rowan asked.

I was half floating, half supported in his arms, but I needed to stand on my own; all this emotional fuckery was not helping me utilize my common sense. "No," I said. "You can let go."

He released his grip, slowly until, quite delightfully, I went under. Dirt, grime, sand, and the dead man's blood lifted away from me. I thought briefly of sharks but remembered I was with someone just as lethal.

"There's only one body in the tent," I said, realizing there was no way I was going to swim to my freedom. Or run. I could barely keep my head up out of the water to talk. "What if your people come back?"

"They won't tonight." Starlight flashed through his eyes. "And tomorrow I'll add another body."

I jerked. "You mean kill someone else—"

"I'm not a monster, Eva. That man I killed in the tent stood by and watched while Prominus attacked Amari. He laughed as my sister was being helplessly beaten. I should have killed him sooner."

Not a monster...

I rubbed my arms in the water and watched Rowan inspect the horizon and the beach. His gaze softened when his eyes found mine again.

"Where will you get a body?" I asked.

He cleared his throat. "There are the graves of your people, the ones not given a proper burial. I will take a body from the ground so at least one of them will be able to transcend."

I was speechless.

"Do you think the worst of me?" he asked, crossing his arms over his broad chest as the water gently licked at the waist of his shirt.

All but my head was under water. "I've seen what you can do."

"Oh, have you? Other than the man in the tent... have you seen me take the life of another?"

"I... I—" Huh. No, I hadn't witnessed him doing anything untoward to anyone. Even on the trek across Aldira to the sea, he was merely a name uttered during a threat—nothing more.

"I've heard the rumors," I said defensively.

"Ah. So your opinion of me is based on what you've *heard*, not what you've seen."

Oh, stars above, it was. I was *that person*. "I just saw you slit a man's throat without any hesitation." I rubbed water out of my eyes. "I mean, is it not true? Are you not a killer? Should I not be terrified of you, or trying desperately to escape?"

He smiled ever so slightly. It was glorious. "Yes," he said softly. "You should run. Far and fast."

His eyes met mine, moonlight shimmering in his irises, and I couldn't hold back a shiver. What was it about him that turned me into an indecisive dumbass? His good looks? Had to be. I was just lonely for Zoleya. That was all.

"You are cold, Eva."

Not bothering to protest, I was back in his arms as he waded out of the water toward the beach, our clothes dripping. I felt so very heavy, but he moved as if I weighed nothing.

"I can't go back in that tent," I said.

He paused—probably not wanting to go back in the tent either. "You have to rest, though. And I need to dress your wounds again with dry bandages."

"Please." I looked toward the funeral pyre that had burned the dead, heat from its dying flames stretching out like fingers to beckon us closer. "Can we at least sit there a moment and get dry?"

I was asking a lot of this man who was already risking his life for mine, and I could see the conflict in his eyes. I thought he might say no, but he swallowed hard and then headed for the last pyre where no one would see us behind the mound of smoldering wood.

Rowan dropped to his knees, almost as if forgetting I was still in his arms, and his gaze centered on the burning embers.

"Those who left us through this fire were all good people," he said.

"They've transcended?" I hoped I was using the word properly.

"Yes."

In Aldira, when you die you are dropped into a pit six feet deep, and after a few words—if you are lucky—you are forgotten about.

Rowan raised an eyebrow and searched my face, which I realized was much too close to his while I remained cradled against him. I wiggled free and backed up enough to see him clearly; this man was not who he had been pretending to be. I knew that now. I was looking at the real Rowan, the man who made my heart skip a beat and my breath catch. The man I'd fallen for rather dangerously and needlessly. But being caught in his gaze was like staring at the sun.

"I'm sorry for your loss," I said softly.

His fingers rose, then tentatively touched my cheek. "You've suffered loss as well, Evangeline."

I sighed. Regretted the sigh. Wished I knew what to say.

"And for that, I'm sorry, too," he added. "Truly. I never wished any harm to come to you, or anyone you care about."

The weight of his apology sent me reeling. My hands anchored in the sand behind me barely supported my body as every cell absorbed those words, words that somehow, in some way, were everything.

The fire crackled and I tried not to think of what was in the smoke as my hair dried. Rowan disappeared for a moment and when he returned, I stole glances at him through heavy eyelids as he wrapped the wound on my leg, then my foot, and slipped blue liquid into my veins. I thought of Zoleya. I craved the feeling of having Alexander in my mind. I wondered if Kade had truly escaped.

"Why me?" I asked, abandoning those thoughts to give Rowan my full attention.

He knew what I meant. Saving me on the ship, giving me his knife on the beach, risking everything to give me medicine, hiding me from his people…

When his eyes met mine, instead of saying anything, he just shook his head and sadly smiled.

It was all the answer I needed.

When I awoke, the moon was gone, the wind had picked up, and I was shivering next to a near-dead fire. Morning was approaching, and that otherworldly hue it cast just before the first rays of sun made everything a murky gray.

Pulling myself upright, I turned to see Rowan sound asleep next to me. His long lashes fluttered in a dream, his expression peaceful, his body vulnerable as he lay curled up on his side, arm underneath his head. I wondered when he had last slept. I wasn't sure how long I'd been in the tent, but he'd stood outside keeping watch every minute, claiming to be guarding the souls of the dead when in fact he was guarding me and Amari. I wanted to know more about him. What he liked to eat, his favorite color, who his parents were, and why he chose the life of a Raider. I wanted to wake him and see the gray of his eyes, hear what his voice sounded like after being asleep… and then I thought of Alexander.

Quite ridiculously, some strange wave of guilt washed over me that made no sense whatsoever. Did I also have feelings for the Sage who took me into the freaky realm without asking?

I was a mess.

Rowan said something in his sleep, and I was drawn to him again, barely able to look away. Could I fall for two people?

A fluttering sound caught my attention, drawing my gaze away from the man sleeping at my side. Dragonfly wings brushed past my eardrums and an exquisite purple and black creature moved before me, swaying side to side as if trying to tell me something.

"Zoleya?" I whispered, nearly bursting into tears. It was her. I knew it in my heart.

The dragonfly flew up and down as if in an exaggerated head nod, then flew toward Rowan, eyeing him head to toe.

"It's safe for us to meet in the Between," I said softly, desperate to talk to her but knowing it wasn't the right time. Rowan's hand twitched and I worried that at any second he might wake up. "But later. Okay? Come to me tonight when the moon is high. I'll make sure my body is safe. I have so much to tell you."

The dragonfly's movements became erratic; Zo was worried about something.

"I know what you're thinking," I said, "but he's not what you think."

The Dragonfly moved side to side, wings humming frantically. It took to the air and flew over the embers of the pyre, and that's when I saw it; Raiders. Eight of them. Marching toward us.

I froze, knowing by their unhurried gate that I was seeing them before they saw me. I contemplated running into the dark but heard voices behind me too; we were surrounded. Any moment now Rowan and I would be visible on the beach—and he'd be tortured for committing treason by helping an Aldiran.

Without a second thought I removed the kopis from the holder at his thigh, thus jolting him awake. He sat up, eyeing me in confusion, and before he could get a word out, I dragged the sharp blade across my palm.

"Eva, what are you—"

Then I slapped him. Hard. My blood splattered his face. "Bastard!" I screamed, jumping to my feet.

Rowan put his palms out in surrender, eyes blinking up at me in a way that made my heart nearly break in half.

"I'm sorry, I don't know—" his question caught in his throat when he noticed that his people were aware of our presence and approaching rapidly, then his eyes widened with the sudden understanding that I was risking my life to save his. The very same thing he'd done for me.

"No, Evangeline... please don't do this," he begged under his breath.

"Come any closer and I'll kill your commander!" I yelled at the Raiders who were now circling and closing in. "I'll take his head!"

All weapons were drawn, but not one Raider seemed deterred by my warning.

"I mean it!" I yelled.

I kept Rowan's weapon trained on him, placing it mere inches from his neck. He was on his knees, and I stood over him, my legs shaking but not buckling. I could decapitate him in one breath if I wanted to. It would be so easy; kill him in a second and be done with it, and not long ago I desired that very thing...

I tried to recall that feeling to hide how opposed to killing him I truly was.

"Evangeline, they'll slaughter you for this," he said quietly, not falling for my act.

I crouched slightly, moving the blade an inch closer. "Bastard," I hissed loudly but did not look him in the eye.

Shadows fell over us.

"Commander, what is going on?" asked the man whom I recognized as Terens.

Terens had black stones for eyes, was stocky and thick in the neck, his head was half shaved and he was covered in black tattoos. He had a sick gleam in his eyes that he could not hide; he was clearly excited by the prospect of Rowan losing his head.

"Stand down," Rowan ordered, putting his hands up in defense. "She's just a harmless girl."

I let out the most insane laugh I could muster. Dug deep for it.

"Harmless? Is that why you had me chained up in that cage like the other men? You took everything from me, and you will pay!"

"Is this Evangeline Quillene?" Terens asked.

The men beside him tensed, taking me seriously now—as they should; I did kill quite a few of their comrades while fighting for me and Zoleya in the meadow.

"Back off!" I warned, knowing there was no fighting my way out of this one. My body was weak, but at least my voice was strong. "I'll take your commander's head, just like I took the heads of the others. Brothers, were they?" I claimed Max's horrific actions as my own. "Filthy fucking Raiders. All of you! I'll take *all* your heads!"

I lifted my arm in the motion of beheading Rowan, certain that his instinct would kick in and he'd defend himself—but he didn't budge. He just stared at me blankly while I started to swing, then had to pull my arm back in horror at the last second. One of the Raiders dove at me, knocking me off balance and sending the Kopis flying from my hand just after it nicked Rowan's shoulder.

Then I was attacked on all sides and didn't fight back.

Rowan's gaze met mine, in awe as I was dragged to my feet. It was then that I knew I had saved him.

Hands held mine behind my back. Someone punched me in the stomach, and I lost all ability to breathe. Another fist punched me in the face hard enough to see stars. I tried not to notice the horror flash through Rowan's eyes when Terens fashioned a rope around my neck.

"You're off your game this morning," Terens said, seeming somewhat disappointed that his commander was still breathing but delighted over my capture. I got a good look at the side of his head, including the lines of a sun-faded star tattoo, the lines jagged as if whoever tattooed him did so on a rocking boat. "Letting some girl sneak up on you? Maybe you need to get some rest."

Rowan slowly stood, hand pressed against the cut on his shoulder. I couldn't tell if most of the blood on him was his or mine, and it was nearly impossible not to ask if he was okay.

"What should we do with her, Commander?" One of the Raiders asked.

I had the feeling he might fight for me so I shook my head at him hoping to convey that it would be a really bad idea.

Rowan conjured up that stone-cold expression that accompanied his legendary lethal cutthroat persona, and I watched all emotion drain from his features as he casually stretched his neck and straightened his spine. Suddenly, he was not the man who had cared for me and dreamed next to me by the fire. He was the monster that the legends were born of—which I had come to understand was just a well-played role. Quite possibly, the real monster was the one heading toward us now.

Shoulders rigid, jaw clenched, Rowan stared at a dark presence that consumed the beach and nearly turned the air to quicksand; Captain Vallerik was making her way toward us, black hair billowing out behind her, silver and gold jewelry dazzling against her dark skin. She parted the sea of men with a sharp snap of her ringed fingers, nails long enough to be daggers.

"What have we here?" she asked, giving me the once over as a sneer tugged at the corners of her red-painted mouth.

I kept my bleeding hand in a tight fist.

"This is the Aldiran who killed the Grakke brothers," Terens told Captain Vallerik, sounding quite proud of himself for relaying this information. "She attacked Commander Rowan while he was guarding souls, and I suggest we behead her immediately."

I noticed Rowan stumble back slightly, eyes widening in horror for the briefest second. It took him a moment to school his features into what could have been merely mild annoyance. "I can speak for myself, Terens. Keep your suggestions to yourself."

Blood was oozing through his shirt, dripping between his fingers onto the sand.

Captain Vera Vallerik tipped her head curiously to the side, studying him a moment before lowering her eyes into a glare at me. She was a stunning woman who could have walked right out of one of the fairy tales my mother used to read me. One could almost forget that she was pure poison.

"Your name?" she asked, voice as sharp as the fingernails she toyed against my throbbing cheek.

I simply stared back, trying to calm my pulse.

"Speak." Terens tugged on the rope around my neck, making my eyes water.

I could see that Rowan was ready to defend me, so instead of speaking, I spat at Captain Vallerik's face—which she must have taken offense to because the world became very dark after that.

41   KITKUN

Imatla, the all-seeing, all-knowing God of all gods only rewards those of undisputed loyalty with an afterlife of splendor.

— THE BOOK OF IMATLA

Hanuk ordered me not to leave the village. Muma ordered me not to leave the kitchen. Not that I could do either because I had burns that felt like fresh Mordorain on my legs, and I was shaking so hard I could barely stand.

I'd lit myself on fire. Lit. Myself. On. Fire. What was I thinking?

"You risked your life. For me," Elke said for the hundredth time.

Oh, right. Elke. Big brown eyes, shy and delicate, a kindness about her that was extraordinarily admirable... I'd turned myself into a human candle for the little sister I loved more than anyone in the whole world.

Love made a person do such stupid things.

Elke was gently applying ointment Muma had made out of honey and boar's fat to my legs. It was sticky and it smelled, so I pretended that its odor was what bothered me the most.

"Sera would be dead, too, without you. And the Yoann's new baby. They weren't prepared. None of us were," Elke said, dabbing very carefully at the peeling skin on my thigh. "You know that cottage with the broken boy? It's been abandoned. The whole family fled before sunset so they wouldn't have to offer their youngest child. Hanuk's drum calls to them but is unanswered. He's sending warriors to retrieve them."

"Brave," I muttered under my breath.

"At least they haven't angered the gods so far, but I suspect it's only because your fire magic has appeased them. Maybe there won't be any more sacrifices for a while."

And on and on she went. I lay flat on my back on the kitchen table, the tortoise peeking out at me from his shell where it lounged on my chest, its slight movements the only thing keeping me grounded to the earth. I kept seeing Muma's face when I closed my eyes, haunted by how it held no expression of grief when I'd offered myself for sacrifice in place of Elke. Now, as she busied herself at the cookstove and avoided catching my eye, I finally knew how she felt about me.

The night crept into the kitchen and sent everyone off to bed. I remained stretched on the table rather than squished in with my sisters and Mother, and the breeze drifting in through the window felt good on my blistered skin. Elke had put a pillow under my head and her scarf around my feet. Hesutu had lit a fire in the hearth to keep the kitchen warm. Nita had fed me a honey cake before saying goodnight. Mother had simply patted me on the head and wandered off.

And then I was alone.

But I was not scared when I heard him pull open the door and wander in like he owned the place. I kept breathing the same way. Kept staring at the moldy spots on the ceiling.

"You've got some explaining to do," said Hanuk.

He sat down at the creaky bench alongside the table, his breath hot in my ear, the sour smell of him taking over anything remotely pleasant. I felt the hard earth below us shake as his massive body settled, the gold bands that circled his wrists and ankles rattling. I kept my eyes trained on the ceiling even though my focus had shifted to the tortoise and the firestick pressed between its belly and my chest.

"Where did you get it?" Hanuk asked. His voice was barely a whisper, but it shuddered through me.

"I don't know what you're talking about," I said, feigning a yawn.

He pressed his fingertips to my neck, long greasy braids falling around his face. "Your heartbeat says otherwise, Kitkun."

I heard him rustle around and half expected to see his knife glint in the moonlight before it slashed my throat. But instead, he held something over my face, rubbed the top with his thumb, and made a little flame dance up between his fingers.

"I have fire magic, too," he said.

My breath caught and I tried not to bolt upright.

Hanuk stood, the mass of him remarkably steady and cat-like as he headed for the bunches of dried herbs and flowers hanging from the rafters. "How many will die because of you?" he asked, allowing the firestick to get a little too close for comfort to the easily ignitable dried plants and timber.

"We are your family, Hanuk," I said, trying not to show fear while reminding him that we were cousins, even if not by blood.

"My devotion is to the whole of the Ouray people. Our connection is inconsequential."

In seconds he could set the whole house on fire. And that would probably set half the village on fire. Mother, Elke, Hesutu, Nita… they would die, and just like it had been for the death of my father, I would be blamed.

The tortoise squirmed. I reached beneath him and retrieved my firestick, holding it up like I was raising a white flag in surrender.

"Ah, smart girl," Hanuk whispered, marching back to me and plucking the firestick from my hand.

I watched him examine it closely. "If I hadn't lit myself on fire, would you have gone through with it? Would you have sacrificed Elke?" I asked, my voice sounding as small as I felt while prone and vulnerable on the kitchen table.

Hanuk caressed the firestick like it was a long-lost friend. "When our Goddess Nvula speaks, I must listen and obey. There is no other choice."

"We all have a choice."

Brown watery eyes met mine. "Not if you want to keep people in line, Kitkun. Those before us—the ones who set the planet on fire—got out of line. They went against the rules and look what happened; our planet got sick. Our ancestors had to migrate to a new land, most of them dying along the way. The human race nearly died out completely. I won't let that happen again."

He was as stupid as he was devoted. "It wasn't actual *fire* that set the planet on fire," I said.

"The machines sent the gods into a rage, so they unleashed holy terror upon the land. Now, only our obedience and sacrifices appease them. When we pour blood and send the smoke of the living to the Goddess of the Sky, she asks Imatla to allow us life for another day." Hanuk's voice was a low grumble. "I don't need a history lesson, Kitkun, I study The Book every day."

That he did. And he spouted off the same old words relentlessly to all those forced to listen. I was a believer in the gods—Nvula presented herself pretty clearly by sending rain to save my life—but some parts of the book did not ring true. I wished I could read so I could verify if what Hanuk was saying was accurate.

"Now, tell me where you found this," he said, pulling his head back a bit when the tortoise snapped at his nose. "And, how did you know what it was?"

I thought of Eva and the sea people; I couldn't share my knowledge of them with Hanuk because I'd made a promise. Besides, I liked knowing something that Hanuk didn't.

"On the ground," I said. "Half a day's walk past the stream."

"You are lying, Kitkun."

"No, I'm not," I challenged, trying not to flinch because yes, I was lying.

"I let you feed your family and pretend to be a hunter for the sake of your father. I turn many a blind eye to the things you do, but not this. Now, tell me where it came from, or I will burn this house and everyone in it."

The tortoise squirmed. "By the waterfall," I said. "The last pool before the stream heads off toward the sea."

Partly true. It was also a place everyone was terrified of, so I hoped Hanuk would leave it at that.

"These things aren't just lying about," he said. "They are usually buried deep in the earth. Did you dig for it?"

"No."

"It was just… there?"

"Yes." I swallowed hard and turned away from Hanuk. "On a rock."

It was the wrong thing to say. I knew it as soon as the words left my mouth.

"That means there are others here. But it can't be the tribe from the South. They would never venture up this way again. So, it must be strangers. Our village could be at risk." Hanuk was talking to himself, the wheels spinning in his brain.

"The Wejukah protects us," I reminded him, thinking of the ring of poison air I'd been nearly caught in a few times.

"If *you* can get through it, so can others," he said, rising.

How did he know?

"The fish you bring back aren't from our stream," he said as if reading my mind. "I know you venture close to the sea. I can smell it on you when you return."

I had no reply to that, so I changed the topic. "Where did you find your firestick?"

"It was given to me by my father." He put the two firesticks side by side to compare them. Then, to my surprise, he handed mine back to me. "You must keep this now that you have become a pleaser of the gods. Tomorrow, you will take me to the place you found it, and if you trick me, Kitkun, or if you don't take me where I want to go, I will offer your mother and sisters for the next sacrifice whether the sky changes or not."

And with that, he left.

I lay awake long after, rolling the top of the firestick with my thumb, watching the little flame burst to life over and over. "What should I do?" I asked the tortoise.

In reply, it ducked inside its shell.

42   Evangeline

Wherever I was, it was pitch black.

For a moment I thought I'd lost my arm, but then I realized it was asleep beneath me. I eased up off it and it prickled back to life. Breathing deep, I kept myself calm and tried to sit up, but my forehead connected with wood and so did my knees; I was in a crate.

Although wisps of air reaching me through the cracks meant I was still above ground, I knew that being buried alive would soon follow. It was a punishment the Raiders were legendary for.

Panic clawed at my mind, and I couldn't stop my body from thrashing about in my enclosure. Elbows, palms, fists, anything I could move was accompanied by a high-pitched wail that I never knew I could produce, along with a string of threats that the Raiders were probably laughing at. Tears poured over my swollen cheek and broken lip as my knuckles cracked against the crate, sending a warmth over my face that I knew was blood.

Stop.

I was pulled toward the light of Alexander at breakneck speed, colors swirling and churning past us in the Between. His light wrapped around mine, soothing and releasing the terror that had gripped me so violently. I was somehow sobbing in the freaky realm with no breath, and he said nothing until I had calmed down.

"You have good timing for once," I said after a very long while.

His light shimmered around me. *Eva, you'll be okay. I'll make sure of it.*

Here, in the meeting of minds, I felt no pain, but the gravity of what was going to happen to me in the physical realm was still crushing. "I'm… I'm not ready to die," I admitted.

Then I won't allow it. My people have you in a crate in the middle of camp. Captain Vallerik is trying to decide what to do with you. But—

"Rowan… is he all right?"

The light of Alexander surged brightly then dimmed. *Yes. Rowan is fine.*

"Can you see him? Do you know for sure?" I felt desperate for reassurance. Did I do the right thing? "Did Captain Vallerik believe that I had attacked her commander and beheaded her beloved Grakke brothers? Was my acting convincing enough to eliminate any notion that Rowan may have been trying to help me? Did I… hurt him?"

I can assure you that he is not mortally wounded and is quite safe.

I felt my anxiety ease slightly. If I died, then at least it wouldn't be for nothing. "Okay. Good."

Listen, Evangeline, I'm going to get you out of there. I promise.

The vast darkness surrounding us seemed to pulse, and my gold light moved in closer to Alexander's indigo blue. "You can't if you are putting yourself in danger. Are you not committing treason right now by bringing me here? Do your people know what you're capable of?"

Do not worry about me. Only one other person knows what I am, and he would die before ever giving me away. Your loyalty is infallible as well, judging by how fiercely you protect that other Sage.

Zoleya…

I had to change the subject to avoid any thoughts of her.

"What do you look like, Alexander? What do you do? Are you a cook? A shoe polisher? A builder?"

He chuckled. I couldn't hear him laugh, but I could feel it somehow. *I'm of average height, I boss people around, can't cook to save my life, only polish my own shoes, and can build anything out of nothing. I'm also not going to let anything happen to you here in this realm, or on Earth. Please know that, okay?*

"There is nothing you can do except keep me company once in a while. They're going to kill me, Alexander, and you'll have to let them. You can't risk yourself for me. All I ask is that you find some way to let the rest of my people go. Can you do that? Let them have a fair chance at life. The little boy that tends to your captain… his brother is back at my camp and desperate to have him back. Can you make that happen, please?"

As if a tsunami rushed in, all at once I could feel Alexander's emotions pouring over and through me. He carried an enormous mass of grief and sadness for his people, along with a feeling of helplessness and empathy for mine. He bore the weight of the world on his shoulders and was crippled by an intense worry for those he loved. He was pure, brave, and selfless… and I wondered if I might drown in everything I suddenly knew about him.

But as quickly as he let down his guard, he built it back up, and I felt the world spinning madly out of control.

I will do my best for your people, and you must do what is best for yourself. That means that you need to tell the truth when they come for you. He communicated quickly, as if he was running out of time. *Tell anyone who will listen to you that Rowan tried to help you and that he attempted to heal you in that tent and you were just pretending to attack him. Tell them that you weren't the one to take the heads of the Grakke brothers. This way maybe you can barter with your life and—*

"Never. Your people will torture him."

Eva, please…

"I could never live with myself if that happened. I won't turn against him."

But why? You know nothing about him. He's a—

"I've seen into his heart. I've looked into his eyes. And I— well, I just… I would take my own life if it came to it."

I too was completely stunned by my admittance of what was the honest truth.

You really would, wouldn't you?

The word came out easily and shocked me to the core. "Yes."

Silence. What did Alexander think of me? That I was crazy? Brave? Lovestruck and foolish?

"Rowan is someone who can make a difference in the world," I said, meaning it fully. "I can feel it. He's important. He's… somebody worth saving."

Again, silence. The light of Alexander swam around me, pulsing in between blue and purple fragments of his guarded memories and thoughts.

Okay, he said. *We'll do it your way.*

"Thank you."

I will free your people, and I will free you, Alexander said. *You just have to trust me.*

"Do I have a choice?" I teased.

His reply was serious and one that I knew to be true. *Unfortunately, yes.*

43 KADE

I met a girl that I could love. Her name is Holly. She is the most beautiful person I've ever laid eyes upon. I wish I didn't have to keep her a secret and could shout her name from the tallest cliff, but she'd be hung for capturing my attention.

I know what the Nihila expect of me, but am I to also pretend that I am not human?

— *JOURNAL ENTRY, KADE, AGE 16*

Was ripping through the jungle on a rampage and smashing everything around me to dust an option? Because, besides that, I really didn't know what to do. Never in my life had I felt such extreme anger, not even when my marks lit up in the presence of Atomica.

With the help of Beast, Max, Dominic, and Lucky, Amari and I had evaded the Raiders and then circled back, only to find Eva being dragged away by Captain Vallerik and her crew. Eva was as good as dead, and I wasn't the only one raging because of it.

"They're going to kill her," Max spat. "And I'm going to kill each and every one of those Raiders so hard their ancestors will feel it. I'll paint the entire island red with Raider blood. I'll crush every Raider bone until nothing remains but—"

"Stop," I said, even though I agreed wholeheartedly. I had to calm Max down. He was turning on Amari, pointing at her with his knife and preparing to lash out at her, and she was in no position to counter the attack. "Use your head," I said through gritted teeth. "Amari is the only thing keeping Eva safe right now."

Max's cheeks were so red that his freckles had disappeared. "Safe? Are you insane? Was I the only one who heard her claim to have killed those brothers just to save Rowan's ass? Why? Why would she do that? What is it about that guy?"

The same question had been slamming around in my head hard enough to make it throb, and the answer I kept gravitating toward was unbearable.

"I don't know, but we have to think things through. We can't just go on a rampage and try to kill everyone." As much as I would have taken immense satisfaction in that.

The monkeys dangling above us were yapping and a fat red bird was singing some dumb song. They were increasing my irritation as much as Max's temper. I needed quiet. I needed Max *and* the jungle to shut up.

"It's better than nothing, Kade," Max raged, eyes burning holes into the female Raider on her knees, nearly blue from trying to catch her breath. "So, unless you have a better idea, I'm going to kill everyone, starting with this one!"

Beast got between Max and Amari, his massive size blocking Max from lashing out. He stepped forward and pressed his meaty hand against Max's chest.

"Eva would be very disappointed in you right now," he said.

It was only a few words, but enough to fell the forest of rage that was Max. He stumbled back, turned, and marched off into the trees.

With Max gone, Amari toppled over and stared up at the sky. Running had taken everything out of her, making her look even worse than before. She was still deeply injured and needed protection, and I hated that it was up to me.

"He won't harm you," I told her, entire body vibrating—I had to calm down. I wouldn't be able to help Eva if all I could see was red.

Amari muttered something unintelligible and tried to rub her eyes only to quickly drop her hand in exhaustion.

Beast got down on his knees next to her as the jungle crawled around us like a moving blanket. "Aye, ye rest for a minute. I'll keep watch, I promise."

"As will I," said Dominic.

Amari nodded and closed her eyes. I doubted she trusted us, but she was too weak to resist.

"So, what are we going to do now?" said a small voice.

I nearly jumped out of my skin and turned to see Lucky standing behind me. He was practically ghostlike, pale, with eyes so bloodshot they were nearly glowing red. The kid looked like he'd been chewed up and spit out by a couple of sharks, and if I felt anything for anyone other than Eva at the moment, it might be a bit of sympathy for Lucky.

"Don't worry, Lucky. We'll rescue her," I said, meaning it fully, feeling the bite of my marks.

Damn this cursed situation I'd put myself in. If I could go back to the ship and be chained up across from the girl with the honey hair, the strange, lithe creature who was braver than any of the men in the hold and whose eyes met mine and stole my vision for anything else, I would kill her. Right there and then. Then carry on with my mission and not be burdened with these… feelings.

"What about my brother?" asked Lucky.

"Huh?" I was startled out of my thoughts, teeth aching.

"My little brother," Lucky clarified.

"We'll rescue him, too."

"You got a plan to make that happen, Kade?" Dominic asked.

Stars above. "Do I look like I have all the answers?"

Beast sighed heavily. "Look, emotions be flying high right now, I git it. But if we don't band together and git to thinkin' things through, we're gonna lose the Missy."

I drew in a deep breath. He was right, and I couldn't go back in time to fix it.

"Dominic and Lucky—take Amari back to camp and make sure she's okay."

Dominic nodded in agreement. Lucky squeaked something out.

"Guard her with your life. Understand?" I added. "She's our insurance with Rowan."

"Yes," they acknowledged in unison.

"Beast; you, me, and Max—if he returns—will go back to the Raiders camp. We'll find Rowan. He'll know what to do. He must have a plan to get Eva free, and he'll need our help."

Amari struggled to her feet, but she was so deathly white I thought she might pass out at any second. "Rowan can't help you now," she said, placing her hands on her knees for support. "Eva will be heavily guarded until her death. There will be eyes on her at all times."

"We rescued Prominus. We can rescue Eva."

Amari's eyes lowered into a glare. "Prominus? The monster with the chapped face who was punished by the whip?"

"Yes."

Before I knew it, a flash of short black hair flew at me, and only because she was injured did Amari not connect her fist to my face. Dominic caught her and Beast helped hold her back while she writhed like a wildcat caught in a trap. I just stared, stunned by her reaction.

"That piece of shit beat a woman in the hold just for the fun of it," Amari roared, and tears were streaming down her cheeks as she fought to breathe. "She was one of his own people! We were punishing him for that, and you idiots freed him. Freed him! Then the bastard came back and found me while I was sleeping… and…"

All at once her body crumpled in defeat. Dominic let her sink to her knees. Beast put his hands up and stepped back. I just stared at her, stunned.

"You're all idiots!" she spat.

Well, she wasn't wrong there.

"I'm so sorry," said Beast. "We couldn't have known. We thought we be doing the right thing by freeing the bloke."

Amari put her palms to the earth, trying her best to not tip over. "If he's a part of your alliance, I'd rather walk into the sea with weights tied to my feet than be anywhere near him."

"Wait… are we talking about that big guy? The one that wanted to fight Eva at our camp?" Dominic asked, clueing in a bit late to the conversation.

I nodded. Beast huffed.

"Prominus did that to you?" Dominic motioned to Amari, her swollen face and bruised body.

Amari gave him a 'you really are stupid' look, then sighed.

Dominic ran his hand over the top of his shorn head, eyebrows knitting together. "He's not of our people or our beliefs, and certainly not a part of our camp. You're safe from him. You have my word."

Amari laughed. "You Aldirans like to 'give your word' a lot, don't you? Not sure what it's worth though." Her eyes met mine. "Or how honest it is."

"You have no choice but to take it," I challenged.

Her gaze was piercing. "Oh, really?"

My body bristled defensively. "Really." I hoped my glare was an obvious warning for her to keep our little secret to herself.

Silence hung between us for a long moment.

Finally, Beast spoke. "Well, we done got that sorted out, aye? Prominus be a dead man in my books."

"And mine," I said, recalling Prominus' eagerness to fight Eva and the gleam in his disgusting eyes. "I'll happily get rid of him the next chance I get."

Amari looked relieved—until the leaves behind me shook. When her eyes widened in alarm, I didn't have to turn around to know it was Max. I could feel his presence. The overwhelming mix of hate and rage blended with the kind of loyalty that takes on a life of its own surrounded him like a cloud.

"I won't kill her," he said, referring to Amari.

He must have taken his excess anger out on a tree because his knuckles were scratched and bloodied while his voice was even-toned and deadly calm.

"Good choice," I said, finding myself taking a step back from him when his amber eyes met mine—the kid was a bomb waiting to go off.

"Have you got a plan to get Eva back yet?" he asked.

"Yes."

Max pulled a long blade from the holster at his waist, the silver gleaming like the death wish in his eyes. "Then it's go time."

44  KITKUN

Take from the earth only what you need and tread lightly. Learn the melody of the trees, the voice of the water, and the hum of the dirt. Sing to them from your heart, and they will give back to you.

— THE BOOK OF IMATLA

Hanuk had a built-in lie detector in his shriveled-up pea brain. If I started to wander off course—hoping to lead him away from the sea people—he knew. He'd grab me by the throat with his meaty hands, feel the pulse in my neck, and his eyes would roll back as if the gods were filling his mind with my thoughts. I thought it was just for show to impress the five warriors he'd brought along, but every time he asked me if we were going the right way and a sputtered 'yes' squeaked from my throat, he knew I was lying.

So, I kept my mouth shut. I tried to go south over the stream that led to the sea, but all of a sudden my lies, or 'tricks' as Hanuk called them, weren't necessary. He'd found tracks.

Now he was the one leading the way, following bent branches and things broken or moved on the jungle floor either by my feet or Eva's and the man she called Kade. He saw clues I couldn't see and smelled things lost to my senses.

His uncanny sense of tracking—the only thing I admired about him —brought us to the edge of the Wejukah. The shells on our wrists whistled a low, eerie warning not to go any farther, and only then did I breathe a sigh of relief.

273

"Others have gone through," Hanuk said as his warriors shifted uneasily behind him, terrified of the Wejukah, and rightly so. "Did they survive, Kitkun?"

I played dumb. "Uh, I don't know what you're—"

His sweaty hand lashed out and grabbed my throat again, and this time not to check my pulse. "The people you stole the firestick from," Hanuk whispered into my ear. "You know where they are. They made it through the Wejukah somehow and they're on the other side. I can feel it. Now, you lead me to them, or I'll send a warrior back to the village to pay a visit to your mother and sisters. It would be very unwise to attempt to defy me or harm me, *Huntress.*"

He released his grip, and I stumbled back, imagining all the ways I'd like to see him suffer. But I was just a tiny mouse amid a pack of lions. Stupid, posturing, oiled-in-odd-places lions. I would not be intimidated. I would not be scared or—

"Kitkun!" Hanuk roared. "Take me to the people who made this trail!"

I nodded and got my feet moving, then found the markings I'd made with the jade rock not far from the place Eva had slipped through when she found the waterfall. I knew the spot between the stones where the air was still breathable, a tiny gate in the poison wall that made a fence around Black Mountain. I headed in, shell whistling on my wrist, but the warriors stopped.

Hanuk spun to face them, reading their faces and the lifetime of superstition wormed into their DNA to never enter the Wejukah. Even if they wanted to follow me, I doubted their arms and legs would cooperate with their muscled heads.

"Go back to the village," Hanuk ordered his five 'fearless' men, all wide-eyed and antsy. "The gods will allow me passage through the Wejukah because I am their mortal voice, but they will fill the lungs of my warriors with stones."

The look of terror and relief on the warriors' faces was rather hilarious.

Hanuk kept blathering. "And since Kitkun has pleased them, they will allow her to pass through as well. She will lead me to that which I seek. If I am not back by the time the sun has set twice, you are to burn the house of her family to the ground with them in it."

"Yes, Hanuk," they muttered in unison, and in a blur were gone.

I whirled on Hanuk. "You don't mean that… you can't… Hanuk, what if something happens? What if—"

Hanuk put up his hand to cut me off. "You've gone through the Wejukah many times, Kitkun. Yes?"

No point lying now. "Yes."

"Well, then lead the way."

I could get rid of him, right here, right now. Lead him into the poison air and stick my knife in his back, then run back to the village and get to my mother and sisters before the warriors did. I could beg Muma to follow me into the jungle…

Except I knew in my heart that no matter how much I begged, Muma would never leave.

So, I put one foot in front of the other and marched ahead with the wishful thinking that Hanuk would get hungry and bored, possibly missing the trail that connected Eva's camp to the sea people on the north beach—but he found it.

And now I had no more secrets to keep.

45   EVANGELINE

All my life I had been strong, able to rely on the power of my mind to overcome and see the light at the end of the tunnel. But now, all I could think about was that I was going to die. And rightly so. I'd survived the Raiders' ship and been given a second chance, and even though Zoleya claimed to be fine and well taken care of, I'd certainly failed her… again.

"I'm sorry," I kept repeating, because as shitty as it was, I wouldn't change a thing.

I'd given up banging on the crate, instead content to wallow in my misery. When the air changed and I was pulled upright into the light, yanked to my feet so fast the blood rushed away from my head, it took a moment to adjust my eyes to the sun full in the sky. Trembling with pain and confusion, I blinked into focus a group of people surrounding me, each face wearing the unmistakable expression of hate.

I was indeed in the middle of the Raiders' camp, just as Alexander had said. Fires roared beneath pots of water and bundles of roasting fish. Laundry was hung neatly from lines to dry. Small buildings and sleeping platforms peppered the cleared space, and many hammocks were strung between trees. It was spotless, too. Organized. Completely the opposite of how I used to think Raiders lived.

Terens was the one who had pulled me out of the crate. He had me by the hair and I didn't bother struggling. There was no point. I tried not to wince as he practically dragged me to where Captain Vallerik sat on an ornate gold chair plunked in the middle of a patch of dirt.

"Will you tell me your name now? Or would you rather go back in the crate?" she asked.

Her hair was polished and twisted into what looked like hundreds of writhing snakes as black as her glimmering eyes. The sun at her back cast a golden halo around her slender figure, making her appear almost angelic—only this woman was no angel. Even her people feared her.

"You already know it, but for the sake of posterity, my name is Evangeline Quillene," I said, voice cracking.

"Evangeline Quillene," she repeated, testing the words on her tongue, tasting them before swallowing and inhaling deeply. "You claim to be the one who took the heads of my boys, yes?"

My stomach flipped with the lie. "Yes," I said as firmly as I could.

Something wavered in Captain Vera Vallerik's eyes. Something… terrifying. "We have punishments for people like you, but I feel they all would be too swift of a death for my liking. I'd like to drag it out. Over a few weeks. Maybe longer."

I tried to stop my legs from shaking. "Go for it," I challenged. "But no matter what you do, it won't be as satisfying as how that blade felt in my hand when it went through the necks of those men."

Her glare was piercing. I held my ground.

"She's lying," said someone in the crowd.

I blinked at the sea of faces, all shiny from the heat of the day.

"Who speaks?" asked Captain Vallerik.

A man stepped forward. Older, short, thick glasses, skin the color of coconut husks. "She did not kill the brothers. It was a young man described to be approximately five foot eleven, with tanned, freckled skin and wavy reddish-brown hair. He was an Aldiran destined for the arena. Unfortunately, when he was in the hold, we couldn't get a name out of him."

He was talking about Max.

There was muttering amongst the Raiders. Captain Vallerik put up her hand and the entire earth fell silent. "Go on, Cyrus," she said.

Cyrus flared his nostrils and rubbed his brow wearily. "There were two witnesses, Captain. I recorded their account of the death and put it in a report that I spent a good hour preparing. I don't know why I bother writing all this down if—"

"Are you suggesting that this girl is lying?" Captain Vallerik interjected.

Cyrus sighed heavily. "Yes."

Captain Vallerik let out an amused huff and returned her attention to me. "Why are you trying to protect such a heinous person, Evangeline Quillene?" she asked, getting up close enough for me to know she'd recently eaten a banana.

I kept my mouth shut. My eyes focused on her forehead.

"Giving your life for another? Hmm." She eyed me differently now. "Well, that is rather admirable and brave—and unusual for an Aldiran. Too bad you will suffer for it."

"That sort of behavior is deserving of a warrior's death, don't you agree?" Rowan had stepped out from amongst the crowd, face a sheet of ice, eyes even colder. A rush of nervous silence fell over the camp. "We reward bravery amongst our own. I think that we should consider lessening the terms of punishment because of it in this case—"

"She is an Aldiran." Captain Vallerik smoothed her hands over the sides of her intricately sewn, buttery leather dress that crossed seams at her chest. "She's a stupid, love-sick, little girl who is trying to protect the vile creature who murdered my boys." Her daggered fingernails gripped my face. "Give me a name and I will make your death swift."

"I'm not protecting anyone. I'm not lying."

Captain Vallerik slapped me hard enough to see stars. "Tell me now and spare me the hassle of killing every single one of your people. Because I will. I'll start with the ones I currently have in the keep, then hunt the rest, exterminating every Aldiran on this island most horrifically. And I'll let you die last so you can watch their torture and fully feel the weight of your decision."

"It was me," I said, practically sputtering. I had to keep up the lie that I was waist-deep in now. "I killed those men, so get on with it and take your revenge out on me. Leave my people out of this, you bitch."

Another slap across my face. Someone yelled "whip her," another yelled "burn her," and when my vision cleared, Captain Vallerik had an expression on her face that could only be described as absolute abhorrence.

"You're going to regret killing my boys, and you're going to regret calling me that."

She pointed the tip of her knife at my pupil, about to start removing pieces of me, starting with my eye.

"Oh, for the love of the Sea, just stop," said Rowan, feigning boredom.

Captain Vallerik raised an eyebrow and turned her head ever so slightly to see him, but she kept her blade an inch from my eye.

"If you kill her, she'll be useless to us." Rowan inspected his fingernails, his voice frighteningly calm as he leaned casually against a palm tree. "It's obvious the girl is lying, so—"

"I'm not lying!" I yelled. "I hate Raiders! I'll kill all of you! I killed those men and—"

Rowan snapped his finger and Terens stuffed fabric in my mouth so I couldn't speak.

"As I was saying." Rowan crossed his arms over his chest. "She is lying. I say instead of making a mess of her we use her as bait. Her people will try to rescue her. So, why don't we let them try? Let's use her to lure them in. We will find the one who truly did kill the Grakke brothers and eliminate them all in the process. Easy as that."

No. No! Rowan was right. Kade and the others would come for me. They would all be captured.

I tried to scream through the gag but it was hopeless. My words were choked off.

"Hmmm, yes. Yes. Was she not chosen for the arena?" asked Cyrus, shoving his glasses up higher on his beaked nose. "Is this not the girl you dragged us across Aldira to find?"

Rowan shrugged his shoulders. "Possibly."

"Yes, I believe she was," Terens interjected, his beady eyes dancing in his fat skull. "We lost a few good people hunting this one down."

"Ah yes, the dangerous female," said Cyrus, speaking like he'd rather have a nap than be worrying about something so trivial as this.

"Dangerous?" Captain Vallerik's eyes lit up. She stepped back and examined me head to toe. I felt naked as the day I was born under her stare.

Rowan cracked his neck as if bored and stood away from the tree. "Yes. When we get back to Cal de Mac she'll fetch top dollar in the arena."

"Ah," said Captain Vallerik. "You have hopes of returning home."

"We all do, Captain."

Captain Vallerik assessed the mood of her crew, all of them waiting expectantly for her to speak. I could practically see her trying to choose her words, conflicted between just being rid of me or offering them the all-powerful hope.

"My brilliant commander is right," she said, addressing her loyal subjects. "This girl will lure in the rest of the surviving Aldirans, and we will seek justice for the Grakke brothers."

A muffled response. Some head nods. A few yawns of boredom.

"And," Captain Vallerik's voice grew louder, seeming to claim every available space in the jungle. "Since this is our home until we can rebuild the Whydall, why don't we make it...*cozy*. Let's carry on with tradition. Evangeline Quillene will fight Prominus tomorrow at high noon. They can battle to their deaths. And oh, what gory and glorious deaths they will be!"

Now cheering erupted from the crowd that morphed into a chant. *Fight, fight, fight, fight...*

I sought Rowan's face amongst the crowd, only to see the back of his head as he headed for the beach. There was nothing he could do, and his dismissal brought home the fact that yes, I was most certainly going to die. At least, though, since the Raiders did everything at high noon, Zoleya would have a chance to come to me tonight so I could properly say goodbye.

46  EVANGELINE

My cage was on the edge of the clearing where overhanging palm fronds offered a bit of shade. My gag was removed and I was given water, then fish of some sort—burned and raw at the same time—and bananas too green to eat. I was threatened with the gag again if I uttered a word, so I stayed quiet because no one would listen to me anyway. I had to pee, but I'd be damned if I was going to do that in broad daylight.

Besides my engorged and painful bladder, my leg throbbed, and I could tell by the increasing redness that the infection was back. Last night I heard Rowan tell Kade that I needed three more injections, and by my calculations I was long overdue for the second. As I dreamed of the sweet taste of victory that would come from defeating Prominus, I would probably succumb to the wound on my leg before I even go the chance to fight.

The afternoon heat was stifling. Sweat dripped into my eyes as I stared at the faces of Raiders passing by. They were busy building and burning things, cooking, cleaning, hunting, and fulfilling every wish of their captain with an orderly efficiency I couldn't help but admire. Which one of them was Alexander? Was he one of the men washing clothes? Or was he a part of the group taming back the jungle to clear the land? I didn't have a physical description, so I didn't know what to watch for, but I thought for sure I would know him if I saw him. I assumed the connection we shared in the realm—or what he called the Between—would give me a solid hint as to his identity in this realm…

I'd dozed off with my head on my knees when a familiar voice startled me awake.

"She must be cleaned up before the fight," said Rowan.

He stood before the cage and made a flippant hand gesture in my direction. His golden hair had been tamed and his slim-fitting trousers and button-down shirt tucked in at the waist were spotless and pressed. His appearance conveyed complete calm and control, the only marker of the stress he was under showing as dark shadows under his eyes.

"Just because we are stranded on this god-forsaken island doesn't mean we should act like beasts," he continued, speaking to people coming up behind him. "I can smell her from here."

Captain Vallerik, followed by Lucky's little brother and the short man known as Cyrus, stopped to stand next to Rowan. Captain Vallerik's jewels and chains clanged around her neck and shone in the filtered sunlight. She was decked out in fighting gear, with knives sheathed at her waist and heavy straps criss-crossing her chest and thighs.

"I can smell her from here, too. But so what? It doesn't matter," she said.

"Actually, it *does* matter. We have a code of ethics, remember? Allow me to make preparations, Captain." Rowan inspected his fingernails, feigning mild interest in my well-being.

"I detect a tone from you, Rowan." Captain Vallerik dismissed the short man and he walked on ahead. "Are you still angry with me about Amari? You know the laws. I was just following protocol."

"As am I," Rowan countered.

Captain Vallerik grinned. "Ah, yes. Well played. Well, go on then, you can be the girl's keeper. If she escapes, it'll be your head, though. I'll look after Prominus—he could use some freshening up as well. In fact, I'd like him to shine like a polished blade while he tears this little Aldiran to shreds. And really, I guess the dogs would appreciate their dinner freshly washed."

With that, she turned on her heels and headed for the beach.

"Dogs?" I muttered. "Did they not drown?"

One of the three Raiders posted to guard the cage grinned sadistically at my question.

"Not all," he said. "The two we're nursing back to health will find your carcass pretty tasty."

"Mind your business and get back to work," Rowan ordered, and the smile left the guard's face.

Rowan eyed the cage, the trees behind it, the dirt it sat upon… everything except me. His eyes would not meet mine—which was good. He was playing the role, as I had. Only the slight tremble in his hands as he pressed his fingertips to the bridge of his nose told the truth.

He snapped his fingers and two of the guards were instantly at his side.

"Take her to the healer's shack," he ordered. "Bind her hands and don't let her out of your sight. I'll send further instructions."

I was pulled from the cage, my hands fastened behind me, and then I was dragged to the small building the Raiders had erected for their wounded. I struggled for show and to maintain an ounce of pride even though I knew it was futile.

Shoved inside, the smell hit me first. There were all sorts of minty and floral scents, along with something cold and sharp. Once my eyes adjusted to the dim light, I could see four beds on the floor—one of them occupied by someone very thin and quite possibly dead—and a small ancient woman in the corner before the case of medicine. She had it open and the blue light emanating from it lit the strange vials and her deeply lined features. As I was slammed down onto one of the beds, she glanced briefly my way and then went back to whatever she was doing.

Flat on my back, the guards secured my hands to a hook on the wall over my head, then stood a few feet away, arms crossed over their chests, eyes daring me to try and make an escape.

Their smells added to the stink of the shack.

"Get out," the old woman said after a while.

"She's dangerous, Aunnie," said one of the guards. "We must make sure she doesn't—"

"Doesn't what? Try to run with her hands tied to the wall? Fart in her sleep? You stupid baboons, get the hell out of my shack."

I gathered that nobody disobeyed Aunnie, because the guards left, shutting the creaking and crooked door behind them without further question.

"You're the one that is to fight tomorrow?" the old woman asked, her voice deep and scratchy.

"Yes," I answered, relieved to be lying down even though my arms were falling asleep again. At least I was in the most perfect place for Zoleya to come and take my consciousness to the freaky realm—no one but this old woman would see my eyes rolling back in my head.

The old lady laughed. "Oh, this ought to be good. I got a feeling about you. Always did."

Always did? What did that mean?

Before I could ask her what she was talking about, Rowan breezed through the door, and when his eyes met mine all but him was forgotten.

"Aunnie," he said, bowing his head respectfully. "This is Evangeline Quillene."

"I figured as much," said Aunnie, sucking on her brown teeth.

"She needs preparations for the event tomorrow."

"You mean the 'slaughter'," Aunnie replied.

Rowan bristled. "She has a chance at winning."

The old lady laughed.

Trying to maintain composure, Rowan cleared his throat. "Anyway, I am going to look after things in here for a few minutes. You are needed on the beach. Terens has had an accident, and I've left orders for him to not be moved until you've assessed his condition."

The smile left Aunnie's face and she sighed heavily, knees cracking as she got to her feet. She barely came up to Rowan's ribs at full height, but despite her size there was something giant and ferocious about her.

"Terens is an idiot," she spat. "Did he trip over a grasshopper again? Fall out of a two-foot tree? Grab the wrong end of a blade? The moron. Maybe he should do us all a favor and just go walk the plank."

"Our ship is underwater," Rowan reminded her.

"Exactly," she said with a huff, and with that, she was out the door.

Rowan wasted no time grabbing the case and unlocking it. He filled a syringe to the top with blue liquid while I glanced over at the other person in the room, who remained unconscious.

"It seems that your healer doesn't like Terens," I said, stating the obvious.

Rowan was on a mission and had no time for small talk. "Here, bite down on this," he said, putting the wooden handle of a small knife between my teeth. "I need to get this medicine to the wound quickly. It's hours past due."

My wrists were up over my head so I assumed he would untie them and feel around for a vein, but he was pressing at the skin on my leg, his eyes yet again avoiding mine. I muttered against the knife handle when I knew what he was about to do. "No…"

"I must. I'm sorry."

Then he jabbed. He stabbed that needle right to my damn bone and I couldn't contain the scream that erupted from deep in the pit of my stomach. For a moment, darkness clouded my vision, and when I could finally see again, he jabbed once more.

Agony. A rush of cold through my veins.

But as quickly as the pain came it began dissipating—the medicine was working quickly now. I concentrated on breathing slowly, and Rowan removed the knife handle from between my teeth.

"I'm sorry," he said, and there were tears in his eyes.

"It's okay," I muttered, feeling exhaustion on every level.

He placed the vial back into the case, and I noticed it was full again. What sort of sorcery was this?

"You need one more injection," he said. "The last one is twice as much, but you can handle it. After that, you will be good as new."

I watched him busy himself with replacing the bandage on my foot, then clinically feel my forehead for a fever—which was a waste of time.

"Don't worry about the last injection," I said, knowing that if he got caught his fate would be worse than mine. "I'm going to die anyway."

This angered him. I could see his jaw tighten. "Do not say that."

"I can't beat Prominus."

"I am going to help you, Evangeline."

"There's nothing you can do—"

He pressed his fingertips to my lips and the cold exterior he tried to hide behind slipped away. "Don't say that. Don't give up hope, please. I will free you before it gets to that."

I turned my head to the side, unable to meet his gaze. "I won't chance you getting caught."

"Evangeline…"

"Just let me die. Let my leg kill me. Do me that kindness."

"No."

His hands were on my cheeks, holding my face so I had no choice but to stare directly into his eyes. So badly I wanted to rake my fingers through his dirty blonde hair, brush a thumb over his pillowy mouth, and wipe at the tears clouding his beautiful gray eyes. The need was so strong, so powerful, I wondered if my heart might slam right through my chest.

"You must fight to live, Evangeline. For me. Please." His hands remained on my cheeks and he leaned in, pressing his forehead to mine. "I'll free your people. I'll keep Kade Thorn and the others safe. I'll do anything you want. Anything. Please… Fight. Fight for your life right now, and if it comes to it, in the arena, too. Do this for them. For me. For yourself."

His pleading awakened something deep within me. Something strong and powerful. And the look in his eyes when he pulled back to study mine triggered a will to live so forceful that if I hadn't been tied to the bed, I would have soared up through the clouds. There was fathomless emotion in his eyes, and it was the same sort that I had seen in Zoleya's when she told me she loved me.

"Okay," I said, barely able to speak through a flood of tears. "I will fight."

He smiled with a combination of relief and pride, and it lit the whole dismal room.

"Good."

There was the sound of commotion outside and Rowan pulled his hands away just as Aunnie kicked open the door. She headed for the case, patted it lovingly, and if she noticed it had been tampered with, she said nothing.

"How is Terens, Aunnie?" Rowan asked, still kneeling, eyes glistening and unable to pull his gaze away from mine as he straightened his shoulders.

"Stupid as ever," she said sharply. "A complete moron. Got his foot stuck in a hole coming out of his tent and fell face-first on a rock. The dumbass got himself a bump on his forehead and a twisted ankle."

I noticed the slightest grin tug at the corners of Rowan's mouth. "Will he be relieved of his duties?"

Aunnie plopped down in her corner, sitting cross-legged. "No. Not enough bodies as it is around here. Now, off you go, Commander. I've got Inez and Willa coming to clean the girl up and no man needs be hanging around for that."

Rowan pulled in a deep breath but didn't move.

"Did you hear me, boy? Or do I gotta box your ears to get them to work?"

Rowan rose to his feet, and I could see Aunnie noting his reluctance to leave.

"I trust she will be in the best care," he said, lowering his gaze on the old woman in a way that said more than words ever could. "When the preparations are done, I will return with some fighting strategies to share with her."

Rowan's absence from the shack felt like a knife to the chest.

Aunnie's ancient beady eyes met mine from across the room. "Ha. Strategies my ass."

Inez and Willa didn't care for me, nor I for them. They weren't happy being tasked with the mundane chore of washing a lowly Aldiran. My dignity took a hit but at least afterward I was clean. My head no longer itched from sweat, and my hair was brushed and scented with the same soap most of the Raiders smelled like. They wound it all into a tidy braid at my back—Inez pulled extra hard with her beefy, chapped hands but I didn't give her the satisfaction of tears—and my fingernails were scrubbed and my feet looked like feet again. The buckets of water were black afterward, and if I cared what they thought of me I would have been mortified.

Gone were my shredded pants and stained shirt, and now I donned the same apparel as the Raider women; a sturdy but breathable pair of black pants, long enough to cover the wound on my leg—which neither girl treated any less roughly than the rest of me—that fit close but not tight to the skin, and a breathable black shirt of the finest cotton, low cut at the neck and armpits for ease of movement, nipped in at the waist but a bit too snug across the chest for my liking. I had never worn anything finer. The stitching was impeccable, the fabric soft and the blackest black. I almost said thank you but the scowl on their faces held my tongue.

Aunnie, however, praised Inez and Willa for making me "smell and look better than the hair-covered pig-dropping" that I was before getting washed up. At one point, I'd caught her looking at my leg while I stood naked in the bucket with no means to cover myself. She assessed the scar, then eyed the other battle wounds I'd gathered. I thought I saw her smile.

Aunnie ordered the girls to secure me back to the bed, then had them remove the bedpan from beneath the other occupant in the room, who, due to lack of movement, I still assumed was dead.

"Oh, he sees you, don't worry bout that," said Aunnie when the girls had left, as if she'd been reading my mind.

"Excuse me?"

"Jin. On the bed over there. He falls ill quite often. Slips into a dream state where no one and nothing can wake him. If he's not watched and cared for, he'll dehydrate and die. Anyway, when he comes around, he can tell you everything you said and did. So watch yourself."

"But he can't *see...*"

"He sees as well as I do," she said.

Well, that was comforting.

Aunnie rose and went to Jin. She placed a cloth over his eyes and adjusted the thin sheet covering him. I noticed the intravenous hooked up to his arm keeping him alive and wondered if Rowan had done that. Jin didn't budge when Aunnie tenderly wiped the drool from his mouth and dabbed at his eyes.

With features strikingly similar to Rowan's, Jin could have been a brother. His body was much thinner than Rowan's though, cheekbones razor sharp and arms as thin as twigs, but his full lips, shape of nose, and jawline were similar. Was Jin tall? I couldn't tell, and I had to turn my eyes away when Aunnie began rubbing him with oils, making his bare, hairless chest gleam.

The pungent smell of menthol and something woodsy filled the air. It brought forth a memory of my mother rubbing the lotions and oils onto Delia's tender skin that had filled me with hope that she might survive. The memory was as sharp and painful as the injection, forcing me to realize that if I survived burying my family, I could survive this too. Hell, it was amazing that I made it this far in life, and being in this shack with my hands tied up over my head was better than being buried alive in a damn wooden crate.

I shivered.

"Yes, you got lucky," said Aunnie.

I had no idea what she was talking about.

"You would have been six feet under by now, howling where no one could hear you," she clarified, opening a different bottle of oil that smelled floral. "And probably missing a few more body parts than just an eye."

Was this ancient woman reading my mind?

"Uh, I don't know if you could say that I'm *lucky*." I gave a fierce tug to the rope holding my hands secure and kicked out with my bound ankles—Inez was proficient at knots.

"Your eyes are open," said Aunnie, "but you do not see. Well, give it time."

"What are you talking about?"

She pulled the sheet up to Jin's chin—who I swear was actually dead—and was about to say more but instead cocked her head to the side and perked up her ears. "No more questions. Someone is coming."

I didn't hear a thing. But sure enough, within seconds the door flew open, and standing in the entrance haloed by the afternoon sunlight were two Raiders.

"What's this about?" Aunnie was not pleased with the interruption.

"Cap'n wants the girl back in her cage," said the tallest one.

"*The girl's* name is Evangeline, and you shall address her as such. Now off you go. The preparations are not yet complete." Aunnie rose to her full height of four feet.

"I need to follow orders," said one of the men as he stepped fully into the shack.

Aunnie moved in front of him and stared up. "If you touch her, Samson Jaron Pickers, I will put you over my knee and spank that flabby heiney of yours so hard you won't sit for a week."

Samson Jaron Pickers paused mid-motion, eyeing Aunnie, conflict pulling his thick eyebrows together. "But I've Cap'n's orders, Aunnie. I can't disobey *her*."

"You're not disobeying, you moronic dumbass. You can take Evangeline when I'm done with the preparations, and you can tell Vera to come and talk to me if she has a problem with that."

"But—"

Aunnie glared so hard at Samson Jaron Pickers that he shut his mouth, bowed, and left with the other man in tow.

"Well, I guess we better get on with it," Aunnie said as the door shut.

I wished this woman would make sense. "Get on with what?"

"Ack. Playing dumb doesn't suit you, Evangeline Quillene. Now put this in your mouth."

Cold, withered hands practically jammed a dirty stick between my teeth, cutting off all my questions. My pant leg was rolled up, and that familiar glint of light from the medicine case caught my breath.

"Rowan's late," Aunnie said before she jabbed my leg with the needle and injected the blue liquid. "Which is odd, because he's never late. Never."

47   KITKUN

At your temples, leave flowers at the feet of the God of War, stones at the feet of the Goddess of Fertility, and thorns at the feet of the God of Love, for this confuses the God of Chaos.

— THE BOOK OF IMATLA

I discovered that there were things besides tracking that Hanuk was good at; he had the uncanny ability to sense where every slithering creature was, no matter how high up it hung in the trees and then kill it in one breath with his blow dart. Navigation came easy to him too, quickly deciphering north from south even though the sun was directly overhead. And he could climb trees like a cat and move through them like a monkey.

I had every reason to be scared of Hanuk. But I wasn't.

I wasn't, I wasn't, I wasn't…

At the sound of voices, Hanuk was up in the trees before I was. We were just outside Eva's camp, now silently watching two men drag an injured woman they called Amari to their shelter. Even though she was hunched over, Amari's size was impressive. She was taller than Hanuk, had a sturdy build, and despite her obvious injuries, did not appear physically frail. I could see the intense curiosity come across Hanuk's face as he watched her, sniffing the air when she passed beneath us. I half expected him to spit-shine his puffed-up chest.

He was ridiculous.

"You've known about these people for a while, Kitkun?" he asked once we climbed back down and they were out of earshot.

I nodded.

"They are the bringers of the firestick?"

I nodded again.

"Have you seen them with any other strange objects?"

The eager tone in Hanuk's voice made me nervous. "No. I promise."

With a deep breath he drew his ridiculously oversized blade and absentmindedly wiped it on his leg, which I'd come to learn was something he did when he was thinking. I could practically smell his thoughts igniting and fizzling out over and over.

"We must find out if they have any other objects. Do you have a weapon, Kitkun?"

The hair rose on the back of my neck. "Of course," I muttered.

"Good. Then maybe you can regain some of the pride you lost when you allowed your father to die," he said.

Low blow. I felt the horror of that day deep in my gut. How badly I wanted to show Hanuk with my bare hands around his neck just how much pride I had retained…

But I dutifully bowed my head.

"How many strangers have you seen? Did you count them?" he asked.

"Just five or six. Six, I think. Not sure."

Hanuk knew I didn't have a knack for numbers and let out a huff, not caring if I was right or wrong. Killing ten people or less was easy for him, so it didn't matter anyway. "We'll eliminate them all, huntress Kitkun, and you will rise in ranks at my side. You will follow my lead. Do exactly as I command."

My mouth fell open wide enough for a fly to brush my molars. "What? No. No… you can't kill them, they're people like we are and—"

"They are a threat to our way of life, Kitkun."

Hanuk began marching ahead so I ran to catch up, carelessly snagging my forearm on a bush of thorns. Ignoring a stinging line of beading blood, I lunged and grabbed him.

He spun to face me, throwing me off. "Do not be a fool, Huntress. This must be done."

I said the only thing that came to mind. "Then you'll anger the rest of them, and they'll come for you. They'll come for all of us and—"

I was shoved so hard I fell back on my butt. A very angry Hanuk straddled me, his words spitting venom. "I thought you said there were only six. What aren't you telling me?"

"Only *six* at the camp those two men were taking that injured woman to. On the north beach, there are, um… more. Many more. And they—the sea people, well they call themselves Raiders—they… well, they, um…"

"Out with it!"

My mind raced. "They have the gods on their side. I've seen it. They walk right into the sea and come right back out." The pressure of Hanuk's body on mine eased up a bit, so I continued. "We cannot risk angering the God of the Sea. The blood we would pay for that would be far too great."

"The God Idis is on their side?" he muttered to himself, eyes glassy. His nostrils flared and spittle hit me in the forehead when he spoke. "Take me to them, Kitkun," he said. "I must see this with my own eyes."

As I led this heinous, ruthless, despicable, power-hungry maniac toward the sea people, I hoped for their sake that the gods truly *were* on their side.

 48 KADE

Today I broke it off with Holly because she didn't fit into my agenda. There were tears in her eyes when she told me that someday I would find the person who would shove me off course and obliterate everything I thought I knew, and I laughed in her face. She must think me weak. But I've learned that I am anything but.

— JOURNAL ENTRY, KADE, AGE 17

With the sun high in the sky, we had minimal shadows to keep to. Beast, with his flaming red hair and beard, was silent and stealthy, but his sheer size was hard to hide. Max was a ball of fury, so full of rage he was reckless. At least my marks were content for the moment, allowing me to move unhindered. But I knew that could change in a breath.

Circling wide through the jungle to avoid being noticed, we came to where we'd rescued Prominus. Things seemed strangely lax at the Raiders camp. Guards were no longer posted every few feet around the perimeter, and the fires were merely red coals. We found a group of men clearing more land and building what seemed like an animal pen, and another group playing cards in the shade of a tree.

"Something don't feel right," said Beast.

Indeed, it didn't.

We snuck across a trail leading into a small clearing of tall grasses and dropped flat to the ground when we heard voices getting closer. Two Raiders were dragging a felled tree out of the bush and were too involved in their conversation to notice us hiding merely a few feet away.

"Do you really think that girl killed the Grakke brothers?" said one of them, grunting with exertion.

"Ha, nope," answered the other.

They were talking about Eva, and I had to put my hand on Max's shoulder to remind him to be still.

"The fight tomorrow should be interesting, regardless," said the man closest to us. "I put money on the girl lasting about four minutes before Prominus tears her apart."

"Four minutes? I give her sixty seconds in the arena, total. I mean, you saw what Prominus did to Amari, and she'd take the two of us in a fight. Just sayin'."

There was a huff. Branches snapped. A huge spider crawled past my nose. The breeze carried the scent of the latrine toward us.

"Yeah, but Prominus took Amari by surprise," said the Raider in the lead, breathing heavily. "If Rowan traveled inland for this Eva girl, she must be an exceptional fighter. He's good at picking them."

"True, but Prominus has the advantage of having no morals whatsoever. So, I'm still going to keep my bet at sixty seconds."

Their voices trailed off as they walked past.

"They're building an arena," whispered Beast. "That's what the pen be for."

"Yeah," said Max. "And Eva will be the first to die in it if we don't do something. Now."

I tried to gather my thoughts, but it wasn't easy with two yapping mouths and the jungle noise clouding up my head. "Shut up and let me think."

Max sat up and flexed his arms, cracking his knuckles as if preparing to fight. "There's no time for thinking."

"What do you suggest, Max?"

"Kill everyone."

"That's stupid," I retorted.

Beast said nothing.

Max fastened his hair back behind his head, sweat pouring in rivers down his cheeks. "They're throwing Eva to the wolves, so why shouldn't I rage my way in and start swinging? If I kill enough of them, including Prominus, I can at least eliminate some spectators and Eva's opponent."

"They'll just find someone to replace him," I said.

"Well, better safe than sorry."

Max made to leave so I grabbed him by the shoulder and slammed him to the ground. The punk was wily and solid, but he wasn't trained like I was. He swore as I pressed my knees to his back and pulled his arm tight behind him.

"If you get caught, we're screwed," I hissed close to his ear. "You need to be a part of this team, Max, and that means you must follow my orders or it's your throat that will be slit next. Understand? I'm not about to let your idiocy cost us our lives, especially Eva's. So, if I say sit, you sit. If I say move, you move. Got it?"

"Yes, sir."

The respectful tone in Max's voice wasn't what I was expecting.

"It's about time you took control," he added. "I was having doubts about you."

It was all I could do not to slam his pretty, freckled face into the ground. "For now, we wait. We sit here and do nothing until we can move under the cover of dark." I moved off of Max, sat back, and put my arms around my knees. A bird was singing like it was a lovely day in paradise. If I wasn't concerned with being caught, I'd throw a knife at it. "Then we free Eva," I said, stating the obvious, drawing in a deep breath to steady my nerves. "And, Max—"

He raised an eyebrow, a slight grin cocked on his face as if he knew what I was about to say. "Yes?"

"Once we get Eva safe, you can kill them all."

Waiting was infuriating, and the setting sun couldn't have come fast enough. We snuck back around to the far end of the Raiders' beach where the tent for their dead still stood. There were no fires lit and no one was guarding souls, but I had a feeling Rowan would show. So, we watched. Counted the seconds until the stars came out. Then, suddenly, without any warning, the sky started to blow apart with streaks of color. Was Atomica attacking and setting the island on fire? Was I too late and it had weaponized? Had I failed the Nihila and Mother Earth? I was ready, every muscle coiled and about to spring…but my marks remained quiet.

"What the hell is going on?" Max cowered behind me.

Patterns of dizzying colors exploded through the sky with near-deafening popping sounds.

"Ah, it just be fireworks," said Beast casually.

Fireworks?

"For celebration," Beast clarified. "They be small bombs of sorts that get lit on fire and shot up into the sky where they can blow up. Fun stuff, really. They be harmless to us here on the ground. It's just for show."

This was *not* the work of Atomica.

Thank the stars.

Although the sound was loud and unnerving, the sky danced with a spectacular array of colors and patterns of light. Max stared open-mouthed with the wonder of a child, barely able to look away.

"What the heck are they celebrating?" he mused.

There was a cacophony of angry voices followed by more explosions that didn't produce a light show overhead but shot hazardously into the trees. A palm tree turned into a massive candle.

"Oh, somebody screwed up," said Beast.

And it was then that I clued in to what was actually happening.

"Rowan is creating a diversion..." I said, and left the shadows of the trees to head out onto the beach.

Max and Beast stood guard on the cold sand while I snuck up next to the tent that housed the dead. Listening closely for signs of life, I heard nothing, so I crouched low to the ground and rounded the corner to the front entrance—only to come face to face with Rowan.

His eyes were wider than usual and he seemed out of breath.

"Took you long enough, Kade Thorn." He looked up and down the beach somewhat nervously. The flames overtaking the palm tree were climbing to towering heights as fireworks showered the sky. "You look like hell."

"And you may have set the island on fire."

"Amari?" he asked.

"She's back at our camp with Dominic and others. They're tending to her."

"And who is with you hiding in the trees?" he asked intuitively.

"Two that are willing to do whatever it takes to rescue Eva. Which I hope you have a plan for."

Rowan nodded and motioned for me to enter the tent. I brushed the canvas flap aside and walked in expecting to see nothing but the empty bed Eva had once occupied, but many faces stared back at me instead.

"What the—?"

"Your people," Rowan clarified. "I promised Evangeline that I would free them, and so I have."

Three women, all clutching each other and shaking like they were facing the hangman's noose, stared at me with eyes as big as plates. Their clothes were torn, hair dirty, and one had blisters all over her arms. Worse yet, three blokes that were in the hold with me and Eva on the ship wore expectant expressions beneath their bruised faces, and all appeared close to fainting. Plus, smelling like rotting chicken stew and looking just as awful, were five young lads—no, make that six, one was skinny enough to hide behind another—all gleaming with sweat and as terrified as the women.

"Kids?" I glared at Rowan. "Are you joking?"

"They're all yours," Rowan clarified.

Did he think I was a babysitter?

While many unblinking eyes watched my stunned expression morph into anger, I had a difficult time refraining from punching Rowan right in the face. What the hell was he thinking? I didn't want anything to do with these people. They were not "mine," and I didn't have time to waste on them. I had to free Eva and find Atomica and not worry about anything else.

"Take them to your camp, Kade Thorn. You have four more minutes before their disappearance is noticed," Rowan said. "I cannot yet get to the boy the captain has taken a liking to, but I will. There is another man, but he—"

"Isn't this sort of bad timing?" I interjected.

"There is nothing you can do for Evangeline. They've put her in a cage on the edge of our clearing—which looks like it might be accessible from one side but it's a trap. Captain Vallerik knows you will come for her, and she is waiting. You must go back to your camp and stay there."

"Stay there? And just let you look after Eva?"

Rowan nodded. "Yes. Three minutes. Go."

"What aren't you telling me, Rowan?"

His eyes shifted downward briefly. "I promised her your safety too."

Of course. Eva, in her impending doom, would be worried about me.

My heart burst in my chest with the desire to hold her, keep her safe from everything and everyone—and my marks stabbed at me fiercely. "She'll never win against Prominus."

"I know. I will stop it somehow."

"How?"

"That, I'm not sure of, but I will find a way. Now go. Lead your people to safety."

How could I walk away from Eva? I couldn't. My feet simply wouldn't move.

Noticing this, one of the women took a few tentative steps toward me. When I simply stared and did nothing, she came closer and dropped to my feet.

"We are forever in your debt, Kade Thorn. Thank you for saving us."

Ugh. Ridiculous! I had saved no one, only strayed so far from my purpose my name should be taken from me.

Fuming, I pulled her upright and clutched her by the shoulders as if to shake some sense into her, but her big blue eyes sought mine and all at once my heart felt something it shouldn't. Sympathy? Regret? I could have been looking down at Holly, telling her I could never see her again, watching the color drain from her face as I broke her heart. What the hell was wrong with me?

Oh, right. I was human. Sorry, Mother.

"Can all of you walk?" I asked, releasing my grip on the woman and addressing the misfits all blinking back at me with great expectation.

"Yes," was the collective reply from all but the skinniest of the boys. His feet were a mess and he was so short he'd only slow us down.

"We have a camp, but it's a long trek through the jungle. You all must help each other along the way and not utter a single word during the journey." I looked at the small boy, wishing his desperate appearance didn't affect me so. "Name?"

He muttered something unintelligible.

I motioned for him forward. "Come here." The poor kid trembled, thinking he was in trouble, and I was right; his feet could barely hold him up.

"Is this really how you treat children?" I hissed at Rowan, now wanting to punch him for an entirely different reason.

"This child was worse before we took him. We found him in a back alley tossed in the trash in Port Hayes like garbage, nearly dead. I guess that's how you treat *your* people."

I had no words. None.

So, I reached down for the kid and hefted him up onto my hip like I'd seen mothers do with their kids. Except I had no hip. So I swung him around onto my back and told him that if he let go I'd leave him for the centipedes and wild boars to chew on. Skinny legs wrapped around me and tightened in fear when we marched into the trees to where Beast and Max stood in shock to greet us. As I began leading the way to camp, my marks burned and I quietly reminded them that this was part of the plan. The more people on my side, the more chances I had of finding and eliminating Atomica.

But it was complete crap.

49 EVANGELINE

I was imagining what the sky might look like with the fireworks going off, flat on my back in the healer's shack, flexing and tensing my leg—which almost felt brand new—when Terens was brought into the shack with burns on his hands. His pals were having a good laugh at his expense as Aunnie ordered him to sit down on an empty bed.

"How come your boys were able to drag a crate of fireworks out of the ocean, but a chest of medical supplies that could save us all is lost to the fishes?" Aunnie complained, inspecting his blistered skin.

Only the shaved sides of Teren's head didn't turn pink with embarrassment. He had scrapes on his cheeks and thick neck, and a bandage around an ankle that he favored. "I told you, Aunnie, some things didn't survive the storm. Many crates were smashed—"

"Ugh, just shut up, Terens. The only person who likes the sound of your voice is you."

I could have listened to this old woman insult people all day long and had to laugh—which wasn't missed by Terens. His beady black eyes practically lasered a glare right through me. He was so mad that I had to laugh again.

"Why is she still here and not back in the cage like Captain Vallerik requested?" he asked as Aunnie applied ointment and bandages to his hands.

"And why are you so clumsy?" she shot back. "Accidentally setting off a crate of fireworks? You could have set the whole jungle on fire, you know."

Terens gulped audibly. "I'm not clumsy. We dried the fireworks out but that makes them chemically imbalanced and—"

"I think you're the one who is chemically imbalanced. Why Vera keeps you around is beyond me," Aunnie said, and I bet she was the only one who got away with calling Captain Vallerik by her first name. "Now, off you go. Keep your wounds clean and your nose out of trouble, Terens."

Terens stood and his foot caught in the corner of the blanket, almost sending him to the floor. Aunnie tossed up her hands in dismay and I couldn't suppress another chuckle.

Face twisted with rage, Terens spun to face me. "You go ahead and have your laugh now, because I'm going to have the last one when that brute rips into you tomorrow."

"At least I'll die fighting with honor and not because I tripped over my own feet," I said.

Terens growled and drew his knife. He lifted his arm, ready to stab me through the heart.

"More idiocy, Terens? Really?" asked Aunnie.

Terens' hand began to shake, but he lowered the knife.

"Ah. That's the first good move you've made all day. Keep it up and—" Aunnie stopped mid-sentence, eyelids fluttering. "Uh oh. Something has happened."

Bursts of yelling came from outside and the shack door swung open.

"The Aldirans have escaped," said a breathless female, cheeks mottled and just as red as Terens'. "All of them. Cap'n's pissed. Your presence is required."

I couldn't hide the sudden shiver of excitement that ran through me. Had Rowan come through? Had he freed my people? Funny, I initially had just wanted numbers; people to help me find Zoleya or become potential Guardians. Now, I was truly elated for no other reason than their safety.

Maybe I'd done something right?

My smile was uncontrollably wide... until Terens got on his knees and clutched my jaw so tightly I thought my bones might actually snap. I was surprised by his strength and tried my best not to show fear.

"I know it was you," he hissed. "But how did you make that happen *from in here?*" His black eyes searched mine, breath hot on my cheeks. "You had some help. Care to elaborate?"

I tried to spit at him but his grip only tightened.

"No matter." He let go. Stood. "I'll have your people back here by dawn. Well, pieces of them anyway." He yanked open the door and disappeared into the night.

The body on the bed not far from mine—the person I thought was dead—jerked upright.

"I hate that guy," he said, wiping drool from the corners of his mouth.

I instantly liked this skinny non-dead person whom Aunnie referred to as Jin. "Me too."

"Terens is a poop-smear on a buzzard's arse," said Aunnie.

And I decided I liked her, too.

I was back in the cage. The moon was full and bright, and the fires roared as Raiders went about their duties, eager to be ready for the fight tomorrow. I wished I was back at camp with Beast and Kade, but the metal bars meant to hold livestock were unbendable and the gaps were too small to fit through.

Flicking away a crawly thing, I tried to get comfortable. At night the jungle came to life, and tonight green bugs gravitated toward my cage, hard-shelled critters that were sort of scaly like fish. They didn't bite, but that only meant something that did would come for them.

Sure enough, a green snake slithered past, eyeing me before gulping down some victims. It was all I could do to not scream, instead repeating the words Kitkun had said to me when we'd first spoken;

everything green—except the toad with the bloodshot eyes—is pretty much harmless.

Harmless. Yes, I had much more to worry about than a hungry little reptile.

"Ha. I'm locked up with a snake and I'm not having a complete meltdown," I said out loud to no one.

The snake slithered closer to me now that the bugs were gone. There was nothing to distract it from the sweating defenseless girl with a phobia of its kind. However, as if understanding my fear, it moved to the farthest corner and coiled up, facing away from me. How odd.

When I managed to get my heart rate to slow, I tried to tune it out, as well as the Raiders who had begun buzzing around me like flies on honey.

"You excited for the big event?" said one of them, marching up to the cage and banging some sort of tool against the bars. His teeth were brown and cracked, and a long scar ran down his arm. He was young, maybe Rowan's age, and could have been good-looking despite the teeth if he weren't wearing such an ugly expression.

The clanging sound was deafening. I tried to ignore him but he swung again, even getting some irritated responses from his peers, who were gathered around the fire.

"I'm on watch tonight," he said, spitting his words. "I don't need to sleep, so maybe I'll keep you company."

He swung at the cage again. I gripped handfuls of the earth to keep from cowering at the sound, and the snake began to crawl over my hand. I could not show fear, not now when that was exactly what this Raider wanted.

The man was spitting insults, and the snake was now curling around my wrist.

Green things are safe… green things are safe…

I took in a deep breath and slowly got to my feet, hand with the snake behind my back. I prayed the thing wouldn't crawl up into my hair as I fought to conceal the panic in my voice.

"Are you pestering me because you're jealous?" I said to the young man, and his comrades around the fire fell silent.

"Jealous?" he scoffed. "Jealous of what?"

"My bravery. My strength. Yeah, that's right; you know you couldn't withstand two minutes in the arena with Prominus. You'd shit your pants before your weapon was even drawn. I can see it all over your chubby baby face."

He grabbed hold of the bars of the cage, the tool he'd been banging it with falling to the ground. "Come a little closer, bitch, and get a better look at my face."

Perfect. I would do just that.

I moved forward with my hands in front of me, and the snake, sensing the true threat, turned its head toward the Raider, who was too focused on his hate to notice the green creature hissing in his direction. This man was hell-bent on grabbing a lock of my hair so he could tug it violently and give my face a good slam into the bars—I'd learned that trick early on in life—so I got close enough for him to do just that. But before he could grab me, I thrust my hand forward with the snake, and the little creature lashed out, its fangs striking the guard's nose with alarming accuracy and speed.

I put my hands back behind me.

The guard stumbled back, screeching in pain. "Bitch! You *bitch!*"

"See? I don't even have to touch my enemy to make him fall! Is anyone next?" I yelled, hoping the snake wouldn't bite me now— harmless? I think not.

The guard was off and marching to the shack, no doubt to receive medical help from Aunnie. Snake unseen and not knowing exactly what happened to their pal, the others now kept a respectful distance from the cage.

I was shaking in my boots as I got back onto my knees and lowered the snake to the ground. I thanked her silently and hoped she would just slither away, but she returned to the corner, eyeing me as I eyed her.

"Nice trick," said a thin voice. The young man who eerily resembled Rowan stared down at me, white as a ghost and paper thin. "Not many people know how to use a snake as a weapon."

"They're easy maintenance," I said with a smile that I didn't feel.

"Makes sense." He moved closer and kneeled before me to get to eye level. "We weren't properly introduced in the shack. I'm Jin, but then again, you knew that. Aunnie told you a bit about me. You thought I was dead."

As he spoke, the oils Aunnie had coated him with wafted in closely. "I'm Eva."

"Pleasure."

Jin's voice was similar to Rowan's but lacked his authoritative tone, and perhaps his consonants rolled off his tongue a little slower. With golden blond hair that was slightly frizzy and similar gray eyes that were alert and blazing, even in the dim light I knew I was looking at a sibling.

"I'm a twin," said Jin. "Two minutes younger."

There were sideways glances from the men at the fire in Jin's direction, and I couldn't help but feel worried for him. He seemed so fragile, like he might break in half with a stiff breeze.

"Should you be talking to me, Jin?"

He glanced back at the men. "They won't lay a hand on me as long as my brother is alive," he said proudly.

"Rowan," I choked out in a weak whisper.

"The one and only." He gave me a gentle smile. "I must say… your leg is looking much better. It should be fully healed by the morning."

My pants covered my leg. "How do you know what my leg looks like?" I asked, and the snake in the corner seemed to lift her head in curiosity.

Jin blushed, or the addition of logs on the fire cast him in an orange hue. "I'll admit, I have seen a lot of you," he said sheepishly.

Aunnie mentioned that Jin didn't miss a thing even though he appeared dead. I thought it was the senseless blabbering of an old woman. But…

"How is that possible?" I asked.

Jin shrugged his shoulders. "I, uh… don't know. I see a lot. More than I should." He stared at his feet a moment then lowered his voice into a whisper. "I'm glad Rowan is helping you."

"As am I. Your brother is a good man, Jin."

"Yes. I'm glad you think so."

"Do you know where he is?"

Jin paused a moment, eyelids fluttering. "Uh... no."

I spoke as softly as I could. "Tell me something, Jin; does Rowan like to torment Terens? Does he do things like dig holes outside Terens' tent so he can twist an ankle? Or somehow set off fireworks so that Terens could be blamed?"

Jin smiled deviously and whispered, "Maybe."

I laughed inwardly.

"But don't tell Terens. He's a bit of a poor sport."

I nodded. "The secret is safe with me."

Jin seemed to be craving company, just as I was. So I scrambled for small talk. Dug around for a question to keep him with me.

"So... do you decide to become a Raider? Or is it forced upon you?"

His smile faltered—oops. Wrong question.

"We are born into this life. Chosen by blood." Jin rose to his feet and made to leave.

"Wait... do you know who Alexander is? He's a Raider in your tribe."

Jin stumbled back like I'd hit him, eyes growing wide. "You've met Alexander?"

He knew exactly who I was talking about. My heart beat madly. "Yes."

Jin paled, if that was even possible. "Uh... that snake is still in the cage with you, by the way."

He was trying to change the subject. Maybe Jin didn't 'see' things while he was unconscious, maybe he was a Sage like Zoleya, and was able to see through the eyes of others. Maybe Jin was Alexander.

"Please, Jin, is it you? Are you Alex—"

I didn't get a chance to finish my question when a voice like a thunderstorm bellowed from the shack. It was Aunnie yelling at Jin to 'get his skinny butt back into bed or she'd lay a whippin' on him like he'd never forget'.

"She loves me. She'd never hurt me," Jin said with a forced smile.

Then he turned and walked away.

50 EVANGELINE

I could feel a Sage pressing against my mind and quickly made sure I was lying flat on the ground—but it wasn't Zoleya. Alexander pulled me into the Between, his indigo light rushing to envelop me in a blanket of comfort.

"I know who you are," I said right away, getting to the point.

His light pulsed. *You do?*

"Yes. Don't play games with me. You were just here."

He tensed. *I do not play games.*

"Just tell me I'm right then. Verify who you are."

I can't. It wouldn't be safe. For you or me.

"But Aunnie knows, right? That's why she protects you."

How do you—

"And your twin… he protects you."

My twin? Who do you think I am, Eva?

"Jin."

Oh, he replied, seeming disappointed.

"Am I wrong?" I asked. "I mean, it makes sense that—"

I felt Zoleya. Her light was rushing toward us, and I was racing for her, pulling away from Alexander without any hesitation. Our connection was a rainbow of color blowing apart like a bomb, bundles of light like thunderbolts. I met Zoleya wholeheartedly with chaos, relief, and overwhelming delight, allowing her to immediately rummage through my thoughts and go through my memories. In seconds she learned what I'd gone through and where I was on Earth, while quickly investigating the Sage sharing the space with us.

Meanwhile, Alexander's light shifted around Zoleya like a dog sniffing a rear-end, trying to figure her out.

"This is Alexander," I told Zo, even though she already knew that.

If this wasn't awkward, I didn't know what was.

Like a mother's arms, protecting and shielding, Zo seemed to fold her light into a concrete box around me, keeping Alexander at bay.

Who are you, really? she asked him.

Alexander's light grew brighter, and he boldly pressed up against Zoleya, which, to my surprise, made her dim ever so slightly—he was demonstrating his power. *I am as Eva says. And you are?*

I am someone who also cares very much about Evangeline. Zoleya seemed angry, which was an emotion from her I'd yet to encounter. It made me wonder if she'd gotten too much sunlight in the physical realm and wasn't under control. *You must leave her alone. You are putting her in danger.*

She needs me, Alexander replied, and I could feel his energy shift and grow stronger. *And I would never bring her any harm.*

Don't make me force you to go, Zo warned.

"Uh, do I have a say in this?" I asked but was ignored.

The two Sages pressed up against each other, and I wondered what a fight would look like in this realm.

I can see through her eyes, said Alexander. *I can control her body. Can you?*

Zoleya froze, all color and light ceasing to move. *No... that's not possible, only—*

I could feel Alexander gather strength and display it in a way that seemed to fill every space of the vast darkness with his indigo light. Zoleya released me from her hold, and to my surprise, she shrank away.

It's you that must leave, Alexander demanded.

He is right, Evangeline. I'm sorry, but I will come to you another way...

Then, with what seemed like a massive pulse of energy, he shoved Zo away, and faster than I could think, her light disappeared.

And her sudden absence was excruciating.

I felt myself unraveling. Yelling inwardly. Swearing in the freaky realm, which felt a whole lot of right and wrong in the most ridiculously inexplicable way. Alexander remained distanced from me. We were two separate beings hovering in the Between, now wary of each other.

Nobody can be trusted, he said once I had calmed down.

He was right—himself included.

"I don't want to be here anymore." I was angry. I wanted Zoleya back more than I wanted to know the identity of this Sage who had just acted like a schoolyard bully. "That other Sage… she…" I couldn't say another word about Zoleya. I was putting her in danger every time this male got anywhere near my memories. "You know what? No. It doesn't matter. Just leave me alone!"

Suddenly I was back in my body.

The snake had curled up on my chest and was hissing at a guard who was poking me to see if I was still alive. I had no energy left to be afraid of it.

The fire crackled loudly, and the Raiders' voices softly carried through the night. Eventually, they grew bored of tormenting me, and the only company that remained was the snake. I risked touching it. I ran a finger along its back and it couldn't have cared less—which just wasn't normal.

"Zoleya?" I said softly, finally clueing in.

She'd watched me through butterflies, dragonflies, and maybe a mouse once or twice. Why not a snake?

I nearly laughed out loud when the snake moved its head up and down in a nodding motion.

"You had to visit me in the form of my nemesis?"

The snake stuck out its tongue in reply.

"I appreciate you coming to check on me. And just so you know, I'm not aware of the physical identity of that male Sage, Alexander, but I told him to leave me alone. I think… well, I'm pretty sure he'll respect that."

"Making friends with the jungle creatures, I see," said Rowan.

I hadn't noticed him approach the cage. I sat up and the snake slithered off my chest. Even though I knew Zo was in control of the scaly creature, I wasn't disappointed with the distance.

"Oh. Well… *snakes*. You know how they are."

Rowan smiled weakly, his fear for me overriding any actual joy. "No, I do not know snakes. Well, except for a few human ones."

"Like Terens?"

Rowans couldn't hide his dislike. "Yes. One of the worst." He looked over his shoulder at the men gathered by the fire. The noise had died down and they were doing their best to try and eavesdrop. "I'm going to get you out of there. Okay?" he said, voice barely a whisper. "You won't have to fight Prominus."

I felt a burst of hope. "How?"

He winked. "I just have to get the key, create another diversion, and then you can run."

"Well, that sounds easy."

"Yes." His fingers gripped the cage as though he might rip it in half, then, remembering he was being watched, he let go, stood back, and crossed his arms over his chest.

"Was that you… the fireworks?"

His eyes flickered mischievously in the dim light. "Yes."

I felt my throat close up. He was risking a lot for me. "My people?"

"Are with Kade Thorn."

I felt immense relief. "Thank you."

He nodded, gaze holding mine, and I could see him… *him*… not the commander, not the legendary killer, but the true person he was behind his mask.

"And after I escape, what about you?" I asked.

"What about me?"

How and when had I gone from wanting to kill him to being worried that I might never see him again? "Don't you want to be free, too?"

"Free of…?"

I spoke as quietly as I could. "This life you were born into. I mean, we're somewhere where we can make our own choices now and not be told how we must live."

His face darkened. "These are *my* people, Eva."

"I, uh… *we,* could be your people instead."

The thought was spoken the moment it came to my mind, and I should have kept it to myself.

Rowan's voice lowered, and gone was any warmth or kindness from his face. "I am a Raider," he said after a long moment. "By choice."

"I can see through your façade, though. You're no killer. You're not this scary monster that Aldirans tell stories about around campfires. You're—"

"Stop. That's enough."

My chest tightened. He eyed the snake, then spoke over my head to the jungle so his eyes would not meet mine.

"When it's time, you run. You go back to Kade Thorn and remain strong. You build walls. You protect yourself and your people, and you do what you do best, Evangeline."

He was walking away, and I felt a bit sick. "And what might that be?"

"Fight."

51 KADE

— JOURNAL ENTRY, KADE, AGE 14

I was winded by the time I made it back to the Raiders' camp, sweat running off my skin in rivers. I'd snuck away from Beast and the others and headed back to enemy territory because Rowan's instructions to stay away and let him handle things weren't sitting right. I couldn't leave Eva to the wolves, and sitting around babysitting a bunch of kids was ridiculous. So, I decided I would act as backup somehow in case Rowan couldn't get Eva free.

Since morning was approaching, I snuffed out my torch and left it on the edge of what seemed like a small meadow just outside of the Raiders' camp. Thinking I was alone, I carefully moved through the tall grasses and almost walked into the backside of a Raider standing guard at the perimeter. His head whipped around just as his hand raised his weapon, but I was quicker, and with the lingering shadows of night on my side, plunged my blade into his heart.

The man fell dead at my feet, and I was surprised by the sudden onslaught of disgust I felt for myself. It had been nothing to kill him. I hadn't even hesitated or bothered to counter his move with another that would simply render him unconscious. I realized as I stared down at the man that he and I shared common ground; he was simply doing what was expected of him, as was I.

This thought caught and held, making me wonder who was in control; me, or the hunter that the Nihila had bred me to be? And what did that mean for Eva or those I decided to care about? What would happen to them if I fulfilled my destiny? What would happen to them if I didn't?

I heard a group of Raiders returning from a search party, so I got down on my knees, feeling the warmth of the dead man's blood on my feet. Hopefully I blended into the dark of the grass just out of reach of their torchlight.

The Raiders were frustrated. They'd been trying to track me and Amari but were completely defeated. Raiders knew currents, tides, ships, and storms, but they didn't have a nose for land. Tracking was beyond them. The group of people I'd taken back to camp were clumsy and loud, and the stink of them alone would have led any Aldiran worth their weight right to them—but these Raiders were comically hopeless.

There were two men ahead of me and two behind. Another group of Raiders were heading back into the jungle to search for their missing prisoners, but they were venturing inland, which was completely in the wrong direction.

"Idiots," I said, then froze when something snapped to my right and a light brushed over my hand—someone else was in the meadow with me.

"Stimps?" said a husky voice. "Where you at?"

I crouched lower as the torchlight passed over me again, glinting off the fallen Raiders' knife. I knew it had alerted the man who was now coming my way, but I was ready. I'd take him down—but not kill him.

Ten feet. Eight feet. Four. Three… I lifted my arm, my knife aimed at the hard flesh of the man's thigh, but something blunt hit the back of my head and I fell forward. I was vaguely aware of a knee pressing into my back and something tightening around my neck as I fought to remain conscious.

"Got one!" said a female voice victoriously.

Even with my air being cut off, I could still fight. Propelling myself upright, I flung the female off my back and got to my feet. I grabbed at the rope around my neck, got hold of the free end, and yanked her toward me so I could slam my forehead into her nose. As she fell, I dodged whatever object was coming at my head again and started swinging, slamming my knuckles into jaws, chins, and throats. Three Raiders were down, and I sensed another one behind me. Spinning around, my elbow connected with a forehead, and I kept my footing even though a sudden sharp pain in my side took my breath. A blow with some sort of blunt weapon cracked one of my ribs as I saw a knife come at me, so, steadying myself, I dodged a strike and pinned the hand of its holder between my bicep and injured rib, then twisted the knife holder's arm outward before dropping to my knees. Then I slammed his wrist with the palm of my hand, snapping a few bones in his arm.

The Raider was screaming, and as I turned to run, I came face to face with five more of them, all armed to the teeth and snarling. I felt a power surge within me that was like nothing I'd ever felt before. I knew it was my marks, and the sensation that I could become nearly as lethal and devastating as Atomica was nearly crippling. Now, I fought not only the Raiders but the sudden realization that I was as unnatural as the abomination that nearly ended the Earth. We were one and the same.

"Stand down or the dogs will rip the Aldiran to shreds!" yelled one of the men who had retreated out of reach to stand behind his comrades, a coward with a tattooed head and wrapped ankle. "The girl. Evangeline. She's why you're here, isn't it?"

I threw someone off my back, and the knife in my hand jabbed a chest three times in rapid succession. I broke a man's neck and felt my muscles ripple with power as I knocked another two unconscious with a single blow—I could kill them all. Easily.

The coward barked. "If I don't return to my captain in three minutes, she will feed the girl to the dogs. And, as fast as you are, you'll never make it to her in time. Is that what you want?"

I willed my limbs to remain still as the group around me receded slightly. I could tell my marks were about to take over, and soon my hands would end up covered in blood, just as they had been when I made the journey to the Red Stone all those years ago. I couldn't put Eva's life in jeopardy.

"She's part of the plan!" I yelled at the marks, screamed actually, reminding them for the billionth time that Eva needed to be alive and they needed to release their hold on me. "Trust me."

The tattooed man simply looked amused by my outburst. "Plan? Right. Okay," he said, grinning.

And I was back to being just Kade, taking another hit to the ribs, feeling a rope being fashioned around my neck again, hands bound, knees kicked out from beneath me—and this time I did not fight back.

EVANGELINE

The first rays of morning sun broke through the eerily quiet camp, and everyone except the three guards watching me were still asleep. I was confused. Rowan said he was going to create a diversion and get me out of the cage, but now the cover of night was gone and he was nowhere to be seen. This wasn't good. Not good at all.

I eased upright and stretched my wounded leg, shocked to find no pain or swelling. It felt so sound I had to tug up my pantleg to see if I'd actually even been wounded; all that remained was a thick pink scar. Incredibly, the horrible wound on my foot was gone, too. What had Rowan injected me with? And why had he risked so much for me if he wanted me to run the second I was free? Why had he wasted such powerful medicine on someone he had no intentions with?

As the sun grew hotter and morning began slipping away, the camp slowly sprang to life. The two girls who had washed me the night before were back to wordlessly tidy my hair, clean my face, and force-feed me fish. Terens was back too, a horrible scowl on his face but thankfully no severed heads in his hands. I saw Jin wander out of the shack with Aunnie close behind him, and they headed for the beach without even a glance in my direction. Captain Vallerik sauntered by too, silver and gold jewelry shining as bright as her polished hair and silk black dress, weapons clanging around her waist and chest, not saying a word. For a moment, I wondered if I'd been forgotten about.

I felt the presence of Alexander pressing against my mind.

Evangeline?

I leaned back against the cage and closed my eyes, waiting to be taken from my body, still suspecting this was Jin. "Yes. The coast is clear."

Are you all right?

I could hear him—but I could still feel my body. How was this happening? I hadn't been taken to the other realm. I wasn't surrounded by his light, just vividly aware of his voice in my mind and the air around my physical body. "How are you doing this? How can I hear you and—"

Eva, I have no time for explanations. Just answer me; are you okay?

My body was tingling, waiting to be separated from my mind, but the vast expanse of the freaky realm never appeared, so I spoke out loud, unsure how to answer him any other way. "I am for the time being. Rowan was supposed to free me, but I haven't seen him."

There will be an opportunity any minute now for you to run. You must head in the opposite direction of the beach and go into the jungle. At the far end of camp there is a tent with a blue letter 'C' painted on the side. In it are provisions; water, food, and a knife. Take them and go.

"Alexander, my eyes are open right now. I can hear you in my mind and I haven't gone into that… other realm. Please, tell me who you—"

Colors burst vividly behind my eyes, canceling out the sun, canceling out the air as I was dragged into the Between at lightning speed.

I've no time for questions! Now, do you understand what I'm telling you?

His light was pulsing, shifting madly between every color of blue there was.

"Yes. The tent with the letter C. Got it."

I felt him exude relief, and the world came back into view.

Any minute now… he said.

Then he was gone from my mind.

And now I could smell smoke strong and thick, the wind bringing it inland from the beach. There was some sort of commotion coming from that direction too, voices shouting and one of the dogs I had yet to see barking, then yelping madly. The guards at my cage were standing and on full alert when Rowan strolled directly toward them looking like he hadn't slept in years. There was such ferocity on his face we all flinched. My breath hitched.

"I'm going to get the girl prepared for the fight. Unlock the cage," he demanded.

There was nothing familiar on his face. I could have been a worm on a hook and nothing more. I hoped his ice-cold demeanor was for the benefit of the guards and the few still gathered around the fire tending to boiling pots.

The young man who'd been bitten by the snake hesitated. "What's going on at the beach, Commander?" he asked, clearly on edge, nose swollen.

Rowan scowled. "I don't know. But you would probably be more useful there than standing around guarding this Aldiran. So go."

He did as he was told. The other two guards made quick work of taking me out of the cage and binding my wrists with rope and chaining my ankles.

"Is that necessary?" Rowan asked.

"Captain's orders," said the larger of the two. "She doesn't want to take a chance with this one."

"Ridiculous," Rowan said, then he roughly dragged me toward one of the fires where a woman sat sharpening knives. Reaching down, he dipped two fingers in the ash and dragged those two fingers from my hairline above my left eye, down to my jawline.

"That's not going to help her in the fight," said the woman.

"Maybe you'd like to take her place?" Rowan growled in reply.

The woman put her hands up in defense, then stood and marched off.

"What's going on at the beach?" I asked quietly, because now fragments of Captain Vallerik's voice could be heard, and it seemed like the entire camp had begun heading that way.

Ignoring me, Rowan fashioned some sort of thick leather strap across my chest. I noticed his hands were trembling ever so slightly. "You'll have two knives and a sword," he said robotically, loudly so anyone wanting to eavesdrop wouldn't have to strain too hard to hear. "They will be given to you at the start of the fight. Prominus will have the same."

Now there was booing and hissing coming from the beach, and the two guards keeping close to us had their weapons drawn.

"Okay?" I said, my curiosity piqued as well.

"We will go over the rules, and—" Now there was cheering, and Rowan was completely irritated by it. He turned to the guards. "Oh, for heaven's sake. Go see what is happening," he told them flippantly, and only the slight twitch at his jaw gave him away—he was nervous. Was this the diversion he was creating?

The largest of the men cleared his throat. "One of us must stay. Orders—"

Rowan drew his weapon and in a blink, it was trained on the guard's neck. "You take orders from me. Go or lose your head."

With a respectful nod, the man headed for the beach. The other followed.

And, it seemed that for the moment, we were alone.

"Now what?" I asked.

Rowan was leading me behind the healer's shack where he made quick work of unlocking the chains from my ankles and untying my wrists. "Now you run."

My feet would not move. I stared back at the gray eyes holding me captive far more than any cage ever could, because I knew that my disappearance would be blamed on him. He'd pay the price for my freedom.

He sensed my conflict. "Go, Evangeline. Most of the guards are on the beach. You must head for the jungle. Remember, in the tent marked with the letter C you will find—"

"What's going on here?" Terens had come around the corner of the shack, his head tipping to the side, his bandaged hand holding a kopis just like the one Rowan always had at his waist. I was startled by the interruption, but not as startled as I was by the fact that Rowan had repeated Alexander's words; *the tent marked with the letter C*. My mind was reeling.

"Just strategizing with my fighter," Rowan said quickly.

"Are you really?" Terens was skeptical, body tensing in alarm. "I think you have a soft spot for the girl. Were you thinking of letting her go, Commander? Because that would be treason."

Alexander's voice flooded my mind; *Run, Eva... please....*

I was stuck. Glued to the ground. Unable to move.

Rowan sighed heavily, trying to convey indifference, but I could see right through it. And so could Terens.

"Leave, Terens," he said. "I'm busy here and I'm sure you have a hole to fall into somewhere."

Terens noted my unshackled hands and feet and the key in Rowan's hand. "Traitor," he said, eyes lowering into a challenging glare. "I've known it for a long time, and now I finally have proof. You're a traitor!"

Rowan moved toward him, slowly drawing his blade and stepping in front of me. "Go, Eva."

"I knew it," Terens hissed. "Your little play-acting on the beach was ridiculous. I didn't buy it for a second. The mighty Rowan Alexander Vallerik bested by a simple Aldiran? Impossible."

Rowan was saying something and shoving me behind him, but all I heard was his name, his *full* name, and it slammed into me with the force of a tornado: Rowan *Alexander Vallerik?*

Rowan. Alexander. Vallerik.

"Dammit, Eva, you have to run!" The tremble in Rowan's hands was now in his voice.

I knew his secret.

I knew *him.*

And I couldn't leave. Oh, gods above and the devil below, I couldn't leave him. He would be tortured beyond all imagination. I had to act, and act fast.

I lunged for the knife at Rowan's waist and, in a move I'd practiced on Zo a thousand times, got behind him and had it pressed up against his throat in the blink of an eye.

"Gullible fool," I hissed loudly into his ear, hoping he wouldn't struggle. I could feel the muscles in him tense and knew that in seconds the knife could be turned on me if he decided to fight back. I could feel the power in him rippling like lightning ready to snap free of a storm cloud. "You men are all the same. A girl bats her eyelashes and you become putty in her hands."

Terens laughed and clapped his hands together. "Oh, come on. Do you think I believe that you're *playing* him, again? Haven't we done this already?"

Thank the stars Rowan didn't move. I could feel his heart pounding as I glared at Terens and sought some reply that would sound fierce, even though I was nearly melting against the body of the man I most certainly cared deeply for.

"I don't care what you believe, you hideous maggot."

"Hideous maggot? That's all you got?"

We'd caught the attention of Aunnie, who had come around to the back of the building. Our eyes met, and if I didn't know better, I'd think the old woman was encouraging me to keep up my act.

"Yeah," I said, shaking. "Actually, comparing you to a maggot is insulting to the maggot."

Aunnie giggled over that.

"What kind of idiot do you think I am?" Terens growled. "I know you're trying to piss me off so you can distract me from what's really going on here, and I'm not falling for it!"

I pressed the knife tighter against Rowan's neck, shaking so hard I was worried I might cut him. "You want to take a chance, Terens? Gamble with your commander's life? I'd like to see how that goes over with your darling captain. Who is also his mother, correct?"

By now we had the attention of a group of Raiders who had returned from the beach, and my opportunity to run had most certainly vanished—not that I would have anyway. So, I had to make this look good. I had to ensure that whatever I did, Rowan would not be perceived as a traitor.

"Now back off, Terens, or I'll kill him," I warned.

The grin left Aunnie's face as she tried to read my true intent while gauging Rowan's safety. "Let's all calm down," she said.

Terens' eyes lowered into a glare, singly focused on me. "You've got a thing for him, don't ya? He was setting you free and you didn't run because you're worried about the repercussions it would have on him. Ha! Oh, that's something. Here you are risking your life for no reason because you're both going to die."

You're going to have to cut me.

Alexander—Rowan's—voice slammed into my mind, and it was so overwhelming I almost dropped the blade.

Or better yet, kill me. You've got seconds, Evangeline…

"No," I said aloud, to Rowan, to Terens.

"Well, damn. I have no problem removing both your heads," Terens said, lifting his heavy blade and getting ready to swing it. "I mean, I'd rather see you suffer, Rowan, but if it has to end this way, so be it."

"Terens, you stupid sac of festering pus, drop that blade!" Aunnie ordered, and she marched right up in front of him despite the possibility of her head being removed from her body. "Do you think you're going to kill the captain's son? What in the dingbat depths of hell is wrong with you?"

"Stand down, Aunnie," Terens said, his shoulders heaving. "Rowan was about to let the girl go, and I'm—"

"And you're being an absolute idiot. She's got a knife to his neck and is clearly using him to try and escape. Have you rocks in your head? Did you snort some of that acid rain and it's fried your puny little brain? Now back off or I'll lay a whipping to ya you won't forget."

Four feet of gray hair and weathered skin became the most frightening thing I'd ever encountered. Terens was about to argue, but Aunnie put her hands on her hips and turned to the guards who had now gathered behind me and Rowan. "And what about you idiots? Are you all just going to stand there while your commander gets his throat slit by our main attraction? He obviously doesn't want to damage her before the fight, so please be careful as well and don't create any reason to postpone the event. I've been looking forward to it all morning."

The men were slow to approach, and I was doing my best to look crazed, like I might truly cut Rowan. They were trying to figure out a way to remove me from him—gently.

"They're faking! This is all bullshit," yelled Terens.

Cut me... Rowan said into my mind. *Make it deep.*

"Fake. Fake! Traitor!" Terens wouldn't shut up. The guards hesitated, all ears. More people had gathered. Terens kept yelling, pointing out that my hands were untied, and quickly starting a ripple of speculation through his people. I saw Captain Vallerik heading our way, someone quickly filling her in on what was transpiring, and the look in her eyes was pure evil. She would do worse to Rowan, her own son, than simply banish him from camp like she'd done to Amari—her daughter.

Aunnie will heal me... Rowan said. *If you truly wish to save me, do it. Do it now!*

The old woman was staring at me, and ever so slightly, she gave me a nod.

So, I dragged the blade across Rowan's throat.

53 EVANGELINE

The Raiders were gathered around the small arena they had built, which consisted of felled trees with hacked-off branches protruding brutally inward like spikes. The fence surrounded a square patch of bare earth with the odd tree root bulging upward. There was a small knife at my hip, another strapped to my leg, and the leather strap Rowan had fashioned around my chest secured a sword to my back that was nearly as tall as I was. The knives, I knew. The knives I had faith in. Fighting with them was something I was trained to do. But this strange sword was nothing like I had used before. It was foreign, clumsy, and heavy in my hands, and required more muscle than I had. It was meant for men like Rowan.

Rowan…

There'd been so much blood.

He'd slumped to the ground. Blood poured from his neck.

So. Much. Blood.

Was he dead? If so, did it matter if I lived another day?

My heart threatened to implode. It was all I could do to remain standing. To not throw my body to the ground and curl up in the fetal position. Cutting Rowan was one of the most horrific things I'd ever done. I could still feel the resistance of his skin as I dragged the blade across his throat. Funny… I'd gone from wanting to kill him with every fiber of my very being, to becoming haunted that I may have hurt him. Worse yet, I felt the absence of him in my mind.

I closed my eyes and let the chanting of the Raiders wash over me, then I called out to him. Softly, not moving my lips, I silently pleaded for him to give me a sign, a word, a color, *anything* to let me know that he was alive.

But the only response I got was the sun reaching its apex in the sky.

I called out for Zoleya too, even though I knew it was futile. She could not risk visiting me in the realm, and in the physical plane, she couldn't risk powering up to save me. There was nothing she could do.

The Raiders were eager for blood. Prominus was shoved into the arena and stood at the opposite end, hands and feet shackled with a rope around his neck that he struggled against like a rabid bear. His eyes were wild. His face was red and chapped, his lips white with blisters. He was a mountain of ugly fury.

"Are you ready for some entertainment?" yelled Captain Vallerik.

All eyes lifted to where she was perched on a platform up and over the heads of her lowly subjects. From there, she surveyed her flock while the little boy—Lucky's brother—fanned her. If I took five steps closer, I could throw the knife at my ankle. It could make the distance and pierce her heart...

As if reading my mind, Terens passed her up a shield. Some metal monstrosity intricately carved with skulls and the Raiders' lion head symbol now protected her chest.

Captain Vallerik stood and spoke. "For today's match, we have Prominus fighting Evangeline Quillene. To unknowing onlookers, this might seem like an unfair fight, but Commander Rowan has assured me that the girl can hold her own just as well, if not better, than any man here. Now, I'm a fair woman..." disjointed muttering rumbled through the crowd. "And normally I would make sure our opponents matched in weight and skill, for it is not the way of our people to have a blood bath for no reason. But..."

The crowd hung on her every word. Prominus stared at me, foaming at the mouth in anticipation.

"Evangeline Quillene has slit the throat of your commander and claims to have killed the Grakke Brothers. So, if her blood is spilled unfairly, so be it. And... if for some reason she is victorious, well, then Prominus will finally get what Amari could not give him—death."

I searched the cheering faces of Raiders, hoping to see Rowan's, but no gray eyes met mine.

"And what does the winner get?" yelled someone.

Captain Vallerik smiled. "Ah… yes. In our beloved Cal de Mac, the victor would receive a coin to someday buy his—or her—freedom. But since coins mean nothing here, the victor will just receive freedom."

The Raiders didn't like that, and they booed their disapproval.

Captain Vallerik put up a jeweled hand to silence them. "That freedom will be in the form of a fifteen-minute head start into the jungle, and then anyone who cares to join in the hunt for the victor's head is welcome. Terens will take the lead."

The cheering was sickeningly exuberant.

Captain Vallerik's gaze met mine. She grinned. "Now, it is customary for opponents to shake hands first then retreat to their corners until the countdown. Fighters, do you understand?"

I nodded. Prominus nodded.

"Shake," ordered Captain Vallerik.

Prominus stalked into the middle of the arena. The sheer size of him was alarming, but worse yet was the gleam in his eyes; he was enjoying this.

"Claiming the death of the Grakke brothers, eh? You protecting that kid, Max?" he hissed under his breath.

"Be a man and keep that secret to yourself," I said.

He chuckled. "Nah. You're gonna have to kill me to keep my mouth shut, bitch."

I didn't even have the will to reply to that. What did it matter now, anyway?

Prominus rolled his shoulders and cracked his neck. "I am going to drag this out and give these sadistic fuckers a good show while I destroy that pretty face of yours. Then I'll spill your secret. That should really get them going."

"Shake!" yelled Captain Vallerik.

I put my hand in Prominus' sweaty palm, our fingers tightening. "I'm not going to fight you," I said softly. "You can do whatever you want, because I'm going to die anyway. You won't get one drop of sweat out of me."

He shoved my hand away. "Lies." He spat at the ground. "You're a little bitch who lies!"

I went back to my corner, leaving the sword sheathed at my back, and called out to Rowan one more time in my mind—to hear nothing.

My heart sank lower. My feet became heavier.

Then the countdown began.

Three.

Two.

One…

54 EVANGELINE

Prominus charged toward me. I put my hands up over my head and waited for him to hit. I had let Zoleya down, I killed Rowan, and nothing mattered anymore.

The wind was forced from my lungs when Prominus' shoulder slammed into my diaphragm, sending me flying backward to land hard on my spine. The pain was horrible, but not as bad as the lingering feeling of that knife in my hand as Rowan's blood poured from his neck. I felt a void so severe it shook me to my soul. What had I done?

I saw stars when Prominus got hold of my hair and began dragging me around like a rag doll. Encouraging the Raiders to yell, he pumped his free fist, basking in premature glory. He hit me a few times—a couple of jabs to the jaw and one dead center of the solar plexus—but the force was insipid. He was holding back, biding his time and dragging it out like he said he would.

I remained as limp as an overcooked noodle, telling myself it was part of my plan, but also, I really didn't have the vigor to fight back. Exhaustion after absolutely everything—the voyage on the ship, losing Zoleya, running and hiding and worrying and starving and Alexander being Rowan, and Rowan being a Sage, and Kade and Beast and Max and Crow and the Scouts and my mother, father, and baby sister—it all caught up to me all at once. My performance of not caring if I lived or died was believable because perhaps, it was true.

My arms and legs dangled listlessly when Prominus let go of my hair and then lifted me up by the armpits. The prick was certainly enjoying my pain, so I thought that at least I could give him the opposite of what he desired. I rolled my eyes. I laughed when he open-hand slapped me. I sucked in a breath when his knee slammed into my ribs before tossing me to the ground, and I didn't cry out.

Straddling me, the smell of him was almost making it harder to breathe than the pain in my ribs. He balled up a fist, then slammed it into the ground next to my head. "Fight me!" he spat.

"Nah." I tasted blood. "I kinda like it when you hit me."

Prominus wanted me to struggle. To beg and cry. Unsheathing the sword at his back, his massive arms strained to hold the monstrosity upright as it gleamed in the sunlight. He was a sweaty, muscled beast right out of the 'G' section of Zo's encyclopedia under the heading "Gladiator."

"I'll just lop off your head and be done with you then, yeah?" he said, spitting flames.

I shrugged my shoulders. "Eh, might as well."

He swung and chopped at the earth, fury and anger spilling out of him. "Fight me!"

I was damn near shitting my shiny new pants. "Nah," I said nonchalantly, blowing dust off my fingernails—I would piss him off as long as possible. This I did for Amari, for the other woman he attacked in the cage, and for anyone else who had been one of Prominus' victims.

The idiot didn't know what to do. I'd taken the fun out of it for him and he was completely disenchanted. Getting up off me, he stormed around the arena, lashing out at a man too close to the fence. "How about you? Care to get in the ring?" he asked, grabbing a red-faced Raider by the throat.

Captain Vallerik slammed the butt-end of a walking stick against her perch. "Time out," she yelled, claiming everyone's attention.

I stayed where I was, pretending I wasn't having a hard time breathing. My strategy had at least shown some of Prominus' weak points. He favored an ankle that seemed a bit swollen. He held the sword with his right hand, and when he'd grabbed the man by the neck, he'd transferred it to his left, so I suspected he wasn't in good command of his left arm. He was strong, no doubt about it by the way the earth had been pummeled and chopped around me, but he was slow, and with the sun in his eyes his vision was greatly impaired. But did that matter?

"Rowan? What do I do?" I said under my breath, hoping for any sort of response. "Drag this out and fight back like my heart wants to, or give in and join you swiftly in death?"

There was no reply.

I was vaguely aware of a commotion not far from the west side of the arena, but I kept my eyes on Prominus and waited for him to realize that if he put away his need for sadistic gratification, he could just kill me and get a head start to freedom—stupidity was yet another one of Prominus' weaknesses.

Really though, I had a knife. I could use it on myself and forego the ensuing torture.

"We want you to give us a show, Evangeline Quillene," said Captain Vallerik, standing close to the edge of her perch, massive palm fronds over her head shaking with the breeze. "Maybe this will give you some incentive."

She motioned across the arena in direct line of the sun, and I had to squint and wipe the sweat from my eyes to see what she was pointing at. When I realized what it was, my heart dropped to my toes.

"I believe you call him Kade?" she said sweetly.

Beaten and bloody, there was the man I'd slept next to since we'd arrived on this god-forsaken island. Kade. My friend. My partner in this hellish existence. They had him strung up between two trees, arms stretched out and away from his bruised body. Now I knew that he was the reason for the commotion on the beach not long ago.

I got to my feet, feeling my stomach churn as Prominus doubled over with a sick laugh.

"Here's what's going to happen, Evangeline Quillene," said Captain Vallerik, eyes shiny as polished coins. "You fight Prominus and kill him, or Kade Thorn will be whipped until there's nothing left of him. I'll let Terens strip the flesh from his bones."

Just to prove this was no joke, Terens tore Kade's shirt at the back and with a flick of his wrist, sent a sharp lick of leather across his bare skin.

Kade gasped but didn't yelp, and his mismatched eyes met mine, blazing with anger.

"Sorry," he mouthed.

Terens whipped him again, and this time Kade's eyes rolled back in his head.

Trying not to puke, I turned to Captain Vallerik and stared at her with so much hatred and revulsion I probably looked as insane as Prominus. "I'll kill you for this," I hissed. "That's a promise."

Beaming, she elegantly returned to the edge of her seat. "Ah... there's the fire. Maybe now we'll see the warrior our dear commander dragged us across Aldira for." She put up a hand to make Terens take pause, as he was about to whip Kade again. "That's enough, Terens. Come, the real fight is about to begin."

You need to tire Prominus out even more, Evangeline...

Rowan's voice was in my mind! I jerked my head around, once, twice, searching for those gray eyes in the crowd.

Don't speak. Just let me help you.

"I'm so sorry," I said as Prominus carefully inched toward me.

I'd removed the sword from its sheath and held it across the front of my body. Prominus thought I was talking to him.

"Sorry? You talk like you have a chance, bitch," Prominus spat.

You do have a chance. And don't be sorry. I'm okay. Look to Kade and then to the left...

He was there. A white bandage circling his neck. The sight of him alive made everything broken, hurting, and bleeding go completely numb.

Prominus is already tired... and the heat is getting to him... keep it up...

Indeed, Prominus was sweating heavily from exertion. Dragging me around the arena and swinging at the dirt had taken its toll.

I moved around the edges of the fence as if dancing, going from one corner to the next, keeping my breathing steady as I made Prominus dance too. He liked the encouragement from the crowd as he swung his blade back and forth to try and intimidate me. I took my time, testing my sword, moving it in circles to judge the weight and get used to the feel. When Prominus lumbered closer, my confidence increased when I was able to quickly dodge him. The sweat was pouring off him and his breathing was heavy. I would tire him out a bit more before throwing him into a blind rage. Take away all his rational thought. Make him stumble—and I knew exactly how.

After a few more laps around the arena, I reached up for a tie binding the longest braid at the back of my head and released it, letting the waves tumble to my waist. I left the smaller braids at my temples intact so I wouldn't be blinded. "You don't really want to hurt me, do you?" I said innocently, even batting my eyelashes.

Prominus jerked as a switch flipped in his head. He spat and pawed the earth with his feet like a bull ready to charge. I made sure he was focused on all things feminine about me as I adjusted the tone of my voice. "Do you really want to fight *an innocent girl*?"

Yes. Yes he did. The bastard's fire was fueled, and he was raging. His blade swung, and I countered, able to block the blow before recovering and swinging upward, nicking his thigh ever so slightly. Insanely, this elated him. A grin broke out over his red face, exposing teeth black and brown like raisins shoved into his gums. He came at me again and I blocked his blows, spinning on my feet as I crouched down, leading him closer to the end of the arena and beneath Captain Vallerik's perch. I had my eye on the fence, on the spikes just waiting to impale his sweaty flesh, if only—

If only I wasn't the one backing up. Prominus was gaining on me, and the sword was becoming increasingly heavy. He was swinging harder, and my shoulder felt like it might come loose with every move I countered. The blade was foreign, and awkward, and it didn't slice through the air like the knives I was used to.

Let me in your mind... said Rowan. *Take a hit and fall to your knees... open the door to your mind for me...*

With both hands on the sword, I blocked a blow from Prominus and allowed the force to knock me flat on my back.

"Ah, now we get to business," Prominus said.

I closed my eyes as colors swam through the back of my vision, and all at once I was propelled to my feet with stunning force. As if watching the world through a dusty window, I saw my arm wielding the sword, my body reacting in a way that I had no control over. I could feel Rowan in my head. I could feel him controlling me, moving my limbs. He was in my heart. In my tendons and muscles. Coursing through my veins. Seeing through my eyes and expanding my lungs. And I welcomed it.

Rowan was fighting Prominus, using my body and reacting far quicker than I ever could. Prominus' eyes grew huge as we backed him into a corner and the blade in my hand swung, nicked his calf, then sliced his shoulder. The ability to counter what Prominus was about to do before he barely even moved was incredible. Rowan was incredible.

Prominus was furious, his eyes narrowing into slits as he roared like a wounded bear. My arm was swinging in ways I never imagined, catching Prominus' weapon at the perfect angle and sending it flying from his hands. It was euphoric. The sensation of Rowan taking over, of being able to feel him and everything that was going on around me was indescribable. I was soaring…

Until suddenly, he was gone.

I felt my body lurch forward and the sword drop from my hand. Every muscle went lax, and I was suddenly so exhausted it was all I could do to breathe. What had happened?

"Ah, you want to fight hand to hand now, is that it?" said Prominus, saving face as he tried to recover from being seconds away from death.

Where was Rowan? I backed away and scanned the crowd, looking for the place where he had stood. To my horror, I saw two Raiders holding him up. The bandage on his neck was completely red and his eyes were closed.

I'm okay… it's okay, Evangeline. I'm just not fully healed…

"Fight, Eva! You can take him!" yelled Kade, and Terens quickly shut him up with a lash to the back.

Prominus kicked our swords aside. "I like it better this way." He lurched toward me. "I can feel your flesh rip and your bones break under my hands. Your screams will be so much sweeter closer to my ears."

I steadied myself, straightened my shoulders, and sighed as theatrically as I could. "God, Prominus, you're such a bore. Is that supposed to scare me? The smell of you is far more frightening than your male posturing. Did you shit your pants? I mean… I'm not one to judge, but if fighting loosens up your bowels that violently maybe you better take a time out."

His switch flipped again. He charged at me with no strategy whatsoever, and I ran and leaped up onto the log fence while withdrawing the knife at my hip. He was a little too close when I threw it, but it embedded itself into his shoulder. This didn't slow him, though. All I'd done was kick the hornet's nest. He grabbed me and pulled me off the fence, which forced me to fight with everything I had. One hit to the head served with intention from those meaty fists and I wouldn't be able to see straight enough to fight back. I evaded his swings and leaped free of his lunges, but he caught me by the hair and slammed me to the ground. He was a cat playing with a mouse now, flipping me onto my back, laying flat over me and pinning my hands up over my head. I squirmed beneath him, but his weight was too much. My lungs gasped for air as the bastard sunk his black teeth into my shoulder—he was biting me! He pulled back to assess my horror before sinking his teeth in again, so I slammed my other shoulder into the knife handle sticking out of him. Howling, he drew back and spat a mouthful of my blood in my face.

"Kill her! Kill him!" roared the crowd.

But Prominus just pressed harder against me as he gathered my wrists together in one of his hands. I knew what was coming next and realized every bone in my face was about to be crushed with a few blows. So with my last breath of air, I put all my energy into swinging my right leg up, using my other as a lever, and twisting my body away from Prominus until the crook of my knee was around his throat. This threw him off balance. He was off of me, but I held on. With both arms pulling my leg as tight as I could and every muscle focusing on strangling Prominus, I could do nothing when he began flipping around like a fish. I was knocked against the fence, barely missing a spike, and slammed to the ground… but I held on, squeezing, pulling, using everything I had to hold the crook of my knee around his neck. The big lug of muscle began to fade. After what seemed like forever, he grew limp and his body began to convulse, fingers and legs twitching until… he stopped breathing.

Still, I held on.

I squeezed until I knew he was dead. And then I squeezed a bit more.

The crowd cheered and booed. And as I let go, I felt the world spin madly beneath me. Crawling away from Prominus, I was barely aware of someone else coming into the arena until my hair was gathered up and used to haul me to my feet.

"I guess our commander was right to pluck this one from Aldira," said Terens, his voice silencing the incensed crowd. "She has won against a male three times her size!" He tugged me by the hair and then shoved me away. The whip at his waist was dotted with Kade's blood. "But do we grant murderers their freedom? Even if it is only a head start? I think not. What say you, Captain?"

Captain Vallerik was judging the faces of her people, gauging their reactions. "We are people of our word, Terens," she said simply.

I looked toward Kade. His eyes met mine, and I thought of the ship, of all of us in that hold, arms chained up over our heads… and now here he was, strung up between two trees about to have the skin whipped from his bones whether I won or not.

"This girl must die," Terens said. "She must not be allowed freedom, especially after what she did to the Grakke brothers!"

Captain Vallerik rose to her feet. Her gaze passed over Prominus' unmoving body and then to our swords on the ground not far beneath her perch. "You, Evangeline Quillene, will fight Terens," she said.

Terens laughed.

I crouched down to feel the earth between my fingers, calming my shaking legs and taking a pacifying breath. The knife I'd stabbed Prominus with was at the far end of the arena, and I could see Terens noting that. He removed the sword from his back and threw it to the ground, as well as the knife at his waist.

"Fine. Let's fight, Eva," he said, lapping up encouragement from the crowd. "Are you watching, Commander Rowan?"

I glanced briefly into the crowd to see those cold gray eyes lit with rage.

Terens puffed out his chest. "I want you to see her fall. I want you to acknowledge that I was right and that traveling inland for this little girl you call a warrior was a waste of time. It's why we're stuck here on this island!"

Evangeline, would you please shut this snake up?

I couldn't help but grin, and I must have looked rather cocky as I straightened my spine and unlatched the leather strap from my chest, letting it fall to the ground. Terens was as stupid as Prominus, with no thought in his head except to teach a girl a lesson. He marched toward me favoring his twisted ankle, intent on swinging, but I could see what he was about to do before he did it. My legs, even though every muscle in them was trembling with exhaustion, were still strong, and I easily delivered three roundhouse kicks to Terens' solar plexus before he could even blink. All muscle, weak fighting skills, and too much arrogance made him an inferior opponent. I let him recover, mostly because I needed time to plot my escape as I circled as close to Kade as possible.

"You just got lucky," Terens muttered.

But he was scared. There was fear in his eyes. Despite that, he came at me again. I let him get close enough to grab me, then swung my arms up through his and brought my wrists down hard, releasing his hold as my elbow met his throat. While he gasped for air, I lunged for the knife at my ankle, but instead of driving it through his heart, I gave him another roundhouse kick to the ribs.

Terens was on the ground, eyes rolling back in their sockets.

"Was that a good enough show for you? Or do you really want me to kill him?" I hollered to the incensed Raiders, to Captain Vallerik.

Booing. Spitting.

I moved to Terens, straddling him like Prominus had done to me, and held the knife up over his chest. Now the jeering stopped and you could have heard a pin drop. I made to stab Terens in the heart, but I had my eye on Kade, specifically the ropes stretching each of his arms to a tree. With a deep breath, I gave Kade a slight nod, then swung my arm out while flicking my wrist, releasing the knife at just the right time—and cutting clean through one of his ropes.

Kade didn't miss a beat. He pulled his arm free and lunged for the knife now embedded in the sapling behind him. In the seconds it took for everyone to realize what had happened, he'd cut his other arm free.

I didn't wait to see what happened next; I had to get to the swords and slice my way out of the arena.

Balling my hand, I punched Terens as hard as I could and moved off him. Kade was holding his ground, so I dove for the swords beneath Captain Vallerik's perch, glancing up momentarily to see her shocked expression.

"Don't let her get away!" she yelled to her men.

Two Raiders had jumped into the arena, and I readied the sword, but no sooner had I gotten into position when they both fell flat on their faces. Out of the corner of my eye, I saw Terens struggling to stand, and then he, too, jerked like a bee stung him before falling forward onto his face.

Someone was in the trees.

I would have laughed if I wasn't so terrified.

"We're under attack!" yelled Captain Vallerik.

The sharp sound of whistling cut through the air as Raiders started falling. Captain Vallerik scrambled down from her perch and held her shield up over her head. Now everyone standing—including Rowan— was solely occupied with protecting her. Darts were coming from the trees, and just before I hopped the fence, I noticed one sticking out of Terens' neck.

With Kade at my elbow, we ran for the jungle. We passed Raiders' tents, their fires simmering, cooking pots left unattended, and I paused at the tent with the red letter 'C' to dash inside; there was a sack of provisions, just as Rowan had promised.

Rowan. I was leaving him behind. And suddenly my feet forgot how to move. My mind crashed again, and a horrid empty feeling came up to strangle the air from my lungs.

"Hurry," said Kade, grabbing me by the hand and tugging me ahead.

The leaves and trees instantly enveloped us, becoming a living blanket of protection as the shouting of the Raiders faded. I stumbled then tripped, my knee now threatening to give out completely and the bite marks on my arm and shoulder bleeding… ribs throbbing and head spinning…

Are you safe? asked Rowan.

"Yes," I said, gulping for air and ducking from a vine. "Are you?"

Kade turned back to eye me curiously. I touched my head to pretend that maybe the knocks I'd taken were making me sputter nonsense.

I think that whoever is in the trees was trying to protect you… said Rowan. *It seems that you have made some other friends on this island besides the snakes.*

I laughed. Then dropped to my knees and threw up.

Kade, nervously glancing overhead, paced, waited till I was done, then plucked me up into his arms. "I've got you. Just rest."

Yes, rest now, Evangeline. Kade Thorn will keep you safe.

I closed my eyes.

55  KITKUN

All faithful to Imatla must accept the words of its preacher, for it is this mortal who is well-read and all-knowing who is the closest to the gods.

— THE BOOK OF IMATLA (OR SO HANUK CLAIMS)

The green darts took a man's sight for hours.

The red poisoned him to death slowly for days.

I was glad Hanuk only had green darts—until the battle began between Eva and the red-faced man named Prominus. What was wrong with these Raiders? Was forcing two people to fight to the death their way of sacrificing to the gods? I thought the Ouray's customs were horrible, but this suffering through a painful death, egged on by the torture of someone you cared about, was barbaric. I mean… whipping Kade to make Eva fight? That sort of cruelty was something people did thousands of years ago. Where was their honor? If this senseless pain was for sport, then they deserved the poison.

Every one of Hanuk's darts hit its mark. His desire to give Eva time to escape was just as great as mine—but for different reasons. "I want her," he said under his breath when she strangled the red-faced man with her leg. We'd been hiding in the trees, him studying the sea people and looking for forbidden objects, and me keeping my blow gun ready. I'd never seen Hanuk's eyes grow as wide as they did when he saw Eva, and when she began to fight, I thought his brain might explode. He was looking at her as an exceptional sacrifice. One that might earn him much more favor than a chicken or village girl. She was worth a thousand firesticks—and that could get him one giant leap closer to the gods.

"You have proven your worth today, Kitkun," Hanuk said once our feet were back on the ground and the Raiders were far behind us.

We were following Eva and Kade's trail. I purposely smudged a footprint that marked the direction they had gone, patting the last remaining dart in my pocket. "Thanks."

Hanuk noticed a bend in a leaf, and then a dot of blood that was practically imperceptible to the human eye. He deeply inhaled, smelling something lost to my senses.

"This way," he said.

I could cover up all the tracks I could see, but it wasn't going to stop Hanuk. Every muscle and tendon in his body was bulging beneath his skin. His bare upper half, covered in traditional scars and tanned nearly as brown as his eyes, gleamed with a thick sheen of moisture that wasn't from the heat of the day or exertion. It was from the intense desire for Eva's blood.

Now I, too, could see her trail. Kade was bleeding—his back sliced clean open—and Eva had multiple wounds, including bite marks on her arms. They were leaving red marks everywhere. And they were slowing down. Getting clumsy. I even noticed that in one place they must have fallen to the ground, because at a wide, bloody splotch, two sets of tracks became one. Was Kade carrying Eva?

"We need to go back," I said, mind racing; I couldn't let Hanuk catch up to them.

"Yes. After we kill the man and capture that girl."

"You can't just take her," I said, but knew it was a waste of breath.

"I run this land. It is my duty to keep our people safe, and I will have the girl because she is a valuable offering. Once she is secure in our village, I will come back with our warriors and eliminate those barbaric sea people."

"Hanuk, I beg of you, please, let's just go back and let them be—"

He spun around and the remainder of my sentence was slapped from my mouth. "Are you going to cause me trouble, Huntress?"

Hanuk had never hit me before—choked me, yes—but never

swung with actual intent to cause me pain. I'd egged him on and got him close to raising a fist once or twice, but I'd convinced myself that he would never *really* hurt me.

I tasted blood.

Pressing my fingertips to the corner of my mouth, they came away red. I was stunned.

"These are wicked people," Hanuk continued, eyes wild. "You saw what they did to their own! Killing to appease a god is acceptable. Killing as punishment for breaking laws is acceptable. But pitting people against each other in a *game*? Making a sport of death? It's wrong, Kitkun. You know this. If they are capable of these things, then what else can they do? They walk into the water and come back out unscathed, which means Idis truly is on their side. What if they have the Goddess of the Sky too? Would Nvula allow them to move like the birds? Control the wind and command the Mordorain? It is far too dangerous to let them live."

I just stared at him in awe. He had no regard for human life, which was the very thing he claimed was appalling about the sea people. He also claimed to trust the judgment of the gods, but he was doing anything but. He only spouted nonsense to support his heinous wants and desires. I suspected he truly did not care about the gods' will and just wanted to be the only one in power connected to them, and that made him just as bad. Maybe worse.

Hanuk was about to say more, but an unnatural snapping sound followed by a slight moan had him crouching into stealth mode. He was a cougar on the prowl, sneaking toward the sound, knife in his hand... and then suddenly he was breaking into a run. I could barely keep up, practically diving through the trees behind him until I collided with his backside.

Gathering my wits about me and wiping my eyes, I blinked into focus what Hanuk had cornered.

Kade had Eva in his arms and he was on his knees. At the sight of us, he released her and then drew his knife and stood, barely. He was shaking, one eye was swollen shut, and it seemed that any moment now he might pass out. Eva was a mess too. Her eyes were rolling around in her head. She tried to stand but could barely even lift her arms let alone straighten her legs. I was again angry at the people who had done this to her—to them—and angry at Hanuk for cornering and terrifying such wounded souls.

"S-stay back," Kade warned, the ornamental designs on his skin kind of glowing.

"I just want the girl." Hanuk crept forward. "You won't get hurt if you walk away."

Kade took in a breath and got into a defensive position. He would die for Eva, that was clear—which would most certainly happen if he fought Hanuk.

"No," I said, getting in between them and putting my hands out. "Please, Hanuk, there is no need to fight."

"Stand down, Kitkun," Hanuk warned.

"We are not murderers," I reminded him.

Eva was struggling to her feet. "What do you want with me?" she asked.

I knew that she would protect Kade by freely going with Hanuk. But that would certainly result in her death too.

Hanuk played upon her bravery. "You both are too weak to fight me," he said, taking another step closer, causing Kade to shove Eva behind him. "No one will die if you both do as you're told. All I want is to take the girl to my village."

"When hell freezes over," Kade spat.

Hanuk continued. "Walk away." He flexed his muscles, cracked his neck, and assumed his most intimidating posture. "Or you will die by my knife."

Eva put her hand on Kade's shoulder. "Kade, just let him take me and—"

She didn't get a chance to finish. Kade charged forward and swung at Hanuk with everything he had, but Hanuk brushed him off like he was swatting a fly. When Hanuk's fist connected with Kade's jaw, Kade hit the ground, but he was oddly clutching his ribs and not his jaw.

"Run, Eva," Kade muttered, trying to get up.

Eva remained where she was, watching breathlessly as Hanuk marched toward Kade and positioned his blade over Kade's heart.

"Stop!" Her voice was raw with panic. "Don't hurt him and I'll walk next to you. Hurt him and you'll be carrying me the whole way back to your village and I'll fight you every second."

This appealed to Hanuk's laziness.

He stood and stepped back from Kade. "All right." He paused for a moment to ponder the strange markings on Kade, then scratched his head before turning to me. "Bind the girl's hands, Kitkun."

Numbly I crept toward Eva, her eyes not meeting mine but staying focused on Hanuk the entire time. I had to step on her foot to get her to look at me, then directed her gaze to where the blow gun rested in my side pocket—the green dart loaded and ready. She understood.

As I stood behind her, I removed the leather cord holding my hair back as slowly as I could, then pretended to tie her hands with it. Hanuk didn't see me place the dart in Eva's hand instead.

"He will kill you..." I whispered to the back of her neck. "Act now."

I gave her a shove toward Hanuk, and the big lug, staring at her in wonder, wasn't prepared for the dart that impaled him in the neck.

He dropped to his knees and was out cold in seconds.

"Holy shit," Eva said, collapsing against me.

I'd never heard that term before, but I assumed that, given the circumstances, it was a compilation of emotions mixed with awe and relief rolled into two tidy little words.

"Yes, holy shit," I repeated.

"Kitkun, that was you... in the trees?" Eva asked, breath sounding ragged in her lungs. "Did you save me and Kade from the Raiders?"

I nodded. "Me and Hanuk did. But for very different reasons."

She fell to her knees, legs too tired to hold her up. "Thank you."

Kade was struggling to his feet, and the look in his eyes went from wanting to kill me to silently thanking me.

"What does he want with me?" Eva asked, motioning to Hanuk.

I was embarrassed suddenly. Embarrassed to tell her that my people sacrificed living creatures—sometimes humans—to the gods. Saying it aloud made it seem even more… horrific.

"Hanuk wants you for bad reasons, Eva. You must not let him take you to our village."

Kade had Hanuk's knife in his hand. "I'll solve that problem," he said.

Without a second thought, I let go of Eva and stood before Hanuk, spreading my arms out protectively.

"No. You cannot kill him." What was I doing? This was the perfect opportunity to get rid of the person who caused me so much grief. I could let Kade kill him and wander off on my own. Live my life how I wanted to.

But my family would die. Elke would die.

The three of us stood, blinking at each other, a million questions burning on our tongues. Eva was just about to ask one but suddenly the shells at our wrists began to whistle.

"We are in danger," I said, pointing to the sky that was quickly turning green, then to the shell on Eva's wrist. "We must seek shelter. The Mordorain is coming!"

Kade said some word I had never heard before, and Eva took in a deep breath. "Death from above," she said as if she was alerting someone, but there were only the four of us here.

Sure enough, the first trickle of rain came down. Like a light mist, it fell through the canopy of trees, warning every living thing in the jungle to run for cover. It was always regular old water to start, clear and clean and soothing to the skin—but soon it wouldn't be.

I knew this side of the island like the back of my hand. There were places to hide. But Hanuk…

"Show us where to go," Eva said, helping Kade to his feet—or was he helping her? I couldn't tell which.

I looked down at the mass of muscle passed out on the ground. Mom, Elke, Nita and Hesutu would pay the price for Hanuk's death. I couldn't let that happen.

"Please, Eva… help me. I can't leave him here."

Kade was frantic, desperate for somewhere to hide and about to walk away. "He tried to kill me and wants to kidnap Eva. To hell with the bastard."

More strange words.

Eva made to come back to me—because her heart was pure and she would probably risk her own skin to save that of a man who intended to sacrifice her to the gods—but Kade was holding her back.

"You'll die without me," I said, eyeing both of them as the rain came down harder.

It was the honest truth.

"I know where we can take cover," I added. "Help me with Hanuk and I'll take you there."

Lightning cracked through the sky; a warning that we better hurry.

With Eva and I pulling on one arm and Kade pulling on the other, we dragged Hanuk through the jungle. Eva stumbled, Kade said more strange words, and I used every single speck of energy I had to keep momentum. The rain was turning Kade's bleeding back to pink rivers, and the shells were screaming so loud we couldn't talk above them. I pulled, tugged, and stumbled toward the tree with the seven trunks, woven as if in a thick braid. It stood not far from the Wejukah, and I knew that five paces from its core directly south, we would be safe. At one point I was pretty sure I was the only one dragging Hanuk when Kade had to help Eva, and I could barely breathe over the panic rising in my chest. When we made it to the tree, I fell to my knees and began clawing at the earth.

"This is it!" I yelled.

Kade joined in, our fingernails scraping back weeds and black dirt. He yelped, and sure enough I felt it seconds later: the Mordorain was starting to fall.

"Kitkun, there's nothing here."

Eva was on her hands and knees too, barely able to breathe, her body draped over Hanuk's to try and protect him.

My skin was on fire. "There is a place... it's here, I know it! I just —it's a l-latch... a-a handle... a—"

I found it. A smooth piece of metal that twisted in my hand, which I then tugged upright. I threw back a trap door, scattering the clawed earth that had turned into muddy rivulets.

"Down here, hurry!"

I dropped down into the dark, tugging on Hanuk as Eva and Kade helped shove him into the dark behind me. Eva practically fell in after, and Kade, bearing a lashing of Mordorain on top of the one from the whip, pulled the door shut over our heads.

Then only the sound of labored breathing filled the dank air for a pained moment. When I could finally catch my breath, I fumbled for the lantern I knew was hanging on the wall. The rain pouring above us sounded like hammers falling.

"We're safe in here," I said.

Finally, I found what I was looking for. Trying not to scream from my stinging skin, I knew I had to act fast.

"And where is 'here' exactly?" asked Kade, unable to hide the panic in his voice.

The firestick made quick work of igniting the lantern, and soon golden light illuminated the small metal hiding hole. I'd utilized places like this one many times. They were all over the island. Some were badly corroded and often filled with so many crawling insects the Mordorain might have been preferable to the bites, but this one was nice. Airtight. Clean.

"I call it a hiding hole. They're all over this land." I tried to remain calm as I untied the pouch I always kept at my waist that was packed with the aloe plant. "Some aren't always safe, but this one is."

Eva was whimpering. I passed Kade a piece of the plant and he promptly addressed her burns. I addressed mine, and then Hanuk's. I smeared the gel over his square face, his wide neck, and his stupid oily chest... then, with Kade's help, we got him over onto his stomach and tied his hands and feet together just like I'd watched Muma do with our last pig. After addressing the burns on Hanuk's back, I moved to help Kade but was met with protests.

"Your wounds... they need attention, too," I said.

Kade grumbled something. His shoulders remained slouched and he stared at Eva where she lay passed out. I ignored his complaints and put the gel on his back, avoiding the wounds from the whip. I realized then that he was scarred in ways unimaginable; this wasn't the first time he'd been whipped. Oh, the pain he must have suffered… I could have cried for him, but instead pretended not to notice.

"That man, Prominus… he, uh, bit Eva," I said, barely able to swallow past a lump in my throat. "Who knows what kinds of diseases he might have."

From a small shelf, I retrieved a white box filled with bandages and some sort of goo for wounds that was ancient but still efficient. Kade snatched it from my hands and moved to tend to Eva even though his burns and open wounds were much worse; there was a streak of blood on the wall that he'd been leaning against.

I lit another lantern, and now we could see the strange writing on the walls left behind from a time that history tried to erase. Little shelves with odd ornaments hung above a bench made for short people to sleep on, and nooks and crannies held interesting artifacts from Before, along with jars of dried fruits I'd left behind over a month ago. Of all this, Kade only saw Eva. He cared about nothing else.

Shaking with exhaustion, he got her onto the bench, poured anti-septic over her wounds, then applied the goo and wrapped clean bandages over the places where Prominus' teeth had sunk into her skin. When he was done, Eva wasn't moving.

"I won't hurt you," I said, carefully moving behind him to assess the deep gashes on his back from the whip. "And I am sorry those people did that to you. We are not barbarians like they are."

Kade let out a weary chuckle. "No? Hanuk proves otherwise."

"Hanuk has ulterior motives. The rest of us aren't so… eager."

"Is he going to die?"

"No. The dart just makes him sleep."

Kade winced as I cleaned his back, and the two long gashes running from his shoulders to his waist brought tears to my eyes, too.

"It's not so bad," Kade said, as if reading my mind. "I've had much worse."

The markings on his skin were hot, and whether they were tattooed, branded, or both, I couldn't quite tell. I'd never seen anything like them. "At the hands of your own people?" I asked, wondering if the marks also pained him. They were so strange.

"Aldira is a complicated place."

I did my best to tend to his wounds, but I really needed Hesutu's needle and thread to stitch a few places back together.

"Thank you," Kade said when I was done. "You saved our lives."

The rain poured harder. We both shivered. "It's my honor."

Hanuk jerked, but his eyes remained closed. A crack of lightning shook the hiding hole.

"You rest," I said to Kade, who could barely keep his eyes open as he tried to remain prepared to fight Hanuk. "He's out cold, but I'll watch him just in case."

"Let me bind your hands first."

Did he not trust me? After all I'd done? "Like I said before, I won't hurt you."

"I know. But if the big guy wakes up and sees that you're helping us, he might be a little pissed at you. And since you won't let me kill him—"

I didn't know what 'pissed' was but assumed in context that it meant "angry," and he would be entirely correct.

"Hanuk's men will hurt my family if he doesn't return to our village," I confided. "I will be blamed."

Kade seemed to give this some thought. "Well, when he wakes, you'll pretend that you were overtaken by me and Eva, and then you go back to your village with the dirtbag and look after your family. I won't kill him, Kitkun, unless he comes near Eva again. Then I won't think twice."

I gulped at the amount of passion in his voice. What would it be like to have someone care about me the way Kade cared about Eva? "Yes. That is fair," I sputtered.

Kade nodded. I handed him some rope.

"Tell me about your village, Kitkun," he said as he made multiple knots around my wrists.

"It's on the other side of Black Mountain—have you seen its peak?"

Kade was lying down next to Eva, his eyes closing. "Yes. I climbed a tree the other day and stared almost straight up to the clouds to see it. It's beautiful."

"It is," I said. "My people are the Ouray, and we live at the base of the mountain…"

I told him all about it even though he was sound asleep.

Hours passed.

When the rain stopped, I nudged Eva with my knee to wake her up and pointed to the trap door. "You must go before Hanuk wakes," I whispered. "The sedative won't last much longer."

Hanuk, even tied up, would be a tornado in this small metal box.

Startled and confused, she sat upright and rubbed her eyes. She was so pale. Her eyes surrounded by dark shadows. She tentatively shook Kade awake, and he inched upright, wincing.

"It's safe?" Eva asked, looking up at the hatch door.

Hanuk flinched—he was beginning to come around, which was too bad because both Kade and Eva could have used much more rest.

"Don't worry, the Mordorain is neutral a few minutes after it hits the ground. It's safe."

Eva stopped to hug me. "Thank you, Kitkun."

Hanuk was jerking awake, now struggling against the ropes.

"Quickly now," I mouthed silently.

Jerking madly like a fish caught on a hook, Hanuk was struggling to flip over onto his back. When he finally did, Eva and Kade were gone.

I slumped against the metal wall, and when I felt the weight of Hanuk's watery brown eyes, I blinked a few times to pretend that I was just waking up, too. My gaze fell to his, and when he noted the rope around my wrists, he let out a low growl.

"Did they hurt you, Huntress?"

What? Was Hanuk inquiring as to *my* well-being? I was almost too shocked to speak. "No," I said quickly. "But they have escaped."

He noted the aloe plants emptied of their life-saving gel. "Mordorain?"

I nodded.

His eyes widened. "You made those people bring me here, didn't you Kitkun? That man—Kade—he would have taken my life, but you convinced him to drag me here, to this place, where you could safely wait out the rain. Although you were careless and let the girl steal the dart from you, you also saved my life, Kitkun."

And all this time I'd thought Hanuk was as thick as a stump in the smarts department. Maybe I was wrong? He'd figured a few things out without my help, but I wouldn't divulge the more accurate details.

It hit me then—quite horribly—that I was glad to see him awake. And it wasn't just because I was relieved that my mother and my sister's lives would be spared.

"Uh-huh," I muttered. "You kind of gave me no choice with your whole 'going to burn your family to the ground' rant."

He shrugged his shoulders as he took in the strange writing on the wall of the hiding hole. "You have proven yourself worthy," he said, and I could have sworn he sounded sincere.

It didn't take him long to work the ropes free from his wrists, then undo the ones at his ankles. Instead of dragging a knife through my ropes, he gently untied the knots. Then, in a way that made me want to vomit and scream and scrub my face every hour for the rest of my life, Hanuk did the strangest thing; he kissed me. Thankfully not on the lips, because if that were the case I'd have to cut off my whole face, but on the forehead.

"What was that for?" I asked, horrified.

He sucked on his teeth and cracked his muscled neck. "I need a competent partner. Someone I can rely on in life." He glanced around the hiding hole at the objects from *Before*—things I knew nothing of but coveted—and a sly smile came over his face. "A woman who understands the world. Someone to have my children and warm my bed. Maybe that person is you, Huntress."

A whole-hearted NO was just about to escape from my lips, but something stopped it—self-preservation perhaps. "You're my cousin," I said instead.

Hanuk laughed. "Only in title. Not by blood. You are of marrying age, Huntress, and I am offering you the world. Will you not consider for one moment what life could be like at my side?"

It would be hell.

But it would be a hell I might have some control of.

I would be throwing my life away like so many girls in our village did. I would never have the chance to pick someone I loved. But... maybe I could change things. Maybe I could demand things of Hanuk that would make a difference to everyone on the island.

I tested the waters. "I'll consider it, if—"

Hanuk was hanging on my words, and I suddenly felt a sense of power over him.

"Yes?" he said eagerly. Too eagerly.

I took in a deep breath and held his gaze. "When we go back to the village, you must promise to never harm my mother or my sisters. Never use them against me. Never threaten them. Ever. Forever."

"Done."

"And no more sacrificing humans."

His lip curled into a snarl. "I cannot control the wants of the gods, and I dare not defy them."

Then I needed to learn the wants of the gods and interpret them in my own way. "Okay, then you must teach me to read. I want to know the Book of Imatla through its letters and not your words."

He pondered this a moment, then smiled. "You are worthy of such knowledge, so, yes."

He was so close I could feel his breath. I tried not to cower. "Okay. Good."

His meaty fingers touched the corner of my mouth and the blood dried there from when he'd hit me. An emotion I'd not yet encountered washed over his face and softened his features ever so briefly.

"You now have my word and my heart, Huntress Kitkun," he said. "Witnessed by all gods."

And now, I was scared of him.

56 EVANGELINE

Approaching the fire surrounded by familiar faces felt like going home. Beast was the first to pull me into a tight bear hug. His beard was soft against my forehead as I melted against him, and I released tears I could no longer hold.

"Holy raspberries, we missed ye, Missy," he said, voice catching, arms tightening around me.

"I missed you, too, Beast."

To my surprise Max hugged me next, quickly but warmly all the same.

"I'm sorry about the Grakke brothers," he said, hands on my shoulders, eyes brimming with remorse. "You took the blame for what I did and… damn, Eva, you went through hell because of me." Anger then consumed his sadness, making him vibrate. "I'm sorry I didn't kill every one of those Raiders so you could have gotten free sooner."

"Killing them isn't the answer, Max," I sighed, patting his cheek.

Max and Kade exchanged a look I would have to question another day. For now, I just wanted comfort and peace.

Dominic, grinning ear to ear, sparkling clean and head newly shaved, gave me a friendly pat on the back and a quick once-over to assess my well-being. Assured that I wasn't in any immediate distress, he handed me a cup of water and asked to see my leg; the healer in him was desperate to understand why I wasn't dead. "Whatever kind of medicine those Raiders have, I want it," he said.

Lucky was tending the fire, stoking it lovingly, eyes meeting mine through the wavering heat. "My brother?" he asked.

I felt tired right to my core. "Alive. But…"

"It's okay," he said. "We'll get him back. I'm just glad you're alright."

Amari nodded in agreement. "As am I." She wasn't so pale, but she still had a long way to go to heal. I noticed she kept a healthy distance from Max.

I was introduced to the six boys huddled together in the shelter that Beast had had fortified, as well as the women and men Rowan had also helped escape from his camp. But my head was too weary to remember names.

Everyone fell silent when Kade and I took a seat by the fire. We recounted the events of the last few days. We told them about the fight, the death of Prominus, and what we knew of Kitkun, Hanuk, and their village, but we left out the fact that I might be hunted by Hanuk; there was just no point in causing any more worry or stress.

When there was nothing left to say, Amari moved next to me. Her bruises were fading and the swelling in her eye had considerably diminished. I learned that she had helped fortify the shelter, and that she'd been trying very hard to fit in even though Max threatened to kill her every chance he had.

"He's dead. For sure?" she asked.

She was talking about Prominus.

I recalled the feeling of his body going limp and watching his lips turn blue as I squeezed, and I rubbed my knee that would ache for a very long time. "Yes," I said.

"You're very brave, Eva."

"I'm not brave, Amari. I was just doing what I had to do. Just like you."

Her eyes met mine—a storm gray that made my heart thump. "What of my brother?" she asked.

The thought of Rowan made everything around me disappear. He'd flashed through my mind briefly before the rain and then again in the hiding hole but hadn't since. I was desperate to hear his voice in my head. See and feel that joining of our light in the Between that was so vivid, so blissful… And erase the feeling of that knife cutting through his neck—my knife—his warm blood on my skin… My hand still shaking…

"Eva?"

"Rowan? Yes, he was well when I left. Terens accused him of being a traitor, but I made sure those accusations didn't pan out."

"Thank you."

"And Jin, your other brother… he's okay, too," I added after a while.

Amari took in a deep breath and patted the back of my hand. She sensed there was more to the story but didn't press. "Tell Rowan I'm fine," she said. "Tell him I will survive here, with you and your people."

I was confused. "I'm not sure how—"

"I know what Rowan is, Eva," Amari said, lowering her voice. "So, when he comes to you, please, just tell him I'm okay. And that… that I love him."

I pulled in a deep breath. "Yes. Okay."

She stood and headed for the shelter, crawling in amongst Beast and the others to sleep. Max had curled up by the fire and his eyes were closed, but Lucky and Kade were still wide-eyed awake. Exhausted as I was, I felt the overwhelming need to be alone.

Sneaking a good distance away from the camp, I lit a torch and headed for the sea. I felt like I'd been holding my breath for days when I came out of the green onto the beach, the moon so bright I could see the rocks towering around the cove and the expanse of water shimmering like polished glass. Pulling off my boots, I dug my toes into the sand at the water's edge, the wind ruffling my hair. I cleared my mind. Pictured his face.

"Rowan."

Without announcing his presence, without those colors crashing through my mind and stealing my vision, I could feel him surge through me.

The sky is beautiful tonight, he said.

It took a moment to remember to breathe again. "Why is it that you can speak to me this way and I'm not passed out with my eyes rolling back in my head? I thought a Receiver and a Sage could only fully communicate in the Between."

When we connected in the other realm, something happened. It joined us in a way I cannot explain. I have met Receivers before, but never have I had a connection like this. You're different somehow.

"Or maybe *we're* different? I mean… I can feel you." Warmth spread to my limbs. My hands and feet tingled.

He was seeing through my eyes. When I lifted my hand to my lips, it was him, taking over control, feeling my mouth with my fingertips and sighing. *Is it okay if I do this?*

"Yes," I shuddered.

I can feel you, too, through your hands. And I can sense your emotions.

The intimacy was staggering. "Are you okay?" I asked, nearly breathless. "Your neck…"

Hmmm. Yes, he answered. *I am perfectly fine, Evangeline. Aunnie treated me. You did not sever an artery or do any permanent damage. Three more treatments and I will be as good as new.*

"Oh, thank the stars."

I must know something. There were moments when I could see a strange man through your eyes. You were in a dark place with him, a girl, and Kade Thorn. You kept blacking out so I could not get the whole picture.

"There are other people here. A tribe who call themselves the Ouray. They were the ones who shot the darts at your people and rescued me. When the Mordorain came, the girl, Kitkun, hid us in an underground hideout."

Can I see this for myself? Rowan asked.

I selected memories and replayed them, sensing his rage as he watched the interaction with Hanuk and our escape from the Mordorain. I showed him what I knew of the Wejukah, and of Kitkun. I even let him see a vision I would forever hold dear; of my people safe and sound by the fire… because of him.

And the Sage… the female that comes to you. Who is she?

I quickly put up a wall, guarding my memories of Zoleya. "Please don't. She… is off-topic. I'm sorry, but you must never ask me about her. Pretend she doesn't exist, for my sake. Please."

His reply was honest. *Yes. Okay.*

Silence. But the blissful kind.

You will have to go south, Eva, Rowan said after a while. *Get as far from Kitkun's tribe— the Ouray—as possible. I do not think Hanuk is the kind of man who will give up on trying to find you.*

My chest constricted. "I… I don't want to go any farther away…" *from you,* I wanted to add but didn't.

A flash of blue burst through my mind.

Terens seeks revenge, and Captain Vallerik still wants your head. With them searching for you, as well as Hanuk, you will need to disappear.

"Come with me."

I would. But…

He paused, and suddenly a vision was so clear in my mind I wondered if I was there. Rowan was in the healer's shack, looking at Jin on the bed who appeared as dead as dead could be. Aunnie was hovering and pressing a cloth to his forehead, and Rowan's hands rested on Jin's delicate arm just above the intravenous feeding his veins.

"You have to protect your brother," I said.

Captain Vallerik has no need for the weak. If I am gone, she will dispose of him. Since I cannot look after him without Aunnie's help, I am bound to my people. Besides, even if Jin wasn't dependent on me, going anywhere near you would only put you in more danger; Captain Vallerik would hunt us both. She wouldn't rest until I was punished for being a traitor.

"But Captain Vallerik is your mother. She's *Jin's* mother. How can she—"

Only by blood, Rowan said bitterly. *She does not care if Jin lives or dies. She only cares about strength and power and serving Cal de Mac with honor. Her children are not her priority.*

A comet burst through the sky and I focused on it, taking Rowan's mind elsewhere, wanting to ease his anguish just for a second. "We could go far away… together. We could hide where they would never find us. Take Jin and Aunnie and that case of medicine with us. I'll keep you safe." I said, but I knew I was being unrealistic.

I felt him sigh in sadness, and the desire to go to him was so intense I could barely keep my legs beneath me.

That would be a dream…but I can't be selfish with you, Eva. Look where it put us already; stranded here because of my… desires. From the moment I saw you on the streets of Nora fighting off derelicts trying to rob your caravan, I wanted you. Warrior or not, fighter or not, I dragged my people across Aldira to find you because I had to see you again. You would not leave my mind. I told myself it was because you would make me a wealthy man when I put you in the arena, but it was more than that. So, so much more. When I couldn't let you die in the hold of my ship, I told myself I was just doing what anyone would for another human. And when you walked away after saving my life, the feeling of loss was so great that the only thing that got me through was repeating to myself that you'd be dead soon and I'd be free of whatever spell you had cast upon me. That, or I figured I would find you and just kill you myself. End the torture gripping my mind and get it over with.

I stared at the sky, completely shocked at what I was hearing but comforted by the confession; Zoleya had nothing to do with our capture, she really was just a victim of circumstance.

Rowan paused and seemed to gather his thoughts. *But, Evangeline, when you were taken out to sea by a rip tide, the absence I felt was paramount. I slipped inward, deep into my mind, searching for something to ease the pain. And then I found you again. Who knew you would be a Receiver? And that not only would I be taken completely with what I saw of you but what I could feel and know of you as well? Every time I came into your mind, I fell deeper. And there was no going back when Kade delivered you to me half-dead. Your leg… your injuries… were because of me. I couldn't look at your face, otherwise I could have never given you those injections. The pain I'd caused you— and had to cause you again—was as excruciating to me as any torture. I knew I had to do it to save you, that the medicine was what you needed, however... oh. I'm sorry, Evangeline. So very sorry... for everything.*

I was too stunned to speak. Too short of breath to breathe.

I know I am saying too much, but we are stranded here, and it might be for a long time. Your survival depends on knowledge. You need to go far away from me. You need to be with people who are strong and who care for you deeply. Someone who can keep you safe. Someone like—

"Hey, are you worrying about Zoleya again?" Kade asked.

He'd come up behind me, startling me and causing Rowan to send a flash of blue through my mind. I'd hoped there weren't tears on my cheeks, but by the look in Kade's eyes, there were.

"We'll find her," he said.

I could feel Rowan so intensely I'd begun to shake. He was still there, surging through my limbs, making my fingers twitch, making the sky behind Kade completely black.

"Whoa...are you okay?" Kade asked.

Shivering, I attempted a shallow breath, my legs wobbly beneath me. "I don't think so," I said honestly.

Kade pulled me toward him, pressing my head to his chest.

I think it is time for me to leave.

"No!" I said, confusing Kade and desperately clinging to Rowan with every synapse in my exhausted brain. "I mean, no. I'm not okay," I said to Kade.

With a gentle smile, he pressed his palm to my forehead. "You're not burning up. I think you're just tired, Eva."

"Don't leave me," I muttered. "Please..."

Kade took my words as an invitation, and his mouth was suddenly on mine. Every color in the world slammed and flashed behind my eyes as the presence of Rowan consumed my mind and practically stopped my heart. I pictured that it was Rowan's hands on my face, Rowan's mouth on mine, Rowan's storm gray eyes searching mine when I pulled back...

Only to see the mismatched hazel and green gaze of Kade.

I will leave you in Kade Thorn's capable hands. Just know you have my heart, Evangeline Quillene. Now and forever.

Then Rowan was gone.

I put my hand on Kade's chest to steady myself and he gasped as if it pained him. The marks on his skin were hot, and I was about to pull away, but he held my hand in place, holding it there while he inhaled a shuddering breath.

"We're in this together, all right?" he said.

I nodded, too full of tears to speak, too tired to explain that I was devastated by the incredibly empty feeling Rowan had suddenly left me with.

Kade lit a fire on the beach. Next to crackling flames and smoke twisting up into the sky, he curled up around me on the blanket he'd placed on the sand. I didn't flinch when his arm draped over me or when a little green snake slithered up against my legs and curled up, too.

57 EVANGELINE

I would remember this morning for a long time.

The breeze woke me first, cool against my cheeks as the warmth of Kade's body at my back staved off its bite. The sky was silky threads turning slightly orange as the sun came up behind the green, and it cast the sand and diamond-flecked sea in a golden glow. This island, this place, was beautiful. Breathtaking. But what was even more so, what reached in and grabbed my heart, filling a small corner of the vast cavern of emptiness Rowan had left behind, was *my people*. They were milling about, stoking the fire, dipping clothes in the water to wash them, washing themselves, running after crabs that had poked their heads out of the sand… all without even a whisper. I assumed their silence was to allow me and Kade to sleep while they—under the guise of chores—kept watch over us.

In that moment, we had become our own village. We protected each other.

We were okay.

And so was Zoleya. She had people around her too, and she was safe for the moment. If she was in danger, I would feel it. Every inch of my skin would be crawling right to my inner core and I would be consumed with her distress. Was it possible that Zo was safer now than she'd ever been in Aldira? Maybe… just maybe… being stranded here really was better for her?

The snake lifted its head, yellow eyes meeting mine.

"Don't move, Eva…" said Kade.

He was awake now too, his muscles tensing as he noticed the scaly creature pressed up next to me. One of the boys had grabbed a stick and was about to try and lure it away. The whole camp came to a crashing halt over this little harmless snake, and I had to laugh. After all we had endured! It was so surreal. So perfect. But… so unbearably, horribly, deathly-lonely without even the slightest hint of Rowan's presence in my mind.

"She's harmless," I said to those who had gathered around, my throat choking with impending tears.

The young boys were interested in the snake, while Max was far too eager to kill it.

"Sit," I said to them all. "Please, everyone… just… sit."

The boys sat down so quickly it was alarming. The women settled in around Amari, who seemed to be their pillar of strength. Dominic and Beast were confused but did as they were asked, as did Lucky. Max, however, kept his knife tight in his hand and that murderous look in his eyes.

"Max, please," I repeated.

Running a hand over his knife, he was confused as to why I wasn't freaking out. He held his breath as I put my hand out to the snake, who then slithered toward me and curled up around my wrist.

"She isn't dangerous," I said.

As if to prove this, the snake rubbed her head lovingly against my cheek, wiping at the tears I realized were now falling freely. Max, stunned beyond belief, fell to his knees and dropped his knife.

For a long while we were all silent, feeling the heat of the fire, the heat of the sun, the heat of the moment…

"What now?" said Amari after many minutes had passed.

I stared out across the sea, to where I thought Aldira might be, far off in the distance, to the place I'd called home all my life… We would go back there someday, that was a promise I'd made to Max that I would keep. But for now—

"We need to move our camp south," I said, drawing in a deep breath, eyeing each expectant face. "The Raiders will be searching for us, and since we don't know much about the Ouray people, I'd rather not have any run-ins with them either. We need to move as far from them as possible, and maybe search for survivors along the way."

"I'll follow you anywhere," Max said, hand over his heart.

"As will I," said Beast.

There was a nod of agreement from everyone, their belief in me so powerful that for a moment, I thought I could fly…

Until the weight of what was being expected of me fell heavily.

"What about my little brother," Lucky asked.

"We will get him back. I know it's hard to believe, but for now, he's in good hands. I promise."

Rowan's hands. Stars above, my chest absolutely ached at the thought of never seeing him again, never getting the chance to be with him without the threat of death looming behind our every action. Was there a ray of hope that somehow, someday, our paths would cross?

The snake curled farther up my arm, slithered across my shoulders, watching, listening…

"So, what's the first order of business for today then, Eva?" asked Kade.

I got to my feet, wanting nothing more at that moment than to run off, be alone, and beg Rowan to come back into my mind… But instead, I reached for Kade and pulled him to his feet to stand next to me. I needed him. I couldn't do this by myself.

"Yes, what do we do now?" asked Amari.

The sun lit each beautiful face that was staring back at me. I gathered my breath and spoke from a place sincere and honest, hoping I was making a good decision for everyone—including Zoleya.

"Now? Right this very moment? Well, now we dance. We eat. We swim, rest, laugh, and do it all over again. We enjoy today like it's our last and keep it in our hearts forever. Then, tomorrow, we rise with the sun and work hard to do whatever it takes to make sure we have many more days like today."

Nods of agreement. Sighs of relief. Smiles. Kade's hand gently patted my back.

Then I felt it. Felt *him*.

Evangeline... Rowan's words were a whisper against my mind, making my hands and toes tingle with what I knew to be goodbye; *Good luck.*

Visit
www.heathermckenzie.com
for updates on the next book in this series

Thank you...

This novel would not have seen the light of day without Haley Bueckert and Emily Bueckert. Their input is something I will cherish forever and made this book what it is today. Thank you my darlings for going above and beyond and being there for me when I needed you most. Your kindness and support carried me through many rough patches—I'm so grateful for your patient wisdom. Thank you, Hubs Extraordinaire Byran, who looked after reality while I lounged about in dreamland—I am grateful for you more than you could ever know. Thank you Mumsy for believing in me, and thank you Shelley McKenzie and Josh Bueckert for your valued opinions. I am so blessed to have you all as a family. Your love is what carries me forward.

A big thank you to Shannon Snow for reading the first version of this manuscript and offering much-needed encouragement. Big thanks to Melanie Newton and the girls at CTP Publishing, who got me started on this author journey, and who I am forever grateful for. Thank you Jennifer Walker, Thoenn Glover, Ross McKenzie, Bonnie Cannam, Bonnie deVos (RIP Beautiful soul) Reanne Averay-Jones, Keiran Averay-Jones, Darryll Newsham, Deb Pietrusik, Mia Fillan, Martin Andrew, Rick and Myrna Bueckert, Kristin Smith, Jessica Powers, Jennifer Rees, Marni MacRae, Damian Jackson, Roxanne King, and my cat friends. Also, thank you House of Hebyzie for publishing this novel and putting it out into the world—you rock.

Last but not least, thank you, dear reader, for embarking on this journey with me. This story was a labor of love and I truly enjoyed every minute dreaming it onto paper. I am so grateful to be able to share it with you!

Heather

Heather McKenzie is the bestselling author of the darkly romantic thriller novels *Serenade, Nocturne,* and *Rhapsody.* She pulls from her extraordinary experiences as a musician to fuel ideas for writing fantasy and contemporary fiction. Currently residing in Alberta Canada, she paints abstract art and writes songs in her spare time. You can find her at:

www.HeatherMcKenzie.com